Books should be returned or renewed by the last
date above. Renew by phone **03000 41 31 31** or
online *www.kent.gov.uk/libs*

Libraries Registration & Archives

The House Across the Street

The House Across the Street

LESLEY PEARSE

MICHAEL JOSEPH
an imprint of
PENGUIN BOOKS

MICHAEL JOSEPH

UK | USA | Canada | Ireland | Australia
India | New Zealand | South Africa

Michael Joseph is part of the Penguin Random House group of companies
whose addresses can be found at global.penguinrandomhouse.com

First published 2018
001

Copyright © Lesley Pearse, 2018

The moral right of the author has been asserted

Set in 13.5/16 pt Garamond MT Std
Typeset by Jouve (UK), Milton Keynes
Printed and bound in Great Britain by Clays Ltd, Elcograf S.p.A.

A CIP catalogue record for this book is available from the British Library

HARDBACK ISBN: 978–0–718–18924–2
TRADE PAPERBACK ISBN: 978–0–718–18925–9

www.greenpenguin.co.uk

To Olive Bedford, my dear fan in New Zealand,
who over twenty years has become a friend,
confidant and almost a mother to me.

To celebrate her ninetieth birthday she will be
coming to England to visit family and me.

She is a source of inspiration, and I doubt
she will ever become an old lady.

Prologue

Bexhill-on-Sea, 1964

At the bang of a car door out in the street, Katy glanced out of the bedroom window.

It was the old black Humber she'd seen several times before, and two women were getting out and walking up the garden path of the house opposite. She was doing some ironing up in the front guest room; her own bedroom was at the back of the house and all it overlooked was the garden. Her younger brother, Rob, claimed she was nosy, always people-watching, fascinated by their comings and goings. She denied this, but she did find the house across the street very mysterious.

Mrs Gloria Reynolds, the owner, had a lovely dress shop in town called Gloria's Gowns, just two doors away from the firm of solicitors where Katy worked as a secretary. Her shop, and the fact that she was a very glamorous divorcee, was more than enough to make her interesting to Katy, but the clincher was that she had the oddest visitors and guests calling at her house.

The driver of the black Humber wasn't remarkable. Dumpy, grey-haired, middle-aged and wearing the same tweed coat she'd worn on every other visit. She struck Katy as the kind to be married to a doctor, vicar or other professional; she imagined her having a cut-glass BBC accent, and spending her spare time gardening.

But the women she brought here couldn't be more different from her or Mrs Reynolds. Mostly they were far younger, often quite shabbily dressed, and sometimes – like the woman today, who was limping – they could appear injured. Once, in the summer, when Katy was weeding the front garden, a woman had arrived with not just a black eye but her whole face swollen and distorted.

Some of the neighbours had also noticed odd visitors. Some thought Gloria must be helping women who had just been released from prison, or that they were women with serious diseases. Prostitutes, alcoholics, women who had lost a child, all had been suggested to Katy. Yet most of the neighbours felt that Gloria had a heart of gold, and whatever reason prompted these women to come to her house, it had to be to help them.

To Katy's shame, the exception to this rule was her own mother.

Hilda Speed was known for her sharp tongue; some would say she never had anything good to say about anyone. Whenever Gloria's name was mentioned she pursed her lips in disapproval. 'No better than she should be,' was what she always said. She was suspicious of Gloria's red fox coat, her very high heels, her pencil skirts and her chestnut-brown hair, which Hilda was convinced was dyed to cover up grey hair.

Katy moved closer to the window, watching through the net curtains as the older woman took the younger one's arm and led her up the garden path. She wished she could see this woman's face, as it was difficult to assess someone's age from a mere back view, but she thought she was young as she wore tight ski pants and a leather jacket, and her long dark hair was tied up in a ponytail.

The older woman opened the front door with a key. This was another thing that Hilda was suspicious of. She always said, 'What sort of woman allows people into her home when she isn't there?' And Gloria couldn't be there today as it was the last Saturday before Christmas and the busiest time in a dress shop. Rob had joked to Katy that their mum was so crabby the only visitors they'd ever get at their house was if people knew she would be out.

As the two women disappeared inside the house, Katy returned to the ironing while considering the mysterious visitors. She was in the habit of chatting to Gloria whenever she went into her shop. Just the previous month she'd bought a beautiful emerald-green chiffon dress for going dancing at Christmas.

But Gloria was the kind of woman who was more interested in other people than in talking about herself. Katy did know she had two daughters and a son. The daughter who lived in Hastings had two small children, and her son was up north somewhere. But as much as she had always wanted to ask about the people who came to her house, she couldn't. She didn't want to admit she spied on Gloria – and besides, it was rude to ask personal things of someone you didn't know well.

Katy felt Gloria might be a marriage counsellor. She certainly was easy to confide in. Katy had always hated her red hair, but she had Gloria to thank for telling her it wasn't carroty but strawberry blonde and very pretty. Two years ago she had picked out a pale green summer dress and suggested Katy try it on, to prove her point. Katy did, and loved it, because suddenly her hair seemed a less brassy colour. She bought that dress, and it had become her favourite, inspiring her to buy other clothes in the same colour. She was so very grateful to Gloria for giving her new confidence in her looks.

Just recently Gloria had also advised her to leave Bexhill. 'It's full of old people, and the dullest town in England,' she said with a big sigh, waving one hand to the street outside, which seemed to be full of pensioners. 'Get off to London, share a flat with other girls and have some fun. The only blokes you'll meet at the Saturday dance at the De La Warr Pavilion will be grease monkeys, labourers and the like. Anyone with any gumption runs off to London, these days. That's where it's all happening.'

Katy knew Gloria was right. Most of the girls from her class at school were married now, some with two or three children. They'd all married local boys, got council houses, and their lives were set to be repeats of their parents'. That wasn't the kind of future Katy wanted. She and her friend Jilly were always talking about broadening their horizons, and maybe it was time to start now.

'There's no maybe about it,' Katy said aloud. 'You've got nothing to tie you to Bexhill.'

Rob was home from university for Christmas; only last night he'd said he didn't think he'd come back any more because their mother was so cranky. But if Katy went away too that would leave her dad at Mum's mercy. Already henpecked and ridiculed, he was likely to spend longer and longer in either the office or his shed to avoid her. Her brother might think their mother was cranky, but he really hadn't seen just how nasty she could be to their father. She always kept it down when Rob was home.

Hearing her mother calling out downstairs, Katy went to the door.

'Did you want me, Mum?' she called down the stairs.

'Surely you've finished the ironing by now?'

Katy moved so she could see her mother. Everything about Hilda Speed was sharp – her tongue, features, eyes and her mind – allowing her to miss nothing. Even her body seemed to be all sharp angles. She was too thin; her knees and elbows were like weapons. Although only in her late forties, she appeared older because she so rarely laughed or even smiled.

'Just doing the last sheet,' Katy said. 'Why, have you got something else you want me to do?'

'No, I was just checking what you were up to.'

Katy rolled her eyes with irritation. For her entire life her mother had always liked to keep tabs on her. Coming home from school, running a message, anything outside the house always had an allocated time, and if she wasn't back within ten minutes of that time, she was questioned. It was as if her mother couldn't bear the thought of her running into a friend or neighbour and stopping for a little chat.

'I'll just put the sheets in the airing cupboard and then I'll be down,' Katy replied. She finished the last sheet, put the pile of ironed things in the airing cupboard, then went to her room. She wanted to put off going downstairs again so she sat at her dressing table, looking at herself in the mirror.

Her friend Jilly had always encouraged her to enjoy her

'pale and interesting' look rather than complain how long it took to achieve even the faintest hint of a tan in summer. Now, at twenty-three, she had finally accepted her looks: straight, long golden-red hair, the sprinkling of freckles on her nose, the pearly colour of her skin, and her green eyes. She actually liked her eyes; everyone admired them, as they were large and lustrous. She was also grateful she'd been blessed with brown eyelashes and eyebrows, as so many redheads had blonde ones. She was slender too, and her legs were long; it would've been better if she was two or three inches taller, instead of a miserly five foot two, but no one could have everything.

She didn't feel she'd inherited anything much from her parents. Rob was a replica of their dad at the same age: five foot nine, well built, with dark brown hair and eyes. Hilda had brown eyes, and she had said that her hair used to be chestnut before it went grey. But Katy had a heart-shaped face, while her mother's was oblong. Hilda's nose was sharp, Katy's small and well rounded.

'As long as you don't get as difficult as Mum, or as soft as Dad, you'll do,' she told her reflection.

'Katy!'

At the sound of her shrieked name, Katy sighed. It was a few days yet till Christmas and her mother was already going into a tailspin. No wonder Rob said he didn't intend to come home for the holidays any more.

I

January 1965

'Fire! Fire! Get up, get up!'

Katy woke with a start at her mother's shrill command. She leapt out of bed and grabbed her dressing gown. As she put her feet into her slippers, she heard her father speak.

'For goodness' sake, Hilda! The fire is across the street, we aren't in any danger. Leave the children in peace.'

His plea was one of weariness, and Katy's heart went out to him. He'd been in the office until late for the last few days because his engineering company was having an audit.

'You wouldn't think to jump into water even if your feet were on fire,' Hilda retorted. 'Lazy oaf!'

Normally Katy reacted to such nasty remarks like a red rag to a bull, but just now she only wanted to see the fire.

Rob emerged from his room as Katy passed his door. 'What on earth is going on?' he said grumpily, clutching at his pyjama bottoms as if afraid they would fall down.

'Fire, but Mum's probably overreacting,' she replied. 'Let's go and see?'

But as they stepped into their parents' room they were astounded to see it was almost as light as day from the blaze across the street.

'Oh my goodness!' Katy exclaimed, her mouth dropping open at the scene outside the window. Vivid scarlet and yellow flames were licking up the front of the house and illuminating the whole street. Set against the night sky it made a terrifying picture. This wasn't some little kitchen fire, but a real inferno.

'I can't believe it,' Katy burst out, her voice shaking with emotion. 'Poor Mrs Reynolds, I just hope she isn't still in there. Did someone call the fire brigade?'

'Of course I did,' their father said, pulling his trousers on over his pyjamas. 'I may be an oaf, but I can manage to dial 999. And now I'm going out to check on whether she did get out – and if she has, I'll be inviting her and the neighbours on either side back here.'

Katy heard the steel in his voice and turned back from the window to look at him. 'Good for you, Dad. Can I help in any way?'

'No, you and Rob stay here in the warm with your mother,' he said, glancing at his wife who had got back into bed as if nothing unusual was happening. 'It looks like it's freezing out there.'

He was right; away from the blaze the pavements sparkled with frost.

'Please God, tell me she got out.' Katy felt faint at the thought of what might have happened. There were a few neighbours out there looking at the blaze, but she couldn't see Mrs Reynolds amongst them. She turned towards her mother. 'She's not out there, Mum! Did you spot her when you first saw the fire?'

'No, but it was already blazing away when I woke, so she probably ran to someone's house.'

Katy nodded. She hoped that was the case. 'Usually on a Saturday night she goes to her daughter's. Let's just hope she did this time.'

'Since when did you get to know that woman well enough to find out her movements?' Hilda asked, her voice sharp and disapproving.

Katy looked at her brother and rolled her eyes. It was typical of their mother that she would be more concerned with finding out how her daughter knew a victim, rather than expressing sympathy for their plight.

'Seeing as her shop is only two doors away from the office, it would be very rude if I never spoke to her,' Katy said curtly. 'I like her, she's very interesting to chat to, and she's got two daughters — one's twenty-three, like me. But it's the older one who she goes to on Saturdays; she lives in Hastings.'

The bell on the fire engine drowned any response from her mother. Katy turned back to the window to see more people arriving to look at the burning house. A police car drew up right behind a second fire engine. Two policemen jumped out to move the crowd further down Collington Avenue.

The blaze was so fierce now that Katy could feel the heat even through the windowpane. As the firemen unrolled their hoses, she saw her father talking to old Mr and Mrs Harding. The pensioners lived in the house attached to the burning building. They were looking fearfully at the blaze, huddled together with coats over their nightclothes, clearly afraid their house would soon be consumed by the flames. She guessed her father was urging them to come over the road and wait in the warm.

Rob came over to stand beside Katy at the window and squeezed her forearm, his silent way of communicating his disapproval that their mother hadn't gone out there too, to try and help in some way.

'I'll go and put the kettle on,' Katy said. She needed to do something, just standing watching a house burning down seemed awful. 'Dad might bring people back, so maybe I should make some sandwiches too. Would you like something, Mum?' she asked.

'Some cocoa would be nice, and a slice of that fruit cake I made this afternoon.'

Katy merely nodded confirmation that she'd heard and made her way downstairs. She didn't understand why her mother was taking the fire so calmly. Even if she didn't approve of Mrs Reynolds, surely she would care whether she was alive or burned to death? As for the Hardings, they'd lived here for about fifteen years before Katy was born, and she and Rob had often gone to their house after school for tea. In fact, they thought of them almost as stand-in grandparents. At their age it must be awful to think their house and all its treasured contents might be destroyed.

As she filled the kettle, Rob came down to join her. 'Sometimes I wish I was still five,' he said sadly, his mouth downturned. 'Back then, I didn't know that other mothers cared about their family, and sang, danced, or chased their kids round the garden. I can't believe she hasn't gone out there with Dad to see if she can help. What's up with her, Sis? She must have a heart of stone. Was she born that way or did something happen to her?'

'I don't know, Rob,' Katy sighed. 'I used to pray at

Sunday School that she'd change. The worst of it is that I almost don't notice how cold and hard she is any more. It's only because this is something so dramatic – so serious and so damaging for everyone affected – that it's reminded me just how peculiar she is.'

'I'm definitely not coming back in the holidays any more,' Rob said. He was in his final year at Nottingham University, studying horticulture. 'Each time I come back it's like a punishment, not a joyful homecoming. I'll miss you and Dad, of course, but I can't deal with her any longer. She snipes at me, as if she resents my life. I don't think she's ever asked about my friends, or how I find the work, or even what my digs are like. All she does is clean and polish.'

Katy saw that her brother was close to tears and she embraced him. He was three years younger than her, but they'd always been close. They had not been allowed to go and play in other children's homes when they were little, so they'd believed all mothers were like theirs. Later, when they were allowed to play outside and they learned it wasn't so, they found their own ways of compensating for a difficult mother who rarely showed any affection.

Rob was clever, he could make things out of next to nothing – soapbox carts, bows for archery, stilts and many other ingenious toys – which made him popular. Katy found her niche by being daring, climbing trees, knocking on doors and running away, and acting the clown to make the other kids laugh. Although very different in temperament – Rob being shy, while Katy was outgoing – they made a good team, supporting each other and sharing their resources.

'I've been considering moving to London,' Katy admitted. 'Funnily enough, it was Mrs Reynolds who put the idea in my head. She said Bexhill is the dullest town in England and I ought to be whooping it up in a big city. She was right: Bexhill is dull. Dancing at the Pavilion on a Saturday night is as good as it gets. The only boys I ever meet are the ones I went to school with, and half of them are married now with a couple of kids.'

'I'd suggest you came up to Nottingham, as I'd love you to be there, but I don't think it's a very good place unless you are at the university. Besides, I won't be there after my finals this June. London is where everything is happening now, so I'm told.'

Katy smiled at her brother. 'I wouldn't want to cramp your style in Nottingham. And anyway, if I go to London you can come and stay with me there.'

As Katy buttered some bread for sandwiches she thought about her parents. Katy had once got a sneaky peek at their wedding certificate. They were married in July of 1941, and she had been born in March the same year, four months earlier. As she understood it, that wasn't unusual then; they said people lived for the moment, and many women found themselves to be pregnant after their man had been sent off abroad. But it was extremely hard to imagine her mother ever having being swept away by passion. She was so totally disapproving of pre-marital sex. When she'd tried to explain about the birds and bees to Katy, she looked and sounded like she was almost choking at the thought of such things. Perhaps she'd had a hard time, though, being on her own with a new baby.

But that didn't exactly explain why her dad had ever

been sufficiently attracted to Hilda to even speak to her, let alone sleep with her. Albert was almost Hilda's exact opposite: kind, caring, soft spoken. He was a tall, handsome man with thick dark hair, good teeth and a ready smile.

She longed to ask her mother about those days and her romance with Albert, but Hilda wasn't the kind to confide in anyone; she found personal questions an affront, even if they were from her children.

It wasn't just the problems with her mother that made Katy want to leave home. She also longed for the hustle and bustle of London. Here in Bexhill she felt she was under a microscope. If it wasn't her mother cross-examining her, it was friends and neighbours constantly watching her.

Bexhill wasn't just dull, it was dead! A story had gone round that the police had once pulled the vicar in for questioning because he was out after nine on a winter's evening. They were convinced he was a burglar, and refused to believe he was visiting a sick old lady, until he took off his scarf and showed his dog collar.

That story had always amused Katy. And yet, despite the town's shortcomings, she had affection for it. Aside from the sea, it had wide tree-lined roads, at least where she lived, and more lively towns like Hastings or Brighton were only a bus ride away.

Rob had left the kitchen to take their mother her tea and cake. As he came back into the kitchen, Katy was brought back to the present.

'Looks like the fire is coming under control now,' he said. 'But no one in there could've survived.'

Katy ran into the sitting room and looked out of the window. Rob was right, the flames were no longer licking as vigorously up the front of the house, and the blaze in the front room appeared to have died down. A lump came up in her throat; even if Mrs Reynolds was safely at her daughter's, losing her home and all her personal possessions was terrible. But much worse was the possibility that such a lovely woman had died in the fire. That was too tragic to even contemplate.

Rob came up behind her. 'Mr and Mrs Harding won't be able to go back into their house,' he said thoughtfully. 'It might not have burned down as such, but the smoke will have damaged everything. They are old and frail, and I don't think they've got any family to go to.'

Katy could think of nothing to say to that, so she pointed out she had sandwiches to make. They both turned away from the window and the devastation outside and went back into the kitchen. Rob stoked up the Rayburn while Katy started on the sandwiches.

'Are you going to tell Mum and Dad you won't come home for the holidays again?' she asked her brother. 'Or will you just make excuses each time?'

Rob looked sheepish. 'I think the excuses route. I'm not as brave as you.'

'I think it's more diplomatic, actually. I mean it won't make Dad so sad, will it? I don't like the thought of walking away from him either, but I suppose parents do expect their kids to leave at some time.'

'Maybe Mum will be nicer to Dad once they are alone?' Rob suggested.

Almost as if he'd heard his name being mentioned, the back door opened and Albert came in on a blast of icy-cold air. 'Brrr, it's freezing out there,' he said, rubbing his hands together. 'Mr and Mrs Harding are going along to the Bradys, down the road. They play bridge with them, so it's better for them than here.'

'What about the Suttons?' Rob asked. They were the couple who lived on the other side of number 26.

'Well, as their house isn't attached to number 26 it hasn't been damaged. They went in with firemen to check it. They said it stinks of smoke but it's okay. Anyway, they are going to their daughter's until it clears. She's on her way.'

'Did the firemen find out if Mrs Reynolds was in there?' Katy asked.

Albert frowned. 'They don't know yet. Mrs Harding said she was at home earlier in the evening, as she heard her television. It was switched off later, so hopefully that means she went out. But the firemen can't get in there just yet to check. We'll just have to cross our fingers that she's safe somewhere else.'

'Do they have any idea of how it started?' Rob asked.

'I heard one of the policemen say they suspected arson. But they won't be able to confirm or rule that out until the fire is properly out and the house has cooled down.' He paused, his dark eyes glinting with what looked like emotional tears. 'If it was set deliberately and Mrs Reynolds died in there, I would want to personally throttle the person who did that to her.'

When Katy woke up the following morning, for a moment or two she thought she'd been dreaming there was a fire. Church bells were ringing down at Little Common, summoning the faithful to eight o'clock communion. She felt she ought to be angry that they'd woken her at eight on a

Sunday – after all, she'd only got back to bed at five this morning. But there was something comforting about the bells, as if nothing really bad could happen within the sound of them.

She got up and went into the spare room to look out of the window. But there it was, worse than she'd expected, a blackened, still smoking wreck of a house, the roof half caved in, windows gone and the once neat front garden trampled and full of burned debris. Even through the closed window she could smell that dank, half-charred, half-chemical smell of ruin.

It was too early for people to be out – and bitterly cold, too – and, as Rob and her parents appeared to still be asleep, she went back to bed.

By eleven that morning it had begun to snow, and Katy sat up on the window seat in the sitting room watching what was going on in the street. Aside from people coming to look at the burnt-out house, there were several firemen. Katy got the idea the house was either too hot or too dangerous to go in, as they stood in groups outside. There was police activity too, mostly knocking on the doors of residents on that side of the road, though a young constable knocked at their door to ask what they'd seen the previous night. There were also men in civilian clothes looking up at the house and these, Katy assumed, were building inspectors or surveyors.

It was just after lunch when Katy brought a cup of tea into the sitting room, intending to sit and read a book. She saw policemen coming out of number 26 carrying someone covered up on a stretcher.

She almost dropped her tea in shock, because by that

time she and the rest of the family were certain there couldn't have been any fatalities. But then, to her further horror, a second stretcher was carried out.

Just to look at the faces of the police and firemen was to know they were as distressed as she was. She saw that while she and her family had been eating their lunch at the back of the house, a big pile of burned furniture and what looked like doors had been hauled out of the house and added to the debris in the garden. So presumably the firemen had found the two bodies beneath it all.

Sobbing, Katy ran into the dining room where her father and brother were sitting in the armchairs either side of the fire reading the Sunday papers. 'There's two bodies,' she blurted out. 'The police just carried them out.'

Both Rob and her father were too shocked to speak for a moment or two. They just stared at her as if not understanding.

'How absolutely dreadful,' Albert said eventually, his voice hushed and shaky. 'Her poor family! Do you think the other body was her daughter?'

Katy began to cry. 'The daughter she usually goes to on a Saturday night has two small children. She once said they never stayed overnight, so I doubt it was her,' she sobbed out.

'There is another daughter, and a son,' Albert said thoughtfully. 'She said the daughter was a career girl. I seem to remember she was going in for law. The boy lives in Manchester.'

'Yes, that's right, I remember she told me that too,' Katy said. 'She even suggested I try to get legal secretarial work, as it's better paid than normal stuff.'

'So if it was arson, someone is responsible for two deaths,' Rob said, his face set and flushed with anger. 'That is such a horrible thought, here in Bexhill of all places, where nothing happens.'

'Don't let's talk about this in front of your mother,' Albert said in a low voice. 'I couldn't bear to hear her going on and on about it all evening. She's had a thing about Mrs Reynolds ever since I went over there to fix an overflowing cistern.'

'Where is Mum, anyway?' Rob asked.

'She just went out for a walk,' Albert said. 'Heaven only knows why, when it's so cold. But there was no talking to her; I even offered to go with her, and she nearly bit my head off. But she should've been home by now, it's nearly dark.'

'I'll go and make a start on laying the tea,' Katy said. 'Not that I feel like eating anything after seeing those two stretchers.'

2

Katy woke to find a dull grey light in her room and knew immediately it had snowed in the night.

As a child she had always been thrilled by snow, but after the events of the previous day she couldn't have cared less if there had been an earthquake or a hurricane during the night.

Flora, a woman at work, had once told her that her next-door neighbour had died unexpectedly. 'I felt as if I'd been kicked in the stomach,' she'd said. 'But it was very odd, because we were never that close.'

At the time, Katy thought it was a weird thing to say. Yet that was just how she felt now: winded, sore inside, yet unable to grasp why she should be so affected. Was it because she had wanted to know more about Gloria Reynolds? Or because she felt guilty she'd watched her so often?

But death was new to Katy; until now she'd never experienced it. Both sets of grandparents had died before she was born. So maybe it was this way for everyone?

She thought she would ask her friend Jilly, because she came from a big extended family that discussed anything and everything. She would know if Katy's reaction was normal.

When she got up and drew back the curtains, despite her mood she was moved to see a thick white blanket of snow covering the garden.

The bare flower beds, the old lawn roller, the apple tree, fences and her father's shed were all magically transformed into a winter wonderland like a scene from a fairy tale. Yet it didn't seem right that the world should look so pretty when something so awful had taken place such a short while before.

An hour later, Katy was trudging down the road to get to work wearing a pair of tartan trousers under her dress, two jumpers and her brown winter coat, plus a green woolly hat, gloves, matching scarf and wellington boots. Her indoor shoes were tucked in her handbag. Snow on a Monday before the gritting trucks could get out meant some of her workmates living out of town might not come in today, so that meant she'd have more work than usual. A depressing thought.

Yet, despite the cold, she was glad to be out of the house, as there had been a tense atmosphere over breakfast. Usually her mother's bad moods were signalled in advance by banging plates and cupboard doors, and sooner or later an outburst would erupt. But today hadn't been like that – no noise, not even any sniping – in fact, to an outsider it would have seemed calm and ordinary. But Katy knew better; she'd observed the humourless smirks, felt the concealed venom. This was when her mother was brewing up for something.

Rob said he'd heard their father arguing with her late last night. He couldn't hear well enough to discover what it was about, though.

Katy thought their mother was probably bad-mouthing Mrs Reynolds again, as she had on Sunday morning, when

Albert had lost his patience. He always said it was bad form to speak ill of the dead.

But if Katy had thought going to work would be a distraction, she was wrong. The tragedy had been reported on the local news, and as everyone in the office knew Katy lived in Collington Avenue, right across the street from the burnt-out house, they were eagerly awaiting her inside information.

Even Mr Marshfield, the senior partner, came out of his office purposely to ask questions. Normally the only time he spoke to Katy was to summon her for dictation.

'Mrs Reynolds was a client,' he said, looking very concerned. 'Such a bubbly woman, I liked her very much. And it seems her daughter died with her?'

Katy had never heard the man admit he liked anyone before. She and the other girls had nicknamed him 'Eeyore' because, like the dour donkey in *Winnie-the-Pooh*, he was a complete pessimist, and his long, thin face never broke into a smile.

'It's not been confirmed who the second woman was, Mr Marshfield. I hope it wasn't her daughter, but then whoever it is, she belongs to someone. The police seem to think the fire was started on purpose, but why would anyone want to kill such a nice woman?'

'A jilted lover, perhaps?' Mrs Edwards, Marshfield's secretary, suggested. She was a hopeless romantic, buying wedding magazines to drool over the pictures and plan her sons' nuptials, even though none of the four was even going steady. She also had a vivid imagination fuelled by reading lurid thrillers.

'Maybe having the dress shop was just a front,' Sandra,

the dopey filing clerk, suggested. 'She might have been a spy!'

'Yes, that's extremely likely,' Mr Marshfield retorted with sarcasm. 'Now get on with your work, Sandra, and make sure you put the correspondence in the right files.'

All through the day the subject of Mrs Reynolds' untimely and horrible death came up. Nothing much ever happened in Bexhill so it was hardly surprising that any-one who had even the most tenuous link with the dead woman wanted to discuss it. People who had never been in the office of Franklin, Spencer and Marshfield before made excuses to do so – so many, in fact, the staff were forced to lay newspaper by the office door to soak up the snow they tramped in.

It was on the way home – earlier than usual, because it had begun to snow again – that Katy's mind turned to the last time she'd actually had a conversation with the shop-keeper. She'd gone into Gloria's Gowns in late November to look for a dress to wear to go out dancing at Christmas. She could see Gloria in her mind's eye right now, a volup-tuous lady with an hourglass figure. That day she'd been wearing a red sheath dress with a wide black patent-leather belt and matching high heels, her chestnut hair fixed up as usual in a beehive, red-and-black dangly earrings, and her make-up so well done her complexion looked flawless.

'So glad you called in, Katy,' she said. 'Because I've got the perfect party dress for you.'

She pulled an emerald-green chiffon dress off the rail and shook it to show off how the fabric fluttered. 'A great contrast with your pretty hair, and look at the way the skirt swirls.'

As always, Katy was bowled over not just by the way that Gloria knew what would suit her customers, but how she made each one feel special.

When Katy came out of the changing room in the dress, which fitted her like a glove and made her feel like a Hollywood star, Gloria clapped her hands with delight.

'I thought of you as soon as it came in,' she said. 'It is perfect for you: the colour and the fit. But, my dear, you should be wearing it somewhere far more exciting than Bexhill.'

She went on to say how she sensed that huge changes were happening in England, starting now in London. 'I felt it last time I was there,' she said. 'Finally, the whole prissy fifties Doris Day thing is over. They've got gorgeous little shops opening up everywhere; they call them boutiques, and the outrageous, sexy clothes are made by young, talented designers. Then there's the discotheques, too – dance halls are old hat now. If I was your age, Katy, I'd be up there like a shot to join in.'

Katy had seen articles in glossy magazines to this effect, but Gloria's enthusiasm made it seem so much more real and attainable.

'But there's my job at the solicitors,' Katy said. 'What if I couldn't find such a good one in London?'

'Don't be daft, Katy, there are thousands of solicitors in London, and you'll find a job that will pay you twice as much as you get here, because good secretaries like you are like gold dust. My Elsie is a legal secretary, so I do know what I'm talking about.'

'But there's all my friends here. London can be very lonely, I'm told.'

'Oh, Katy, a girl like you will soon make new friends. You share a flat with some other girls and – hey presto! – soon it will be parties, dancing, meeting ambitious young men who are going somewhere. I bet the only men who ask you to dance at the Pavilion on a Saturday night are either grease monkeys or work in a shop.'

Katy preened in front of the mirror, swishing the skirt, loving the way the dress felt, even if it did cost over two weeks' wages. 'I must admit I've met a few mechanics, farm labourers, and even a dustman,' she said with a grin. 'Certainly no one that sets my heart racing. But then I might not find that in London either, and my mum and dad wouldn't like it if I left.'

'You must live your life for yourself, not your parents,' Gloria said firmly. 'You look like a model in that dress, enough to break any man's heart. Besides, your dad will only want the best for you, he'll know that Bexhill is a bit staid for young people.'

That evening, after the conversation with Mrs Reynolds, Katy did daydream about going to London. She imagined herself and her friend Jilly in a smart flat whooping it up all night at weekends. The pair of them discussed it and thought they could go up for a reconnoitre in January, as both had a few days' holiday left. But then their minds turned to Christmas shopping and what they would wear to the Christmas and New Year's Eve dances, and they hadn't spoken of going to London since.

Now, as Katy trudged home through the driving snow, she felt so desperately sad that she hadn't found time to pop in to see Gloria Reynolds before Christmas and thank her for her suggestions. As it was, she was never going to see the woman again, and she expected the shop would close down. It was going to feel like a bright light had gone out in the town. Perhaps she really ought to move to London now, it would be a way of honouring that lovely woman.

A blue-and-white panda police car was parked outside her house.

'There's my daughter now,' Katy heard her mother say as she hung up her coat and took her wellington boots off just inside the back door. 'But she won't have seen or heard anything, she sleeps like a log.'

Katy went into the sitting room to find her mother there with two policemen. She'd made them a tray of tea and even put biscuits on a plate. The fire was blazing away and the deep red carpet and gold brocade three-piece suite made the room look very sumptuous and welcoming.

'This is Katy,' her mother said. 'I told the police you wouldn't have seen or heard anything.'

'No, that's right, I knew nothing about it until Mum shouted for us to get up,' Katy said, looking at the older policeman. She had met him briefly once before, when he'd come into her office to make some inquiries about a break-in further down the high street. He was around forty, tall, broad-shouldered and bald, but with nice twinkly brown eyes and a warm smile. She knew his name was Sergeant Ransome. 'It's a terrible business; I do hope you catch the person who started it.'

'We are still gathering information. Just now we are trying to build up a picture of Mrs Reynolds. Did you know her, Katy?'

'Yes, I often bought clothes from her shop, and I liked

25

her,' Katy said. 'I think everyone did. She was very warm and friendly.'

'Did she ever tell you anything about her personal life?'

Katy shook her head. 'Not exactly personal, only that she had two daughters – and a son, too, in Manchester. She usually went to the daughter with children after work on a Saturday evening. I believe that daughter lives in Hastings. The other one, Elsie, is a legal secretary in London. But I don't know the first daughter's name.'

'When you were out of an evening in Bexhill, did you ever run into Mrs Reynolds? In a bar, at a dance or anywhere else?'

'No. Never.'

'Your office is only two doors away from her dress shop. So did you ever hear any gossip about her? About her men friends, who she went out with?'

Katy glanced at her mother. She had a feeling she might have suggested to the police that their neighbour was a maneater.

'The only gossip I've heard I believe to be entirely unfounded. I'd say it came from pathetic, spiteful women who were jealous because she was such an attractive, charismatic and successful woman,' Katy said firmly, looking away from her mother.

There was an awkward silence, the only sound the fire crackling. Katy glanced again at her mother and saw she was tight-lipped and frowning. She knew then she'd be in trouble later.

Sergeant Ransome suggested they talk in private and led her out into the hall, shutting the door behind him, leaving the other policeman with her mother.

'I sensed you were nervous of saying anything further in front of your mother,' he said. 'But go ahead now, tell me anything you think is important. And, unfounded or not, did you ever hear of Gloria Reynolds having an affair with a married man?'

'No, I never did,' Katy said firmly. 'I'm a bit shocked that people would say such things when she has just died.'

'Yes, but if it is true, that man could be her killer,' Ransome said evenly. 'Few people are murdered by total strangers; it's almost always at the hand of someone close to them.'

'Has anyone told you about the visitors she had?' Katy asked. 'I shouldn't imagine it was any of them, as they were always women and they usually came in an old black Humber with a middle-aged woman driving.'

Ransome looked surprised. 'No, no one else has mentioned this. Are you saying they were visitors as in guests, coming for a drink?'

'No, I don't think so. And anyway, mostly they came during the day when Mrs Reynolds was at her shop. The older woman had a key.'

Ransome frowned. 'How often did this happen?'

'I've no idea, because I only saw it occasionally, on a Saturday, and only then if I happened to be looking out of the front window. But I've seen the Humber at the house several times when I got back from work.'

'What were your thoughts on why the women came?'

'I wondered if Mrs Reynolds could be counselling them about their marriages, maybe, or if they were women just out of prison. She was very kind and caring, you see. I mean other neighbours mentioned it too, and some implied quite nasty things. But I don't believe Gloria Reynolds had a bad bone in her body.'

'Would you recognize any of these women who called, if you saw them again?'

'The older lady, the car driver, I would. But I don't think I'd know the women who came with her.'

'The car number?'

Katy shook her head. 'Sorry.'

'Well, that has all been very helpful. If you think of anything else, please call me,' he said, handing her a card with the police station phone number on it and his name.

'I will,' she agreed. 'I hope you catch whoever did it. I can't bear the thought of that lovely lady dying in such a horrible way.'

The family's supper that evening was eaten in a strained atmosphere. Rob grimaced at Katy, which she took to mean this was how it had been all day.

Silence continued; Katy felt her mother was about to burst into one of her tirades, almost certainly directed at her.

'I think I'll go back to Nottingham tomorrow,' Rob said suddenly. 'I've got a project to finish and I need some information I'm more likely to find in the library there.'

'Good for you, son,' Albert said. 'Easier to get stuck into the new term if you have a few days' grace to get settled back into hall.'

'What would you know about it?' Hilda said waspishly. 'You've never been anywhere near a university hall.'

'How many men of my age got to university, with war looming?' Albert replied. 'I was the same age as Rob is,

28

back then. Just because I didn't go to university, it doesn't mean I can't imagine what it's like.'

'Joining up for war would've been a lot harder than going to university,' Rob said, as always trying to be the peacemaker. 'My generation is getting it a lot easier.'

Katy looked at her mother, wondering how she could twist that to make her husband look like a failure. He had been in the Royal Engineers during the war. When he was demobbed, his uncle took him on at his engineering company in Hastings, and got him to complete a full apprenticeship at the workshop and at night school. He was the managing director of Speed Engineering now, and under his direction the company had gone from strength to strength. This was why they had the big house in Collington Avenue, why Katy and Rob had gone to private schools, and why Hilda had never wanted for anything. Yet all she ever did was snipe at her husband.

Albert looked from Katy to Rob. 'I, for one, am very glad neither of you had to endure the war. All I want from my children now is to see you happy. And if that takes you away from Bexhill and your mother and me, that's okay with me.'

The disapproving snort from her mother goaded Katy.

'So glad you agree, Mummy,' she said with saccharine sweetness. 'Just today I was thinking of finding work and a flat in London. I've got a few days' holiday owing to me so I might take it next week and go up there to check things out.'

'More fool you, that's all I can say,' Hilda said, standing up to gather up the empty plates and clattering them together. 'You've got a good job and a nice home here. People live in squalor in London.'

29

She swept out of the dining room with the dirty plates. Albert, Rob and Katy exchanged glances as they waited for the sound of banging crockery which would follow.

'Are you serious, Katy?' Rob whispered.

'I wasn't until she started,' Katy said. 'I'm sorry, Daddy, but it's becoming unbearable. Anything is preferable to coming home to this every night.'

'I don't blame you,' Albert said quietly. 'I would like to get up and go, too. There is nothing for me here any more, but I promised "for better or worse" and I have to keep that promise.'

'You don't have to, Daddy, she's doesn't deserve your loyalty.' Katy raised her voice over the sound of banging pots and plates. 'You get a flat in Hastings and I'll come and live with you.'

She saw the flicker of hope rise and then fade on his face. 'I can't do it, Katy. It's so tempting but it wouldn't work.'

'You think she'll go to Speed's and make trouble?'

'I know she will.'

'You say you want us to be happy, but how can we be when we know what she puts you through?' Rob said. 'You should make the break.'

All at once they realized the banging had stopped and their mother must have heard what Rob said. He groaned, wiping his hand across his face.

Katy felt a wave of nausea wash over her. All of them knew Hilda didn't take criticism lightly. One way or another, she would make them pay for what had been said.

The next morning, Rob and Katy left the house with their father at eight thirty, with the plan he would drop Rob at the station and Katy at her office. Although none of them voiced it, they felt a huge sense of relief at getting out of the house together. Snowploughs had cleared the busier roads, and although the piled-up dirty snow at the kerbs was ugly, it was a lot less dangerous.

Usually Hilda baked a cake for Rob to take back to Nottingham, wrapped sandwiches for the journey and fussed over him. But not this time. She'd been like an iceberg on the previous evening, dumping some of Rob's unironed shirts on his lap with instructions to pack them, before flopping into an armchair and remaining in total silence for the rest of the evening. She hadn't even said goodbye to any of them this morning.

In the past when she had been really nasty, Katy had begged her father to seek help for her. He always quoted the proverb: 'You can lead a horse to water but you can't make it drink.' He insisted he had tried and failed many times.

'I'm dreading going home this evening,' Katy said after they'd dropped Rob off at the station and were driving to her office. 'She'll be worse than ever with Rob no longer there. You know she usually keeps a lid on it when he's home. Why can't we get a flat, Daddy? Surely it must be even worse for you than it is for me?'

He didn't reply until he pulled up in front of her office. 'She had a difficult childhood,' he said, his face lined with anxiety. 'Maybe if I'd been more understanding when you kids were little, or clamped down on her when she first started these tantrums, the problem might have been solved.'

'You always blame yourself, Daddy.' Katy reached out

and stroked his face tenderly. 'You are a good man, a wonderful father, and you've been the most tolerant husband, too. You have nothing to reproach yourself with. You are only forty-five, still young enough to meet a lady who will value you. Divorce is nothing now, there isn't even any stigma to it like there used to be.'

'Let's see how she is tonight,' he sighed. 'I must admit I am at the end of my tether. Maybe I should talk to a solicitor and get some advice. But not at your firm, Katy – we don't want them knowing our business – maybe a firm in Hastings.'

Katy's spirits lifted a little, as this was a major breakthrough; he'd never even admitted before that he'd considered divorce.

'I'll see you about six,' she said. 'And drive carefully.'

Katy was given a divorce statement to type up later that same day. It was from a Mrs Byrne, a client divorcing her husband for unreasonable behaviour, and by coincidence her complaints against her husband were very similar to those her father had to live with.

'There's no joy in him, he complains about everything. He doesn't want to go anywhere; he's so nasty about my friends and the neighbours when they are really nice to him. I'm so glad I've got a part-time job as it takes me out of the house, but every night I wish I didn't have to go home and see him.'

Katy's eyes prickled with tears as she read the statement. She wondered if the divorce judge would think this was nothing to complain about, yet she knew her father was at the end of his tether just as Mrs Byrne said she was, too.

Later, when she took the typed statement to Mr Marshfield, she couldn't help herself; she had to ask him the all-important question.

'I found Mrs Byrne's statement very moving,' she said, hoping he wouldn't snap at her. 'I can imagine how miserable it must be to stay with such a difficult man. But tell me, sir, do you think she will get her divorce on grounds of unreasonable behaviour?'

Mr Marshfield put his elbows on his desk and his hands together, almost as if he was praying. He did this all the time when he was thinking, and everyone in the office found it funny.

'No, I think the judge will dismiss it,' he said after a few moments. 'After all, Mr Byrne hasn't beaten her, or been unfaithful.'

'So he would think a wife should put up with her husband's callous behaviour? And what if it was the other way round, and Mrs Byrne was the nasty one? Would her husband be granted a divorce?'

'Interesting question, Katy,' he said, giving her one of his very rare smiles. 'I suspect the husband might be treated more sympathetically by the judge, but what would his friends and relatives think of him? A henpecked husband is always a figure of fun.'

Katy wanted to ask him what he'd do if his wife was a joyless cold shrew, but that was too impudent, so she thanked him and left his office.

Katy didn't go home after work but called on her friend Jilly instead, to sound her out about going to London.

Jilly worked as a nurse at the local vet's. Her ambition

was to get a job nursing sick animals at a zoo. While she knew her training and experience didn't actually run to caring for elephants, monkeys or any other wild animal, she was always reading up on different species.

'Come on in,' Mrs Carter, Jilly's mother, said, welcomingly when she opened the door to Katy. 'She isn't home yet, but she soon will be. Will you stay to tea? I've made a big stew.'

Within minutes Katy was sitting at the kitchen table, a mug of tea in her hand, and thinking, as always, that Jilly's mother was the polar opposite to her own. Mrs Carter had no sharp edges, she was billowing plumpness with a pretty face, curly fair hair and an almost permanent smile. The Carters' home was a council house, and different in every way from her own home. The untidy small living room never smelled of lavender polish, the curtains drooped from the rail because some of the hooks were missing, and a very hairy dog called Ruin monopolized the sofa. But more than once Katy had wished this was her home. If it wasn't for Jilly having her heart set on working at London Zoo, Katy would say she was mad to leave her family.

Jilly and her young sister, Patsy, came in together and threw their coats on to the banister while still continuing an argument about a jumper Jilly believed Patsy had borrowed without asking and torn a hole in the sleeve.

'Enough!' Mrs Carter yelled from the kitchen. 'Do you want Katy to think we have no manners?'

'Katy's here?' Jilly called back and came running in to hug her friend. 'What a lovely surprise. I didn't expect to see you till the weekend. Tell us about that fire. Isn't it awful that Mrs Reynolds died in it? And they said on the news this afternoon the other person was her daughter, the one who worked in London.'

Jilly was often described as 'striking', which she hated because she was sure they meant 'plain'. She wasn't exactly pretty, because her face was very angular, her nose a bit too big, and her eyes very prominent; plus she was five foot seven tall, taller than most girls. But she seemed unaware that she'd been lucky to inherit her mother's shoulder-length blonde, wavy hair and her startling azure-blue eyes. The description 'striking' was given more because people never forgot her. She was a force of nature, firing out questions, wanting to get things done. She did everything at speed, but when anyone had a problem and wanted someone to talk it over with, she was also the best listener.

'I suspect Katy came here to avoid talking about the fire,' Mrs Carter said. 'I bet that's all you've heard since it happened?'

'Sorry,' Jilly said, looking chastened. 'I didn't think of that.'

Katy suddenly felt better about everything. Jilly always had that effect on her. They had met at thirteen when they joined the Girl Guides on the same day. One glance at each other bonded them, and a year later they were asked to leave because they were so disruptive. They couldn't help themselves, so many of the other Guides were goody two-shoes who sucked up to the Guiders and worked diligently and quietly to get more badges, while Katy and Jilly much preferred doing handstands, cartwheels and playing leapfrog outside, and encouraging other potential rebels to join them. Their final indiscretion was to light a campfire much too close to a cherry tree in the church hall grounds, and it caught fire.

Hilda didn't approve of Jilly; she said the Carters were 'not our sort', and claimed Mr Carter had been a bookie's runner. Katy neither knew nor cared what a bookie's runner was, and she continued to think of Jilly as her best friend, even though Jilly had gone to the local comprehensive while she went to fee-paying Hamilton House School. Katy had found the best way to deal with her mother's prejudices was to avoid bringing up the subject so, while seeing her friend as often as she could, she just didn't mention Jilly at home.

Yet Katy often felt bad that the Carter family's affection and generosity towards her were never reciprocated by her family. She felt compelled to tell Jilly what her mother was like, and why she couldn't invite her back to Collington Avenue. But it shamed her to think that was necessary.

Jilly only shrugged. 'Maybe she had something bad happen to her, to make her that way,' she said with her usual generosity. 'It doesn't worry me, anyway.'

As always, Katy felt happy to be with the Carters for a few hours; it would be bliss not to guard what she said, or to try and appease her mother.

'So what's brought you round in the middle of the week?' Jilly asked her, running her fingers through her blonde hair, as the woolly hat she'd been wearing had flattened it. 'Fed up with the police presence in your road, or is Rob getting on your nerves?'

'Neither of those two. Rob went back to Nottingham this morning, and I've decided to give finding a job in London a go. I hoped you might join me.'

'Oh wow, would I ever!' Jilly exclaimed, and both mother and daughter made whooping noises.

'She's been hoping for this for months,' Mrs Carter said.

'And I'll get a room to myself, if she leaves,' Patsy added.

Katy immediately felt just a little jealous that Jilly always had her family on her side, whatever she wanted to do. 'I've got a week's holiday owing to me,' she said. 'I think you said you've got some, too. So how about we go up there to reconnoitre?'

3

'Good luck and have a good time, girls,' Albert said as he dropped his daughter and Jilly off at the station on Saturday afternoon.

'Thanks, Dad,' Katy said, taking her small suitcase from her father. 'I'll phone tonight so you know we are safe, but if Mum answers I don't suppose she'll tell you.' She stood on her tiptoes to kiss him. 'I hope she isn't too mean to you.'

It had been a strange week. On the 24th there was the bombshell of Winston Churchill dying. It made her father very sad, as he'd admired him so much.

But since the evening when Rob said he was going, the atmosphere at home had been poisonous. Dinner practically thrown at the table, drawers and doors banged, and then when Katy said she was going to London on Saturday with Jilly Carter and that they would be staying in Hammersmith with Mrs Carter's sister, Hilda revved up the banging, the sighing and added abuse, too.

'You'd stay with a relative of that guttersnipe!' she exclaimed.

She carried on muttering about mice, rats and bedbug infestations until Albert ordered her to stop it.

'You are being ridiculous,' he said. 'There is no reason to suppose these people have a lower standard of living than us. Besides, Katy has made up her mind to go, and unless you start being a little more pleasant and encouraging, you may very well find that when she does move away, she won't even come back to visit.'

Albert chuckled at Katy now as they said their good-byes. He appreciated her saying she hoped her mother wouldn't be mean to him. 'Don't worry, I've lived with her moods for too many years to get distressed by them. But while you are away, I'm going to try and talk about our future together. We certainly can't carry on like this.'

Once the girls had found a compartment on the train all to themselves, Katy sighed with relief. 'I thought Mum was going to try and stop me,' she admitted to her friend. 'I expected her to play ill or something; she's done that before now when I said I was going somewhere special. You are lucky your mum is so well balanced.'

Jilly looked lovely today. Although she was only wearing her old navy-blue coat, she'd added a shocking-pink woolly hat and matching scarf, and even her lipstick was the same colour.

'She's had to be well balanced; my dad's been in and out of work all their married life. The building trade is like that, especially in the winter.'

'Then I don't suppose she'll really want you to move out?'

Jilly laughed. 'Oh, she's not like that, she makes jokes about how I eat three pounds' worth of food a week and only give her two pounds ten shillings. She wants me to work at London Zoo as much as I do. Speaking of which, I've got a surprise for you. They rang me late yesterday afternoon and I've got an interview there on Tuesday morning!'

Katy whooped loudly with joy. 'How wonderful. We'll have to celebrate that tonight.'

'I expect Mum's already been on the phone by now to tell Auntie Joan about it. She'll be thrilled and baking a cake or something.'

Katy already knew that Mr and Mrs Underwood, Jilly's Auntie Joan and Uncle Ken, adored her as they had no children of their own. So the girls would be made very comfortable and be fed really well, but the downside, as Jilly had pointed out, was that they wouldn't be able to stay out half the night, or come back roaring drunk.

But then, this time in London wasn't supposed to be about going out dancing or drinking in clubs. Jilly had her job interview at the zoo, Katy would be calling on employment agencies to find a job, and then they needed to find a flat.

Later that same day, tucked up in bed, with Jilly in the twin bed beside her, and traffic still humming outside even though it was nearly midnight, Katy felt she'd made the right choice in coming to London.

Mr and Mrs Underwood – or Joan and Ken, as they'd insisted she call them – were really kind, jolly people, and their Victorian terraced house was as cosy and warm as they were. They had already said the girls could come back and stay for as long as they liked once they'd started their new jobs, so they could find a flat at their leisure. But both girls were determined to find somewhere in the coming week. They had great plans for decorating it to their own taste and throwing parties.

Jilly's relatives, however lovely, were very strait-laced.

Just this evening Joan had spoken very disapprovingly of seeing a girl in the grocer's wearing the new miniskirt.

'I couldn't believe a girl so young could be that brazen,' she said in horrified tones.

Jilly and Katy had to choke back giggles. They both intended to shorten their skirts in line with what girls were wearing here, the moment they were settled in London.

Sunday was spent with Joan and Ken. They went for a bracing walk together along the riverbank towards Chiswick. It was very cold and the sky was the colour of lead, but it was good to see that even in a big city there were open places to walk. After a huge lunch, the rest of the afternoon was spent watching television and dozing by the fire. Then on Monday the girls roamed around Hammersmith. They had been advised it was a good, central area to find a flat and nowhere near as expensive as nearby Kensington.

They were a little daunted initially by how scruffy everywhere was, but a flat-letting agency they went into told them not to be put off by that. 'I have a very well-appointed one-bedroom basement flat in a very tidy road for just eight pounds a week,' the man told them.

That seemed cheap enough and they went to see it straight away, only to be horrified by how damp and dark it was.

'It was probably well appointed to him because he had a very reptilian look about him,' Jilly said as they scurried away. 'And the landlady was a dragon, too!'

They had a coffee before venturing into any further agencies, and kept laughing about the landlady, who had said she wouldn't tolerate male visitors, parties or loud music.

'It was so cold, too,' Katy said. 'And the stink of mould! We'd have people backing away from us because we'd picked up the smell on our clothes.'

On Tuesday they left home together at nine to go to Hammersmith tube station. Jilly was going off to Regent's Park for her interview at the zoo, and Katy to Oxford Circus to enrol at some employment agencies. They arranged to meet back home in the late afternoon.

By two o'clock Katy had been into four agencies and given all the details of her present and past employment, typing speeds, exam results and her personal interests, and she was feeling jaded. She'd been tested in typing and shorthand, and they all said her speeds were impressive. But none of the agencies had talked about specific companies that needed someone with her skills. All they'd said was that they would ring her at Hammersmith when they had something lined up. She guessed that she was being a bit naive to suppose they'd grab her with both hands, there and then.

She went into a Wimpy Bar for a hamburger and coffee, tempted to just go and look in the shops afterwards. But eating gave her a boost and it occurred to her that it might be smart to return to each of the agencies to ask if they'd found anything for her. If nothing else, it would make her look really keen. Employers were supposed to like that.

The first agency said they had been ringing around for interviews but were unable to pin anyone down as yet. The second looked at her askance, as if astounded she'd have the nerve to come back without being asked to. But the voluptuous blonde receptionist at Alfred Marks, the third agency, gave her a huge smile and said her colleague was just about to telephone the number in Hammersmith to ask her to ring them back to arrange an interview.

Half an hour later, Katy came out of the agency unable to stop grinning. She had an interview the next morning as a legal secretary for a firm of lawyers in the Inns of Court. She'd heard staff at her solicitors speak about this historical home for lawyers that hadn't changed in hundreds of years. In films she'd caught an occasional peep into the Dickensian chambers there, and it had always appealed to her.

But setting aside the interesting working environment, the wages of a legal secretary were almost three times more than she currently earned. The agency had said they were impressed by her typing accuracy, as there was no place for mistakes on legal documents.

Katy was so thrilled she went into Peter Robinson's at Oxford Circus and bought a black-and-white mini dress. As she was short, it was only about an inch and a half above her knees but the chequered styling was up to the minute. She would never have found such a dress in Bexhill.

'I've got the job!' Jilly yelled as Katy came through the door. 'There were four other girls for an interview, but they picked me!'

Katy threw her arms around her friend. 'I was sure you'd get it, you are such a good animal nurse.'

Jilly drew back from her, laughing, her eyes shining. 'Says you who have never seen me treat any animal. The closest you've come is seeing me feed Ruin.'

43

Katy couldn't help smiling. Ruin was a rather ugly, mottled brown mongrel, with a very soppy nature – unlike the animals Jilly would be handling at the zoo.

'Well, you tell me so much about the animals, it's like being there with you,' Katy laughed. 'And I've got an interview tomorrow. How about that!'

Over dinner, a delicious shepherd's pie, Jilly told them all about her interview.

'There was a panel of five people,' she said. 'I was terrified, because there were four other girls waiting to be interviewed and they all looked more suitable than me. The panel fired questions about hygiene at me, and then how you treat an animal when it is waking from anaesthetic. I almost joked that I'd back out the door if it was a tiger, but luckily I stopped myself in time and admitted that all I could tell them was what I knew about domestic animals. I added that I supposed bigger, wild animals could be at their most dangerous at such a time, so I would expect a more senior nurse or the vet to explain what to do.'

'Heavens above,' Joan exclaimed. 'I can't imagine anyone nursing a tiger. In fact, I don't much like the idea of you near one, either!'

'She can't be a veterinary nurse without getting near the patient,' Ken said with a grin. 'But I'm sure they don't take any risks with wild animals. So did they tell you that you had the job right away?'

'No, they asked me to wait in an adjoining room and I had to do some strange intelligence test. It was stuff like six different objects and you had to ring the odd one out. Or spot the differences between two pictures which, at first glance, looked the same. I can't really see what bearing that would have on nursing sick animals.'

'I would think powers of observation were vitally important,' Joan said. 'I read somewhere that they do tests like that in many schools now, and they can work out your IQ from the results. So did they tell you they wanted you right after that?'

'Yes, one of the men, Mr Metcalf, I think he's the top vet there, came back in the room, checked all my answers, then he smiled and asked how soon I could start. I'll be a very junior nurse there – the bottom of the heap, always working under supervision – for at least a year. But that's what I expected, anyway. And I was so surprised I'd been picked, I could hardly speak.'

'So when did you say you'd start?' Katy asked.

'I said I'd have to give notice in Bexhill, but I thought they would be alright with just a week. So a week next Monday I might be going in there to work. Imagine that!'

'Let's hope I get my job tomorrow, then,' Katy said.

'I'm sure you will,' Jilly said stoutly. 'I'll come up there with you and wait somewhere close by.'

Katy put on a plain high-necked black wool dress the next morning, just in case she was asked to take her coat off at the interview. She tied her hair back in one bunch at the nape of her neck and finished it off with a black ribbon.

'A bit funereal,' Jilly remarked.

Jilly never wore black; she liked bold colours, and once said it was because she hated to be overlooked. Katy didn't think anyone would ever overlook her flamboyant friend.

'Lawyers' chambers are serious places,' Katy retorted. 'Besides, my navy houndstooth-check coat isn't funereal, and they might not ask me to take it off.'

'You might fall in love with a barrister,' Jilly giggled. 'Just imagine! But could you bear a man wearing a wig?'

'They only wear the wig in court, silly,' Katy said. 'And I expect every last one of them is already married, with bad breath and smelly feet. Now let's get going!'

The girls got off the underground at Temple station by the Thames and walked up into Middle Temple. Katy was too nervous to take much notice of the centuries-old buildings, the gaslights or the ancient doorways that led to rabbit warrens of lawyers' offices beyond.

They found the chambers of Frey, Hurst and Herbert easily, as the brass plaque just inside the porch with their name on it was larger than others they'd seen.

'I'll go and explore,' Jilly said. 'If I'm not here when you come out, just wait.' She put her arms round her friend for a brief hug. 'Good luck, and don't forget what my mum always says: "Look your interviewer in the eye, and ask intelligent questions."'

Katy's interviewer, a Miss Frogatt, came to the reception desk to meet her. She was a slender, very smart woman of about forty. Her plain black suit, high heels and shiny blonde bob all spoke of stern authority.

'Good morning, Miss Speed. I have to admit your surname is most appropriate, if the agency has given me your correct typing and shorthand speeds. Come along to my office now and you can tell me a little more about yourself. I will be testing those speeds myself later.'

Her office was spartan compared with others they passed that were furnished with red leather chairs, walls lined with books and enjoyed roaring fires. Miss Frogatt had an uncluttered light-wood desk, a four-tier filing basket and a wall of filing cabinets. Not even a framed photograph of a husband or other family member. But then Katy realized very quickly that the woman was strictly business. It would be hard to imagine her ever unbending enough to share a bit of gossip or to talk about her private life.

Yet despite that appearance she asked Katy questions about the kind of work she did in her present job in an encouraging way.

'Mostly I take dictation and then type up letters about property sales, divorces and wills,' Katy said. 'I have, of course, typed many legal documents, too.'

'That is good.' Miss Frogatt nodded. 'The ones you will be expected to do here are usually for a trial, for the barrister who is prosecuting, or defending a client. I have to warn you now, and this is of vital importance, you must never discuss anything you might hear about in the course of your work, not with anyone.'

'Of course,' Katy said. That was obvious to her; she'd had it drilled into her when she first joined the practice in Bexhill. 'I understand confidentiality is vital in the legal profession.'

'I'm glad you understand that, Miss Speed,' the older woman said. 'Unfortunately, we have had secretaries who have come, like you, from provincial solicitors, where the most interesting documents they have seen until coming to us are divorce petitions. Here we often have very high-profile cases – murders, for instance – cases that are in the news, and however tempting it might be to chat about what you know, it is vital you don't.'

Miss Frogatt tested Katy's typing and shorthand speeds herself in another office, and also got her to fill in an application form. As Katy had only ever worked for the one company, and while at school had had a Saturday job in Woolworths, it didn't take long.

Then Miss Frogatt left Katy alone in the office, not even explaining whether she was to stay or go. After some twenty minutes Katy got a bit scared, and thought perhaps she'd been forgotten or, worse still, that they had expected her to leave.

She was just about to get up when Miss Frogatt came back, and this time her smile was a real one. 'Well, Miss Speed, I've just had a word with Mr Marshfield in the Bexhill practice and although he was surprised you were seeking a new position, he gave you a glowing reference. He said he would be very sorry to lose you.'

'I didn't tell them I was thinking of moving to London,' Katy said, a bit panicked that she hadn't prepared anyone.

'I'm sorry if I've embarrassed you,' Miss Frogatt replied, not looking sorry at all, only rather pleased with herself. 'But I discovered some time ago that one always gets a more truthful reference by putting people on the spot. A written one can often be a work of fiction.'

There was nothing Katy could say in response. In fact, she'd typed up references for people in the past, and sometimes she barely recognized the person being described.

'I've been told they will let you off with two weeks'

notice,' Miss Frogatt went on. 'So if you would like the job, you can start on Monday, February 22nd. Is that alright with you?'

'It's wonderful,' Katy said, without thinking, then blushed scarlet. 'I mean, yes, thank you.'

'Just pop into the last office before reception on your way out and see Mrs Greenwood. She will take down a few more particulars and explain about your wages and working hours. I shall look forward to seeing you on the twenty-second.'

Jilly was waiting outside as Katy came out.

'Well?' she asked, tucking her hand through her friend's arm. 'I'm frozen, so let's go quickly to somewhere warm.'

'I start on February 22nd, I can hardly believe it!' Katy said as they walked quickly away. 'I'll be paid seventy-five pounds a month. I never expected so much.'

'Well, everyone says we get rubbish wages at home. Now did you see anyone you thought might be a friend there? Any nice men?'

'All the women I saw were much older than me, but I saw a bloke who appealed. I'd say he was just a few years older than me, with dark hair, smart suit, nice dark eyes. He smiled at me as I was leaving. But it didn't strike me as the kind of place you'd chat or lark about. It was very quiet, so I'll have to watch myself.'

Later, in a small coffee bar in the Strand, Katy told Jilly about Mr Frey, the senior partner. Mrs Greenwood had taken her in to meet him before she left the chambers.

'He was a bit scary, with a big hooked nose and a deep plummy voice. He shook my hand so firmly I nearly cried out. But he said Miss Frogatt believed I would be an asset to the chambers, so I guess I'd better make sure I am.'

The girls spent the rest of the day calling in at flat-letting agencies and putting their names down. It was very disheartening to find a flat with two bedrooms would be at least twenty-five pounds a week, so they thought they would share a bedroom.

'That is until we meet some dreamboat and want to be alone with him,' Jilly said, arching her eyebrow suggestively.

'Would you do it?' Katy asked.

They often discussed whether they would go 'all the way', but although Jilly said she might with the right man, Katy was too scared. She knew logically that her mother had brainwashed her into believing that every man in the world was so desperate for sex he'd do and say anything to get it. Clearly it wasn't true of all men, but all the ones she'd met at dances were like octopuses, their hands everywhere. She had the idea that she'd know the man of her dreams when he came along, because he wouldn't try forcing her into anything but would just wait till the time was right.

That evening the girls went out to Chelsea. They had heard the King's Road was really exciting, with lovely shops and bars. Their source hadn't exaggerated; compared with Bexhill on a cold February night it was like landing in Las Vegas. Throngs of people shuffled along the pavements just as the girls were doing, admiring the brightly lit displays in shop windows, happy to be a part of it all. All the many cafés, restaurants and bars were packed with young people, and music wafted out from every door.

'I never expected anything like this,' Katy said in awe. 'I wish we could live here. It looks so much fun.'

They stopped to look in a letting agent's window, and as they read the cards displayed they realized it would be far beyond their reach.

'It doesn't matter,' Jilly said. 'We can always visit here – and meanwhile, let's get a drink and find some blokes to flirt with.'

Much later that evening, going home on the tube, they couldn't stop giggling, partly because they were tiddly, but also because of the two men who had plied them with drink. Jeremy and Martin were snooty, upper-crust types who imagined they were doing the poor little country girls a favour just speaking to them. No doubt they thought if they plied them with enough drink they'd get them into bed later, too. However, the girls played up to them, making out they were totally naive and in awe of them. Then, when the men had gone to the bar to get more drink, they slipped out of the pub and ran along to Sloane Square to get the tube home.

'They thought far too much of themselves,' Katy giggled. 'And they both had BO and weren't even good-looking. As Rob would say, "I wouldn't piss on them if they were on fire."'

'I bet they were savage they bought us so many drinks,' Jilly said gleefully. 'I should've told them they'd need chloroform to get us into bed.'

'What a brilliant evening, though,' Katy said. 'I wish we could live in Chelsea, it really felt everything was happening there. Hammersmith doesn't feel that way.'

'No, it doesn't. But don't say that to my aunt and uncle, they'd be hurt. Maybe we should try some other areas?'

'We'll do that tomorrow,' Katy said. 'But now we'd better try and look sober for when we get home.'

4

'I'm dreading going home,' Katy admitted as she and Jilly came out of Bexhill Station.

It was Saturday afternoon, a week since they'd left for London, and although she had phoned home twice whilst they were away, her mother would not engage in any conversation. She didn't even respond when Katy told her she'd got a really good job. She also claimed Albert was out, when Katy was fairly sure he was just in his shed and could be called from the kitchen.

'Well, you've only got two weeks of it,' Jilly said, putting her arm around her friend's shoulders comfortingly. 'And I'll still be around for the first week. Shame we didn't find a flat, but I'll carry on looking when I go back.'

'Your auntie and uncle are so kind saying we can stay there,' Katy said. 'They made me see just how odd my mum is. And I suppose it is more sensible to look for a place once we're there.'

They had looked at more than ten flats in the week, and all of them were awful. One had the bath in the kitchen with a board over the top of it. Some of the others had shared bathrooms with other tenants, and all the flats were grubby, with shabby furniture, dirty carpets and stained beds. When they answered advertisements in the evening paper, those flats had already gone. Yet despite the disappointment of not finding a flat, they'd had a wonderful time in London and couldn't wait to get back there.

After arranging to meet up with Jilly in the coming week, Katy picked up her case and made her way home to Collington Avenue with a heavy heart.

'So you're back, then?' Hilda said as Katy came in through the back door, straight into the kitchen. She was sitting at the kitchen table polishing some brass and looked at her daughter with a sour expression.

'It appears that way,' Katy said. 'I did say I'd be home today.'

'Don't use sarcasm on me,' her mother snapped.

'Well, how about you act a little more welcoming?' Katy retorted. 'Honestly, Mum, you are so nasty sometimes. Is it any wonder I want to move away? Where's Dad? I want to tell him about my new job.'

'Then you'd better go to the police station. He's been arrested!'

Katy nearly laughed, assuming it was a joke. But, of course, her mother never made jokes. And who would joke about something like that?

'Arrested!' she exclaimed. 'Whatever for? Mum, you are scaring me. What is this about?'

'He's been arrested for murder. He killed Mrs Reynolds and her daughter.'

Katy's legs buckled under her, and she had to grab the back of a chair for support.

'My dad would never kill anyone,' she said, and her voice came out thin and shaky. 'Who said he did?'

Hilda shrugged her thin shoulders and pursed her lips.

'They must have evidence; they just came and took him away soon after he came in from work yesterday.'

'But he was asleep when the fire broke out, as we all were.'

'That's what I told the police. But something woke me, so maybe it was Albert getting back into bed.'

Katy looked at her mother in horror. 'You can't believe that. What makes you say such a thing?'

Hilda picked up a small brass jug and began polishing it vigorously. 'I don't know what to believe any more. I never imagined he would have an affair with another woman, but it looks as if that's exactly what he's been doing. So, you tell me why I should believe he didn't kill her?'

Katy felt sick and dizzy; it was as if she was being sucked into some kind of maelstrom, with nothing to hang on to, not even her own sanity. She sat down heavily and rested her head on her hands for a moment to stop the dizziness.

'Mum, even if he had been having an affair with Mrs Reynolds, which I don't believe for a second, he would never kill her. Especially by burning her house down. That was done by someone deranged. He's gentle, kind and so very tolerant.'

'The neighbours all thought John Christie was a good man,' Hilda said. 'But he killed young women and buried them in his house. And he let his poor, simple-minded lodger take the blame and be hanged.'

'Dad is as far removed from Christie as you are from Marilyn Monroe,' Katy bellowed, enraged that anyone could be that stupid. 'I'm going down to the police station now to see him.'

*

Katy ran the whole way to the police station, crying as she went. Although only five o'clock in the afternoon, it was already dark and bitingly cold and there were very few people about.

At the counter in the police station she asked to see her father. The middle-aged, balding desk sergeant at first refused her. But when she started to cry again he said he'd see what he could do and disappeared out the back.

Some twenty minutes passed before he came back. 'Okay, miss, I've put him in an interview room. You can have a few minutes, that's all.'

Being led along passages, and then down some plain stone stairs with a terrible smell of damp, made her father's predicament seem even worse. She saw a doorway covered with an iron grille that clearly led to the cells, straight ahead of her, but she was led off to the right and ushered into a very small, windowless room. All it held was two chairs, a tiny table – and her father.

She had never seen him like this before. Unshaven, and with red-rimmed eyes full of anxiety. He looked older and beaten down.

Katy rushed into his arms. 'Oh, Daddy, how could they even think it was you?'

He hugged her tightly for a moment and then nudged her on to one chair. He took the other chair and leaned across the table to wipe the tears from her eyes with his thumb. She caught hold of his hand tightly, fighting back more tears.

'They found paraffin in my shed,' he said. 'The can was mine; I bought it once, when I ran out of petrol, so it had my fingerprints on it. But as God is my witness, I've never put any paraffin in it. Why would I? We don't have any paraffin stoves. But they also found some material which they said was the same as whatever was used to start the fire. The only material I've ever had in my shed was rags: old pants and vests and bits of worn-out flannel sheets. They showed me the stuff they found. It was like curtain material; it wouldn't have been any use for rags, as it wasn't absorbent, and I'd never seen it before, anyway. So someone put it there to incriminate me.' He paused for a moment, looking at Katy intently. 'I was in bed asleep when it started. I got up five or ten minutes before your mother woke you and Rob, and in that time I rang 999.'

'I believe you, Dad, I know you wouldn't hurt anyone. But Mum thinks you were having an affair with Gloria Reynolds.'

Her father shook his head. 'So the police told me. I wasn't, of course, but I am guilty of not telling your mother I became friends with her. I'm sure you can imagine why! Do you remember the fuss she made when I went over there to repair the cistern?'

Katy nodded; she did remember. It was a couple of years ago, on a Sunday. Mrs Reynolds came over, distraught, because water was cascading down the wall from her bathroom. Albert grabbed his tools and went back with her, but when he returned home an hour later, Hilda was furious with him. She kept up a tirade for the rest of the day.

'From that day on I often popped in to see her, because I liked her. She was warm, funny and kind and always so pleased to see me. She'd had a violent husband she'd run away from, and had to bring her children up on her own.

We often talked about what hell it was living with some-one whose moods were so unpredictable, you never knew when they were going to turn on you. I'd never admitted to anyone before what Hilda was like – after all, it made me look so weak. But I did to Gloria.'

'Oh, Dad . . .' Katy began to cry again. 'I liked her, too; I can understand you confiding in her. But who do you think set the fire?'

'I'd say it was one of the husbands of the women she helped,' he said thoughtfully. 'Or maybe her ex-husband.'

'What do you mean about women she helped?'

'She helped them get away from violent husbands,' he said.

All at once, like a light being switched on, Katy realized that was who the women were; the women she had seen arriving in the black car. 'They came with a plump older woman in a black Humber?'

Her father nodded. 'Yes. Well, I only saw her friend with the black car once, but Gloria told me she often brought women to her. They would stay for a couple of days while Gloria talked to them and helped them to begin a new life. She had to keep it secret, for obvious reasons; the husbands of those women were dangerous.'

Katy realized that at any minute the sergeant would be back to ask her to leave. 'Look, Daddy, we haven't got long. What can I do to help?'

'You can ring my solicitor and arrange to meet him, so you can give him a bit more background – especially what I've said about these women Gloria helped. Until last night I'd never met this criminal lawyer. His name is Michael Bonham; our company solicitor found him for me. He seems a good man. He's hoping he can get me bail at court on Monday.' He took a card from his pocket to give her. 'Mr Bonham has put his home number on the back. Will you ring him and ask if you can see him tomorrow?' He paused for a moment or two, as if considering what else he had to tell her. 'If you could get a couple of clean shirts, shaving stuff and a change of underwear and bring it down here, that would be wonderful, Katy,' he went on to say.

The door opened and the sergeant was back. 'Time's up,' he said.

'I'll come to the court on Monday,' Katy said, going to her father to hug him.

'No you won't, that's why I said to see Bonham tomorrow. Nothing much will happen at the court – it's just applying for bail – so it's better that you go to work.'

Katy wanted to protest, but she knew by his tone of voice he meant what he said. He was trying to keep her out of this, perhaps afraid someone who knew her might see her at the court. She could argue that the whole of Bexhill would know he'd been charged with murder by Monday evening, once the local paper got hold of the story. But she had to leave him with some hope her name wouldn't be tainted, too.

One last hug and biting back tears, she left. As he disappeared with a constable down to the cells, the gate was locked behind them. The sergeant gave her a nudge so she would go on up the stairs and back to reception, and Katy shuddered. If Dad didn't get bail on Monday, how was he going to cope with prison? He was an outdoors kind of man who loved long walks, working in the garden – even when he worked in his shed, he left the door wide open.

But more importantly, how could he cope with being labelled a murderer?

She rang Michael Bonham from a telephone box before returning home. He was reassuring to speak to; his voice was very deep and he was patient with her when she stumbled over words.

'I know my dad could never have set that fire,' she said passionately. 'He would never hurt any woman, even one he disliked. And he really liked Gloria Reynolds; they were friends. He's a very honest man, you must believe that.'

'I do believe that, Katy,' he said. 'I wouldn't want to defend your father unless I believed he was speaking the truth. I suggest that we meet tomorrow, and you give me a bit more background information. You can probably give me a different perspective on Mrs Reynolds, too.'

They arranged to meet at a coffee bar on the seafront at eleven the following morning.

Katy went home then, feeling more alone than she had ever felt in her life before. She was tempted to go to Jilly's and tell her all about it, but she knew that wasn't a good idea, not yet. Rob should know, and she wished she could tell him, but she had no phone number for him. In the past he had always rung home on Sunday mornings. But he'd been so fed up when he left this time, he probably wouldn't bother. She'd sit down and write straight after dinner.

First she had to face her mother again, to try and convince her she was mistaken about her husband having an affair. But that was going to be hard; she knew of old that when Hilda was set against someone, nothing would change her mind.

*

60

Katy left home on Sunday morning just before ten, taking with her the items her father had asked for. She'd written to Rob and posted the letter, begging him to phone as soon as he got it. Sadly, she hadn't made any headway with her mother. Hilda was still stubbornly insisting that her husband was unfaithful. She didn't even seem to understand the implications of being charged with murder; that he could get a life sentence, or maybe even be hanged, without her support. She said she wasn't going to let him back in the house, even if he did get bail.

At one point Katy had screamed at her, 'Do you really believe he set fire to number 26? Because if you don't believe it, then you must help him.'

Her mother's answer had floored her. 'By consorting with that woman right under my nose, he deserves all he gets.'

Katy had been tempted to slap her mother's face to bring her to her senses. But she'd controlled herself; hitting her mother would just make things worse between them.

It was another bitterly cold day, but it was good to be out of the house and away from her mother's malevolence. Hilda had gone on and on about Albert's supposed affair. But if she really believed he was having an affair, Katy thought, why hadn't she tackled him about it before? Only a completely crazy person would wake in the night to see a fire, and jump to the conclusion that her husband had started it to cover his infidelity.

Katy had said this to her. But her mother's answer had been that, although she'd had her suspicions her husband was having an affair, it was only confirmed after the fire

61

because of the way he kept looking sadly across the road at the burnt-out house. And then he'd cried openly when the stretchers were brought out. Katy pointed out that she'd looked at the house sadly too, and had cried, as had probably every single one of their neighbours. Did that make them suspects, too?

After leaving her father's things at the police station, Katy went down to the seafront to the Marine Café. It was one of the few cafés facing the sea which opened all year, and it was renowned for its full English breakfasts. It was Rob's favourite café; Katy always went there with him when he came home for the holidays.

Michael Bonham had said she would recognize him by his dark brown sheepskin coat, and she did immediately. He actually looked as if the coat wasn't his. His hair was cut very short and slicked down with Brylcreem. The knife-edge crease in his navy-blue trousers, and the highly polished expensive shoes, would both have been happier paired with a dark wool overcoat. But Katy had a feeling he didn't want to look like a lawyer, and the sheepskin coat was a prop.

He had got a table in the corner, at the back of the café, where presumably they wouldn't be overheard. Close up he was older than she first thought; he had a lined face, and his eyelids drooped over washed-out blue eyes. Even his hair was white rather than blond. She guessed him to be in his late fifties.

'Mr Bonham?' she said and held out her hand. 'I'm Katy Speed.'

He ordered coffee for them both, asking if she'd like something to eat, too.

'No, thank you, I'm too nervous to eat anything,' she said with a glum smile.

He put his hand over hers comfortingly. 'Yes, I'm sure you must be. But from what I've learned about your father, I really don't think the police can make this charge stick.'

After the waitress had brought them coffee, he asked her to tell him exactly what happened the night of the fire. Then he went on to ask her what she knew of Gloria Reynolds.

'She was a good, kind woman,' Katy said. 'I really don't believe for one moment that she and Dad were having an affair. And even if they were, why would Dad want to kill her? Mum would be terribly angry, of course – but she tends to be angry all the time, anyway – and really an affair would just have given Dad the excuse, if he needed one, to leave her. He wouldn't be worried about Rob and me; we are old enough to be able to cope with divorced parents. Besides, who would kill a woman he cared for just to prevent his wife finding out?'

'It has happened, many times, though mostly when the wife was the wealthy spouse. Speaking of which, your father is quite wealthy. Is there any possibility Gloria could have been blackmailing him?'

Katy looked at the lawyer askance. 'Do you suppose a woman who helps other women get away from violent husbands would even think of blackmail?'

'One wouldn't have thought so, but all kinds of people become blackmailers, Katy. I have to ask if it was possible.'

'Remember, my father is a clever businessman,' Katy said reprovingly. 'He's kind and generous, but not a fool. I don't understand why the police aren't looking for one of the violent husbands? One of them is far more likely to have done it.'

'Yes, I agree with that entirely. But I don't think the police knew she was helping other women. I didn't, until your father told me. This is something I must speak to them about. The very nature of the help she gave needed to be kept a secret. If those violent men knew who was helping their wives to escape them, taking the children with them, they were very likely to seek them out and drag them home.'

'So surely that makes one of them a prime suspect?'

'To us it does. But as I said, the police didn't know about these beaten women that Mrs Reynolds had been helping, at the time of your father's arrest. As far as they were concerned, the paraffin can with your father's prints on it, and the material in his shed – which was the same cloth as was used to start the fire – were enough.'

Katy rolled her eyes impatiently. 'From what you've learned about my father, did he strike you as a stupid man?'

'No, of course not. Far from it.'

'Well, if he had done this terrible crime, would he leave evidence like the can and the cloth in his shed for the police to find?'

Bonham smirked. 'No, I wouldn't think so. And believe me, that is something I will put to the prosecution. You are not like him in looks, Katy, but you have the same direct way of speaking, I like that.'

They talked for some time, Katy telling him about her job at the solicitors and the one she had just got in London. 'I'm not sure they'll want me in either job if this gets out,' she said ruefully.

'Sadly, it will get out, Bexhill being such a small place and your father being a prominent businessman. So first thing tomorrow you must tell the senior partner at your firm. If you tell him before he hears it from someone else, he's more likely to be sympathetic. Okay, he may feel you must go straight away, but maybe not. As for the London job, I see no real reason why you should tell them anything. It won't affect them in any way.'

'What can I do to help my dad?' she asked. 'Will you be talking to Gloria's other two children? I mean they may know what she thought about Dad?'

'I do want to talk to them very much, and as the funeral has been arranged for this Friday I shall go and try to talk to them, and perhaps other close friends.'

'I'd like to go to the funeral too, to pay my respects,' Katy said. 'But I don't suppose I'd be welcome.'

Bonham pursed his lips. 'No, Katy, I doubt you would be. In situations like this it is usually better to keep your distance. But I shall try to talk to the daughter.'

'There was a lady called Marleen who Gloria used to call on at busy times and whenever she needed time off from her shop,' Katy suddenly remembered. 'I got the idea she was a very old friend, not just an employee. She lives at Cooden Beach, but I don't know the address.'

'Now that is useful.' Bonham beamed. 'She might be able to tell me about the woman with the black Humber.'

'I wish I could do something to help,' Katy said wistfully.

Bonham touched her cheek gently with the palm of his hand. 'You could rack your brains to try and remember if Gloria ever mentioned any friends, or even people she disliked. You could try asking other people you know; sometimes a bit of gossip can prove useful. The police did question the immediate neighbours just after the fire, but maybe you know other people in the road who were friendly with her?'

Katy nodded. She couldn't think of anyone just now, but she would mull it over and ask questions anyway. 'I'll do my best,' she said.

'I must go now,' Bonham said, getting to his feet, 'I've got some relatives coming for lunch, and I'll be in trouble if I don't get back to give my wife a hand. Now you've got my number, Katy, if you think of anything, or find out something, however small, ring me! Also, if you do move up to London as you've planned, let me know your address and telephone number.'

Katy walked out of the café with him, and turned down a lift home in his car. 'A walk will do me good,' she said as she shook his hand. 'It may calm me down enough to prevent me attacking my mother.'

Bonham laughed and put his hand on her shoulder. 'This is a difficult time for you, Katy. But keep your sense of humour, and believe in your father, and I'm sure it will all come right in the end.'

At lunchtime on Monday Katy slipped out to get some aspirin from the chemist as she had a thumping headache. After seeing Bonham on the previous day she'd gone round to tell Jilly and her family what had happened, and ended up staying with them for lunch. Even though she'd phoned to say she wasn't coming back, she still got it in the neck when she returned home at about six. Sometimes it seemed her mother had a degree in acting the martyr. She got the whole 'I'm here alone all the time' routine. Katy was tempted to say her mother wouldn't be alone if she hadn't told the police her husband was the arsonist. She didn't say it, though, as she wasn't sure if it was actually Hilda who had told the police.

Then this morning she had to brace herself to tell Mr Marshfield about her father's arrest. She had expected him to be horrified, to tell her to leave right away. But to her surprise he was sympathetic.

'How utterly ridiculous,' he exclaimed. 'I can't imagine anyone less likely to wilfully start a fire.'

'I hope the police and prosecution will see that about him,' Katy said. 'But meanwhile, Mr Marshfield, I had intended to give you a fortnight's notice today because I've found another job in London. But under the circumstances you might want me to leave right now.'

'I realized you were going to move on when we were asked to give you a reference, my dear. But I certainly won't be asking you to leave now, not when you've been such a first-class employee. In fact, if you decide you don't want to go to London because of your father, you may stay with us as long as you like.'

Katy could hardly believe this cold, humourless man could be so kind. It brought tears to her eyes. 'Thank you, sir,' she said in a small voice. 'You can't imagine how touched I am at your reaction. But I'm afraid my presence here might impact on the practice.'

'Why should it, my dear? You have been with us for years and know most of our clients. Your father is a well-respected man, and Gloria Reynolds was a good woman. I believe most people will see this for what it is: a mistake by the police. Now run along and get ready for dictation. The practice will grind to a halt if we don't get letters sent out.'

But the headache had remained, and it was so hard to concentrate when she had so much on her mind. She thought a brisk walk in the fresh air might banish the headache and make her feel less exhausted and fraught.

She bought the aspirin and went down to the seafront. On such a raw day it was deserted, as she'd expected, and the waves were pounding on the beach, threatening to crash over the sea wall.

It was too blustery to walk comfortably so after a few minutes she crossed over and went up a side street. Glancing ahead, she saw a car she recognized pulling in to park further up the street.

The black Humber!

She couldn't believe her luck. Doubling her speed, she reached the car just as the dumpy lady she'd seen so many times before got out.

'Excuse me,' Katy said breathlessly. 'But I believe you were a friend of Gloria Reynolds. May I talk to you for a few minutes, if you aren't too busy?'

The older woman frowned, clearly thrown by being accosted in the street. 'Well, yes, but you do know she died recently?'

Katy realized the woman thought she was from the press and the idea of speaking to a journalist scared her.

'Yes, I do. I live opposite Gloria, I promise you I'm not from a newspaper. I liked her very much,' Katy said. 'But I really must talk to you.'

The woman still looked scared. 'Well, I can only give

68

you a few minutes, as I have appointments this afternoon. But come in out of this wind.'

It was a very ordinary semi-detached house, and as the woman opened the front door Katy noted the decor was from the early fifties, with a spindle-legged telephone table and yellow-and-black contemporary wallpaper.

'I'm so sorry, I don't know your name, but I'm Katy Speed. As I live opposite Gloria, I've seen you visiting there many times. Her death is such a tragedy.'

'Yes, indeed, a terrible thing,' the woman said and her dark eyes filled up. 'I'm Edna Coltrain, and could you be Albert's daughter?'

'Yes, I am. Have you met him, then?'

'Just once, but Gloria spoke of him often and pointed out his home. He helped her out many times; she was very fond of him.'

After all the bad things that had happened, it was so good to hear something good.

'If that's the case, you'll be shocked to hear he's been charged with setting the fire and killing Gloria and her daughter,' Katy said. 'It is madness, he wouldn't hurt anyone, let alone a woman he liked and admired.'

All the colour suddenly drained from Edna's face.

'I'm so sorry, I've given you a nasty shock,' Katy said and begged Edna to sit down while she made her a cup of tea. 'Dad told me about what you and Gloria do. In my opinion, it's far more likely the fire was started because of that.'

Katy went into the kitchen and made the tea. When she came back Edna's colour had improved a little, but she still looked really shaken. Her living room was also stuck in the fifties, with everything either red or grey, and a huge gold sunray concave mirror on the chimney breast. She guessed Edna was about forty-five. Although overweight and short, she had a pretty face with soft dark eyes and beautiful skin.

'I couldn't believe Gloria and Elsie, her daughter, lost their lives in the fire.' Edna took her cup of tea from Katy, but her voice and hands shook. 'I heard talk that it was arson, but I thought it was just talk. And now you say your father has been blamed! Why? Gloria thought he was a sweet, kind man.'

'He is,' Katy said. 'Someone has gone out of their way to frame him; the police found a paraffin can in his shed.'

'Surely half the men in England have some paraffin in their sheds?'

'Well, Dad didn't – we don't have any heaters that need it. Last time he used the can, it was for petrol, and his fingerprints were all over it. There was also some curtain fabric, identical to pieces found at the burning house. I think the person responsible must be one of the husbands of the women you've helped.'

'Oh my God!' Edna clutched at her neck, looking terrified. 'I was always afraid one of them would come after us. I said that much to Gloria, but she said bullies are cowards; they hit their wives but are afraid of everyone else.'

'It seems she was wrong,' Katy said. 'Will you come to the police station and tell them what you know?'

'My dear, I can't do that,' Edna gasped. 'I'd never be able to sleep at night again.'

Katy sat down beside the older woman on the couch and took her left hand in both of hers. 'Edna, from what I know of Gloria, she'd expect you to help the police by telling them all you know. They will look after you.'

'I can't, Katy, I just can't. I have a violent husband, too. If he knew where I was, he'd come and kill me.'

All at once Katy had a better understanding of what Gloria, Edna and those other women had been through. Always looking over their shoulder in case their man came after them. It wasn't an irrational fear, either. Any publicity could alert the man.

'I'm not saying you'd have to speak up in court. Just explain to the police what you and Gloria did. If they know you are afraid of your husbands, they will look after you.'

'Don't you believe that, my dear,' Edna said indignantly. 'We've all been to hospital with injuries and broken bones, and the police have been called. All they do is take the men in, read them the riot act, then let them go, often to go straight home and lay into their wives again. I wouldn't mind betting most policemen hit their wives. They have the attitude that it's a man's right to punish his wife if she's done something he doesn't like.'

'Please, Edna, I'll come with you,' Katy pleaded. 'If you won't go to the police, then talk to Dad's solicitor. I'm sure Gloria would want you to.'

'You don't understand, Katy,' Edna said, wringing her hands. 'Gloria and I succeeded in helping women start over after a life of terror by keeping what we did a secret. Some of these women were from middle-class homes, not just worn-down drudges from slum areas. As such they were married to intelligent, powerful men. The kind of men who have fingers in many pies. What you are asking could jeopardize the present safety of dozens of women and their children.'

Katy suddenly realized Edna and Gloria's partnership was something special. They were brave, selfless women who could have just laid low, happy they had managed to escape cruelty, but instead they had gone out of their way to help others in the same predicament. The deaths of Gloria and her daughter were evidence of the true dangers in doing such work. How could she now expect Edna to put her life on the line?

5

Mr Bonham telephoned Katy at the office just as she was leaving to go home on Monday.

'I am so sorry,' he said, confirming what she had feared. 'I'm afraid the judge wouldn't allow bail, as it is a capital offence. Your father asked me to ring you; he said to keep your chin up and that he believes the truth will eventually come out.'

Katy's eyes prickled and tears spilled over. 'But it's so unfair,' she managed to get out. 'Dad is the most honourable person in the world. He wouldn't have skipped off.'

'I think the judge was aware of that, but he had to be seen to be upholding the law. Your father is on his way to Lewes gaol tonight but he could be moved to Brixton prison in London, as that's where they send most of the remand prisoners who are charged with a serious crime. At least it will be easier for you to see him when you move to London.'

'How will he bear it?' Katy sobbed out.

'He answered that for you. He said, "Remind her I was in the army and it won't be that different." He also said you were to take the job in London and enjoy a new life.'

'He surely doesn't think I'll forget him?' Katy asked, her voice rising in agitation.

'That wasn't what he meant. I think he meant for you to have a good time with your friend, to be young and silly for a change. He's glad you are getting away from home at last.'

Katy pulled herself together and told him about meeting Edna and what had been said.

'I'm not surprised she feels that way; she is right, there is virtually no protection for women who have violent husbands,' Bonham said. 'I can order her to court as a witness, but I'd rather she gave evidence of her own free will.'

'I did give her my address and phone number – and yours, too – in case she changes her mind,' Katy said. 'Maybe on Friday, when she's thinking about the funeral that she isn't brave enough to go to, she'll feel ashamed and want to help.'

'Yes, maybe,' he said. 'I fully understand why she is afraid; goodness knows, her friend dying in a fire is enough to terrify anyone. Getting men punished for cruelty to their wives is the only way to change our society and send out a message that it won't be tolerated.'

Rob called from a telephone box on Tuesday night, and it was lucky that Katy answered, as Hilda might not have let her speak to him.

'I wish I had phoned on Sunday, like I always used to do,' was the first thing he said, his voice shaking with emotion. 'I only got your letter this morning, and I could hardly believe they'd arrested Dad. Why didn't Mum send me a telegram?'

'She's still doing that stubborn thing,' Katy said cautiously, as she was sure her mother was listening. 'I'm so relieved you've phoned at last. I only found out about the arrest when I got back from London. Dad wouldn't let me go to the bail hearing, as I told you in my letter, but I'm sorry to say he didn't get bail, after all. He's in Lewes gaol on remand.'

'What a nightmare this is,' Rob said, and Katy was fairly certain he was crying. 'What can we do, Sis?'

Katy told him about seeing Edna and how she hoped the woman would speak up for their father. She also said how kind her boss had been. 'But word had got around about Dad already,' she told him. 'I saw a couple of the neighbours chatting in the street, and they stopped as I went by. Clearly dishing the dirt.'

'How can people be like that?' Rob asked. 'Over the years, Dad has helped so many of the neighbours. Are their memories so short they've forgotten how kind and generous he is?'

'Is that Rob?' Hilda barked out from just behind Katy. 'Let me speak to him.'

Katy handed over the receiver. There was no point in saying anything further to Rob, she'd told him all she knew, and maybe he could influence their mother to go and visit Dad.

She went upstairs, wishing Rob was here with her. Something told her that the incident with the gossiping neighbours wasn't going to be the only one. So little ever happened in this town, people enjoyed having something juicy to talk about. Katy was fairly certain that by the end of the week every person who knew her father would be convinced he'd had a torrid affair with Gloria. Perhaps they'd even suspect her of blackmailing him, just as that stupid policeman had suggested.

*

75

On Thursday evening Katy was just thinking about having an early night, as she'd promised to go out with Jilly the following night, her friend's last one in Bexhill, when the phone rang.

Katy went into the hall to answer it as her mother grunted it wouldn't be for her.

It was Edna, and she sounded as if she'd been crying. 'I've been thinking about Gloria and your father all week,' she began. 'I want to go to Gloria's funeral tomorrow, but since her death was reported in the newspapers I'm scared who might be there.'

Just the fact she'd telephoned gave Katy hope that Edna might yet help her father.

'There will be police watching, looking for anyone suspicious,' Katy said. 'So you'll be safe enough.'

'Maybe that's so, Katy, but I don't think you fully understand what both Gloria and I went through for so many years, and why I am so afraid.'

'I'd like to hear about it,' Katy said gently, aware the woman's voice was shaking with emotion.

'Gloria was far more to me than just an acquaintance or even a friend. She was more like the sister I never had, because we went through the same horror,' she began. 'You see, we met in the accident clinic of a hospital in central London. It was in 1950. We both had the kind of comfortable middle-class life that others envy, but that night we were both badly hurt, beaten by our well-educated, professional husbands.

'I had a broken arm, cracked ribs and had nearly lost my sight from a punch. Gloria had been kicked so badly all over that she could barely stand, let alone walk. As it

76

happened, our children weren't with us earlier in the evening when the attacks took place. My two were stopping the night with a friend; Gloria's were with her parents. If not for the children being away, I doubt we'd have sought medical help; we'd have done what we always did, patched ourselves up and hoped for the best, or waited for the next morning to get medical help when the kids were at school.'

Katy could hardly believe what she was hearing. She didn't know Edna well enough to make a judgement about her, but it was truly shocking to think glamorous, kindly Gloria could be beaten by her husband. 'Oh, Edna,' she gasped, 'that is awful. But please go on.'

'I don't want to keep you, I'm sure you've got better things to do than listen to me droning on, but I just want you to understand how it all came about. Gloria and I lived about four miles from each other. I was in Hampstead Garden Suburb, while she was in Primrose Hill. That night, we'd both chosen to go to a hospital well away from where we lived so we wouldn't run into anyone we knew. That's how bad it was!'

'But why should you be ashamed, when you were the victims?'

'In general, people don't see it that way,' Edna said, her voice cracking with emotion. 'They think you must've goaded your husband, done something really bad. No one understands that this can flare up because of something as simple and harmless as the dinner being five minutes late, or a shirt not being ironed.'

'Then you must've lived in fear?'

'Both of us did, always appeasing, trying to smooth things out so our men wouldn't fly into a rage. To be truthful, I often wished for death. His, preferably, but often the beatings were so bad I thought it would kill me. Yet it's miraculous just how much punishment the human body can take. But meeting Gloria that night, recognizing that her injuries came from the same source as mine and that she was a similar age and came from the same background as me, was sort of comforting. Like I wasn't the only pathetic creature unable to fight back. She told me later she felt the same, and as we had a long wait for treatment, we talked. Baring our souls, really. It was the first time I'd ever admitted to anyone that my husband the bank manager was a brute. Gloria's husband was a dentist. Two men who had gone to good schools, had all the advantages. They couldn't even be excused because they'd had a terrible time in the war. Both of them had been given desk jobs.

'Anyway, I guess we knew we'd hit rock bottom, sitting there in pain, our faces damaged, wearing expensive clothes and surrounded by drunks with injuries from fighting. Then Gloria took my hand and said, "Edna, meeting tonight like this is fate. I believe it means we have to get ourselves and our children to safety."'

Edna paused for a few moments and Katy felt she was struggling not to break down, determined to tell her just what Gloria and she had meant to each other. Katy wanted to hear it; she not only felt that getting close to this woman would help her father, but she needed to know what exactly had made someone kill Gloria and her daughter.

'That night was the turning point.' Edna's voice was stronger now. 'We not only grew tougher and braver together, but we also talked to the hospital almoner who gave us an address of someone she thought could help us.'

78

Katy was astounded by what she had heard. If she'd met Edna in any other way, place or time she would've thought of her as a middle-class woman who had never had a moment of grief or sadness in her life. Appearances could be so deceptive.

'You became like the woman who helped you?'

'We did eventually, but that was several years later. Right then we had to focus on our own problems. A few days later, Gloria and I went together to meet a Miss Dunkin in King's Cross. She was old, at least sixty-five, quite frail, but she was a real heroine. She'd quietly been assisting beaten women for years, using her own money to help set them up in a new life.

'She told us that many of her women didn't have a penny; they'd often run off with their children in just what they stood up in. Fortunately, both Gloria and I had nest eggs. We'd had the foresight to put a little away before we were married, and we'd been siphoning money from the housekeeping, even from our husbands' pockets when they were drunk, into Post Office accounts.' She paused and gave a humourless laugh. 'When we admitted that to each other we began to laugh, because we'd always felt so guilty about doing it. Yet after what our husbands had done to us it was nothing!'

'So this lady, Miss Dunkin, what did she do for you?'

'She knew of a house in Hastings we could go to for two weeks. She said it was a bit rough. But if we went together, with our kids, she thought it would give us time to think about what the next step would be.

'She was right about it being rough. It was! An outside lavatory and no bathroom, but the sun shone the whole two weeks, and to us it was heaven. The kids loved it, they had so much fun on the beach together. But for Gloria and me it was heady stuff, we were free at last. No more tensing up when our men came through the door, afraid of another row that would end in a beating.'

'Did you tell anyone where you'd gone?'

'We rang our parents to say we were in a safe place, but didn't tell them where in case they accidentally let it slip out when our men contacted them, as we knew they would. The kids couldn't contact their friends, either. Not that they seemed to care. Not one of them asked after their father.'

'And when the two weeks were up?' Katy asked.

'By then we'd already made up our minds we weren't going back to London. We found a house to rent nearby, one with a bathroom, booked the kids into a local school for September. I got a job in a hotel, Gloria in a shop in Hastings. We shared everything: our children, food, and what little money we had. We lived like that for four years, and we were all very happy.'

'How did you end up in Bexhill, both in nice houses?' Katy asked. She imagined the only way to get a nice house was to get married, so she thought perhaps both women had met someone else.

'Gloria was the lucky one, her husband died suddenly of a heart attack. She said she ought not to gloat that she was lucky, but I said gloat away, he deserved death after all he'd done to her. Anyway, the house and everything went to her. She then had the wherewithal to buy the house in Collington Avenue, and later to start her dress shop. As for me, I rent that little house you came to, and I got a job as an almoner at the hospital.'

'Ironic when it was an almoner who helped you?'

'That wasn't a coincidence. I had always known an almoner dealt with many social problems, and I felt I was made for the job. I was, in fact, a trained nurse before my marriage. I did another couple of courses to get the extra qualifications needed. Gloria and I were so fortunate compared with other women in our position, we were able to have a brand-new start. Not all families are as supportive as ours were; many people still believe it is a husband's right to discipline his wife and she should grin and bear it.'

'So did you plan then to seek out beaten women?'

'Not at all, at least not consciously. But a few years ago in the hospital I was called down to Casualty to talk to a woman, because the nursing staff had said she was very badly hurt, and they needed me to sort out someone to look after her children. She had a six-week-old baby in her arms, a toddler clinging to her coat, and her face was so bloody you couldn't see her features. She really needed hospitalization, but this would mean the children being taken into care. I'd seen other women in this state get themselves patched up and go home, just as I had in the past, because they couldn't bear the thought of their children being taken from them.

'So all at once I knew what I must do; help this woman in just the way I'd been helped. I took her and her children home with me. I rang Gloria and we agreed that we needed to do this. Someone had to.'

It struck Katy then that, as Gloria's husband was dead,

the finger of suspicion for the fire was pointing right back at her father. Edna was happy talking about herself and Gloria, but would Katy be able to get the woman to agree to help Albert?

'That was very noble of you, Edna,' she said.

'No, not noble, we both needed to do it. Often the women would stay a day or two and then go home. It always made me mad when they said, "But I love him," like that was a good reason to allow someone to beat and frighten you. But now and then we would get a woman who was ready to really start again; all she needed was encouragement, and being shown the ropes to get National Assistance and a place to live until she could work again.'

She paused, and Katy could hear her breathing was heavy.

'But, Katy,' she began again, 'once wife beaters are alone, without their punchbag, they can't function. They will move heaven and earth to find their woman. They say it's out of love. They even believe that with all their heart, so much so they convince others too, and that is the danger point. Neither Gloria nor I ever attempted to get a divorce, because that would've meant our husbands finding out where we were. It's been fifteen years, and yet I still shake in my shoes at the prospect of Graham knocking on my door. He escaped paying me maintenance, he got to keep our house for himself, and most people would say he came out of it well. But I know he will never see it that way. By now he'll have turned it into grief that I took his two children from him. Never mind that he often hit them too, and they never want to see him again. He will have rewritten his story now, and he will fervently believe he is the injured party. And I would bet he's still trying to find me.'

Katy thought that was the saddest thing she'd ever heard: a grown woman terrified of a man who had once promised to love and protect her, the father of her children.

'I take your point, Edna, and I fully understand why you are scared. But you must go to Gloria's funeral tomorrow. Imagine how upset Gloria would be that you weren't there, after all you've been through together? You'll just blend in with her customers and other friends. You will be safe.'

There were a few moments of silence before the woman spoke again. 'You know, Katy, you sound a lot like Gloria, she was always able to talk me round. That first night in the hospital, I would've gone back to Graham but for her. She held me steady until we made our plans to go to Hastings. She didn't let me waver.'

'Well, hold that in your heart tonight. And tomorrow whisper to her that I would've come too, but I was afraid her children wouldn't want me there.'

Edna sighed. It sounded to Katy like resignation.

'Okay, I'll go,' she agreed. 'Thank you, my dear, for listening to me going on. Will you come and see me before you go to London?'

'I'd love to,' Katy said, thinking that would be the time to tackle Edna about helping her father. 'Now stay strong tomorrow.'

'Who was that?' Hilda shouted as Katy put the phone down.

'Just someone from work,' Katy called back. She felt emotionally drained, and she certainly had no intention of sharing Edna's story with her mother. Hilda would never understand what would possess a woman to risk her life to help others.

She went up to bed then, and as she lay in her warm, pretty bedroom, she couldn't stop thinking about women who were trapped between giving their children a secure life and needing to keep quiet about the beatings they had to endure.

'I want to do something to help,' she whispered to herself as she turned out her light. 'But first I have to find some proof about who really did kill Gloria.'

Michael Bonham mingled easily with the mourners as they gathered at St Peter's for Gloria Reynolds' funeral.

It was another very cold grey day, and many of the women wore fur coats; he noted at least three minks. Given what he now knew about Gloria, it was hardly surprising there were so few men. About eight of pensionable age had plainly just come along because their wives had expected it of them. He counted around ten businessmen – maybe suppliers for her business, because they appeared to know one another – and two other men who he was sure were plain-clothes policemen keeping a watch. But the majority of the mourners were women.

A few other older couples arrived; he suspected they were neighbours by the way they reacted to one another. Then the two hearses arrived, and another car behind them.

Bonham watched the undertakers carefully remove the two flower-covered coffins, placing them on trolleys, and at that point it brought home to him the scale of the tragedy, a mother and daughter consumed by fire.

The young woman clinging to her equally young husband's arm, her eyes swollen from crying, was clearly the remaining daughter. He knew her name to be Janice Plowright, and that she had two small children, though they weren't with her today. As he looked around further he saw another young man arrive. He was slender, with untidy, too long dark auburn hair, wearing a dark suit that looked too big for him. He was out of breath, as if he'd run some distance. He thought that must be Paul Reynolds, the son who was at university in Manchester, because he was making a beeline for Janice and her face brightened a little to see him. Bonham guessed his suit was borrowed; no young man in his twenties anticipates his mother dying and has something suitable to wear for the occasion.

The funeral service was brief. It was clear the vicar had never met Gloria Reynolds or Elsie, her daughter, and that he hadn't been given much information about their characters or personality. Gloria's son tried to say a few words but broke down soon after he started and went back to sit beside his sister.

The hymn chosen was 'Love Divine, All Loves Excelling', and from what Bonham knew now about Gloria it was appropriate. She'd helped other women, not for money but because she was a loving, kind person. No wonder Albert had dropped in to see her frequently. Bonham thought he might have too, if he'd known her.

Albert had said little about his wife, but Bonham couldn't remember any case before when the wife of the accused hadn't telephoned or turned up to see him to try and help prove her husband's innocence. That, to him, spoke volumes about her character.

Bonham was entirely convinced now that Albert was innocent of the crime. All he had to do was to find something, or someone, to prove it to the police.

It was so cold standing at the graveside that many of the mourners left immediately the interment was finished. Bonham watched the daughter, Janice, and the son, Paul, allowing themselves to be embraced by people, and as the crowd thinned he approached Paul.

'May I offer my condolences?' he said, shaking the young man's hand. 'Frank Chivers. I'm afraid I didn't know your mother very well, but my late wife liked her very much and I know how sad and appalled she would be at Gloria's death.'

He knew it was underhand to lie about who he was. But if he was to save Albert, he had to get a little closer to the family.

'It was good of you to come,' Paul said, and his greenish-brown eyes brimmed with unshed tears. 'My sister has arranged for us to go back to the Black Swan. I hope you will join us.'

The lad's manners were impeccable and made Bonham feel ashamed of deceiving him. 'I would like that, thank you,' he said.

Around twenty or so people went back to the private room at the Black Swan. A fire had been lit and it felt quite cosy; only a few sat down, everyone else gathered in groups, taking glasses of sherry from the waitress who circulated. The conversation was very muted.

'My brother tells me your late wife knew our mother.'

Bonham was startled to find Janice at his elbow, he hadn't seen her approach him.

'Yes, that's right, I just wish I'd met Gloria too, she sounded like such a lovely woman.'

'She was kind and giving, always ready to help people,' Janice said. 'I don't know how Paul and I are going to cope with losing her and Elsie. It feels like the bottom has fallen out of our world.'

'How did you feel, hearing the police had arrested her neighbour, Albert Speed?'

Bonham waited, fully expecting vitriol and rage. But to his surprise Janice shook her head.

'It's nonsense. Albert could no more have set that fire than I could. He and Mum were great friends; I know Mum was really fond of him, and I got the impression he felt the same.'

'One can't always be sure two people feel the same,' Bonham said carefully.

'I saw them together on at least ten occasions and, take my word for it, they were great friends. He was good for Mum, a great listener. He did little jobs for her, and she made him laugh, something I don't think he got much of at home. As far as I'm concerned, the police have made a huge blunder.'

Bonham gulped. After what the girl had said, he knew he had to come clean about who he was.

'I agree totally,' he said. 'But in view of what you've just said, I have to admit the truth about who I am.' He managed to tell her in just a few well-chosen words, but the shock on her face made him feel ashamed at having tried to hide his real identity. 'You are right, Janice, Albert Speed is a kind and gentle man and he was fond of your mother. But I hope you can understand why I felt I

87

had to come here today and meet you and your brother? And why I couldn't say straight out that I was defending Albert?'

'You should be ashamed of yourself. It was underhand,' she said sharply. 'But as there were police at the service keeping watch, both my brother and I feel that even they know they've got the wrong man.'

'I need to tell you also that Katy, Albert's daughter, wanted to come and pay her respects today too. She liked your mother very much,' Bonham said, 'but she didn't dare come in case it made you angry.'

'Yes, Mum told me about her, too. She said Katy was a sweet girl who, luckily for her, took after her father, not her shrew of a mother.'

Bonham half smiled at the reference to the shrew. 'I need to push the police into looking harder for your mother's real killer,' he said. 'If you or your brother can help with that in any way, I'd be so grateful.'

'You do know what Mum was involved in?'

'Yes, I do,' Bonham said.

'Well, it seems to both Paul and me that it has to be one of those evil men.' She looked at Bonham defiantly. 'It's a good job our father died, or he would've been the prime suspect.'

'Did your mother ever say she'd seen anyone suspicious hanging around?'

'No, but then she wouldn't, she always tried to protect us kids. She never talked about her life with Dad, and so we never told her how much we all remembered about it.'

'Just before the fire, and over Christmas, did she seem worried about anything?'

'No, not at all. She was her usual happy self, thrilled to have the three of us home for Christmas. She'd gone to town on the decorations and presents because the shop was doing so well. We discussed booking a holiday cottage in Devon for us all in August, and she mentioned she was going to London on a buying trip in February. She wouldn't have been making plans like that if she was worried about something.'

'Would you be prepared to speak out for Albert if it comes to trial?'

He waited. This was the point when even the most ardent supporters backed down.

'I would, gladly,' she said, without any hesitation. 'Elsie and I both knew Albert was married, but we secretly hoped he'd leave his wife and maybe he and Mum could be happy together.'

'Were they having an affair?' he asked gently. He knew such a question was likely to offend.

'No, they weren't. Albert was far too proper for such a thing and I think Mum might have been too badly bruised for an affair, anyway. But she used to light up when he called. I'd never seen her do that before with anyone.'

'Thank you, Janice,' he said. 'You are delightfully direct, and if I might just have your address, I will be in touch in a few days' time. Meanwhile, I am so terribly sorry for your tragic loss, it must be well-nigh impossible to come to terms with. But I must say too that I really admire your strength, grit and humanity. Few people would consider the plight of someone like Albert at such a time in their lives. You, your children and your brother will all be in my thoughts in the coming months.'

'Just speak to Mum's friend Edna before you leave?' Janice asked, her eyes brimming with tears. 'She is the one person who knows the backgrounds of all the women she and Mum helped.'

6

Katy looked all around her before even stopping at Edna's gate. It was the evening of the funeral, and she thought if anyone was going to be spying on Edna, tonight was the time they'd do it. But the street was deserted; it was too cold for anyone to be out, so she knocked on the door.

When Edna opened the door it was clear she'd been crying. It was not just that her eyes were suspiciously pink, but there was sorrow and dejection in every line of her body. As soon as the door was shut, Katy put her arms around the older woman to hug her.

'It must've been awful for you,' she said comfortingly. Edna leaned into her, shoulders heaving as she started to cry again. 'But I bet you are glad you went, and I'm sure Gloria's children felt better for you being there.'

'Oh, Katy!' Edna said after a few moments. She straightened up and dabbed her eyes. 'I was quite proud of myself for holding it together all day, but a little while ago, when my Claire phoned, I couldn't hold back any more. She couldn't come today, and my son was abroad. Gloria was like a second mother to them both. Just as I was to Gloria's children. Claire has taken it very hard and she wanted to talk over the past.'

'About their father?'

Edna shook her head. 'Oh no, we never speak about him! She talked mostly about all the good times we shared with Gloria and her children. She said what hurts her most of all is that she never told Gloria how she felt about her, and now it's too late. I know just what Claire means; I feel the same, and all those good times are gone forever.'

They moved into Edna's living room at the back of the house and sat down, Katy on the sofa and Edna in an armchair.

'Your father's lawyer came to the funeral,' Edna said. 'Such a nice man. Janice had quite a long chat with him; she admitted to me just before I left that both she and Elsie had wished Albert would get divorced and marry their mother. Gloria and Albert weren't having an affair, I hope you realize that? They were just good friends. Janice intends to make a statement to that effect for your father. She said too that I must help in any way I can.'

Katy felt a huge sense of relief. 'But how do you feel about that? Are you still scared?' As much as she wanted Edna to support her father, she didn't like the idea of the woman being frightened.

'Yes, I am scared, but I must help. We all agree that Albert would never set a fire; he mustn't be punished for something he could never have done. We set out to save women from bad men, so we must support the good ones. I'm going to the police station tomorrow. And meanwhile, I have something I want to give you.'

Katy watched in puzzlement as the older woman got out of her chair, turned it away from the wall and began unzipping the loose cover and rummaging inside. She pulled out a grey notebook.

'You probably think I'm suffering from paranoia, Katy, but the information in this book could get people hurt.'

'What's in it?' Katy asked. 'Something to do with the women you've helped? If so, shouldn't it go to the police?'

'If I felt I could trust the police not to go blundering in, I would give it to them. But I can't. Yes, it is to do with the women. In fact, it's a complete record of who they are, where they once lived, what their husbands did to them, and where they are now – at least the ones we know about. But it could cause immense distress in the wrong hands.' She opened the notebook at the first page. 'See here, Susan Mitchell, of Highgate, two children aged four and six. I picked her and her children up outside Camden Town tube station in August, two years ago. She was on crutches. Four weeks earlier her husband had pushed her down the stairs and broken her leg. He then kicked her all over and left her lying in terrible pain, completely helpless on the hall floor, while he went out. Her six-year-old got a neighbour and she took Susan to hospital. Luckily for Susan, our friend there put her in touch with us. She didn't contact us straight away, not until her husband hit her again and broke her ribs. She was trying to stop him beating her little son!'

'Oh, Edna!' Katy exclaimed.

'It was him turning on the children that made her realize she really had to get out,' Edna said. 'That is often the trigger for making a final decision. As I said to you on the phone, many women stay and put up with appalling injuries, because they have children and nowhere else to go. Usually they have no money, either. Almost all of our women were living in north-west London, as Gloria and I were, too. They came to us through our contact at the Whittington Hospital in Archway.' Edna looked back at the notebook. 'I brought Susan down here; she stayed with Gloria for two nights before I got her and the children into temporary accommodation. By the time her leg and ribs were mended, she'd been fortunate enough to find a live-in job as a housekeeper where her children were welcomed. I heard from her last summer, and she sounded very settled and happy, in Scotland. Like Gloria and me, she had not attempted to get a divorce or any maintenance payments for the children, out of fear of her husband.'

'So this book has all the details of all the cases?' Katy asked. She could see that if the police showed Susan's details to her husband, he was likely to set off immediately to get her back.

'Yes, but not all the women end up happily like Susan. You will find it disturbing to realize just how many women end up going back to their men. Some people claim that they are weak women, or even that they need the excitement of living with a volatile man. I wouldn't make a judgement on that – there are as many different reasons for returning to the war zone as there are months in the year – but Gloria and I soon discovered we couldn't save everyone.' She handed the book to Katy. 'Do what you will with this; all I ask is that you wait until I've moved away. I'm going to make my statement about Albert on Monday, then I'll leave here within two weeks.'

'You're leaving?' Katy exclaimed. She hadn't expected that.

'Yes, Katy, without Gloria I feel lost and very alone. I want to be nearer Claire and her children, so I handed in my notice at work today. This is just a rented house, so there's nothing to tie me to Bexhill.'

Katy hardly knew what to say. She understood that fear and the loss of her dear friend were good enough reasons, but somehow she'd thought Edna valued her job too much to leave. She looked down at the notebook in her hands. 'Then I wish you a happy new life,' she said. 'I'll do as you say and hold fire with this until you are gone.'

'I wish you every happiness in London, too,' Edna said with a smile. 'You get out and paint the town red; do all the living Gloria and I should've done instead of settling for marriage with a bully.'

Michael Bonham telephoned Katy at the office on Monday afternoon to tell her that Edna had called in at the police station that morning and made her statement.

'She said Mrs Reynolds thought a great deal of Albert, and so did her children, and that it is completely illogical for anyone to think he would set fire to her house.'

'Does that mean Dad will be able to get out of prison?'

'I'm afraid not immediately, but I should be able to get bail for him at the next hearing.'

Katy wished she could tell him about the notebook Edna had given her. He could take it to the police so they could investigate the husbands in it. But she'd made a promise to Edna, and she must stick to it. Besides, she hadn't read it all herself yet and another few days wouldn't make much difference.

Katy felt quite sad on her last day at Franklin, Spencer and Marshfield. She took in a box of cakes to share round, and she was touched by how genuinely sorry everyone was that she was leaving.

'I always thought you'd be here until you had your first baby,' said Mrs Randolph in Accounts. 'It won't be the same without you.'

'It was time to expand my horizons,' Katy said, giving the woman a hug. 'But I'm going to miss your mothering.'

In fact, she realized she would miss all her workmates, even dour old Mr Marshfield. Mrs Randolph might be her stand-in mother, but every single one of the staff had other qualities she was going to miss. She'd taken pleasure in shopping with the girls, or going for a drink after work. Friendly advice from the solicitors and articled clerks. Manicures during the lunch hour by Rachel, the telephonist. She'd learned so much working here, enjoyed lots of laughs along with moments of frustration and irritation. There had been times when she'd burst into tears and been comforted by someone, and then there was the chatter, learning a little more about each of them week by week. She just hoped that her new job would turn out to be as good.

The staff had organized a whip-round for her, and along with a big 'Good Luck in Your New Job' card, signed by everyone, they'd bought her a red leather vanity case for all her make-up and beauty products.

'If you come back to Bexhill during the week any time, pop in to see us all,' Mr Marshfield said as she was leaving. 'And if the new job doesn't work out, don't be afraid to ask me for another reference.'

'I'm going now, Mum,' Katy said on Saturday morning.

Her packed case was in the hall, but her mother was cleaning the windows in the kitchen, her way of showing she wasn't the least concerned or saddened at her daughter leaving home.

'I'll ring you on Sunday,' Katy added.

She watched her mother on the little stepladder, her slender frame rigid as if she was using every bone in her body to show her indignation at her daughter leaving.

'I might be at church,' Hilda said.

'Then I'll ring until you do answer,' Katy said. 'You don't fool me, Mum, I know you are sad I'm going. But don't be like this, or you might lose me forever.'

Katy half turned to the door, expecting some sort of angry retort, but to her surprise she heard her mother get down off the stepladder. 'I can't help it if my worrying comes out like disapproval,' she said.

As Katy turned to look at her, she saw a softness in Hilda's face; her lips were quivering as if she was about to cry. She reached her mother in a few quick steps and put her arms around her. Hilda remained stiff, but she didn't pull away.

'I'll be fine, Mum,' Katy said softly, caressing her mother's cheek. 'Little birds have to leave the nest sometime.'

'You'd better go now or you'll miss the train,' her mother replied.

To Katy that was as good as a kiss or saying, 'I hope you get on alright.'

Katy arrived at Joan and Ken's house in London just before one o'clock. Jilly came haring down the stairs to greet her, bouncing with excitement. She looked lovely in a turquoise wool dress Katy had never seen before, her blonde hair tied back with a ribbon of the same colour.

'I thought you'd never get here,' she said breathlessly. 'I've found us a flat, but they are only holding it till two. So dump your case and we must head out. I'll tell you about it as we go.'

As they hurried away from Hammersmith towards Chiswick, Jilly explained she'd been told about the flat by someone she worked with. 'It's just down here, close to Ravenscourt Park. Jackie, the girl who lives there now, is going to Australia at the end of the month with her flat-mate, and she asked her landlord if we could have first refusal so he doesn't need to advertise it. I saw it last night and it's really nice. Only one bedroom, and quite small, but it's not dark and stinky. The furniture is nice, too.'

Katy was delighted to hear that the rent was only twelve pounds a week, which was a real bargain.

'Apparently, the landlord, Mr Sawyer, likes long-term tenants who look after the place so he doesn't have to worry about it. Jackie told him we were really quiet and well behaved, so we'd better look like we are,' Jilly giggled. 'Mind you, I've had to work so hard this week that when I get home I just want to fall into bed.'

Shaftesbury Road was tree-lined, and number 8 was one of the smaller terraced houses. The flat they'd come to see was on the ground floor, with a fair-sized sitting room looking on to the street. The bedroom behind it was smaller, but big enough, with two single divans and a huge built-in wardrobe. The kitchen was further down the hall and the bathroom beyond a door to the back garden.

Jackie, Jilly's friend, showed them round while Mr Sawyer was talking to the tenant upstairs. 'He'll love that Katy is a legal secretary at the Inns of Court; he likes his tenants to have posh jobs,' Jackie said with a snigger. 'I told him I was a buyer at Harrods when I first came to see the flat. The truth was I worked in a café nearby, but I did occasionally "buy" stuff in Harrods. Later on, when I got a better job, I told him I'd left Harrods because one of the floor walkers kept coming on to me. Luckily, my flatmate is a florist in Victoria, and Mr Sawyer thinks that's rather grand, as they do flowers for the palace.'

Katy could see why Jilly thought the flat was great. The furniture and decor were much like her home in Bexhill, just as shabby and worn. But Katy had always been happy at her friend's home, and she'd known that for twelve pounds a week they weren't going to get a mansion. Besides, they could tart it up – and it didn't smell of damp and it wasn't dark.

Half an hour later, the girls bounded back up King Street, having signed a lease starting at the beginning of March and paid two weeks' rent in advance as a deposit. Mr Sawyer lived right out at Brentford, so he wouldn't be coming round checking up on them, and the two girls living upstairs were much the same age as Jilly and Katy. So they weren't going to complain about a bit of noise.

'Let's go to Hammersmith Palais tonight?' Jilly suggested. 'We need to do something to celebrate.'

It was Sunday afternoon, after lunch, when Katy finally told Jilly about the developments back home. They were up in their room, lying on their beds, both a little the worse for wear as they hadn't got in from the Palais until one in the morning.

They'd had a fun evening, danced with dozens of

different men, and drunk too much. They'd even arranged a double date with Rob and John, two rather earnest-looking chaps who worked for the Stock Exchange. Neither of the girls were smitten with either of their dates, but the young men were presentable, well mannered and offered to take the girls to the best Chinese restaurant in Soho. As Jilly had pointed out, 'Why spend our own money exploring the fleshpots when we can get a couple of blokes to show us it all?'

Predictably, Jilly was really shocked by Katy's news. She'd known that Mr Speed had been arrested, but not that Katy had kept so much of the story to herself. 'So how is your dad holding up?' Jilly asked. 'And did you hear how Mrs Reynolds' funeral went?'

Katy told her a shortened version of all that had happened, but not about having the notebook. She didn't think it was advisable to tell anyone about that until she'd had time to think it all through properly.

'I can't see why Edna is so scared,' Jilly said, frowning with puzzlement. 'Okay, maybe it was a nutter who started the fire at Mrs Reynolds' house. But I can't see that same nutter going for someone else, too.'

'From what she told me about the injuries these men had inflicted on the women she and Gloria helped, I wouldn't put it past them to go for Edna, too. In fact, she was the more visible one, as she picked the women up in her car.'

'So she's leaving town? Poor woman, just imagine at her age having to start all over again somewhere else.'

Jilly fell asleep a few minutes later. As Katy lay there, awake, her mind turned to what her friend had said. Poor

Edna, she'd been through so much heartache, and had helped so many people. Yet who was there to help her now, when she most needed it?

On Sunday evening, just after six, Edna hurried out to her car with a big suitcase. After putting it in the boot she returned to the house for a box of packed personal treasures. She thought she would get her son-in-law to borrow a van in a few days to fetch the rest of her stuff. She couldn't bear staying here another night, worrying that someone was watching her.

Mr Bonham didn't agree that her life was in danger; he claimed that whoever had torched Gloria's house would find that satisfying enough. He said they'd be too scared to repeat the act somewhere else in Bexhill.

But Edna's mind was made up; she was going to start afresh in Broadstairs with her daughter, Claire, and her family. It was far enough away from Bexhill to never run into anyone she knew. Claire and Roger ran a hotel and they were always short of staff, so for the time being Edna would work for them, just until she got on her feet in the new town.

Remembering she'd left food in the fridge, she went back indoors to clear it out and take some leftovers with her. Then, after turning off all the lights and picking up another bag packed with shoes and a couple of coats, she left the house, shutting the door and locking it firmly.

It was very cold and it felt like it might snow, so Edna wasted no time in starting up the car and moving away. Perhaps for the first time since Gloria had died, she didn't look around her in the dark street. If she had, she might have noticed the dark red Jaguar at the end of the street, if only because expensive cars were rare in her road.

Edna didn't intend to drive all the way to Broadstairs tonight. She had booked a room for the night in New Romney, in a small guest house she'd stayed at several times before on the way to Claire's. As she drove out of Bexhill towards Hastings, she felt a sense of release. By lunchtime tomorrow she'd be with her daughter and her two grandchildren, and a new chapter of her life would begin.

By the time she'd gone through Hastings and the road climbed up towards Guestling, she was feeling relaxed because there was little traffic, and the road was one of her favourites. She often drove along it to Rye during the summer, and she knew it well.

A car overtook her at speed just before she got to Winchelsea.

'Silly man,' she muttered to herself. 'I hope he knows how narrow the road is further on.'

She passed beneath the old Landgate and started down the steep hill, which led to the marshes, when suddenly in front of her a car was coming up the hill with its headlights on full beam, blinding her and blasting on its horn. She had a momentary impression that it was also on her side of the road, giving her no choice but to swerve on to the other side of the road to avoid it. Suddenly, she saw the white-painted barrier seemingly leaping in front of her in her headlights and although she tried to brake and pull the steering wheel in the opposite direction, it was too late.

The barrier smashed with a loud crack and all at once her car was hurtling down the sheer grassy hill towards the river at the bottom. She heard herself scream, and she clung on to the steering wheel in the vain hope she could turn it to stop the fast descent. But the car was just bouncing over rocks, gaining speed as it went, and there was the river, as black and slick as tar in the car headlights.

She felt a spray of icy water as the car landed in the river; the water appeared to be coming in around the bottom of the door. She remembered once seeing someone in this same plight on a film. They couldn't open the door because of the pressure of the water, and although the car seemed to be floating, she could see that the water level was already halfway up the door.

The car headlights were still working for the moment, but beyond them it was pitch dark. She turned her head back towards Winchelsea in the vain hope someone might have seen the accident, but there were no lights that might have been rescuers. Straight ahead of her, across the river, it was just marshland. She put her hand on the horn, but that didn't work; the only sound was her own voice screaming with terror.

As the headlights suddenly went out, instinctively her hand went to the window handle, but as she cranked it round, so a deluge of icy water came in and she immediately felt the car sink deeper. But the window was the only way out. She grabbed hold of the top edge of the window and tried to haul herself up and out. She got her head and shoulders out, but despite pushing up desperately from the driving seat, she was stuck, half in, half out, and the icy water was rising around her all the time.

She realized then she was never going to see Claire, her son Robert or her grandchildren ever again. She was sure the car she'd swerved to avoid was the same dark red Jaguar that had overtaken her before Winchelsea. He must have followed her, raced past her, then turned at the bottom of the hill to drive up again to meet her and force her off the road.

Why did she set off at night? She should have stayed till the morning. So few cars came down this road, and even if one came now, they wouldn't be able to see her and her black car in the river.

The car went down again, bringing the water up to her neck. She screamed for help and tried in desperation to force herself through the window, but the icy water was having a paralysing effect on her. She seemed to have lost all her strength and the will to continue to fight.

That man had got rid of both of them now. It was all over.

7

'So do you think you are going to like this job, Katy?' Joan asked as she passed the vegetable dish around the table.

Katy paused before answering, remembering how scared she was on her first day. Everyone seemed so posh and super intelligent that she felt like a country bumpkin who had no business to be there.

'I was terrified on Monday,' she admitted. 'But I know who everyone is and what they do now, so it's getting easier. I think it will work out okay.'

'I was the same at the zoo for the first few days. I couldn't even find my way around.' Jilly grinned. 'I felt stupid, like I knew nothing about animals. But suddenly it all seemed to fall into place. But they'll probably call me "the new girl" for years yet.'

Ken looked from one girl to the other. 'Well, I have to hand it to you both, you've done so well. You've got jobs you like, and you've found a flat you can afford. Not that we want you to leave, we like having you here. But we admire you for wanting your independence.'

The phone rang in the hall before either girl could answer.

'Who can that be?' Joan said as Ken got up. 'No one ever rings at teatime.'

Ken put on his telephone voice. 'Underwood, may I help you?' he said, making both the girls smirk. 'Yes, she's here, I'll just get her for you,' he said and came back into the living room. 'For you, Katy – some toff, judging by his voice.'

Katy hurried to the phone. It was Michael Bonham.

'Hello,' she said. 'Is this good news – you've managed to get my dad released?'

'I wish it was good news, Katy,' he said. 'And it's not to do with your father, at least not directly. Edna Coltrain's car came off the road near Rye at the weekend. Her car hurtled into the river.'

'Oh no,' Katy gasped. 'Is she –?' She stopped herself, unable to say the word.

'No, she's alive, but only just, it was touch and go. A man walking his dog heard something odd, saw lights by the river and then heard what he thought was a scream. So he rushed down there. The car was almost totally submerged by then and Edna was face down, half in, half out of the car window. Somehow he managed to get her out and gave her artificial respiration. Luckily, another person stopped his car on seeing the beam of the first man's torch and called the ambulance. She's in the hospital at Hastings.'

'You said it wasn't directly to do with my dad, but that sounds as if you think this wasn't a true accident?'

'No, it doesn't seem so. The police think she was deliberately forced off the road. Edna has recovered enough to tell them she thought it was a dark red Jaguar. She said one overtook her at speed just before Winchelsea, and then a short while later what looked like the same car came up the narrow road, on the wrong side of the road, straight at her, headlights blazing. She swerved to avoid him, but he still hit her.'

'How terrible for her!' Katy exclaimed.

'Yes, very frightening, even before she landed in the river. The police found a big dent on her wheel arch and wing, and traces of dark red paint on the bodywork. They also found tyre marks indicating a car turning at speed down the bottom of the Winchelsea road. It's unlikely someone would overtake a car at speed, then double back minutes later unless they were up to something. The dent on the left-hand wing bears out her story, too. If she had hit an oncoming car travelling on the correct side of the road, it would be her right-hand wheel arch which would be damaged. The dark red paint does match a shade of maroon used on Jaguar cars.'

'Heavens!' Katy exclaimed. She suddenly felt a bit faint. 'So this might be the same person who set the fire and killed Gloria and her daughter?'

'It could be,' Bonham agreed. 'Edna was making her way to her daughter's in Broadstairs. I think this person may have followed her.'

'He'd have to be local to know that road so well,' Katy said thoughtfully.

'Not necessarily, he might just have driven along that road at another time. It's a popular scenic route, and people do tend to remember it as being dangerous. So, Katy, I'm sorry I had to disturb you with this news, but I felt you ought to know.'

'I'm glad you did. Will you see Edna? If you do, can you say how sorry I am, and wish her better. I didn't ask, what are her injuries?'

'The shock – and coming so close to drowning – was the worst thing. She banged her head badly on the windscreen, sprained her wrist and has many cuts and bruises. Now she has a chest infection brought on by the shock, I suppose, and the extreme cold. But another minute or two in the river would've killed her. It really was a miracle that someone saw what had happened and helped her. As you probably know, there are no houses down there, just marshland. The chances of anyone coming along on a winter's night were very slight. As Edna said herself, thank God for dog walkers. And yes, I will pass on your message.'

'I bet she's even more terrified now.' Katy's eyes filled with tears, remembering how she had thought Edna was overreacting in thinking the same person who killed Gloria would come for her, too. 'She left Bexhill because she felt someone was going to get her.'

'Well, she's safe now, in a private room at the hospital, and there is a policeman outside to check visitors. She's reasonably calm. But I think she'll feel safer when she's settled in at her daughter's.'

'So does my dad know about this?'

'Yes, I went to Lewes gaol today and told him. It doesn't, of course, actually exonerate him, but it's enough to get the police looking harder at the evidence. Oh, and your brother visited him; that really cheered him up. Rob said he would phone you for a chat about all this.'

Bonham went on then to ask how she was getting on at her new job, and how the flat hunting was going. She was able to tell him she liked the job and they'd found a flat.

He said he would ring or write if there were any further developments, before wrapping up the conversation and wishing her a pleasant evening.

'Strewth!' Jilly said when Katy returned to the living room and told them about Edna. 'Poor lady. Whoever is doing this is a really evil person. Let's hope they catch him quickly.'

After dinner, Katy went up to the bedroom, leaving Jilly downstairs. She got out the notebook Edna had given her and just held it for a moment while she thought what she must do. The book held the original addresses of all the women Edna and Gloria had helped. As long as their husbands still lived in the same place, and if one of them owned a maroon Jaguar with a dent on the wheel arch, that was possibly all the evidence the police would need to make an arrest. But how could she be sure the Bexhill police would come up to London and check cars?

She couldn't. She'd often heard that the South Coast police didn't like to stray into the Metropolitan force's stamping ground. They might request that the Met check the addresses out, but there was no guarantee that would be done. Even Mr Bonham had said one of the failings of the police was that they didn't share information and manpower with other areas. Once she'd handed over this information, she wouldn't be able to get it back. And she'd never forgive herself if they didn't act on it.

'So you do it,' she murmured to herself. 'It can't be that big a task. You only need to check any cars at the addresses of women who left and never went back. They are all within quite a small area.'

Katy knew if she told Jilly what she intended to do, she'd try to stop her. Joan and Ken would disapprove, too. But if she could get all the addresses together without them being aware of what she was doing, then on Saturday she could check them all out. It was going to be difficult to find an excuse to be out on her own all day, but she'd think of something.

She wrote a letter to her father then, telling him about her job, the new flat and how much she was enjoying being in London. Before she signed off she said that Bonham had rung that evening to tell her about Edna. She said she hoped this would help his cause. She really wanted to tell him she was going to look for the damaged Jaguar, but she thought that would worry him. After that she wrote to Rob too, asking how he felt their father was coping, and telling him her news. She begged him to let her have a phone number so she could ring him and they could talk properly.

At lunchtime on Thursday, Katy took a sandwich and the notebook into the staffroom. She had already discovered this tiny room was rarely used, as it was an ugly, airless room holding only a sink, a yellow Formica table, rickety chairs and a very worn sofa.

At the table she opened the notebook at the end, where the most recent women's names were entered. Working backwards, she began to make notes of all those who hadn't returned to their home and husband.

She didn't think she could count the last five women, who had been helped in late November and December. Edna had pointed out that the first month away from their home was always the worst time for beaten women. They missed their old possessions; they had very little money, sometimes almost nothing at all. It was also very lonely and hard for them to manage without friends or family to call on. Suddenly their husbands didn't seem so bad, and they hoped the time away from them had made the men regret their behaviour. So Katy discounted these women, as they may well have returned home by now.

Going through the notebook she pinpointed just six women who had never succumbed to the temptation of going back to their husbands. All their men were real brutes who had finally attacked them so badly they had to be hospitalized with appalling injuries. Three of the women had a child who needed psychiatric help because of what they'd seen their mother go through.

Katy was so engrossed in studying the notebook that she didn't notice Charles Stevenson come into the staffroom.

'What are you swatting up on?' he asked, making her jump. 'And in this dismal hole, too.'

Katy laughed nervously. Charles was the youngest barrister here. He was also very attractive; tall, slender, with dark brown hair and chocolate-drop eyes that a girl could drown in. She thought other more worldly women would call them 'come to bed eyes'. If the way he made her feel when he smiled at her, showing perfect white teeth, was anything to go by, she might even be willing to be led there.

'You made me jump,' she said, closing her notebook and collecting together her *A to Z* of London and her notes.

'Don't go,' he said. 'It's so cold outside I can't face going out, and I was just going to make some tea. Stay and have one with me?'

Katy looked at her watch. 'Just a quick one, I've only got ten minutes.'

She knew he was the most junior of the lawyers there, but she hadn't quite worked out the hierarchy: how they became barristers, what the difference was between a barrister and a QC, what they did to become one, or even what was so special about a QC. Perhaps she could learn from Charles.

He put the kettle on, and looked round at her. 'You didn't say what you were swatting up on.'

'Oh, it's nothing very exciting, just some addresses a friend from back home gave me.'

'And the *A to Z*?'

Katy squirmed a little; he wasn't easy to fob off. 'I was just checking where these people live.'

'You are going to look them up? Why?'

'No, well, maybe. They are addresses from a book that belongs to my friend's mother, and she's in hospital. I said I'd go and see them, if they weren't too far away.'

'Why doesn't she just write to them?' he asked as he finished making the tea. He stood with his back against the wall and crossed his arms. 'Why are you lying about this?' he asked.

Katy blushed. 'Why are you so nosy?' she managed to say. 'If you were in your office and someone stuck their head round the door to ask what you were doing and why, what would you say?'

'Mind your own business, I expect,' he grinned.

'Well, then!'

'Well what, then? Come out for a drink with me after work?'

'So you can grill me some more?'

'Maybe, but more about you. I like to know about people. So will you come?'

'I can't, I'm staying with my friend's aunt and uncle at the moment, and her aunt will have dinner ready for me.'

'Tomorrow, then. It's Friday, so no work the day after. Any excuses?'

'I can't think of one,' she smiled. 'Yes, that would be nice, Charles. But let me drink that tea quickly and get back to work.'

Katy found it hard to concentrate that afternoon; she couldn't really believe that someone as handsome and successful as Charles wanted to go out on a date with her. She wasn't exactly sure if a drink after work was technically a date, but it seemed like one.

Did he take all the new girls out? She could'nt really ask someone, as she was pretty certain that lawyers weren't supposed to fraternize with the office staff.

She could hardly wait to tell Jilly when she got home.

'That's brilliant,' Jilly said, grinning like a Cheshire cat. 'He sounds scrumptious, so go all out to ensnare him. I've got my eye on someone at the zoo too, but he doesn't appear to have noticed me yet.'

'He soon will,' Katy assured her. 'And I'm not into "ensnaring" anyone. He's not one of your wild animals.'

'We can learn a lot from animals,' Jilly giggled. 'They can be trained with treats, and they do hunt for the best available female to impregnate.'

Katy sniggered. 'Well, I won't be letting him impregnate

me. But if Friday's drink goes well, who knows where it might lead?'

'I hope it will lead to a date on Saturday or Sunday for you. Because I've got to work both days.' Jilly pulled a sad face. 'I don't want you to be lonely.'

'I will be lonely without you, but I'll survive.' Katy grinned, relieved she wouldn't need to tell lies about what she planned to do on Saturday. 'But maybe I could meet you from work on Saturday and we could go to Hampstead or somewhere for a drink?'

'I'm a bit stinky when I leave the zoo,' Jilly replied, wrinkling her nose. 'Some of the girls wash and change there, but I'm not mad about doing that. We can go out after I get back here and I've had a bath.'

After dinner, Katy sat down to write to Edna care of her daughter in Broadstairs, an address Bonham had given her. In view of the fact that Edna would be even more frightened now, Katy didn't say anything about the notebook, or her intention to look up some of the violent husbands, only saying how upset she was to hear what had happened to Edna. She went on to tell her about her new job and that she and Jilly would be moving into their own flat in just over a week.

But even as she wrote, her mind was on Charles, considering what she should wear for her date, and planning to wash her hair that night. She was so glad that the beehive hairstyle seemed to have disappeared altogether in London, at least for anyone under thirty-five. Many girls had either the Cilla Black short bob or the 'flick ups' style, if their hair was shoulder length, but Katy had noticed the more trendy girls who wore miniskirts were leaving their long hair straight. That delighted her, as it had always been a nightmare trying to curl her poker-straight hair. She thought she would wear her new black-and-white shift dress tomorrow and run the risk of being told off because it was too short for the office.

That night, as the girls got ready for bed, Katy stuck her fringe down with Sellotape, as it tended to go into an unruly quiff rather than lying straight down. She had butterflies in her stomach now; all the men and boys she'd been out with in the past had been unsophisticated, mostly doing manual work, and often had little conversation. Charles was chatty, but she thought he might find her rather dull and provincial.

She drifted off to sleep trying to think of topics to bring up that would make her seem vivacious and clever.

'So are you going to tell me what you were really doing with that notebook?' Charles asked as he put Katy's second glass of Babycham down in front of her.

'You are an inquisitive chap,' she laughed. 'I've already told you all I'm going to.'

He sat down beside her and took a sip of his pint. The Mitre was very crowded, mostly office workers having a couple of drinks before going home to the suburbs. Charles had brought her to a pub in High Holborn because he didn't want to run into anyone he knew from the Inns of Court.

'I get so cheesed off with all that public-school banter,' he'd added. 'They talk shop all evening, too. When I leave the office at night I like to put aside the cases I'm working on. It seems I'm something of a rarity in legal circles.'

Katy was inclined to believe that too, as he hadn't mentioned anyone from the chambers or anything work-related. While they had their first drink he had asked about Jilly, how long they'd been friends for, and about the flat they would soon move into. He also told Katy he came from a small village in Hampshire, and he had two younger sisters. He shared a flat in Westminster with Mike, a friend he'd made while at Cambridge. Mike worked at the Stock Exchange. Katy got the impression Charles wasn't entirely happy with a career in law, and that maybe he'd been pushed into it by his parents.

'I would point out that being so secretive about your notebook just confirms to me that you're up to something,' he said. 'One thing one learns very quickly as a lawyer is the ability to tell when you are being lied to. I do know that your father is on remand, accused of starting a fire that killed two women.'

Katy's mouth fell open in shock. 'How do you know that?' she asked.

'I have a very retentive memory, and I had read in the press that a man called Speed had been arrested for setting a fire in Bexhill and killing two people. I didn't give it another thought, but then suddenly we have a new girl in chambers called Katy Speed, and she comes from Bexhill. So I knew you were almost certainly a relative. But don't worry, Katy, no one else in chambers knows.'

Katy wished the floor would open and swallow her up. In an agony of embarrassment she tried to explain her side of the story.

'It's okay, Katy, you don't need to try and convince me of his innocence,' Charles said, putting one hand over hers. 'From what I have discovered – because, needless to say, I asked a couple of contacts for the gen on the case – I'd say the police in Bexhill have failed miserably in their investigation. I feel sure your father will be released, without charge, shortly. So I ask again about the notebook. My guess is that you are acting as a detective on your father's behalf?'

Katy felt she had no choice but to tell him the truth about both Gloria and Edna. She explained that the notebook held details of the women they'd helped. Then she went on to tell him that someone had attempted to kill Edna.

'I see,' he said thoughtfully. 'But you can't go around contacting these men. If you did find the dark red car, the owner might very well try to kill *you*.'

'I wasn't going to knock on his door or anything like that,' she said. 'Only to find the car and then inform the police and my father's lawyer.'

'That is still risky. We can surmise this man is quickwitted, observant, patient, has no scruples and he is driven by revenge. I'd say that was a deadly combination. Wouldn't you?'

'Well, yes, but he doesn't know me, does he? I could walk past his house without causing any suspicion.'

'How do you know he doesn't know you? This man took his time planning to kill Gloria. He could've been amongst the mourners at Gloria's funeral, he might have seen you when he was planning the fire. He could have put the paraffin and the cloth in your father's shed because he had observed he was friends with Gloria. That means he could know who you are, too.'

'I didn't think of that,' she said, hanging her head.

Charles put one finger under her chin, lifted it and smiled at her. 'That's why I'm a lawyer. I'm paid to think of all the possibilities. I've also defended and prosecuted quite a few nasty people over the years, so I've had to learn to curb my natural trusting nature. You must learn that too, Katy. But I didn't ask you out to lecture you, so let's drink up and go and find a nice restaurant?'

He had, in fact, already booked a table at a little Italian restaurant just a few minutes' walk from the Mitre. It was cosy rather than smart, with red-checked tablecloths and candles stuck in Chianti bottles.

Judging by the warm way the waiter and the owner greeted him, he'd clearly been there dozens of times before. So Katy suggested he order for her. All she knew about Italian food was from a Greek-owned restaurant in Bex-hill whose owners liked to think they were cosmopolitan by putting pizza and lasagne on the menu, neither of which was very good.

Charles didn't mention the notebook or her father again. Instead, over a starter of garlic mushrooms, he asked her more about Jilly, the flat they were moving into and her interests.

'I'm a nosy parker like you,' she joked. 'I like to observe people; I expect that's why I'm happy in a job that's all about human stories. I also like dancing, reading, swim-ming, and would get seriously into cooking and gardening if I had a place of my own. So what about you?'

He made a comic face and whirled one finger around the side of his head to signify there was little inside. 'I play cricket quite well, and the piano badly. I like reading, and long walks in the country, but unlike you I'm often unhappy at being a lawyer, possibly because I expect more of people than one actually gets. They lie, they cheat, they lack loyalty and they are greedy.'

'So what would you do, if you could change direction now?'

'You'll laugh.'

'I won't,' she promised.

He hesitated, swirling his wine round the glass. 'I'd like to have a market garden, grow and sell trees and flowers,' he blurted out.

'I think that's a lovely thing to do,' she said. 'But you didn't say before that you liked gardening.'

'That was just because you'd said it. As child I loved working in my grandpa's greenhouse, pricking out seedlings, sieving the compost, watering, all that. When I go home I do a bit of weeding, trimming the hedges, but my parents don't really encourage interference.'

'Mine don't, either,' Katy laughed. 'My father watches me like a hawk when I'm weeding, as he thinks I'll pull up flowers. He never lets me make any decisions, like what colour bedding plants to have this year, or suggest something new in the vegetable plot.'

They both laughed, and all at once Katy was aware she really liked this man. It was not just that he was handsome, with a good job, but she had the feeling she wanted the night to go on forever.

They took a long time over the meal because they talked so much. They had chicken with a Mediterranean tomato and basil sauce, but Katy barely noticed what she was eating for looking at Charles. He was so animated when he was talking, so different from most of the men she'd known before who found it difficult to string a sentence together, let alone hold an interesting conversation. Then there were his chocolate-drop eyes that sent delicious shivers down her spine.

She didn't mean to open up about her mother, but suddenly she was telling him how difficult Hilda was.

'My entire life has been spent trying to appease her,' she said. 'It's like that for Dad, too. She is always so nasty and grumpy. She never shows any joy about anything.'

'My paternal grandmother was like that,' he said. 'She made Grandpa's life a misery, and she'd been vile to my father, too. But he got away to Cambridge and stayed away. He tried again with Grandma, taking us kids to see her, hoping that with a new generation she'd be different. But it was no good, she was always complaining and criticizing, nothing was ever right. Grandpa spent as much time as he could in the garden, to get away from her. Even when I was just five or six years old, I saw that. She died when I was thirteen, and to be truthful it was like a weight was finally lifted from Father and Grandpa's shoulders. I remember going over to Grandpa's with my father for the night, just after her funeral; they drank whisky and we played cards. They were both so jolly, laughing about things, teasing me. I stayed with Grandpa a lot after that, helping him in his garden, making bonfires to burn rubbish. He never spoke to me about my grandmother – I don't think he did to my dad, either – but we could both see how much happier he was.'

'I wonder if my dad will go back to Mum when this horrible business is finally over,' Katy said. 'I don't think she's written or visited him. She said she wouldn't have him back if he got bail.'

'I hope for his sake he doesn't. Grandpa only lived another eight years after my grandmother died, and he was the happiest I'd ever seen him then. He should have left her years before, but of course that generation didn't divorce. My father once said he fell in love with my mother because she was always laughing. She never criticized anyone, not even us kids. I find that works so much better; we all just wanted to be good, to achieve things, to make her proud of us.'

'She must be very proud of you becoming a lawyer, then?'

'You know, Katy, if I'd owned up and said I wanted to be a market gardener, she would have been just as proud – probably more, because she could help me. But Grandpa was a lawyer, I think that's why I decided to go for it.'

'Well, I'm sure you are a very good one. And you can break away any time and do what you want to. You don't have to stay. Only don't go just yet; I've only just got to London, and I need to get to know you better first.'

The moment those last words left her lips, Katy wished she hadn't had two glasses of wine on top of the Babychams. It was too forward. In fact, all evening she'd done what she always promised herself she'd never do; she'd told him far too much.

She hardly dared look at him. But when she did, he was smiling.

'That's a lovely thing to say, Katy. You've suddenly made Frey, Hurst and Herbert seem far more attractive.'

*

Charles took her all the way home to Hammersmith on the tube.

As they came out of the tube station, he put his arm around her and pulled her closer to him. 'You are a treasure,' he said softly. 'An undiscovered one, at that, because I don't think anyone has ever appreciated you much.'

He turned her towards him then, and despite people walking past them, he kissed her.

It was the best kiss she'd ever known. It made her toes curl up, her heart beat faster, and created a sensation inside her that felt like she was being gently tugged in a delicious way she'd never felt before.

The kiss went on and on. She didn't want it to end, but when he did break away he still stayed close, his lips on her forehead, his arms tightly round her.

'I've already promised my parents I'll go and see them for the weekend,' he said after a little while. 'I wish I hadn't now, as I'd much rather spend it with you. But maybe on Monday night we could go to the pictures. *Zorba the Greek* is on, and I'm told it's very good.'

'I'd love that,' she said, thinking she'd be happy to sit in a freezing cold bus shelter, just as long as he was with her.

He walked her all the way to Ken and Joan's house and kissed her goodbye, this time even more hungrily.

'I have to go now,' he said eventually. 'Or I won't get a tube back to Westminster. I'll see you on Monday.'

Katy walked up the steps to the front door and watched him walking away. Lean and lithe, despite his thick navy overcoat. He had a good walk – long strides, purposeful – and yet halfway down the road he turned and waved to her, walking backwards for a little while.

Katy put her hands up to her face. Despite the cold, it seemed very hot, and she wanted to shout for joy and dance up and down the pavement.

8

Katy was woken by Jilly hopping on one foot trying to get her jeans on. She had been asleep when Katy returned home the previous evening, so Katy hadn't been able to tell her about the date with Charles.

She waited, expecting Jilly to ask now, but she was rushing, clearly afraid she'd be late for work.

But as she opened the door to go downstairs, she looked back. 'How was the date?'

'Super-duper,' Katy replied. 'But I won't hold you up now – tell you tonight.'

'Can't wait!' Jilly pulled a silly face. 'Go back to dreaming about him.'

Katy lay there for some time, reliving Charles's kiss, but she was so excited that it was impossible to go back to sleep. Yet she also felt guilty about being so happy while her father was stuck in prison. Charles might have advised her against going to look for that red Jaguar, but she couldn't see what harm could come to her by just walking past each of those six addresses. People only ever remembered her bright hair, so she'd pull on a woolly hat and hide it. Besides, she wanted to explore London, and it was a lovely cold crisp day, perfect for walking.

Two hours later, at almost eleven o'clock, with one of Joan's big cooked breakfasts inside her, Katy was standing outside Hampstead tube station consulting her *A to Z*. The first address appeared to be up the hill and facing the heath. She had never been to Hampstead before, and she was somewhat surprised to find it such an obviously affluent area. It was tempting to go into some of the exciting-looking boutiques, jewellers and gift shops she passed, but she resisted, reminding herself she could come here one day with Jilly to look in the shops.

The first address, where Margaret Foster had run away from with her two boys, aged five and seven, was a beautiful Georgian double-fronted house, set back in a walled garden. Katy paused by the tall wrought-iron gate to peep in.

Margaret's husband was a surgeon at the Royal Free, and Katy thought that anyone looking at this house with its shiny, dark blue front door, neatly framed by evergreen ball-shaped bushes planted in stone urns on either side, would never imagine that behind the facade lay violence and brutality. There was a small tree in the centre of the lawn, and beneath it a host of snowdrops in flower, the first Katy had seen this year. She guessed that later in the year the garden would be beautiful because, despite the season and the lack of leaves and flowers, she could see it was carefully tended.

But there was no drive or garage, and no dark red Jaguar parked on the road. Of course he could have parked it at work; maybe she could come back here one night.

The next address was further to walk than it looked on the map, almost at Golders Green. But although this was another affluent neighbourhood, Suzanne Freeman's old home wasn't as lovely as Margaret's. It was a mock-Tudor semi-detached, and it was in dire need of a new coat of white paint. The front garden was very bedraggled, with lots of blown-in rubbish lying around.

A man, perhaps Mr Freeman, was polishing his car on the drive; it was a dark blue Ford Zodiac. The garage doors were wide open and there wasn't a further car inside. She walked swiftly past.

By the time she reached Golders Green and the third address, Katy was beginning to flag. This house was a modest semi-detached with brilliant white nets at the window and a front garden that had been paved over. The car on the drive was an old black Ford.

After stopping for a cup of tea in a café by Golders Green station, she caught the train to Hendon. Two of the addresses were close to the station, and close to each other, which was a relief to Katy as her feet were aching now. She didn't think she could manage to get to the sixth house today.

The fourth address was a very shabby terraced house, and she really didn't think someone living there would own a Jaguar.

The fifth address, number 10 Woodville Road, although only a couple of streets away, was a smart detached house built in the 1930s. It was set high up on a bank with the garage beneath it, and there were steps up to the front door. The drive swept down from the house to the garage door. Even from the road she could see a large shiny new padlock on it. The windows sparkled, with the curtains showing a uniform width at each one, and the drive was well swept and weed-free, suggesting the owner of this property was house-proud.

Yet there was something about the newness and size of the padlock that made Katy feel suspicious and uneasy. She remembered from the notebook that Deirdre Reilly had been hospitalized with the injuries her husband inflicted on her; she'd also told Gloria and Edna that he often locked her in the garage for days on end, sometimes for something as trivial as weeds on the drive or children's handprints on the windows. It was one of her children – a boy called Tony – who needed psychiatric care because of the traumatic things he'd seen.

Aware she'd been standing looking at the house for too long, Katy moved on, but as she got further along the road she saw a man tinkering with his car at the side of the road.

'Excuse me, sir,' she said, an idea coming to her. 'Could you tell me if there is anyone in this road who owns a dark red Jaguar?'

'Yes Reilly, at number 10,' the man said. 'Why do you want to know?'

Katy gulped. 'Well, a man driving a Jag clipped my car the other day and drove off. I wanted to get his car registration for my insurance claim.'

'I can't help you with that, love. I wouldn't know what his reg number is, as he always puts the car in his garage. But it certainly sounds like snotty Reilly. Thinks he's above everyone else.'

Katy felt a surge of delight that she'd got what she wanted. She had seen in the notebook that Deirdre had adopted the name Purcell once she'd left Reilly. All she had to do now was go home, telephone Mr Bonham and ask him to give the name and address to the police. She thanked the man and walked away, back up the road towards the station.

*

Ed Reilly ran down the stairs and grabbed his overcoat and scarf as soon as he saw the girl looking at his house. He knew her, but he couldn't think from where.

It was a couple of moments before it clicked into place. She was the daughter of Albert Speed, the man who had been arrested for burning down Gloria Reynolds' house.

'How did she find out where I live?' he asked himself aloud. 'And what else does she know?'

As he reached the sitting-room window to check what she was doing now, he saw her stop to speak to one of his neighbours, and they both looked back towards Ed's house. He knew then he had to silence her, and quickly.

Reilly was a fan of crime books and he'd read on many occasions that the most successful criminals laid a trail to cast suspicion on someone else. He had been doing a recce of the back of Gloria Reynolds' house, planning how he was going to torch it, when he saw a man come out of her back gate and Reynolds blowing him a kiss.

It was common sense to follow the man; to Ed's delight he lived in the house across the street from Reynolds. Just the way he'd come out of the back door rather furtively and nipped along the back alley, emerging into Collington Avenue further along the street, convinced him the pair were having an affair. All at once he knew what he was going to do. He would set things up so that the man looked like the culprit.

He started the fire in the early hours of Sunday morning, after having got into the shed of the bloke across the street and found his petrol can to put some paraffin in it. He'd left some of the same curtain material he intended to soak in paraffin and stuff through Reynolds' letter box.

Ed left Collington Avenue the second he'd set light to the fabric. But as he reached his car, a street away, he could see the glow of the fire and drove away very happy.

He didn't intend to return to Bexhill at all. But his curiosity about what people were saying about the fire drove him to it, because there was so little in the national newspapers. In Bexhill he couldn't resist asking two or three local people how they felt about such a tragedy in their town, and asked if they knew Gloria Reynolds. Their views were mixed. Some said she was a good woman, others said she was a maneater, but they didn't believe a well-known businessman like Speed could set a fire.

Ed realized he needed to know far more about this man he'd framed. Engaging a plump, gossipy saleswoman in Boots, under the guise of buying cough mixture, he mentioned the fire in Collington Avenue. She instantly began to talk about Gloria Reynolds — what a nice woman she was, how lovely her dress shop was — and asked him if he'd known her. He said he only knew her slightly but couldn't believe anyone would want to kill her. With that, the woman said she thought the police had got it wrong and Albert Speed was innocent.

'I've known him for years,' she said with utter conviction. 'He came in here often, usually with his daughter, Katy. She's all grown up, of course, now. In fact, she works for the solicitors just down the street.'

So there he was, just half an hour later, walking past the solicitors' office window. And there she was, a pretty, dainty girl with long strawberry-blonde hair. Albert Speed's daughter. Katy.

She looked different now, with a brown knitted hat

covering that glorious hair. But it was definitely her. Katy Speed. Now here she was, walking past his house.

What was she doing in London? Had she moved here, or was she just up to snoop? And how on earth had she even found out about him?

As he waited for her to come back past his house, he found his wallet and his keys. Once she'd turned the corner, he left the house to follow her. As he turned on to the main road, she was just crossing over to the station. He caught up with her and was right behind her at the ticket office as she asked for a single to Hammersmith. When she walked to the platform, he bought a ticket too.

Ed stayed at the far end of the carriage, keeping well away from the girl. He picked up an abandoned newspaper and pretended to read it, yet watching her closely. There were only a few people in the carriage, but he knew that once they'd got to Camden Town it would fill up.

She was a small, pretty girl, with delicate features and a peaches-and-cream complexion; in fact, she reminded him of Deirdre when they'd first got married. But he doubted Katy was the docile type, like Deirdre. His new wife had been so grateful to live in a nice house that she did whatever he told her to do. She never worked out that if she'd just fought back or disobeyed him once in a while he might have stopped hitting her – after all, he got bored of her cowering away from him or trying to appease him all the time.

But this girl was a warrior; she had to be, if she was trying to clear her father's name, marching around London, practically putting her head in the lion's mouth. That was the kind of girl he'd dreamed of all his life; one who wouldn't bow down, no matter what he did to her. A fabulous challenge.

How had she got his address, though? It had taken him four years to discover who had helped Deirdre when she ran from him with his kids. He knew that there was a second woman who did the driving, but he didn't know her name. At the double funeral of Gloria Reynolds and her daughter, he mingled with the salesmen friends of hers, making sure he didn't stand out from the crowd. He noted a short, fat woman who looked distraught. The way she kept looking around, as if she half expected someone to pounce on her, was a dead giveaway. Watching her house confirmed it; she was clearly terrified that someone was tailing her. And then, finally, she left with a suitcase once it was dark. He was pretty certain he'd finished her off by driving her off the road. He heard the splash as the car went in the river and saw the headlights go out.

Unfortunately, he still hadn't managed to get confirmation she'd drowned. He had hotfooted it back to London, and the story didn't reach the national press. But even if she had somehow managed to get out of her car and survive, she didn't know anything; she'd have been blinded by his headlights as he drove into her.

Edward Reilly prided himself on being smarter than the average man. He'd proved that fact to be true, as he came from nothing, had only a rudimentary education, and yet he'd managed to amass close on a million if he counted his house and the value of his construction business.

He was born in Dover, and his father disappeared off to sea even before he was born, leaving his mother and grandmother to bring him up in a hideous tenement. Ed's view was that his father must have been a handsome, clever man who made the mistake of getting tangled up with a cheap tart who thought she'd land herself a husband by telling him she was pregnant.

He had this view of his father because he believed he must have inherited his Latino matinee idol looks from him – and the sharpness of his mind too, because he certainly didn't get it from his mother. She didn't have his coal-black hair or brooding dark eyes; she was scrawny and whey-faced. Her eyes were such a pale blue that they appeared almost colourless. She was stupid too, unable to read, and so weak-willed she was a complete pushover. His grandmother was as bad, preferring to spend any money she got on gin.

From the age of five or six, when Ed was old enough to compare how different people lived, he vowed he was going to be rich. The war started when he was seventeen, and if he had been old enough to enlist then, he would've done, for he was tired of trying to scrape a living working on farms. He did a bit of bare-knuckle fighting too, which was lucrative, but he was afraid if he lost his looks girls wouldn't fancy him any more. He thought joining the army would give him the chance to show how tough and brave he really was.

Finally, he was eighteen and able to join up. He came through the basic training with flying colours and was shipped out to Egypt. His looks, a certain rough charm and still more guile soon got him away from the dangers of warfare into supplies and a desk job. Mixing with officers gave him not only a picture of the kind of home life he believed he should have had, but also made him realize he needed to copy the way they spoke, ate, dressed and behaved, or he would always give away his true origins.

It was an officer, Major Royston Hawkins, a man as unscrupulous as Ed, who introduced him to property development at the end of the war. Hawkins had inherited whole terraces of houses in London, many of which had severe bomb damage. Hawkins didn't want to deal with what he called 'the great unwashed' who were his tenants, many of whom hadn't actually paid any rent for the entire war. He struck a deal with Ed that he could have fifty per cent of the profits for managing the properties, but he would be responsible for getting the places repaired and getting tenants to pay the rent.

It was the perfect job for Ed. He wasn't troubled by sympathy for the poor, sick, old or needy. If they didn't pay the rent, they were out. He employed desperate men to repair the houses, and paid them poorly, along with sourcing the cheapest materials for the repairs.

He made money and started a company on his own at the age of twenty-eight that he called Reilly's Real Homes. He bought a few plots of land around London and crammed in as many houses as he could. He met Deirdre at that time. She was convent educated, pretty, and had spent the entire war acting as a housekeeper at a stately pile in Northumberland. Ed knew she would be well up on etiquette and would know how to run the mansion he intended to own before long.

But things didn't go the way he expected. Deirdre became pregnant almost as soon as the ink dried on their marriage lines, and he'd only ever imagined grown-up sons just like him, not squalling babies. Then a fire broke out at one of his properties, spread to three others and a young mother died in the fire, while two children were also badly burned. An investigation proved that the electric wiring was faulty on all the houses. They had been built with such inferior materials that they had to be demolished. Further checks on other houses he'd built proved that many of them were unsafe, and suddenly Reilly's Real Homes was a byword for shoddy building and people were baying for his blood.

He had borrowed heavily, and he had to sell what he could to pay it back, leaving him right back where he started. The dream of owning his own mansion had gone; he took on a salesman's job and had to go home at night to a couple of rented rooms, a bawling baby and a wife who irritated him.

He took it out on Deirdre. At first he was ashamed when he hit her, but he soon found that hitting her relieved the tension building up inside him. It was easy to find reasons to slap her around: the dinner not ready on time, a shirt not ironed perfectly. By the time their second son was born he was back in the building game under a new name, and beginning to make money again. But Deirdre, with her drippy voice, her reproachful eyes, goaded him to new heights in violence.

Ed followed Katy now out of Hammersmith station, keeping well back so she didn't notice him. He could see from her bouncy walk that she was feeling very happy, but he was preoccupied by how he was going to grab her. Obviously he couldn't do it now. It was nearly dark, but there were too many people about – and besides, he had no transport to bundle her into.

He would find out where she was staying, then go back and get his car. Girls of her age usually went out on a Saturday night. He'd get her then. He wasn't too concerned that she'd talk about this to anyone before she'd informed her father's lawyer. She worked for a solicitor, after all, and was used to keeping information to herself. And the lawyer wouldn't be in his office until Monday. If she had intended to go to the police, she would have gone straight to the police station in Hendon. Perhaps she'd lost her faith in the police?

She turned off the main road into a side road. Ed stood at the corner, watching from behind a privet hedge. She went up the steps to a house six doors down. There was a lamp post right outside, so he was able to see quite clearly.

He waited for a few moments, just in case she came out again. When she didn't, he turned and went back to the station.

'What have you been doing today?' Joan asked as Katy came in and flopped down on the sofa. 'You look worn out!'

'Just exploring,' Katy said, 'but I walked further than I meant to. I went to Hampstead. Isn't it nice?'

'Yes, one of my and Ken's favourite places. In the summer we like to walk on the heath and then go for a drink at the Spaniards. When we were younger we used to swim in the pools there. Maybe you and Jilly will do that if we get some hot weather –'

The phone rang then, interrupting them. Joan went to answer it.

'It's Jilly. She wants to speak to you, Katy,' she called back.

Jilly sounded very excited. Barry, the man she liked at the zoo, was having a party that night and had asked if she wanted to go, and to bring Katy.

'I said we'd love to.' Jilly's voice was shrill with excitement. 'But I can't come all the way home to change. Would you bring me some clothes?'

She listed what she wanted, and gave her a telephone number. She said if Katy rang her from the phone box right outside the main gate, she'd come out and let her in through the staff gate. 'Some of the others are also going straight from work and we'll have some drinks here before we all go on to the party. It's only just across the road, no distance.'

It was arranged that Katy would be there by eight. And with that, Jilly rang off.

Joan looked a bit cross that her niece wasn't coming back for a meal. She said she'd made a stew.

'She'll eat it tomorrow,' Katy said to appease her. Joan was a real mother hen, always wanting to feed them. 'She likes the man who has asked us to the party, so she isn't thinking about her dinner.'

'Well, as long as you have some,' Joan said starchily. 'I expect there will be drink at this party and you need something to line your tummy.'

As Katy ate her stew, which was really good, she felt a bit irritated for the first time since she'd arrived here that Joan was a mothering fusspot. She'd had enough of that with her own mother. But in a week's time she and Jilly would be moving out, and she knew she should be ashamed of herself for being so ungrateful.

After the meal, Katy had a bath and put on the green dress she'd bought from Gloria before Christmas. With her hair and make-up done, and her best black patent stilettos, she felt great. She collected up the clothes and shoes Jilly wanted and put them in a bag, then went downstairs to wait till it was time to go.

'Now you leave this party in good time to get the tube,' Joan said. 'And don't let any young men get fresh with you.'

Katy had to bite her lip not to laugh; her mother used that expression. Katy wasn't sure what 'getting fresh' meant. Trying to kiss a girl? Or putting a hand up her skirt?

Reilly looked at his watch for the umpteenth time. It was quarter past seven and he was losing patience.

He was parked right at the end of the road, just around the corner from the main road. He'd already observed there was a semi-derelict house right there, so he could drag her into the front garden, knock her out, then bundle her into his car boot.

But waiting made him nervous.

9

When it suddenly started to rain heavily Ed swore loudly, as it made it unlikely the girl would venture out. But he turned on the windscreen wipers so he could see clearly down the street as far as her house, and decided to hang on, just in case.

At seven thirty, when the front door opened and out she came, he felt like cheering. The filthy night was perfect for abduction; there was not a soul about, and she was battling against the strong wind with her umbrella.

Putting up the hood of his parka, he got out of his car. Without even glancing at her, he opened the boot, remaining there as if looking for something. He could hear the tip-tap of her high heels getting ever closer.

He rummaged in the boot until she was just walking past him. Picking up the tyre lever, he spun round and hit her hard on the back of her head.

She instantly dropped her umbrella and the bags she was carrying, and fell like a dead weight into his arms. He swiftly scooped her up and dropped her into his boot, chucking the umbrella and bags in after her. There was enough light from the lamp post to see her face. For a brief moment he felt a pang of shame, because it was such a sweet face. But only for a moment; he valued his freedom too much to let sentimentality get in the way.

*

Jilly was waiting in the staffroom at the zoo with Amy, a colleague. They both had their coats on, ready to leave, and Jilly could see Amy was growing impatient because all the other day staff had left.

'I don't understand why she hasn't come. She said she'd be here by eight with my clothes.'

'Maybe she got lost?' Amy said, looking in a mirror and tweaking kiss-curls in front of her ears. 'Took a wrong turning out of the tube or something.'

'I want to hang on, but I can see you want to lock up,' Jilly said. 'I can't go to the party in these dirty clothes, anyway, and I certainly don't fancy hanging around in the rain on the off chance she'll turn up.'

'I do have to lock up,' Amy said. 'Right now, too. I'm going on to the party. But maybe you just need to go home?'

Jilly sighed. 'You're right, Amy. I'll wait a bit longer outside, just in case she turns up. Sorry I've delayed you.'

Jilly did stay for a further twenty minutes outside, by the ticket office. But even though she was under a bit of shelter, the wind was blowing the rain straight at her and she was very cold. So finally she walked back to Camden Town tube.

She was cross with Katy, because she thought she'd probably got a call from that new man of hers and wanted to be with him more than her old friend. It was mean of her; Katy knew perfectly well that the object of this party was for Jilly to get off with Barry, and that she couldn't possibly go there in her work clothes.

Her aunt and uncle were watching television by the fire when she got in. They were both in pyjamas and dressing gowns. Joan had steel curlers in her hair, and the room was like a hothouse.

'You're home early,' Joan said. 'And where's Katy?'

'She never came to the zoo. I waited and waited,' Jilly said, slumping down on the sofa and holding out her hands to the fire to warm them.

'But she left here to meet you at half seven, she had your clothes and shoes in a bag. I said to her, "You must be mad going out in this rain," but she just laughed and said she wasn't made of sugar.'

'Well, where did she get to, then?' Jilly asked. 'Could she have got lost on the tube? She doesn't know her way around London.'

'She'd have phoned us, surely, if that was the case?' Ken said. 'Maybe she met another friend?'

'What friend? She hasn't got anyone in London,' Jilly said. 'Well, apart from the chap at work who she went out with last night. Did he ring her today?'

'No, she was out all day; she said she went exploring in Hampstead. No one phoned for her,' Joan said. 'Besides, why would she take your clothes if she didn't intend to meet you?'

They were all silent for a little while.

Ken spoke first. 'Should we report her missing to the police?'

'Don't be daft,' Joan scoffed. 'It's only just gone ten, they'd tell us off for wasting their time.'

'Well, I'm going to have a bath and go to bed,' Jilly said. 'I'm cold and tired. When she comes in, tell her not to wake me, as I've got to work early again tomorrow.'

*

Jilly woke at seven the next morning. Even though it was still dark, the lamp post outside shone through the curtains and she saw immediately that her friend's bed hadn't been slept in.

Now she was really alarmed. She knew that even if Katy had met Elvis Presley, who she adored, and he'd invited her back for dinner at his hotel, she would've telephoned. But then Jilly knew Katy was still a virgin, and a bit old-fashioned too, so she would never actually stay away for the night with any man.

'What shall we do?' Jilly asked Joan as they sat at the table having a cup of tea. 'Should we phone her mother first? Wait a bit longer, or ring the police now?'

'Her mother hasn't telephoned once since she got here,' Joan said thoughtfully. 'So it's unlikely Katy went to her. We can't phone her office because it's Sunday, but it is a bit soon to phone the police.'

'I've got a funny feeling about it, though,' Jilly said. 'What if she was run down by a car and is in hospital?'

'Then they will ring us,' Joan said firmly. 'I know she stuck our phone number on her key ring. She did it in front of me, because she said she can't remember numbers. She doesn't go anywhere without the key.'

'That's true,' Jilly said, pouring a second cup of tea. 'Maybe she'll come charging through the door later with some amazing story of where she's been?'

'If she does, I'll be tempted to give her a clip round the ear for frightening us,' Joan said sharply.

Jilly realized her aunt thought Katy was just a bit wild and off having a good time somewhere. But Jilly knew better; it wasn't in her friend's nature to be thoughtless about others. In all the years they'd been friends, she'd always been the conscientious one.

'I've got to leave for work now.' Jilly got up reluctantly from the table. 'I'll try to ring you later to see if you've heard anything. If you haven't, when I get home we'll go to the police.'

As Jilly was walking to the tube station, Katy was lying on a bed in a dimly lit room that had no windows.

She had come to, with no idea what had happened to her. She'd realized she was in a car boot, because she couldn't stretch out – and anyway, she could hear the engine and the swishing of car tyres on a wet road. The back of her head hurt and when she touched it she found a lump, which felt sticky as if it was bleeding. It was only then it dawned on her that she'd been knocked out by someone and shoved into his car.

The last thing she remembered was walking down the steps of Joan and Ken's house, the wind nearly blowing her umbrella inside out, and thinking that it might have been smarter to put her stilettos in the bag and wear a stout pair of flat shoes.

She had no shoes on now, and her coat was draped over her, like a blanket. She didn't remember anyone taking her coat off, so she guessed the driver of the car had stopped somewhere to see if she was alright. She didn't feel as if anyone had violated her body in any way, which either meant he wasn't a monster, or he was waiting to get to their destination.

Katy was shaken violently as the car went over some rough ground, then stopped. She must have been imprisoned for some time as her legs felt as if they'd been scrunched up for hours.

The boot was opened. But it was too dark, and still raining, for her to see what her captor looked like. The man hauled her to her feet by her arms. She screamed and tried to fight him, but he slapped her hard around the face.

'No point in screaming, there's no one to hear you,' he snarled at her. Then he proceeded to drag her by the arm from his car to a bungalow, which was in darkness. Without shoes she had to walk through an icy puddle, and the stones hurt her feet.

'Why have you brought me here?' she shouted at him. 'What is this about? Who are you?'

'You know exactly what it's about and who I am,' he said as he opened the door and pushed her in ahead of him into a narrow hall. It smelled of damp and mould; the smell of a place that was usually unoccupied. 'So you can work out why I've brought you here.'

'Edward Reilly?' she said, her insides churning alarmingly.

'The very same,' he said as he switched a light on.

He didn't look like a madman or a heavy-set thug with shoulders like a barn door, as she'd imagined. He was undeniably handsome, looking much younger than she had imagined, perhaps early forties. Dark-haired, with dark eyes, clear glowing skin and prominent cheekbones; he was tall, slim and athletic-looking. He had a look of an Italian actor, with his smooth, olive-toned skin and a Roman nose. His black overcoat with a velvet collar was a very expensive one.

She tried to plead with him to let her go – or if not, to at least get her coat from the car, because she was so cold – but he ignored her and pulled her towards the end of the hall and pushed her ahead of him down some steep stairs.

The first impression of the room he pushed her into was that it had been designed as a kind of prison. It was windowless, stark, with brown lino on the floor, the walls painted pale blue, and one dim naked bulb overhead. It was clean, but there was no furniture other than a bed, and a lavatory and a washbasin behind a half-screen.

Without saying anything further, he pushed her towards the bed, backed away and went out of the door, locking it behind him. She heard his feet on the stone steps up to the hall, followed by the clank of a heavier door being slammed shut and locked.

She screamed and banged on the door for some time. But after several minutes or so, it dawned on her that he had gone, driven away. Wherever it was that he'd brought her to, no one was going to hear her screams or her frenzied thumping on the door. She realized she had to calm down, and try to work out a plan. Getting in a state wouldn't help her escape.

But it was hard not to panic and cry. She was cold, and there were no sheets on the bed, just scratchy rough blankets that smelled of mould, and a black-and-white ticking pillow that smelled even worse. Never in her life had she been expected to sleep on such a bed; she didn't even want to touch it. Yet she knew the coldness of her prison meant she had to get into it.

There was no way out other than the locked door. She spent a few moments listening hard at it, but she couldn't hear so much as a car or a dog barking. She tried to remember what she'd seen outside, but nothing came to her other than the long, sleek car he'd hauled her out of, which was likely to have been a Jaguar. She didn't think there was any street lighting, either, because she would've noticed that in the dark.

Setting aside her burning face, the result of the slap he'd given her, and the fact that she was scared because she was locked up heaven knew where, she was also angry with herself for not thinking everything through before she played detective.

It was blindingly obvious that the arsonist and murderer was clever. He'd left no clues to his own identity behind in Collington Avenue, but had framed an innocent man. He must have watched Gloria's house to plan the fire, and then watched Edna too before trying to drive her off the road. So it was also possible, as Charles had suggested, that he'd seen Katy before as well.

Why hadn't she taken note of what Charles said? Only a real fool – or someone far too big for their boots – would ignore the advice of a barrister!

Yet she had gone looking at Reilly's house and asking questions of a neighbour, as if she was invisible. Clearly he must have followed her back to Hammersmith to find out where she was living. Then returned later that evening with his car, guessing she'd go out on a Saturday night. No doubt, if she'd stayed in, he would've bided his time until he caught her alone. She hadn't just been unlucky, she'd been utterly stupid.

If only, when she got off the tube at Hammersmith, she'd gone straight to the police and told them what she'd discovered. Or if not, why hadn't she phoned Michael Bonham and told him? Worse still, she'd left Edna's notebook in her handbag, which was now in Reilly's car along with her coat and shoes. If she had just left it in the room at Joan and Ken's, there was a chance Jilly would work out what she had been up to.

Could there be anything more terrifying than being locked in a cellar, never knowing when you would be killed? He surely did intend to kill her, too. What else could he do with someone who knew enough to get him hanged?

Jilly would be worried when she didn't turn up to meet her at the zoo. But how long would it be before she, Joan and Ken decided to report her disappearance to the police? And how would the police find her? She had never told anyone about the notebook, and she'd hidden it under her mattress because she didn't want Jilly finding it and reading it. The only person who knew there was a notebook was Charles – and he had no idea what addresses were in it.

She took a deep breath and reminded herself that Charles was smart. When she didn't turn up to work on Monday morning, he'd wonder why. Once he found out she hadn't come home on Saturday night, he'd guess she'd been pursuing a lead to help her father. She could almost hear him asking Jilly about the notebook he'd seen. But it wasn't there. He couldn't go through it, however much he wanted to. The only lead anyone had to her abductor was a dark red Jaguar.

In films detectives could find anyone, anywhere. But how could anyone find her, when no one had the faintest idea of where she'd gone today?

She was sure she wasn't in a cellar under Reilly's house

in Hendon; this place had only one storey, and there were no street lights. Besides, they'd been driving for far too long to be in London. He could kill her and dispose of her body long before anyone could find so much as a clue to his home address, let alone this place.

Her stomach lurched and she had to run to the lavatory to vomit. As she bent over the pan, one moment freezing cold, the next sweating, she wished more than anything else in the world that she'd defied Edna and taken that notebook to the police to check out the addresses. How arrogant was she, to think she could solve the crime?

Katy had no choice but to wrap herself in the stinking blankets, as she was so cold. Her head was throbbing and she still felt queasy, but it was the fear which was the worst thing. How would he kill her? Would it be quick? She already knew he'd had no problem burning two people alive, and then he'd tried to kill Edna by running her off the road. What was he cooking up for her?

Katy must have slept. But with no watch, and no window to see if it was light, she couldn't work out whether she'd been asleep for one hour or eight.

Then suddenly, as she lay there, she heard Reilly come through the top door, lock it behind him, then come down the stone stairs to the second door. In panic she leapt off the bed, her eyes desperately scanning the room for a weapon, even though she already knew there was nothing, not even her shoes.

The door opened and, although Katy had thought for a second or two she could spring at him and knock him down, she couldn't move when she saw him.

'Hello, Katy. I'm sorry I had to hit you to get you into my car. But really, you shouldn't go poking your nose into things which don't concern you.'

His deep, pleasant voice seemed more appropriate for a doctor or a solicitor than a wife-beating murderer.

'My father is being held in custody for a crime he didn't commit. Wouldn't any woman try to prove his innocence?' she managed to get out.

He smiled, his dark eyes and white teeth utterly disarming. 'Only some women, the kind of resourceful, brave women I normally like the best,' he said. 'But sadly, your actions are likely to make me lose my freedom, and I can't have that.'

For a brief moment Katy felt she was in a film. He made her think of one of those Nazi officers in war films. Of course he wasn't blond but, in fact, she thought he'd look the part in any uniform. She knew he was a very cruel, evil man, but he didn't look or sound like one.

'Why kill me? I might be of use to you,' she said, hardly able to believe those words came out of her mouth.

He laughed, and passed a carrier bag to her. The bag was hot, and looking inside she realized it was fish and chips, and a can of Coke.

'Is this the last supper?' she asked.

'Maybe,' he said. 'So enjoy it.'

He turned away then, without another word, leaving Katy stunned.

As a totally confused Katy was opening the parcel of fish and chips, back in Hammersmith the telephone rang.

'Maybe that's her,' Joan said to Ken. 'I don't think it can be Jilly, she'll be travelling home now.'

Ken was always irritated by the way his wife constantly surmised who was phoning, instead of getting up and just answering it. He'd been tense all day, waiting for news, and Joan had made it worse by wittering on about Katy's strange family, even asking him if he thought her father really could be guilty of setting the fire and killing two women.

'Then I'd better answer it, in case you say something tactless,' he snapped at her.

As he went out to the hall he saw Joan's shocked expression. Just this once he didn't intend to apologize.

'Hammersmith 4371,' he said.

'Is that Ken?'

Ken assured him it was.

'This is Charles Stevenson. Please forgive me for addressing you by your Christian name, but Katy didn't tell me your surname. May I speak to her if she's in?'

'Ken is just fine. Are you the lawyer at the chambers she works at?'

'Yes, I am.'

'Well, I'm very glad you telephoned, Charles, because Katy has disappeared. She left here yesterday evening at seven thirty to meet our niece from work. But she didn't show up.'

'You haven't seen or heard anything from her in twenty-four hours?' Charles asked.

'No, we kind of hoped she'd gone off to meet you. But our Jilly insisted she wouldn't do that, not without ringing to tell us where she was. I don't know if I should call the police. Don't people have to be missing for more than forty-eight hours before they'll do anything?'

'Yes, usually. But it does sound fishy to me. Is Jilly there, could I speak to her?'

'She had to work today, but she'll be back within twenty minutes,' Ken said.

'Would it be alright if I came to your house?' Charles asked. 'I'd like to talk to Jilly.'

'You mean now?'

'Yes, please. I know it's Sunday night, and you probably don't want a stranger there, but I can probably pull a few strings with the police. I need to speak to Jilly first, though.'

'Of course you can come,' Ken said. He rattled off the address. 'To be honest, it will be a relief to talk to someone rational.'

As Ken went back into the sitting room, Joan glowered at him. 'I'm not rational, then?'

'You haven't been today,' he said. 'According to Jilly, Katy's dad is one of the kindest men on earth. She says no one who knows him believes he's guilty, and I've got a sneaky feeling that Katy's disappearance is something to do with that fire. So don't bad-mouth him, Joan. It would hurt Katy, if she found out – and Jilly won't like it, either.'

Joan just pursed her lips, and Ken sighed. She was a great one for getting the wrong end of the stick and holding on to it.

The sound of a key in the door was very welcome.

Ken went out into the hall and saw it was Jilly. 'Thank goodness you are home!' Ken took her coat, as it was raining hard, and went to hang it up in the kitchen to dry. 'No word from Katy, then?'

'No, Uncle Ken,' she said, and her eyes filled with tears. 'Shall we go to the police now?'

Joan came out of the living room. 'You'll have your dinner before anything else, and that man from Katy's work is coming over, so we'd best let him report her missing.'

'You mean Charles, the man she had a date with?'

'Yes, he phoned just now to speak to her and I told him what had happened. So he's coming over right away.'

'Does he think she's already dead?' Jilly asked, rushing to her uncle's arms for comfort.

Ken held her and rubbed her back comfortingly. 'I'm sure he doesn't,' he said softly. But the sinking feeling in his own stomach suggested that might be exactly what the lawyer thought.

10

'I want you to tell me exactly where Katy said she had been on Saturday,' Charles demanded of Joan, once he had established Katy had spent the day exploring London alone.

They were all in the living room now, Ken and Joan on the sofa, Jilly and Charles facing each other from the two armchairs.

'She said she liked Hampstead,' Joan said. 'In fact, she said she wanted to go there again one day with Jilly to look in the shops properly.'

'That suggests she was too busy doing something else to look in the shops,' Charles said. 'Did she give you any clue what that might be?'

Joan shook her head.

'What about you, Jilly?' Charles asked. 'Girls usually tell each other things.'

'I didn't get a chance to speak to her, not in the morning, as she was still sleepy and didn't say what she was planning to do. Then of course she didn't turn up in the evening as planned.'

'At work she was looking in a battered notebook,' Charles said. 'She had an *A to Z* too, and she was jotting down addresses from it. I asked what she was doing and she said she was going to look up a friend in Bexhill's relatives or something. I knew she was lying. I said I thought she was being a detective to find the person who had framed her father for murder.'

'She certainly hadn't told me that,' Jilly said indignantly. She felt a bit hurt her friend hadn't told her, yet she'd revealed all that stuff about her father to a man she'd only just met. But then Jilly was rushing off to work, so maybe she couldn't have told her. 'What was this notebook? I've never seen it!'

'Later, when we were having a drink, she told me she'd been given it by Edna, the lady who was run off the road and nearly killed. I'm sure you know about her?'

'Yes, we hoped that would exonerate her father.'

'Well, it seems she gave the notebook to Katy. It held all the addresses and details of women Edna and Gloria had helped to start a new life after being beaten by their husbands. Katy finally admitted to me she had the idea of going through that book and checking which of the husbands had a dark red Jaguar.'

'Heavens! Jilly exclaimed. 'Why on earth didn't Katy tell me? So you think she was snooping around them on Saturday?'

'Yes, I do. Worse still, I think it's possible she found the house of the right man, but he saw her and followed her back to this house.'

'Then he snatched her when she left here?' Jilly gasped. 'Oh no, he could kill her!'

'Let's not leap to that conclusion just yet. Now, Jilly, do you know where that notebook is?'

'No, but I'll go and look for it in our room,' Jilly said, her eyes brimming with tears. 'If she'd told me what she intended, I wouldn't have let her do it.'

'Katy is one determined young lady,' Charles sighed. 'If it's any comfort, Jilly, I don't think anything you or I or anyone else said would have stopped her. She was desperate to prove her father didn't set that fire.'

'Poor Katy,' Ken said sadly, as Jilly left the room. 'I wish I'd realized what was going on in her head. If nothing else, I'd have offered to go with her to these addresses. This is all going to affect our Jilly too, as they are inseparable. But what do we do now?'

'I'll go to the police,' Charles said. 'Hopefully, with that notebook – if Jilly finds it – the police can check out the addresses and car owners.'

Jilly was gone some twenty minutes and came down empty-handed, looking very worried. 'It's not there. I've looked in the bed, under the mattress, in every drawer and the wardrobe. There is nowhere else to look.'

Charles's heart sank. Without that book he didn't have a clue where to look. He mopped his forehead with a handkerchief, suddenly overcome by heat. Or maybe it was panic. 'She must have kept it on her. I'll go to the police station now, anyway. But first, Jilly, you must give me Katy's details: date of birth, home address, and a photograph too, if you have one. '

'I've only got one of us taken in a photo booth,' Jilly said, taking it out of her handbag. 'It was from last summer.'

Charles looked at the small black-and-white picture for a moment. It didn't do Katy justice – it couldn't capture that pink-and-white complexion, her pretty eyes and her glorious hair colour – but the two girls looked so happy. This was the kind of picture people kept to remember the moment. He just hoped and prayed they would all get to see her again soon, and have many more memorable moments with her too, but he had a sinking feeling they weren't going to.

'I'll ring you as soon as I've reported her missing,' Charles said, after he'd jotted down Katy's details. He wrote down his telephone number, at home and at chambers, and handed it to Jilly. 'Ring me if you hear anything, if you find the notebook, or if you just need to talk. I won't always be available during the day, as I'm often in court, but leave a message and I'll get back to you as soon as I can.'

Jilly looked up at him, her eyes brimming with tears. 'He'll kill her, won't he? He wouldn't have taken her if that wasn't what he intended.'

Charles couldn't bring himself to admit he thought that was the most likely outcome. 'Katy struck me as being very brave and resourceful, so there is every reason to be optimistic,' he said, with more authority than he felt.

As Charles got into his car to go to the police station in Hammersmith, his heart had never been heavier. If Katy had left that notebook at home, it would be relatively plain sailing to find her. But without it, the old cliché 'finding a needle in a haystack' sprang to mind. He would, of course, find and speak to Michael Bonham. And maybe this other woman, Edna, might remember at least some of the names in the notebook. But that was a long shot.

He wished he didn't feel so involved. It was ironic that he had spent his whole adult life avoiding such feelings. There had been a long list of women, too. And yet he'd always held back from any kind of commitment. He hadn't made any commitment to Katy, either. How could he, after only one evening together? But he had spent the whole weekend thinking about her, which was why he'd rung her tonight. He had a feeling he wasn't going to be able to rest until she was found. He just hoped that she was still alive.

Not knowing whether it was night or day, or what time of day it was, made Katy's imprisonment even worse. She had eaten the fish and chips Reilly brought her, and after that she was so cold she wrapped herself in the blankets and eventually fell asleep. But once again, whether she had been asleep for an hour, or a full eight hours, she didn't know.

She began to cry once she was awake. Her situation was hopeless; she was going to die soon. And she doubted he'd make it a quick and relatively pain-free death. On top of that, she was numb with cold. He might not come back, and she'd die of starvation. What if he came back to torture her?

But after getting the crying and regrets over and done with, she got off the bed and forced herself to do some exercises until she was warmer. Star jumps, bicycling exercises on the bed, even ballet stretches she remembered from when she was much younger.

Once warmer, she felt slightly more hopeful. There were some things she knew. The first was that they must be within ten minutes or so of shops, purely because the fish and chips were so hot. It was also reasonable to suppose that he'd brought them for her around seven in the evening too, as most fish and chip shops opened at that time. That would not include shops in the country – few, if any, of them opened on Sundays – so she was probably on the outskirts of a town.

He also wasn't a stereotypical killer. Even as she thought that, she almost laughed. What did she know about killers? Absolutely nothing! But he didn't look or sound brutish. He was the kind of man she saw daily on the train to work, with a decent haircut, clean-shaven, neat and tidy. He had knocked her out to get her here, then brought her food a little later, rather than killing her right away, which suggested he didn't know how to dispose of her body; it was always said that was the biggest problem in killing someone. Or it could be that he wanted to play with her? In much the same way a cat will play with a mouse or a bird for some time before finally killing it.

She hoped it was the latter, and she decided that was what she should focus on. The longer she could keep him interested in her, the greater were her chances of being found alive. But how could she keep him interested? Maybe by not looking or sounding scared of him?

She remembered Edna saying something about men bullying and beating women to cover up their own inadequacies. She had said she wished she'd fought back or walked out, the very first time it happened. But she didn't, because she believed that she was in some way responsible for her husband's anger.

So what if she acted like she didn't mind being his prisoner? She could insist he get her a heater and some warmer clothes, for a start, rather than begging him to release her. That might disarm him.

Just thinking about that made her feel optimistic. Crying and banging on the door wasn't going to achieve anything.

*

It seemed at least two days or more before she heard his feet on the steps outside the door again. She doubted it was really that long, or she would've surely fallen asleep? But never in her life had she experienced such excruciating boredom for so long. Nothing to do, read, eat, listen to or look at, with a huge side helping of sheer terror thrown in. No cups of tea, no little snacks. She was beginning to understand why solitary confinement sent people mad. And the cold was awful; however much she wrapped the stinky blankets round her, she still shivered.

But the sound of feet on the stairs made her sit up and smooth her crumpled dress, ready for what she hoped would be an Oscar-winning performance of making demands, being charming and showing no fear.

'Hi,' she said as he came through the door. 'You must get me a heater and some warmer clothes, it's arctic in here. And by the way, these blankets stink.'

He stopped in his tracks, not even turning to lock the door behind him. His expression was one of total bafflement.

'Oh, I see,' she said, spurred on, because she felt he really was stunned. 'You expected to find me sobbing? Sorry, I don't do crying. I thought it would be better if we got along. I'll tell you what I want – food, heat, warm clothes and some books – then you can tell me what you are expecting of me. Oh yes, and I'd like my handbag back as it's got my make-up and hairbrush in it. I also need a toothbrush and toothpaste.'

'Who on earth do you think you are?' he asked, and Katy sensed she heard a tiny bit of admiration in the question.

'Katy Speed, legal secretary, that's who I am. Who do you think you are? The new Acid Bath Murderer? John Christie? Who?'

There was no doubt he was a good-looking man, if you went for that dark hair, soulful eyes and chiselled cheekbones look. He reminded her a bit of Anthony Perkins, only not as creepy as he'd been in *Psycho* – and much older, of course. She recalled going to see the film with Jilly twice, and both times they'd been scared out of their wits.

'I came in to ask what you want to eat. Not to be insulted,' he said.

'Oh, sorry! But you bang me on the head and lock me up here and you expect me to be really nice to you? What choices do I get for food?'

'Fish and chips, or sausages and chips.'

'Good job I like them both,' she said and gave him what some men had called her disarming smile.

To her surprise he laughed. 'You are a very unusual girl, Katy. But you don't want to upset me. I can be very nasty.'

'So I believe. Why did you pick on my dad to frame for killing Gloria Reynolds and her daughter? He hadn't done anything to you.'

'Mind your mouth,' he said.

Katy had to force herself not to flinch as he came closer to her. 'You can't expect me not to ask such a question,' she said, more bravely than she felt, 'especially when I'm hungry and cold. So get me sausages and chips, and bring back the other things I asked for.'

His eyes widened momentarily in surprise. Then they narrowed, and his mouth tightened. Katy quaked inwardly, but he turned and walked out, locking the door behind him.

'Now you've done it,' she said to herself. 'No food, no nothing. You always go too far.'

Charles rushed into St Pancras station and caught the 5.15 p.m. train to Broadstairs by the skin of his teeth. He had to stand, as the train was crowded with commuters going home, but he couldn't have gone earlier because he was in court.

It was Tuesday evening now, Katy had been gone for almost forty-eight hours and so far the police hadn't got any leads. They had searched along the road in Hammersmith for clues – a dropped shoe, or anything they could identify as belonging to Katy – but found nothing. One police officer asked Charles how many dark red Jaguars he thought there were in London, if he wanted to check them out one by one? Charles didn't have any idea how many there were, and the figure he was given of 7,000 did make it a very difficult investigation.

Yesterday morning Charles had telephoned Michael Bonham, who was horrified to learn of Katy's disappearance. It was only today that he'd managed to persuade Edna she had to talk to Charles and tell him all she knew. So that was where Charles was going now, to Claire, to Edna's daughter's home.

Michael Bonham had also taken upon himself the unenviable task of contacting Katy's mother. 'Mrs Speed hardly reacted at all,' Bonham had told Charles on the phone. 'She just said, "So like Katy to think she knows best." I ask you! What sort of a mother doesn't at least show some emotion that her daughter has been abducted? If it had been my daughter, I'd be distraught, but also

160

proud of her for having the courage to try and help her father.'

They'd had a little lawyerly discussion about their constant surprise at human behaviour. Then Michael had gone on to say how frail and scared Edna was.

'Her daughter claims she's aged twenty years overnight. She said she shakes with fright whenever someone rings the doorbell. She is torn between wanting to help Katy in any way she can, and fear that the man might come after her again. She's also frightened to tell us what she can remember about the women she and Gloria helped, in case it endangers her and her family in any way.'

'Quite understandable,' Charles had said. 'But we must make her see she is endangering more women's lives by keeping quiet. If her abductor has got that notebook, and I think it's certain he has, it might not just be *his* former wife he wants to hurt but all those women who left their men.'

'I agree,' Michael had said. 'I think you must visit her, Charles, and persuade her. I have tried and failed. She says she remembers none of the details from her notebook, but I don't believe that.'

So now Charles was on his way to Broadstairs, and he was pinning all his hopes on Edna recalling something useful. She must surely remember the more serious cases of battering; the names of the women, and where they came from. In his line of work he didn't forget the worst cases, though he often wished he could.

Bonham had been concerned about the need to tell Albert Speed of his daughter's disappearance, too. Charles had asked him for a couple of days to find her first. It seemed incredibly cruel to tell a man in prison that his daughter was in the clutches of a murderer. But Bonham had managed to get a phone number for Rob, Katy's brother, from their mother and he'd already rung him. Rob had suggested he should come down to Sussex and visit his father to tell him. He had wanted to go to London, to try and help find his sister, but Bonham had talked him out of that, saying for now he'd be more useful staying with his mother and visiting his father. As chilly as Hilda Speed seemed, she might actually be in a bad way and need Rob's help.

Smugglers, the small hotel owned by Mrs and Mrs Unwin, Edna's daughter and son-in-law, was probably very pictur-esque on a summer's day with tubs of flowers by the door and an uninterrupted view of the sea. But in the dark and rain, peering out from the taxi window, it just looked old and a bit shabby; even the lights were sparse and dim. Charles wished he hadn't agreed to stay the night now. He expected a slightly damp, lumpy bed and a shortage of hot water in the morning.

The door was opened by a small, attractive dark-haired woman in her late twenties.

'Mr Stevenson?' she asked, and when he said he was, she opened the door wider in welcome. 'What a filthy night to visit us,' she said, her dark eyes twinkling. 'I told Mother that she should be honoured to have a London lawyer coming down to see her. Normally our guests tend to be a little dull. You'd be hard pressed to have an exciting conversation with any of them.'

'I don't think you'll find my conversation very exciting,'

he said with a smile, already liking this unexpectedly jolly woman. 'But I'll try very hard not to be too dull.'

'Mother is up in her room. I'm afraid she is too scared to be down here with us. But then, if I'd been run off the road purposely and nearly drowned in icy water, I think I might want to stay in a locked room.'

'I'm with you on that,' Charles said. He hesitated before asking, 'So shall I just go up to her now?'

'No, you'll have a cup of tea, or something stronger with us first,' Claire said. 'She's just having her supper at the moment.'

Charles hadn't met Edna before. But even so, when he went into her room, he saw for himself how badly her close brush with death had affected her. She looked like a woman in her sixties, her eyes were dull, and she was wringing her hands nervously. As he went closer to her chair to shake her hand and introduce himself, she recoiled with fear.

'Don't be frightened of me, Edna, I'm here to try and help,' he said gently and squatted down beside her chair, putting his hand on her arm comfortingly. 'You've had a terrible ordeal, and I'm so sorry for that, but now we think this man has abducted Katy. So I must ask you to try and get beyond your fear, for her sake.'

'I want to,' she said in a small voice, her lips trembling. 'I liked Katy very much. If only I hadn't given her the notebook! I intended her to hand it over to the police or Mr Bonham, not to go out looking for the man alone.'

'I think we have both recognized now that Katy is reckless. But she did it for all the right reasons, so we have a duty to help find her.'

'What can I do?' Edna asked.

'Try to remember some of the worst cases you and Gloria came across. Particularly those where, as far as you know, the women didn't go back to their husbands.'

Edna closed her eyes and folded her hands in her lap. 'I find this is the best way for me to unlock the past. Go down to Claire and have some supper. I'll jot down what I remember.'

Downstairs, Claire greeted him warmly and he related what her mother had said.

'She'll come up with something, she always does,' Claire said. 'It remains to be seen, though, whether she remembers the right monster. From what she's told me in the past, they all sound like the Devil's disciples. But sit down, Mr Stevenson.' She waved at the kitchen table. 'I'm going to dish up in a minute, but how about a gin and tonic? Or would you like to see your room first?'

'The room can wait, a gin and tonic sounds wonderful,' he said.

Claire turned out to be a tonic, too. The drink hit just the right spot, the kitchen was warm and inviting, and she was the best of company, funny, irreverent and caring.

'My real job is a social worker,' she admitted. 'We bought this place so that when I decide to throw in the towel, I've got something to fall back on. It's easy to run; we've only got four guest bedrooms, and no one but you tonight.'

'So you followed in your mother's footsteps?'

'Yes, and Mum and I seem to be magnets for the desperate, dispossessed and damned. It may be because of what she went through with my father, and my feelings of guilt at having watched it going on. People imagine a lovely little place like Broadstairs won't have problems like wife beaters, child molesters, cruel parents and all the other nasty things humans are capable of. But believe you me, there's plenty of them here, too.'

Charles agreed. 'Yes, clients who need defending come from every social class and area. It seems we have the dastardly all around us.'

Claire grinned. 'I love that word "dastardly"! Now tell me, what is your connection with Katy Speed? I know you aren't her father's brief.'

'Katy recently joined our chambers as a legal secretary. Against all chambers' rules I took her out for a drink last Friday.'

'Are you trying to help because you feel something for her, or is this a sense of duty?'

'You are direct.' Charles smiled. 'It isn't my normal practice to admit to such a thing, but yes I do feel something for her.'

'Well done, it's always good to establish people's feelings straight off, and I'd say it gives you more determination to find her than the police will have. What are they saying about Katy's disappearance?'

'That it's too soon to be sure if she was abducted. As if Katy would just disappear for no reason!'

'I suppose people do sometimes, but with her father being banged up for a crime he patently didn't commit, and my mother suffering an attempt on her life too, I would've expected them to pull out all the stops to find the real killer.'

They had just finished their supper when Charles heard a bell ring upstairs.

'That will be Mother,' Claire said. 'I think it means she's remembered something for you.'

Charles thanked Claire for the delicious meal and rushed up the stairs.

Edna had a notepad on her lap, and the whole page was covered in her writing.

'It became a bit easier once I recalled what we called "our first". She wasn't the first woman we helped, but the first to never go back to her husband. She was called Sonia Birchill, from Kentish Town. She moved to Brighton, with our help, and changed her name and the children's to Patterson. Nasty as Mr Birchill was, I don't think he could be our man. He couldn't drive, for one thing, and they lived in a council flat with very little money. So even if he learned to drive, I doubt he'd be able to afford a Jaguar – and he wasn't very bright, from what Sonia told us.'

'Have you heard from her since she settled in Brighton?'

'Yes, she always sent us a Christmas card. And about four years ago she wrote and said she had a lovely man in her life, and that her two children were doing well at school.'

'I don't suppose you remember either Sonia or her husband's address?'

'He lived in a block of flats called Denyer House. On the second floor, but I don't recall the number. Sonia lived quite near to the railway station in Brighton, but I can't remember the address; she never put it on her cards or letters. That was a piece of advice we gave all our women, to never trust anyone from their past with their new address. It was safer that way.'

Charles nodded. 'The police should be able to check

them out with just what you've given me. Now what else have you got?'

She gave him nine names in all. To Edna's credit she had remembered all of the women's married names and, if not the actual address of the marital home, she was sure of the neighbourhood it was in. She remembered their children too, surprising Charles by reeling off their names and ages when she helped their mothers. She recalled some of the names the women adopted, and some of the places they moved to. Charles thought she'd done amazingly well, under the circumstances.

One thing she did remember very clearly was the kind of injuries all these women had when they came to her. Charles shuddered when she told him about the imprint of a red-hot iron on one woman's back. Another had her face smeared with paint stripper, and her husband had held her arms until it burned right in so she couldn't wash it off immediately. Broken limbs, weals from being hit with a stick, black eyes, teeth knocked out, and one pregnant woman thrown down the stairs. She lost the baby the following day.

'Ghastly, isn't it?' Edna said when she'd finished, and she wiped a stray tear from her cheek. 'Of course, Gloria and I had received much the same treatment from our husbands, and each time we met one of these poor women we relived it. The police should be made to act in such cases; it makes me so angry to hear how they refer to it as "a domestic". Even if they do arrest the husband, he'll get bail and he's back home in a few hours to give his wife another dose.'

It had been a long, exhausting day and Charles knew he must get to bed to be up early in the morning.

He stood up, leaned over and kissed Edna's cheek. 'You are a very brave, kind lady, and an inspiration,' he said. 'I will do my utmost to get this man not just behind bars but hanged. Also, from now on, you'll find me banging the drum to get help for abused women.'

She smiled up at him and took his hand in hers. 'I'll be praying Katy is found alive and well, and that something good comes out of all this for the pair of you. But I'll be holding you to your promise to bang the drum for abused women; I believe you are the man who could help change attitudes and laws.'

11

Katy was so hungry she thought she could eat a live mouse, fur and all, if one should come into the room. She wasn't merely hungry, she was ravenous, and her mind kept turning to gross and ridiculous things, such as eating that mouse. She wondered whether that was a precursor to going mad.

In books people who were hungry or thirsty always seemed to be in hot places. They saw mirages of dripping taps or fountains. But she was so cold that she wanted to imagine being hot. Unfortunately, she found that impossible. She could easily imagine icy wastes, but she tried not to as that made things worse.

When Reilly had stomped off, she thought he would leave her for an hour or two to punish her for being so demanding. But she'd expected him to come back with food eventually.

But he hadn't come back, and she was fairly certain, despite having no clock and being unable to see daylight, that at least forty-eight hours had passed since then. She had tried to sleep but couldn't, because of the cold. With nothing to do to pass the time, her imagination had taken over. She saw herself getting thinner and thinner until she couldn't stand or walk any longer. Also she had begun to think about the terrifying prospect that he might not come back at all. It was obvious he could solve the problem of what to do with her by just leaving her here to die.

How long did it take to die of starvation? She knew people said you could only survive about a week without water, but she'd never heard how long without food. She supposed it was probably weeks.

The thought of that was truly horrible. Her stomach was already so empty it hurt, and food dominated her thoughts: sausages sizzling in a pan, Sunday roast with golden-brown roast potatoes, or cheese on toast, butter dripping out from under the cheese. She remembered how, when she was about fifteen, she used to read books about life in prison camps and how each day there was a quest for something to eat: a crust of bread, or some potato peelings. When she was reading that, it had never crossed her mind she might one day experience it for herself.

To try and take her mind off food she thought about home in Bexhill. Seen now, while cold and hungry, her home seemed like the most luxurious palace, her mother perfect and loving, cooking meals that were a feast.

Then there was the office in Bexhill, with cakes on someone's birthday, nipping across the road for a sausage roll from the baker's, the lunch breaks spent in the Wimpy Bar; she could smell the fried onions right now, and it made her mouth water.

She had tried very hard to think of something else, but she couldn't, her mind always turned back to food. Yet now and then her thoughts did flit to Charles. Reliving his kiss could take her mind off her hunger for brief moments, as could daydreams of how it might have been if she hadn't gone looking for the red Jaguar. She thought too how upset her father would be to hear she'd disappeared. She knew he would rather spend the rest of his life in prison than have freedom without his daughter.

Even her mother might cry – something Katy had never ever seen. She wondered why it had never occurred to her to sit down with her mother and insist she explain why she was so chilly and sharp. What was it that had made her that way? Now that Katy thought about it, she realized she knew next to nothing about her mother; she had no idea where she'd grown up, or how she had met Albert. What was she like as a young girl? What were her parents like? It was just one big blank.

Remaining scrunched up under the blankets to try and keep warm made her ache all over. She forced herself to get up, to stretch and try to do some exercises, but it made her feel faint, so she lay down again and pulled the blankets back over her.

Then, just as she thought she would never hear the sound again, she heard feet on the steps outside the door. Had he come to feed her, or kill her? Her heart began to pound and she clutched the blankets round her more tightly, as if that would protect her.

'Wakey, wakey,' he said, and the jocular tone was scarier than a snarl.

She peeped out at him. To her shock, he had in his arms what appeared to be an electric fire and a carrier bag, which could contain clothes or food.

Her instinct was to jump up and thank him, but she reminded herself that she would get further with him by being offhand.

'What day is it, and time?' she asked, yawning as if she'd just had a little snooze.

'Thursday and four in the afternoon. I intended to come in yesterday but I couldn't make it.'

'Well, you're here now.' She tried to sound casual, but her eyes were on the carrier bag. It was all she could do not to jump up and rip it out of his hands.

'You are very calm,' he said. 'I expected to find you desperate.'

'Desperate for what?' she said. 'Your company?'

He looked fazed by that and held out the bag. 'Some clothes and food. It was too early to get you hot food but there's a pork pie, cake and some fruit. I'll plug this fire in.'

Trying not to pounce on the pork pie and stuff it in her mouth while standing almost on top of the fire was really difficult. Even if it was only a one-bar fire, she could feel the heat from it almost immediately. She forced herself to move away from the fire long enough to take a brown woollen sweater out of the bag, a pair of brown slacks, and a cream shirt. She put the sweater on immediately and the other things she folded and put on the bed. They weren't new but they were good quality; she guessed they had belonged to his wife. There were also socks and some knickers. The latter were new, three pairs in a sealed cellophane bag from Marks and Spencer.

'Very nice, thank you,' she said and picked out the pork pie with trembling hands. It was a big one, enough for four people, the pastry all golden and shiny. She knew she could easily gobble it all down in about four seconds flat, but that would never do. 'Excuse me,' she said politely. 'I'd rather have this on a plate with a knife and fork, but needs must.'

She bit into it and tried very hard to disguise her sheer delight at the taste.

Nothing she'd ever experienced was as hard as not stuffing that pie down her throat. The meat was perfect, tasty and moist. The pastry melted in her mouth. But to eat a big pork pie elegantly without cutlery and a plate was so hard to do. So after a few mouthfuls she wrapped the waxed paper round it again and put it back in the carrier bag.

'I'll have it later,' she said. 'Now suppose you explain yourself? Why burn Gloria's house down?'

He leaned back against the wall, his arms folded across his chest. 'That bitch took my wife from me,' he said. 'But then you know that. The other bitch, her sidekick, told you and gave you that notebook.'

'Gloria and Edna helped your wife make a new life for her and your children, away from you. But someone had to help them; you nearly killed Deirdre, and your children were suffering to see it.'

'I only gave her a couple of slaps, she had a good life with me. The kids wanted for nothing – bikes, any toy they wanted.'

'Toys don't make up for seeing your mother with broken limbs. Because it wasn't "just a slap", was it?'

'Do you know Deirdre?'

Katy saw a flicker of hope in his face. 'Of course not, how could I? She had a very private arrangement with Edna and Gloria. The only reason I even got to know about her and the other women was when my dad was blamed for killing Gloria. That's why I was hunting you down.'

'Hunting me down?' His voice rose an octave.

'Yes, that's exactly what I was doing,' she said defiantly.

'And what were you going to do when you found me?'

'Turn you in, of course.'

'But you didn't do that, did you? I know, because I was on your tail.'

She realized that making out she'd already told someone where he lived might shorten her life. Being smarter than others was clearly important to him. 'I regret that I didn't go straight to the police station at Hammersmith. My plan was to ring my father's lawyer on Monday morning. But hey, I'm here with you now, so why don't you tell me something about yourself?'

'Why would I do that?' He looked at her hard, his dark eyes like wet tar.

'Because you are unhappy, and it might make you feel better to share it with me.'

'I'm not unhappy.'

Katy sighed. 'You are. I suspect you've always been unhappy, or you wouldn't have started knocking Deirdre about. You miss her still, you want her back. You think that will make you happy again. It won't, of course.'

Katy was just plucking things out of the air to say, half-chewed-up bits of psychiatric jargon she'd picked up here and there. What she really wanted was to eat the rest of the pork pie and the cake.

'I don't want her back, not now; she was a stupid, pathetic woman and I manage fine without her.'

'Who are you trying to kid?' Katy asked. 'You aren't managing at all. You are full of anger. Until you let that go, you'll never be happy or able to get on with a new life.'

Katy sat back down on the bed and patted the blankets

for him to sit beside her. 'You fascinate me, Ed. I can call you that, can't I?'

He didn't move to sit next to her but stayed looking down at her, those inscrutable dark eyes boring into her. 'Yeah, you can call me Ed. What are you playing at?'

'Playing at?' She frowned as if she didn't understand the question. 'I just want to know about the man who intends to kill me. That is what you intend, isn't it? Though I don't really understand why you didn't do it as soon as you caught me. I mean you could've stuck a knife in me, or strangled me and shoved my body in someone's front garden.'

All at once it came to her that he only liked killing at a distance. In a fire, pushing someone off the road. He didn't like to be close up.

'If you think that means I'm going to let you go, you are mistaken,' he said.

Katy smiled. She sensed he hadn't got a plan at all.

'What have you got to smile about?' he asked.

'I've got some food, warm clothes and a fire,' she said. 'After how things were half an hour ago, that's progress. You are also an interesting, nice-looking man. I can see why Deirdre fell for you. What was it about her that made you hit her?'

'Shut your trap, woman,' he snarled at her. His dark eyes became still darker and his face flushed an angry purple. 'I'm going now, and I want no more questions or I won't come again.'

'Please yourself,' she said, more calmly than she felt. 'I only wanted to get to know you better.'

He left immediately, slamming the door behind him. Katy picked up the pork pie again and wolfed it down.

Only when her hunger was sated did she stop to think about what had passed between them. He was certainly a peculiar, troubled character. The way he'd rounded on her for asking him what made him hit Deirdre was interesting. She guessed he liked to forget he'd brutalized the woman he loved, and made himself believe it was Gloria who got his wife to leave him. No doubt Deirdre was a very weak woman, at least at the beginning of their marriage, until she'd finally had enough. Funny he couldn't see that he'd driven her to run away.

But considering why Reilly hurt women wasn't going to improve her situation. Okay, she had some food for now and clothes, plus the fire, but she had no way of escape. And how could anyone find her? She had no doubt Jilly was pushing the police to do something. Michael Bonham would be, too. But their task was close to impossible.

All at once the sheer hopelessness of her circumstances hit her and she broke down and cried. If she was right about Reilly not liking hands-on killing, it meant he was bound to leave her to starve.

As Katy was facing the prospect of being left to slowly starve to death, Jilly was trying hard not to cry as she braced herself to speak to Rob, Katy's brother. A letter had come from him to Katy today, clearly written before she was abducted. Jilly felt guilty about opening the envelope and reading the letter but, as she'd hoped, there was a telephone number in it for him.

She had always liked Rob. At one time she'd had a bit of a fantasy going on about him, but nothing had ever come of it; he treated her like another sister. In the letter he spoke of visiting his father, how stoic Albert was, and about his concern that their mother might be losing her mind. Surely no normal wife would ignore her husband in prison for a crime he didn't commit?

Like Katy, Rob wrote a good letter, amusing, warm and interesting. Jilly was hopeless at writing letters, but then her parents weren't bookish types like Mr Speed. And she supposed that dragon Katy and Rob had for a mother had kept them practising writing letters until they became good at it.

Finally she felt brave enough to ring him.

'Hello, Rob, it's Jilly Carter. I had to open your letter to Katy to get a phone number for you, and I'm afraid I've got worrying news for you.'

It was a relief to find he knew at least some of it. Apparently, Michael Bonham had got his number from Hilda Speed and informed him that Katy was missing. Rob was so happy Jilly had rung him that it was tempting to make light of the situation, to make out she really thought Katy would walk through the door any minute with a long-winded story about the old friend she'd met and gone off on a bender with. But both she and Rob knew Katy wasn't that kind of person.

'So it looks bad,' she said. 'I wish I didn't have to say that to you.'

'I know, even our mum broke out of her usual chilliness to admit she was worried.'

'She rang you? She hasn't even rung here to check if there's any news.'

'I went to Bexhill yesterday, after I'd visited Dad in Lewes,' Rob said. 'Mum's struggling with it all. She was

177

never good at telephoning, especially a stranger's number. So she's basically been sticking her head in the sand. She still refuses to visit Dad, but I suspect that is more out of fear of visiting a prison, rather than not wanting to see him. She is really worried about Katy, too. I could tell by the way she couldn't get her words out. Anyway, Jilly, thanks for trying to give me all this bad news in a kind way. I came back here to Nottingham last night to sort out some things, but I'm going back to Bexhill later today. My parents need me, to keep Dad's spirits up and to stop Mum from cracking. My plan is to try and persuade Mum to come with me to visit Dad. As much as I'd like to come to London and try to help find Katy, I think I'm more use at home with Mum.'

'You are right, there's nothing you can do here,' Jilly admitted. 'I was so happy to get the job of my dreams at the zoo, and then we found a flat and we were so excited, talking about the cushions and lamps we'd buy to pretty it up. We wanted to have wild parties and do all that crazy stuff people do when they first get to London, but all I'm doing now is crying. I'm so scared for her, Rob.'

'Me too, Jilly,' he said. 'Why did she have to think she was Sherlock Holmes? And why, if she was intent on try-ing to find a killer, didn't she just leave a note about where she was going?'

'What if she is dead?' Jilly cried to him. 'I can't imagine life without her in it. And I'm sure you can't, either?'

'No, I can't, we always shared everything until I went to Nottingham. I think that's part of the reason why neither of us were keen on going steady with anyone. We were too busy having fun together.'

'She always told me how much she loved her little brother,' Jilly sobbed. 'Sometimes I was even jealous.'

'She used to tell me she loved you,' Rob said, and his voice sounded shaky. 'I used to be jealous too, so we're both as bad as each other.'

He had to go, as it was his landlady's phone he was ringing from. But he said Jilly could phone Bexhill any time with updates or news. 'Look after yourself,' he said. 'Let's hope in a few weeks' time, when all this is over, we three can laugh about it all.'

Charles had taken a copy of the page of information that Edna had given him and handed it to the police on the same night he got back from Broadstairs. He was disappointed they didn't seem very enthusiastic, or motivated. A curt 'Leave it with us, and we'll look into it' was far too vague for his taste, so he took a few days off work to investigate himself.

So far, with the assistance of an ex-CID friend who still had close contacts in the police force, he had been able to locate the former marital home addresses of three women. At two of these addresses the husband was still living there. Mr Birchill, the one in a council flat in Kentish Town, was massively overweight and barely able to walk; a neighbour said he rarely went out. He had no driving licence, much less a Jaguar.

The husband at the second address, in Hampstead, was a surgeon at the Royal Free Hospital and he had a Mercedes, not a Jaguar. Furthermore, Charles had gleaned from the newsagent further down Haverstock Hill that Dr Foster had been on a cruise in the Caribbean with a girlfriend for three weeks over the Christmas and New Year period. So he couldn't have set fire to Gloria's house.

At the house next door to the third address he was told the Talbots had moved away three years ago. Charles didn't know whether the Mrs Talbot the neighbour was referring to was, in fact, just a girlfriend. Or maybe his wife had gone back to him, after all? Charles didn't know and couldn't really ask. He did ask if they had a Jaguar, though, and was told they had a grey Rover.

The next step was to check the other names on Edna's list against the electoral roll and find addresses for them. This was long and laborious, but he did find another four marital homes, though he couldn't be certain that these houses didn't belong to another person of the same name. He could hardly knock on doors and ask if a wife beater lived there.

He pretended to be doing a survey for the electricity board so he could go straight to the houses in question. At the Edens' house, Mrs Eden was no older than nineteen; she was heavily pregnant and they'd only lived in the house for three months. At the Camerons' home, Mr Cameron was black; a photo on the hall wall proved his wife and children were, too. The Butlers were well over sixty, and at the final house Mrs Seymour insisted he come in and have a cup of tea with her and her husband. Mr Seymour was in a wheelchair, and it was clear they were devoted to each other.

Demoralized, Charles went for a short walk on Hampstead Heath after calling at the last house on his list. He had found in the past that walking helped his thought processes. Knowing that Katy had come to Hampstead on that Saturday morning, six days ago now, pushed her right into the forefront of his mind again, a position she'd slipped out of while he'd been looking for wife-beating husbands.

What had that man done with her?

As a lawyer Charles knew anyone abducting a person almost always meant them real harm. Even those demanding a ransom, who promised to release the victim without harm after the money was paid, still often killed them.

So how could he find Katy? He didn't know who had her, or where he was keeping her; in fact, he knew nothing other than that he had a dark red Jaguar. And that he didn't mind travelling to kill.

But there was one person who might be able to shed light on this killer: his former wife, the woman he beat until she ran away.

Charles took Edna's list out of his pocket and stopped trying to look for addresses for this man. He looked again at what Edna remembered about the women who hadn't returned home.

Claire had said her mother never wrote down the addresses of where the women moved to after saying goodbye to her and Gloria. She said she thought them too dangerous for her to keep, just in case an irate husband resorted to breaking and entering to find any records.

Edna did well to carry in her head so many women's names – both their married names and the ones they changed them to. In many cases she remembered which town they went to as well.

'But which is the wife of our man?' Charles said, looking at the list. Brighton, Hastings, Eastbourne, Lewes and even one in Tunbridge Wells. There was no guarantee these women hadn't moved on somewhere else. Or that they would even talk to him. If they had run and changed their names, cutting themselves off from friends and relatives to escape their husbands, were they likely to take the risk of talking to a stranger who might destroy their present security?

How long would it take him to try and find these women, too? He couldn't take a long leave of absence from chambers. Besides, these women wouldn't necessarily have any idea where the murderer was hiding Katy, either. So it could all turn out to be a fool's errand.

He paused at a big oak tree, leaned back on the huge trunk and looked up. He loved trees, especially in winter without their leaves; the way he could see their bare framework.

Katy was a bit like that: no frills or flounces, a straightforward young woman who said what she thought, did what she thought was right. Fearless, intelligent, persistent. She had a lovely face, such a delicate complexion, pretty hair like spun gold, and clear blue, honest eyes. He hadn't met many honest women in London. Mostly they were out to ensnare a man with good prospects; often they cared more about their appearance than they did about others.

Katy was worth going on a fool's errand for. He had to find her. He was going to find her.

12

The day after Reilly brought Katy the pork pie and other things, then went off in a huff, he returned.

Katy was surprised. She'd eked out the cake, expecting that he would stay away for days. Having the electric fire and warm clothes had improved things, but she wished she had something to read to pass the time.

So when he appeared again, wearing a very wet rain-coat, his hair dripping, and carrying a bag with four paperback books, a toothbrush and paste, and her hand-bag which held her make-up and hairbrush, she didn't pretend indifference because she felt like hugging him. It looked like he was softening; she even wistfully hoped he might release her. That was an unrealistic wish, of course.

She had to wash in cold water, there was no towel or soap, and she could feel her hair getting greasier and greasier. But then did any prisoner expect the Ritz?

'It's good to see you,' she admitted, looking into her handbag. The only thing missing was Edna's notebook, but she'd expected that. She had a pen now, and a mirror. Even though she didn't want to put on make-up, it was comforting to have it. 'Thank you for these things.'

'You are an odd girl, you haven't asked about food,' he said. 'Does that mean you don't want any?'

'Yes, I do want some, please,' she said. 'I was being

polite. It seemed ungracious to ask for food when you'd been generous in bringing the other things I asked for.'

'I'm not going to bring you food any more,' he said.

A cold chill ran down her spine. She looked at him in horror. What sort of a game was this?

'I thought we'd reached an understanding,' she said, trying hard not to cry. 'Look, I know you don't really want to kill me. I've got an idea which will mean you won't be caught. I'll say you wore a mask, and I have no idea where you took me. Then I could say, one night you bundled me blindfolded into your car, and drove a long way, only to release me in the middle of nowhere. I kept walking until I came to a house and asked them to ring the police.'

'You've got it all worked out, then?' The chill in his voice was alarming.

But Katy had to carry on and try to convince him. 'Don't you see? It's a brilliant idea.'

The answer was a hard slap across her face. 'I don't want any ideas from you. You keep your mouth shut and let me decide what I want to do.'

Quick as a flash, and without thinking, Katy retaliated by slapping him back, putting all her weight behind it. 'Didn't you get told as a boy that men do not hit women?' she screamed at him. 'Of course you didn't. I dare say you had a mother who snivelled to your father, and put up with hell from him. Is that why you do it?'

His face was almost black with anger and he came at her, hands outstretched, as if he was going to strangle her. She knew she mustn't back down now; to do so would mean he would beat her black and blue.

'Don't you dare lay a finger on me,' she roared. 'I'm not

afraid of you. But I'm possibly the only woman in the world who wants to understand you.'

He stopped short, then turned towards the door, fumbling with the keys as if distressed. Finally he got it open and left, banging it behind him.

'That's right, run away, you coward,' she yelled at him through the door. 'I bet you've spent your whole life running from people telling you what you are!'

It was only when his footsteps had retreated up the stairs that Katy slumped back on the bed and put her hands over her face. She was horrified she'd gone that far. It was stupid, now he would leave her here. Her slapped face stung and she was hungry. What had she hoped to achieve by all that defiance?

On Sunday Charles decided to contact an old friend, Patrick Bligh. Patrick had been at Cambridge with him studying law. After two years, family financial problems forced Pat to drop out. He joined the police and was very quickly fast-tracked to CID. Charles had expected him to climb the ranks in the force, imagining that one day he'd be a Commissioner, because he had both brains and charm. But a couple of years ago he had left to start up a private investigation bureau. Many of their friends, and his police colleagues, laughed at him and said he'd be skint within a year, but so far he was doing very well.

Getting no response from Pat's number, and guessing he was working on his flat and couldn't hear the phone, Charles got in his car and drove to Ladbroke Square. Pat had bought this basement flat for a song back at the time of the Notting Hill race riots. Although the houses were huge and rather splendid, most of them had seen better days. As for the neighbourhood, that had gone right down the pan. What with war damage, bad landlords who crowded tenants in and didn't maintain the properties, and young people taking bedsitters there, it was looking rough – almost as bad as its close neighbour, Ladbroke Grove, the area all the immigrants stayed in.

But Pat was convinced that one day the tide would turn and it would become an affluent area again. He was probably right, for as Charles parked his car and looked around him he saw several recently renovated houses, and the park in the centre of the square had been tidied up. He'd even heard that Ladbroke Grove was improving and was considered fashionable by young people.

Pat used the front room of his flat as an office, and he'd painted the basement area white with dark blue, glossy railings. He was still working on the rooms further back in his flat. Last time Charles had seen him, he was talking about putting in a good damp course.

Pat answered the door wearing plaster-splattered green overalls. He was a big man, with a round face, sticking-out ears, dark eyes and thick dark stubble on his chin. He'd shaved off his thinning hair and his bald head gave him a villainous look. But his voice detracted from that, as it was straight out of the top drawer. 'What a surprise,' he grinned. 'But a great one, Charlie boy, as I could do with stopping for a coffee.'

Over coffee they did their usual banter, Pat teasing his friend about wearing a wig in court and sucking up to aristocratic barristers. Charles retaliated by ribbing Pat about spying on adulterers and the like.

It was good, however, to see how professional Pat's office was. There were no piles of papers on the floor, or tottering lever arch files. It was all grey and white, with both his and his secretary's desks cleared of clutter except for phones, typewriters and filing trays.

'So what brings you round so early on a Sunday morning? You've got a new bird and you think she might be married? Or you've got tired of the high life and want to join me?'

'There's elements of both of those, with murder thrown in, Charles laughed, and launched into the story. One of the many things he'd always admired about Pat was that he really listened. It was never necessary to repeat anything; he took all the details on board.

It took some time to explain the whole thing, but Pat didn't interrupt or ask for anything to be clarified.

'So what do you think?' Charles asked when he'd finished. 'Can you find out where these women are living now? What do you think the chances are of finding Katy alive?'

Pat put his elbows on his desk and leaned his chin on his hand thoughtfully. 'We both know abductors rarely let their victims go,' he said at length. 'He's a very angry man, too. I wouldn't mind betting he's killed before Gloria and her daughter. The way he set that fire, implicating Albert, it was all a bit polished for a first timer. How did he find out where Gloria was? Bexhill isn't a town people flock to for its beauty or excitement, so running into her by chance is about as likely as me winning the Heavyweight Champion of the World title. I don't suppose the woman he ran off the road got a look at his face?'

Charles shook his head. 'There's so much we don't

know. We can't even be sure that one of these women's names on the list belongs to his wife. It's a needle in a haystack job, isn't it?'

'Yes, but I've got pals who can run bits of info through the system. You said that you'd been told by Edna that virtually all her women came via Whittington Hospital. So that's the first port of call. I expect some of the women will have given false details, but my experience with almoners is that they tend to have elephant-like memories. So let's see if we can get hold of her right now.'

As Charles expected, the almoner didn't work on Sundays, but amazingly Pat managed to get her telephone number from the receptionist by saying it was a police inquiry and very urgent.

Next he rang the number and it was all Charles could do not to laugh out loud at his friend's silver tongue. He apologized profusely to Mrs Haggetty for ringing on a Sunday, especially as he was sure she was on her way to church. Then he went on to say he thought she might have some knowledge that could save a young woman's life.

As Charles watched Pat writing an address, he saw it was in Muswell Hill. He gathered they were to go to the address right now.

'She was wary,' Pat admitted. 'But these women are first and foremost social workers; they mostly deal with the problems no one else can, or will. Her husband will be sitting in on the interview. She sounded a bit nervous.'

With little traffic on the road, they were there in half an hour, and ten minutes of that was spent before they left with Pat putting on a suit and tie and running an electric razor over his chin.

The Haggettys' home was a very well-kept terraced house close to Alexandra Park. Mr Haggetty opened the door to them, a tall imposing man with a shock of white hair.

'This is very irregular,' he said sharply. 'But my wife said she doubted you would have asked to come if it wasn't something important.'

'Quite so, Mr Haggetty. A young women is in terrible danger, and the only person we feel may be able to at least give us a link to finding her is your wife. Now this is Charles Stevenson, a lawyer at the Middle Temple, and I am, as I already told your wife, an ex-policeman turned private investigator.'

Pat had already said that Charles should take the lead in giving the background to the story. As soon as he began to speak about beaten women, he saw deep concern in Mrs Haggetty's eyes.

'Two ladies, Gloria and Edna, actually met in the Whittington when they had been badly beaten, and the almoner who was there at that time put them in touch with another woman who helped them get away from their abusive homes. As a result, these two brave women began to help others.'

He went on then to explain that Gloria and her daughter had died in a fire, and that Edna's life had been threatened, too. Then he went on to describe Katy's involvement and subsequent disappearance.

'I wouldn't have been the almoner at the time Gloria and Edna came to the hospital,' Mrs Haggetty said, looking very concerned. 'But in my time there I have tried to advise many women in the same situation. It is an extremely difficult problem; there is no organization to turn to, and the police see it as a "domestic" and outside their remit. Even if they arrest the husband and charge him with assault, a few hours later he's back home, taking it out on his wife. Because it is so hard, especially for those women with children, to leave and start a new life, a large proportion of them end up returning home. They can't get work without adequate childcare, and they have no money.'

She paused, a little overcome with emotion. This was clearly a problem close to her heart. She wiped a stray tear from her cheek and tried to smile. 'Forgive me, it's hard to stand back from something so serious. I did inherit a bit of knowledge from my predecessor about Gloria and what she and her friend had achieved. It makes it doubly horrifying that she paid for her kindness with her own and her daughter's life. We must do all we can to rescue this young woman. Let's just hope we aren't too late.'

'Did you pass on any women to Gloria?' Pat asked.

'Not directly,' she said. 'I had no way of contacting her, but there was another link in the chain, old Miss Dunkin. Sadly, she was old and frail and I heard she died last year. Since then the only help we've been able to offer women is the addresses of a couple of bed and breakfast places that will take women in an emergency.'

'Then can you recall any of the names of women you met who were badly beaten?' Charlie asked, explaining about the notebook Edna had kept. 'The names they used when they came into hospital.'

'Not really, none stick in my mind.'

'Could you look at these names I've got here and see if they trigger anything?' He held out the list Edna had written.

He couldn't fault how carefully she looked at the names, her lips pursed, as if willing herself to come up with something useful. She handed him back the paper and looked regretful.

'There are several names that ring a bell, but not loud enough to be sure. But all these women will be on record at the Whittington if that is the hospital they went to. I'm sure, if I study the records and see a patient with injuries that tell me she was beaten at home, I am likely to remember more. With luck, we might find the women on your list. I will warn you at this point, sometimes women like these give false names and addresses. But not all. Anyway, I could do that for you tomorrow.'

'Not today?' Charles said hopefully.

She pulled a regretful face. 'We've been invited out to lunch today. But even if I were free, I doubt I'd be able to get permission to dig out old records today. Meet me there at ten tomorrow, that will give me time to get permission.'

As the two men drove away Charles sighed. 'This detective work is tougher than it looks on films.'

'It certainly is,' Pat agreed. 'Ninety-nine per cent plodding. Only one per cent luck. But don't be downhearted, Charley boy, that lady will give you names, mark my words. I sensed she was almost on the point of spilling out stuff as it was, but she just wants to be sure she won't be sending us on a wild goose chase.'

'Us?'

Pat sniggered. 'You think I'm going to let you cock it up alone? But even if we get the right wife and identify this guy, find out if he's got a police record, learn his car registration number and every last thing about him, that doesn't mean we'll find out where he's taken Katy. Presumably, he and his wife have been apart for a long time. He'll have let his anger with her fester, which is probably why he went after Gloria and Edna. So it stands to reason he's got himself this hidey-hole since his wife left him. Maybe his plan was to find his wife and put her in it – who knows? – but it could be anywhere in England.'

Charles was daunted by that; he was used to having a whole case cut and dried before it was brought to him. He hadn't expected this to be quite so hard.

'But if we find out who he is, surely we can issue a press release to get people to tell us if they've seen him?'

Pat turned to him and gave him a withering look. 'Oh, brilliant, Charley boy! Don't you think it's more likely that he'll kill Katy then, if he hasn't already done it? When an animal is cornered, it attacks.'

'So what do you suggest?'

'First things first. We go and get some lunch now. Tomorrow, if we are lucky and Mrs Haggetty pinpoints him, we can stake out his home and then follow him if he goes anywhere. If he isn't at his house, I favour breaking in and looking for something that will tell us where he is. I'm afraid we can't get a search warrant on such flimsy evidence.' Seeing Charles looking so dejected, Pat changed tack. 'But now, tell me about Katy. What sort of girl is she?'

'She looks like a dainty doll,' Charles said with a smile. 'But the similarity ends there. She's brave, tough, determined and bright, too. I couldn't bear it if that creep has hurt her.'

'Sounds like you've fallen for her?' Pat raised one eyebrow. 'I thought the day would never come that you'd get smitten.'

'I've only had one date with her,' Charles admitted. 'She was snatched the following day. So I don't know if what I feel is just normal anxiety for someone I like.'

'No good asking me,' Pat grinned. 'I'm useless with women. My mother keeps telling me it's time I was married. Like you go along to a shop and pick a wife!'

Charles smiled. They both had problems with women. Pat fell for almost every girl he met and smothered her with affection. They soon ran from it. Charles knew he was the exact opposite. He never showed enough enthusiasm; women felt frozen out. Yet it hadn't seemed that way with Katy. He hoped she'd felt something good was there, just as he had.

Later that evening, Charles called in to see Jilly and her aunt and uncle in Hammersmith.

The aunt and uncle feared the worst, but Jilly was a lot more positive and asked to talk to him alone. Charles got the impression her relatives were not pleased that she took him out into their kitchen.

'They chip in all the time, especially my aunt,' Jilly explained as she made him a cup of tea.

She was wearing a pale grey sweater dress, and although she wasn't exactly pretty there was something special about her. Her eyes were red-rimmed, and it was clear she'd been getting as little sleep as he had, these last few nights. But she did her best to be upbeat.

'Auntie Joan means well, but she thinks she's an expert

193

on everything. Yesterday she actually said she didn't think anyone had taken Katy, but that she'd just gone home to Bexhill, because she knows her father did set that fire. I ask you? Is she right in the head? She hadn't thought it through at all.'

'You'd be surprised at how many people refuse to believe what's staring them in the face,' Charles said. 'I was once defending a man who had been charged with armed robbery in a post office. He denied that it was him. Then the day before the trial he suddenly told me it was true. He even said where he'd hidden the money he'd taken. I said he'd have to change his plea to guilty and said I'd go to see his wife and tell her. But his wife would not believe me! She tried to punch me in the chest, and shouted blue murder that her Frank would never do such a thing.'

Jilly smiled. 'My mum's told me lots of people in Bexhill are saying all sorts of things about Albert Speed now; she was even told the other day he was a bigamist! Shame they've got nothing better to do in their lives than making up stuff about innocent people.'

'I'm very glad Katy has such a staunch friend. Don't you worry about your aunt's odd opinions, she's probably just worried that all this will affect you badly,' Charles said. 'Now what was it you wanted to tell me?'

'Only about the kind of person Katy is. She's really strong, Charles, and she can be amazing at talking people round. I couldn't tell you this in front of my aunt and uncle, but about three years ago, Katy and I were picked up at a dance by two Londoners. Compared to local boys they were really something – sharp suits, expensive shoes, and they had all the chat. Anyway, these blokes didn't drive us home, they took us right up to Fairlight Glen – that's the other side of Hastings. They made it quite clear what they wanted.

'I started to cry. I was scared, because one of these blokes had a knife, and he'd already told me he'd use it if I didn't cooperate. But Katy, she started talking like she was a school teacher. She asked why would they want sex with an unwilling girl? She insisted it showed something really bad about a man's character if he had to force girls. She pointed out they were good-looking, well dressed and had a nice car, and they could probably sweet-talk some girls into it. "But not us," she said. "If you insist on doing this, we call that rape, and we'll go to the police and get you arrested. I know your car registration."

'I was amazed, Charles,' Jilly went on. 'She didn't even sound scared. She rattled off the registration number and she told the one with the knife to put it away or she'd have that to add to what she would tell the police. She didn't falter once. Then she ordered them to drive us back to Bexhill.'

'And did they take you?'

'No, as we drove back into Hastings Katy told them to let us out and we would get a taxi. She said on the way home she didn't want them to know where we lived, just in case they tried to get one of us another time. That's what she's like: calm, confident and she just has that way with her. I've got into all kinds of scrapes by being soft with blokes, but she always sees through them. That's why I think she will find a way to outwit this man who's got her.'

'I sincerely hope so, Jilly,' Charles said. 'What you've just told me about Katy makes me feel more optimistic, and I'm going to look at some hospital records tomorrow.'

'Is this at the Whittington, where Gloria and Edna met? Katy told me about that.'

'Yes, the idea is to go through the names in the Emergency Department and see if we can find some beaten women who were treated there. We're looking for the wife of the man who snatched Katy.'

'Can I come and help you?' Jilly asked.

'I'm afraid not, because my friend the ex-policeman has kind of twisted a woman's arm to get her to let us look at these registers. If you are there as well, it might be too much.'

'I understand. I just wish I could do something constructive to find her,' Jilly said sadly.

'I know, but if there's any further stuff, I'll ask you to come along,' Charles said. 'I'll ring you tomorrow night to tell you how it went.'

13

The hunger pains were back, worse than ever. Katy thought it was probably three days since Reilly last came. She'd read all the books he brought and now she was totally demoralized, and feeling ill. Being warm was preferable to being cold, but one minute she was so hot she felt she was burning up, the next shivering. Her whole body ached and she had never felt so scared and alone.

She was convinced now that she would die here; she could only hope that if her temperature continued to soar she would pass out and be oblivious to pain, hunger and her surroundings.

Writing notes in a small pad she'd found in her handbag had occupied her for some time. She noted how she felt, her thoughts on Reilly, Charles, Rob, Jilly and her parents. The things she wished she'd said to people but hadn't. But all at once it seemed pointless, if she was going to die here. No one would ever find and read her notes.

Was Reilly punishing her for slapping him? Somehow she doubted he'd been slapped by many women before, if ever.

Sick as she felt, lying huddled in the blankets on the bed, she still wanted to understand Reilly. What had made him claim to love his wife, yet beat her? Then, when she left him, why couldn't he accept that it was the consequence of abusing her? Added to that, he'd killed Gloria and Elsie, allowed her father to be blamed for their deaths, and he'd tried to kill Edna.

Was he mad? What could have happened to him to make him so twisted?

Aside from thinking about Reilly, she had been having some very strange dreams, believing other people were here in the room with her. Her father, for one, and Rob her brother. She thought it was real when she dreamed about her father, and she called out to him. That woke her to find the room was empty: just her, the bed, toilet and washbasin, nothing else.

Another dream was about a garden, a fabulous one with lush grass and winding paths between brightly coloured flower beds. But she kept walking and walking, and she didn't come to a way out. It seemed the paths just went round and round; there was no end, and no way in or out.

A noise brought her back to the present. She thought she must be imagining it because she wanted someone to come so badly. But then she heard it again, and this time she knew it was real. That light, confident step was Reilly.

This time she couldn't get up. She just lay there, aware he was standing in the open doorway looking at her on the bed.

'What's up?' he said. 'Still got the hump 'cause I slapped you?'

'I don't feel well,' she said, and it came out like a croak.

She heard him shut the door and lock it, then come across to the bed.

'I brought you some fish and chips, and some coffee in a flask,' he said.

That ought to have made her jump up, but instead it made her stomach turn over, as if she was going to be sick.

'Come on, sit up and eat it while it's hot,' he said.

Katy struggled to sit up, but the room began to swirl around, and as he put the newspaper bundle of fish and chips on her lap, the smell of it brought on nausea.

With her hand clamped over her mouth, she just managed to stagger to the lavatory before being sick. There was no food, only fluid, and she sank down on to her knees and leant her head against the cold porcelain of the washbasin.

'Well, that's a waste bringing you food,' he said. He came over to her with a cup of water, and gave it to her to drink. It had barely gone down before she brought it up again.

'Come on, better get back to the bed,' he said and, putting his hands under her arms, he helped her up.

She heard the door close behind him and the sound of the key turning in the lock. The knowledge she was sick and alone again brought on tears she'd held back for so long.

'Don't cry, Katy!'

She hadn't heard Reilly come back in, and she certainly didn't expect such a gentle reproach.

He sat on the bed next to her and wiped her face with a wet cloth that smelled of lemons. 'I think you need to drink some more,' he said. 'I took the fish and chips out, as the smell made you sick. Do you think you could drink some water?'

Gently he helped her to sit up. She drank about half a cup, then slumped back down.

'I brought a bowl down in case you get sick again. I've brought down other things too. Tinned rice pudding – I always like that when I feel poorly – some yoghurt, and some medicine to help settle your stomach.'

Katy didn't even look at the things he'd brought; she just closed her eyes and wished for sleep. She felt him covering her up, and her last thought was that he had been kind to her.

On Monday morning, Charles picked up Pat just after nine and drove to the Whittington Hospital. He'd hardly slept a wink for worrying about Katy. This was now day nine, and his lawyer's head told him she was already dead and her body disposed of. But his heart told him she was waiting to be rescued.

The two men hurried to the Emergency Department, where they'd arranged to meet Mrs Haggetty. They were hoping she still wanted to help them and hadn't changed her mind overnight. Even so, they couldn't be sure she'd be able to get access to the records.

'Have we got permission, Mrs Haggetty?' Charles asked her anxiously as she came down the hospital corridor.

'Call me Irene,' she said. 'And yes, I have got permission to show you the register. I'll take you down there now.'

She led the two men down the cream-and-green-painted corridor, back the way she'd just come, down a staircase, and along another corridor.

Unlocking a door and flicking on a strip light, she led them into a windowless room which was filled, floor to ceiling, with files. Thousands upon thousands of them. Charles groaned.

Irene raised one eyebrow quizzically. 'It isn't as bad as it looks,' she smirked. 'Mostly these are patients' medical notes. The registers we want are just here.' She waved her hand at two shelves filled with big hardcover books. 'These are in year order, and we need 1955 to, say, 1963. Is that right?'

'So just eight books?' Pat sounded positively gleeful. 'I'll take the odd-number years, Charles, and you take the evens. Maybe Irene can flit between us to point out anyone she remembers?'

'Well, I won't know anyone from before 1961, as I wasn't here, but we may find some of the women came here more than once.'

'How much time can you spare?' Charles asked Irene. 'We don't want to interfere with your work.'

'I've got a day off today,' she said. 'Besides, finding a young woman in danger is terribly important.'

By midday, amongst the emergencies and general accidents they had found dozens of women whose injuries appeared to have been caused in a domestic situation. They ranged from broken limbs, knocked-out teeth, damaged eyes and jaws, to cuts and bruises, and burns too. All but two of these women claimed their injuries were accidental. Of the two who admitted their husband was responsible, neither would make an appointment to speak to the almoner.

'That's another problem, you see,' Irene said. 'Mostly I work Monday to Friday, so if these injured women come in at the weekend or during the night, all the sister can do is try to persuade them to come back to see me. Even during the week my work takes me all over the hospital. I could be checking that a frail elderly patient has someone to look after them when they get home, or maybe an unmarried expectant mother needs advice. Sometimes it's just arranging for a district nurse to call when a patient goes home. There is always a lot to fit in. So if the injured woman doesn't choose to book an appointment to see me, or wait, I don't get to see her. We have been known to do follow-ups at home if the injuries are bad enough to warrant that, but we have to be extremely careful. We might just make the situation very much worse if the husband thinks his wife has been telling tales.'

They didn't stop for any lunch, though Pat went and got three cups of hospital coffee for them. Then finally, at half past two, they found a name that Edna had put on her list. Suzanne Freeman, from Golders Green. Half an hour later, they found Margaret Foster.

'I do remember her,' Irene said excitedly, pointing to Margaret Foster. 'Her husband was a surgeon. Look, she even gave a real address in Hampstead Village. She'd been in before, as I recall. Serious injuries, too. She actually confided in me that she lived in fear of him, never knowing when he was going to explode with rage. For years she thought he was just letting off steam because of his stressful work. Everyone else who knew him thought he was charming, caring and almost godlike.'

'Edna remembered her quite well, too,' Charles said. 'She said she settled in a village not far from Eastbourne. But she couldn't remember what she changed her name to.'

'I can find that out,' Pat said.

Spurred on by some success, they carried on with enthusiasm, but without any further results. By half past four they were flagging when Pat found another one of the names on their list. Edna had remembered only the name Deirdre, and that she ended up in Brighton, but she'd said she was a little wisp, and she'd been tortured not just beaten.

'It says here this Deirdre's injuries looked like torture: cigarette burns, rope marks on her wrists, weals on her back, as if from a cane, and a broken arm. So it must be the same woman,' he said.

'I remember her,' Irene said jubilantly. 'Just saying her name has brought her right into focus. A pale face, golden-red hair, frightened big eyes and terribly thin. She had two children with her, I think. Reilly was her surname. I remember that because I loved those Old Mother Riley films when I was a girl. But that address she gave in Horn-sey is a false one. I was worried about her, and checked it out. It doesn't exist.' She paused, looking thoughtful. 'I am surprised she eventually made her way to Edna and Gloria. I really didn't think she had it in her. Worse than that, I honestly expected to read in the papers one day that she'd been found murdered, or had taken her own life.'

They had to call it a day; it was getting late, and they were all hungry.

'Thank you so much for your help, Irene,' Charles said. 'I think we'll run checks on these three. But if we have no luck, maybe we can come back again?'

'Of course,' she said with a broad smile. 'And mean-while, I'll put my thinking cap on and try to come up with some other names. I hope you find her. You will ring and let me know?'

They assured her they would, and left the hospital.

'So who is going where next?' Charles asked his friend.

'Well, I can get a mate of mine to check out the London addresses, to see if the husband has a red Jag. Why don't I go down to Eastbourne tomorrow and find Margaret Foster? You could go to Brighton and look for Deirdre. I'll get the local police checking names. Usually when someone has changed their name, especially if they have children, it pops up in council housing applications or school records.'

Charles looked thoughtful. 'If these two women are always looking over their shoulder, expecting their husbands to track them down, they probably won't want to open the door to us. What do we do then?'

'Play it by ear, I suppose,' Pat said. 'It might be as well to write down our credentials and why we want to speak to them, just in case. Then we can put that through their letter box, if they're too frightened to speak to us.'

Katy woke with a start. She thought it was a dream that someone was in bed with her, but as she moved her hand tentatively to sweep the space beside her, she felt someone close by. The overhead light was no longer on, and she was covered in something warm and soft that didn't smell of mould.

'Who are you? Where have you taken me?' she yelled out in panic.

'It's okay, Katy, it's only me, Ed,' came his voice from right beside her. 'I stayed because you were so ill.'

Katy clutched at herself. She was still fully dressed, and the warm and soft thing over her felt like an eiderdown. 'Put on the light,' she ordered.

She heard a switch and a light came on from below the level of the bed. Enough light to see she was still in the same cellar, and Reilly was fully dressed beside her, except for his shoes.

Too shocked to speak, she could only stare at him.

'How do you feel now? I was worried about you,' he said.

Her mind was whirling. How could a man she knew to be a murderer, who intended to kill her also, stay and keep an eye on her because she was ill? The lamp and the eiderdown, where did they come from? How long had she been asleep?

'You've been out of it for over twenty-four hours,' he said, as if reading her mind. 'I got you to take some stomach medicine, and when you kept that down I fed you chicken soup. Then you went back to sleep, but I thought I'd better stay. So I got the eiderdown and the lamp, also a kettle and stuff, if you'd like a cup of tea.'

She could only nod, too stunned to process the revelation that she'd been lying in a bed with him – and now he was offering to make her tea.

He didn't speak as he was boiling the kettle and making the tea. She sat up and wrapped the eiderdown around her. It was very similar to one her parents had on their bed, with a green-and-white paisley pattern. When she and Rob were small, they used to borrow it to make a den in the spare room. They'd put a blanket over the clothes horse, then the eiderdown made it cosy inside. It was good to have something that felt like home.

'One sugar,' she said, as she watched him spooning some tea into a teapot. 'And pour mine while it's still weak.'

'Yes, Ma'am,' he said and gave a mock salute.

'You are a real puzzle,' she said once she had the mug of tea in her hand and a digestive biscuit. 'How can you switch from being cruel to kind like this? You are a handsome, personable man. Please explain, Ed. I want so much to understand you.'

He shrugged. 'I don't know.'

'Were your parents cruel to you?'

'I never knew my dad; he didn't hang around long enough to even know about me. Mum didn't care about anything but drink. All the men who came into her life while I was young slapped her around. I could see she deserved it.'

'How can you say that about your mother?' Katy exclaimed.

'She was a tart, a drunk, a liar and a thief. We kids had to fend for ourselves. Sometimes her men hit her because she didn't take care of us or our home. Well, it wasn't a home, it was a filthy tenement. But I don't know why I've told you that. Other kids had it bad back then, too.'

Ed got to his feet and Katy realized he felt he'd opened up too much.

'I've got to go,' he said. 'I'm glad you are feeling better.'

A surge of excitement ran through Katy. She felt things had moved on to a different plane, and perhaps now he might let her go.

'Come back soon,' she said. 'I like your company.'

Ed left without saying another word, and Katy felt a bit puzzled. It was true, she really had liked his company.

It felt very weird to be getting to like a man who had abducted her.

Rob looked at his father coming into the visiting room at Lewes gaol. Albert had a worrying grey tinge to his face, and he seemed to have shrunk since he'd been in here.

'Good to see you, Rob,' he said, reaching out to squeeze his son's shoulder in greeting.

'I'd like to hug you, Dad, but I guess that isn't appropriate in here?'

'No, son, but imagine I've given you one.' He sat down across the small table. 'How's your mum?'

'Very nervy, she's not eating,' Rob said. 'I tried to get her to come today, but she wouldn't. If it's any comfort, it's not that she doesn't want to see you, only the stigma of going into a prison.'

'I can imagine,' Albert said, and half smiled. 'Any news of Katy?'

'Charles has got in with an old pal who was a detective. I've got a good feeling about that, but so far there's nothing to report. But tell me, how are you feeling?'

'Proud of my son,' Albert said with a smile. 'Wishing I could be helping to find Katy. Feeling sorry for your mum, because I know she's hurting terribly inside, even if she doesn't admit it. I'd like to be out in the garden, watching the spring flowers come up, and have a pint with you, and eat one of your mum's Sunday dinners. I think that about covers it.'

'You are so strong, Dad,' Rob said, his voice quavering.

'I went through worse in the war. Don't worry about me, Rob, your mum is the one that needs the sympathy. But as we both know, she doesn't make it easy for us.'

They moved the conversation on to books, and it seemed only moments later the bell rang to say the visit was ended.

'Before I go, Dad,' Rob said, 'I just want to tell you Mum's been going to church. She wouldn't admit it to anyone but I know she's praying for you and Katy. '

Albert just smiled. 'Go now, son, and let's hope your mum's prayers get heard.'

Katy had found a length of string in the bag Ed had brought containing stuff for her, and she was amusing herself by playing cat's cradle with it.

As usual, she had no idea how long it had been since Ed left. But she felt well again, and with a kettle, tea and books she was feeling alright and looking forward to him coming back.

Her head told her she was mad to be looking forward to seeing him again. But she couldn't seem to stop the troubling fantasies of him kissing her and the feeling that she wanted it to go further. She had to be really stupid to think there could be a happy ending to this! But if she lay back on the bed and closed her eyes, she could see them walking hand in hand on a sandy beach, laughing as they jumped over waves. Then she would snap out of it, think of her father locked up, of Gloria and Elsie dead, and the terrible things that Ed had done to his wife to make her run from him.

Was she going mad? Could isolation make you love your captor?

'You don't love him, that's absolutely ridiculous,' she said aloud. Her voice seemed to echo around her prison. She pulled off the cat's cradle wrapped around her fingers, as if it was chains.

But even though she knew it was not healthy to begin to think of Ed as anything more than a brute, she still had her ears cocked for his return.

Ed finally turned up after what seemed like hours to

Katy. He was dressed in a pale blue sweater and light grey trousers and he smelled of expensive aftershave. It crossed her mind he had dressed up for her.

'Hello,' she said, smiling at him. 'What's the weather like outside?'

'Slightly warmer than the last couple of weeks, but with a strong wind blowing,' he said.

'You look a bit troubled,' she said, even though he didn't. 'Care to tell me about it?'

'I'd really like a cup of coffee,' he said. 'Care to make me one?'

She laughed, and got up to make it. 'Good job you didn't want tea, the milk's gone off, but some clever prison guard left me some powdered milk that's okay in coffee.'

'When I was a kid, the best treat in the world was tea with condensed milk,' he said thoughtfully. 'I tried it again quite recently but it was horrible.'

'I liked to stick my fingers in the condensed milk tin, and lick it off,' Katy said. 'I still find that scrumptious.'

Ed looked thoughtful as he sat down on the bed. 'Being a grown-up isn't how you thought it would be as a child, is it?'

Katy nodded her head in agreement. 'What did you want most?' she asked. 'I mean when you were a child.'

He sat looking at his hands for a moment or two. 'I remember wishing I had a mother who sometimes took us down to the beach for a picnic. We lived so close to the sea, and although my brothers and I could go there anytime, we used to see other kids there after school with their mums. Their picnics always looked so good.'

'Because you lived by the sea she probably thought you wouldn't see that as anything special,' Katy said.

'She never did anything with us,' he said. 'Even when she had a new baby she expected me to give them a bottle. I'd come home from school and the baby was soaking wet and screaming. She'd be asleep, drunk as a skunk.'

To Katy that was such a sad picture. 'Did Deirdre remind you of your mum?' she asked.

His eyes flashed dangerously. 'No, she didn't. She was about as different as could be. So what's your theory about me, then?'

'I don't have one, Ed,' she said. 'Clearly, you had a miserable time as a kid. But then lots of people have that and they don't all go on to kill.'

'Maybe I didn't mean to kill that woman and her daughter. I just wanted to teach her a lesson for taking Deirdre and my kids away from me.'

'Well, you certainly did that! The worst kind of lesson. And what about her two surviving children? It's a terrible thing you've done to them. Did you hate them because their mother took them to the beach for picnics? Gloria didn't take Deirdre from you. You made it impossible for her to stay with you.'

He lunged at her before she had a chance to move, pushed her back on to the mattress and punched her full in the face.

'No, Ed,' she screamed at him. 'Don't do this.'

He punched her again. 'Plead with me,' he snarled at her. 'That's what women do, wind me up and then beg me not to hurt them.'

'I'm not going to plead for anything,' she spat out, trying to get free of his restraining hands. 'You showed me you could be a good, kind man. Now you've spoiled that.

Hit me, if it makes you feel big, but I won't plead for anything.'

He hit her again, and again. Everything in her line of vision was red, she assumed because her eyes were full of blood. When he'd tired of hitting her face, he hit her chest and abdomen and, although she tried to curl into a foetal position to protect herself, he just hit her back and sides.

'Plead with me, bitch,' he screamed at her.

She wished she could see his face, as she was sure it was contorted with rage. But however much pain she was in, she wasn't going to beg him to stop.

'I'm going to kill you. You do know that, don't you?' he snarled. 'You think you're a cut above other women, but you're not. You are just an interfering little busybody who stuck her nose into something she shouldn't have.'

He got up on his knees and punched her so hard in the stomach that she fell off the far side of the bed. She felt him grab her hair and pull her back on to the bed to hit her again. The bed seemed to be spinning, she couldn't see anything more than a pinkish glow, and she felt herself slipping down into a dark place, with the pain and his voice finally receding.

14

Charles had always loved Brighton, but seen on a wet, windy and cold March morning it didn't have its usual appeal. Everything looked seedy; white-painted houses had a patina of green mould on them, windows needed cleaning, dustbins were overflowing. There also seemed to be far more dog's mess than in London.

Pat had pulled in a favour yesterday evening, and found the addresses of three Mrs Reillys, all of whom had arrived in Brighton from outside the area, between two and three years ago, with children, and applied for emergency council housing. Only one of them had actually been given a council house. Pat's source wasn't able to tell him these women's Christian names, where they came from, or even the children's ages. He wouldn't admit who his source was, either. Charles suspected it was an old flame who worked in the housing department. He thought Edna would be horrified to find out that, after all her and Gloria's efforts to keep their women safe, there were other women out there prepared to hand over confidential information just because they fancied the man who was asking.

He caught a taxi to the first address in the Withdean area of the town. Blythe Street was very grim, with three-storey terraced housing that looked like it should be demolished. He doubted that any of the houses even had an indoor lavatory.

Number 8 was one of the worst; even with the battered front door closed there was still a rank smell wafting out. There were no bells, so he knocked loudly. After getting no reply, he knocked again, this time even louder. A clatter of heels on a bare wooden staircase proved someone had heard him.

'I'd like to speak to Mrs Reilly,' he said to the woman who answered. She looked rough, about thirty, wearing a huge dirty Arran sweater and a pair of jeans, a cigarette in her hand. Her hair was plastered to her head with grease.

'She's on the top floor, you'd better go up,' the woman said, looking him up and down. 'Looks like she's getting a better class of punter!'

Charles wondered if that meant Mrs Reilly was a prostitute. He couldn't blame any woman taking up that career if she was on her own with children to support, but he couldn't imagine any man eager for sex wanting to pay for it in such a dirty, miserable house.

It looked like no one had ever swept the stairs, and the last time the house was painted must have been at the turn of the century. The door at the top of the stairs was open, and he could hear a wireless playing inside. Charles knocked and called out her name.

'Yeah, what is it?' The woman who came to the door was still wearing a housecoat, and had curlers in her hair.

'Are you Mrs Reilly?' he asked.

'What if I am?' she said, sticking her chin out defiantly.

She was probably in her late thirties, and was no doubt reasonably attractive once she'd put her make-up on. But she had a blotchy face, the sign of a heavy drinker, and her body looked like a couple of lumpy pillows, held in rough shape by the belt on her housecoat.

'I'm not sure you are the woman I'm looking for. Would you mind telling me your Christian name?'

'Freda,' she snapped. 'So unless you called to tell me I've won the pools, piss off.'

'I'm sorry I haven't got any good news for you,' he said with a smile. 'And for disturbing you.'

She smiled back, revealing a broken front tooth. 'You're a real gent, don't get many of them round 'ere. What's this other woman done?'

He realized she thought he was a policeman. 'She hasn't done anything wrong, unless you count marrying a dangerous man. I just want some help in finding him.'

'Seems to me most of the women in Brighton bringing up kids on their tod 'ave married a wrong 'un,' she said. 'I often think, whatever 'appened to 'appy ever after?'

'I hope you find yours one day. Thank you and goodbye, Freda,' he said and backed away.

Out on the street he put up his umbrella. He doubted many taxis came this way. Consulting his street map, he found that the second Mrs Reilly wasn't far away, so he began to walk.

Hardy Place was a block of council flats, and by the time he got there he was quite wet, despite his umbrella, and his feet were like ice. The flat he wanted was on the second floor.

This was a neat and tidy place; someone kept the stairs and concrete landings to the flat clean. Even the children's playground on the ground floor was well maintained. He knocked at number 22 and it was opened almost immediately by a tall, attractive woman of mixed race.

He introduced himself, already knowing this couldn't be the woman he was looking for, as he'd been told she was small, with strawberry-blonde hair. He explained he was looking for a woman called Deirdre and asked her Christian name; she said it was Dawn. After a couple of minutes of polite chit-chat, Charles left. He just hoped the last woman on his list was the right one.

She lived close to the station – which, if nothing else, would be convenient if this was a dead end. It would be good to catch the train and head back to London.

Number 83 Station Road was above a greengrocer's shop, with its own front door to the side of the shop. He knocked and waited, hoping this wouldn't turn out to be a waste of time. The door opened and Charles's first thought was that the woman bore a remarkable similarity to Katy. Small, slim, with the same colour hair and blue eyes. But whereas Katy's eyes were azure blue and sparkled with life and intelligence, this woman's eyes looked dull, with dark shadows beneath them. She was wearing a blue sweater and a knee-length, grey pleated skirt. A little old-fashioned for a woman who was only in her early thirties.

'Deirdre Reilly? Now don't look alarmed, I'm a lawyer, and I promise you I am not here to make any difficulties for you.'

She looked panicked. He gave her his card, assured her again that he was here just to talk to her, and asked if he could come in. After scrutinizing his card, somewhat reluctantly she agreed. She said her name was now Purcell.

Deirdre was clearly a real homemaker because he could see the furniture, which must have come with the rented flat, was shabby, yet she'd added cushions, some plants, a few pictures and a bright red blanket over the sofa to make it homely. But two old black-and-white school photographs took pride of place: a girl and a boy. He guessed they were around eight and seven respectively. All she had in her life now.

'No one but me knows this address,' he assured her. 'You and your children are absolutely safe. But I think your husband, Edward Reilly, has abducted a young woman called Katy Speed.'

He told her as quickly and simply as he could who Katy was and all that had happened.

'Gloria is dead?' she said in horror. 'That kind, wonderful woman who helped me so much? I owe my life to her and Edna.' Her eyes filled with tears and she looked at him as if almost pleading for him to say it wasn't true. 'And it was Ed who did it?'

'Yes, I'm afraid so. And unless we can find him, I think he will kill Katy, too.'

'He's a devil,' she said in almost a whisper. 'Even now, three years on, I still think he'll search me out and punish me again.'

Charles told her that Katy lived opposite Gloria, and her father had been arrested for the murder.

'The police are aware now that Albert Speed didn't do it, but he's still on remand until his case comes back to court.'

'Katy lived in the house opposite Gloria's?' she asked. 'Does she have similar colouring to me?'

Charles agreed she did.

'Then I saw her from out of the front bedroom window when I was staying there. She was helping her father in the front garden. I thought how young and carefree she looked, bright and pretty like a spring morning. Because she reminded me of my younger self, I almost wanted to go over there and warn her to be careful before committing herself to any man. The trouble is, she's Ed's type. Oh dear God, I hope he doesn't hurt her the way he hurt me.'

She told him some background about how Ed had made big money from building houses, then the blunders he'd made had caught up with him and he lost it all.

'I met him just before he crashed; he still had a big house and all that. When the business went under, we had to move to a little flat, not much bigger than this one. He didn't like that. The children were born there and it put a huge strain on him.'

Charles nodded. 'I don't have any sympathy for him, but I can imagine what it did to his ego. So did he build up another business?'

'Yes, he went to work for a man in the building trade who was doing much the same as Ed had done, but not cutting corners. Ed did the sales and marketing for him. Then he bought us the house in Hendon. I thought everything was going to be alright then. But of course it wasn't.'

'Does he still live there?'

'I would imagine so, he was very proud of it.' She gave Charles the address.

'Right, Deirdre. Is there anywhere you can think of where he might have taken Katy? Some place he used to go to as a child, or when he had his business. Or even somewhere belonging to a friend.'

'He doesn't have friends,' she shrugged. 'He cultivates people who are useful to him, but he doesn't have that caring instinct normal people have. He seemed so loving and generous when we first met, I thought I was so lucky, but it was all a facade. Not real at all. He only wanted power over me. To bend me to his will. Poor Katy, I wish I could tell you that he'll let her go, but he won't. If I hadn't got away when I did, he would've killed me, and probably our children too. I absolutely know that. I'm sure he tells anyone who will listen that I was the love of his life and all that, but he doesn't know the meaning of the word love.'

'I'm so sorry, Deirdre. Edna was lucky she survived him driving her off the road. She's still terrified, afraid he'll find her. But Deirdre, please think hard, is there anywhere he ever mentioned that he might have taken Katy to? Anyone else who might be able to help me – and the police, too, of course?'

'Is Katy your girlfriend?'

'I only took her out once, just before he snatched her. But I'd like her to be my girlfriend.'

Deirdre made them both a cup of tea. Charles could see she was thinking hard; her brow was furrowed with concentration.

'He was a bit obsessed with Dover,' she said as she handed Charles his tea. 'That was where he was born, and he lived there until he enlisted in the army for the war. When we first got married he took me back there. I thought he was going to be all sentimental about it, and I expected to get some insight into his past. But he got very angry when we were there, ranting about his mother drinking all the time and how he had to take care of his brothers and sisters. The place he lived in as a boy had been pulled down, but he went on and on about how awful it was.

'The odd thing to me was that he kept going back there. He never took me again. He'd just go on his own; sometimes he said he'd been, or was going, but mostly he said nothing, just disappeared. The only reason I knew where he went was when I found petrol receipts in his jacket pockets. There was a card from an estate agent, too. So he might have some place down there.'

'Did he keep in touch with his brothers and sisters?'

'No, he couldn't stand them. He said they were like their mother, always wanting a handout. I've never met any of them; he didn't even invite them to our wedding.'

Charles sensed she knew nothing more about her husband's siblings, and so he moved on. 'Why did you go to live in Hendon? Was there a reason for that?'

'After the war he got to know a couple of Jewish businessmen who lived in Golders Green; I think he was involved financially with them in the building business that went bust. There are lots of rich people living there and I think he had the idea that it could rub off on him, especially as many people thought he was Jewish, with his dark hair and eyes. Of course, he couldn't afford to buy a house there, but Hendon was close by and cheaper.'

'What were his interests, Deirdre – hobbies, that sort of thing?'

'Just money, really, and nice cars,' she said and smirked. 'He liked to make out he was very rich, his Jaguar was part of that. He made our house look grand, too. It was detached and he put all this fancy stuff on it, a thing called a portico with pillars around the front door. He was very proud of that.'

'Sounds like you weren't struck by any of it?'

'No, I wasn't. I found it a bit embarrassing. On top of

that, as soon as we moved in there, the beatings got far worse. I will never, ever go back there. I can't even begin to tell you what he put me through.' She pulled up her sleeves to show him her arms were covered in cigarette burns. 'My entire body is covered in scars. Even if I was to meet a nice, kind man, I could never let him see what's been done to me, I'm too ashamed. Ed's favourite trick was to lock me in the garage. It's sort of under the house, but he soundproofed it, so it was like a cellar and no one could hear me. Even the lights switched on and off outside. He'd chain me to the wall and torture me. Sometimes he kept me in there for days.'

Charles knew she was telling the truth, and it made him feel shaky to think Katy was in this same man's clutches. Could she be locked in that garage?

'Why didn't you run away the first time?' he asked. 'Or even after your first child was born?'

'I often ask myself that same question,' she sighed. 'In my defence I'd been in an orphanage run by nuns as a child, and they made me feel worthless. I was also young when I met Ed, and very naive. When he said he loved me and wanted to marry me, I could hardly believe my luck.

'Back in the early days, he would apologize after beating me, tell me how much I meant to him, and beg me to give him another chance.' She looked at Charles, her eyes filled with tears. 'He told me that he was like it because of stuff he'd seen during the war, and I stupidly believed that. Besides, I didn't have anyone to turn to, nowhere to go. But he got worse as time went on; the children crying, me breaking something, being late getting a meal ready, anything would set him off. It was only when he started hitting

Jane and Tony that I knew I must get away. It's one thing to take a beating yourself, but what mother would watch her children get hurt and do nothing?'

'You are a good mother, Deirdre, always remind yourself of that.'

He felt deeply for her; he doubted her internal scars would ever heal, and she had to be very lonely, just her and the two children, surviving on very little money. But Katy needed rescuing, and her need was greater than Deirdre's. He sensed she had nothing further to tell him, only more tales of beatings and her terror.

'I really must go now,' Charles said. He wanted to check out the house in Hendon immediately. 'You've been so brave telling me all this, and I really hope someone comes into your life before long to make you happy. You've got my card with my phone number. If you think of anything that might be useful, do ring me.'

He took a twenty-pound note out of his pocket and put it on the coffee table. 'Take Jane and Tony somewhere nice for a treat.'

She started to protest, but he leaned forward and put a finger on her lips to silence her.

'It's just a little token of my appreciation,' he said.

She smiled, and this time her eyes brightened. 'I do so hope you find Katy, and that she becomes your girlfriend. I will phone you, if only to ask if that wish has come true for you.'

He moved closer, and this time put his arms around her to hug her. He felt so sorry for her, it made his heart ache.

15

Katy could barely move for the pain. It wasn't just in one place but everywhere, her head and face, her arms, torso, back and stomach, even her legs. She didn't know how anyone could be in such terrible pain and survive. But she needed to use the lavatory, so she had to get up.

With great difficulty she managed to roll to the edge of the bed. By putting one foot down on the floor and pushing up on the bed with her right hand, she managed to stand up. She thought her left arm was broken, as it was hanging awkwardly and hurt like hell when she moved it. She was fairly certain she'd been knocked unconscious and had remained that way for some time, as the blood on her face was congealed now.

It took every ounce of strength and willpower she'd got to reach the lavatory. Once there, on the floor beside the washbasin, she saw the electric kettle and the other things Reilly had brought to make her tea.

Even though her mouth was so swollen and her lips cut, and she doubted she could actually drink tea, the thought of it cheered her. At least she could boil the kettle and wash in warm water.

It took forever to tentatively clean the dried blood from her face, using the face flannel Reilly had used on her when he was being kind. Now she wondered how on earth she could have started to think she'd got him wrong and grown to like him? Every movement hurt so much she couldn't help but cry.

She'd had many low points since Reilly locked her in this prison, but this was the lowest. There was no hope that he'd come back now. Instinctively she knew his visits were over; starvation and pain were all that was left now, before death.

The act of making a cup of tea helped a bit, just by the nature of its normality. But she felt dizzy with the pain, there were spots before her eyes, and it crossed her mind she could be concussed. Surprisingly, the milk hadn't gone off, and she put a lot in the tea to cool it. Even so, it was hard to drink, as her mouth was so sore. Looking at herself in the mirror didn't help; she looked grotesque, with two black eyes, her cheeks and mouth so swollen she didn't think even her own mother would recognize her.

She shuffled back to the bed and drank the remainder of the tea, trying very hard not to dwell on her situation.

But there was nothing else to think about. There was a packet of biscuits Reilly had brought with him, an orange and a banana. The flask he'd brought the soup in, which he claimed he'd spoon-fed to her, was empty.

Fortunately, she didn't feel hungry; that was something to be thankful for, she supposed. Her arm hurt so much she wanted to scream. But when she tried to tear out the lining of her chiffon dress to make a sling, it hurt even worse, so she abandoned that idea.

Lying very still was the only way she didn't hurt as badly. She pulled the eiderdown over her and hoped for oblivion.

*

Charles was back in London at one o'clock. Before he even left the station, he telephoned Pat to tell him he'd found out where Reilly lived and said they should get there immediately.

'Thank God for that,' Pat said. 'I've only just got back myself, and I've got a lot to tell you, but that can wait till I see you. Hop on the tube and I'll pick you up at Hendon station.'

Charles had another phone call to make, and that was to Jilly. He knew she'd been getting more and more upset about her friend, and it might help her a bit to know they had finally got the address of the man who'd abducted Katy.

He thought he would have to leave a message for her, as she'd told him she was often out of the animal medical centre during the day. But to Charles's delight she was there, by the phone.

'That is the best news ever,' she said when he told her that he'd got the address in Hendon. 'Well, it will be, if you can find her.'

She didn't have to add 'alive'; that was on Charles's mind all the time.

'I'll ring you at home, or come over this evening. Keep the faith,' he added before ringing off.

Pat was waiting in his car outside Hendon station. He had a tense look about him, as if he might deck anyone who messed with him. Charles knew that look very well; Pat had often got into trouble back in Cambridge for lashing out.

'What's up?' Charles asked as he got into the passenger seat.

'I think the bastard could possibly have taken another woman,' Pat said. 'And her two children.'

'No! What makes you think that?'

'Remember the doctor's wife, Margaret Foster, from Hampstead? Well, she changed her name to Peggy Ashcroft, and now she's disappeared.'

'Why does it look like Reilly is involved?'

'According to a friend she'd made in her village, a man came to see her sometimes, a good-looking bloke with dark hair. One morning, just after Christmas, she had a black eye and came up with some lame excuse. A few days later she upped sticks, took her kids and vanished.'

'She took all her belongings?'

'Yes.'

'Well, she was more likely to be doing a moonlight flit than anything else. Murderers don't clean out their victims' homes,' Charles said.

'That's true, but where has she gone to? She hasn't contacted her parents.'

'When was this?'

'Just a couple of weeks ago. She was living ncar Eastbourne, so she could have read about Gloria's death in the local papers and panicked, the way Edna did. But my money is on Reilly; she was seeing him, and he hit her. Whether she scarpered with the kids and her worldly belongings, or he took her, remains to be seen. But I'm convinced Reilly was the man she was seeing.'

'Well, it wasn't her husband, we know he was in Florida at a surgeon's convention.'

'Her friend in the village said she was quite surprised that she had a man friend. She said Margaret/Peggy was anti-men. But how did Reilly find her? And why? Was he looking to punish her in some way because of his wife?'

'Maybe the connection between the two women was the Whittington Hospital?' Charles said thoughtfully. 'But let's go to Reilly's house now and have a look around. We might find some answers.'

A few minutes later, they drew up outside the house. Charles saw what Deirdre meant when she said Reilly had tried to make it look like a rich person's house. It stood up on a bank, as all the houses did in that road, but his house had a grand drive sweeping down to a garage under the house. The stone portico around the front door was pretentious, out of keeping with a house built in the thirties, and there were two stone crouching lions either side of it. The front garden was extremely well manicured, mostly evergreen bushes trimmed into balls and cubes. There wasn't one stray weed, sweet wrapper or bus ticket in the garden. Most people's steps up to their front doors would be green with mould in early March, but his looked like they'd just been scrubbed.

'You stay here,' Pat said. 'Blast on the hooter if anyone comes.'

'You aren't going to break in, are you?' Charles was horrified. 'Why don't we just call the police right now?'

Pat grinned wolfishly. 'And spoil my fun? Besides, if Katy is in that underground garage, don't you want to get her out double quick?'

'Of course, but I can't condone breaking and entering. It would ruin my career; I'd be struck off.'

'You didn't see me do it,' Pat said. 'As far as you know, I just knocked on the door. On my head be it!'

Charles watched as Pat went up the drive and rang the doorbell. He wondered what far-fetched story he'd tell Reilly if he opened the door.

Reilly wasn't in, so Pat went down to the garage and banged on that door with a long, thin implement that was clearly going to be used for breaking into the house if the garage proved to be empty. Pat had his ear to the door, and he shook his head at Charles, confirming that he didn't think Katy was in there. Then he disappeared through a side gate and out of sight.

To Charles it seemed like he sat there for hours, worried sick at what would happen if Reilly came back, or a neighbour rang the police to report burglars. In fact, Pat was only gone for twenty minutes, but they were the longest twenty minutes of Charles's life.

'It's incredibly clean and tidy in there,' Pat said as he got back into the car. 'All his tins of food are lined up like soldiers in a row, labels all to the front. His suits and jackets are all arranged by colour, starting with black, ranging down to a white linen one. Each shirt has a colour-matched tie over the shoulder. Poor Deirdre, if she was forced to keep to that regime.'

'Did you find anything useful?' Charles was a bit irritated with Pat's casual attitude, as if this was the works' spring holiday outing and not a young woman's life at risk.

'Some Ordnance Survey maps,' he said. 'Odd, I didn't get the impression seeing that obsessional tidy home that he'd like the great outdoors. They were mostly of the South Coast, and a particularly well-thumbed one was of Kent. In fact, he'd slipped up in his tidiness there; it was folded back to show the coast by Dover. I'd say he'd been study-ing it recently.'

'He comes from Dover. Deirdre said he was obsessed with going there.'

'Then maybe we ought to go there,' Pat said. 'But right now we must take what we've got to the police. Much as I'd like us to find Katy, it requires more manpower than just the two of us. This place needs to be staked out in case Reilly comes back here, and a background check should be run on him, along with his family and connections in Dover.'

Charles breathed a sigh of relief. Pat was so gung-ho, he'd been afraid his friend would want to conduct the whole investigation. 'I hoped so much she'd be here. Did you find anything to give us any further clues?'

'No. I don't think he's taken anyone in there, or even been there himself, for some time,' Pat said, and patted his friend's arm in sympathy at his disappointment. 'It is abso-lutely sterile in there. Not a photograph, not the odd little thing of Deirdre's or the children's still there. Not even some fruit in a bowl. I looked in wardrobes, in drawers, everywhere. For a man who was desperate to find his wife and children, it is remarkably sinister that he's got rid of all their stuff.'

Pat started up the car and drove off. 'I'll go to the police now. I know a lot of the officers, and that really helps to put a fire under them. I don't think it's advisable for you to come too, it might muddy the waters later on. If you'll just give me all the stuff you discovered in Brighton, I can pass it off as my investigation.'

'So what am I going to do?' Charles was a bit irritated that his friend was suddenly so high-handed.

'I thought maybe you could go down to Dover tomorrow and poke around? You're good at talking to people.'

Charles somewhat reluctantly got out his notepad, in which he'd written a complete report of what Deirdre had said to him. He put it on the dashboard. 'Chapter and verse of what took place today.'

Pat glanced sideways and grinned at him. 'No wonder you ended up the barrister, and not me. You always were good at taking notes, looking up details. I'm better at twisting people's arms to talk.'

After Pat had dropped him home, Charles rang Michael Bonham and told him all the latest news.

'Katy's father and brother are frantic with worry,' Michael told Pat. 'I think you know Rob, the brother, is down in Bexhill now – I met him and Albert at the prison. Rob and I went to a local hotel for a drink and a sandwich afterwards so we could talk more. That poor lad is beside himself with fear for Katy. I'll ring him now and pass on all this latest information. But there is some good news: all charges against Albert will be dropped, hopefully tomorrow. Rob is going to stay in Lewes until that is done and he can take his father home.'

'And the mother? Is she going to welcome Albert back?'

'Rob is working on her. He thinks she may be suffering from some kind of mental illness. But Rob has made it quite clear that if she doesn't allow Albert home and treat him with respect, he will leave with his father. I was impressed by the lad, he's strong and forthright, like his sister and father, but even the strongest people can buckle under this kind of strain.'

Charles told him he had to call Jilly and let her know the latest, too. 'She's another one who's frantic with worry,' he said. 'She's had to let the flat go that she and Katy were going to move into. She couldn't afford to pay all the rent on her own, and persuaded the landlord to refund what she'd paid in advance. I think she felt it was tempting fate to try and hold on to it in the hope Katy is rescued.'

'The chances of that are getting slimmer by the day,' Bonham sighed. 'I didn't, of course, say that to her father or brother today. There is always hope, though, especially if the police pull out all the stops now they know it is Reilly behind Katy's abduction.'

Charles rang Jilly after seven when he knew she'd be home from work.

'Any good news?' she said the minute she heard his voice.

'Well, yes, in as much as we know who Katy's captor is and where he lives, and my friend Pat is handing it all over to the police as we speak.'

He told her some more details, as he knew she was desperate to be fully in the picture. 'I thought I'd go to Dover tomorrow and see what I can dig up there,' he said.

'Could I come with you? Please!' she pleaded. 'It will be better for you with me alongside. People are more inclined to talk to a couple, rather than just a posh bloke in a smart suit.'

Charles smiled at that. 'But you have to be at work.'

'I can get my aunt to ring in and say I'm sick. Please let me come, Charles? I want to do something to help find Katy. And women are always better at noting the little details than men.'

'I can't argue with that,' he said. 'Okay, can you meet me at Charing Cross mainline station, at nine thirty? I'll wait under the clock.'

By the time they got to Dover the next morning, Jilly had decided Charles was one of the nicest men she'd ever met. He might be posh and highly intelligent, but he didn't make her feel uncomfortable or stupid. He was kind, nice-looking and he had a good sense of humour. Not that there was anything to laugh about right now, and there wouldn't be until they got Katy back, but with Charles on the case she felt much more confident of a happy outcome.

She had to hang on to the idea that one day soon the three of them would be having dinner together and laughing. Not laughing about Katy being captured, of course – somehow she knew there would never be any-thing funny about that – but about something else. Jilly had to hang on to that, because she didn't dare consider what life would be like without her best friend.

She didn't care that she'd had to back out of renting the flat. She didn't care if she lost her job at the zoo and had to go back to Bexhill and all that entailed. Nothing mattered except finding Katy.

'My friend Pat managed to get me a bit of information about the Reilly family last night,' Charles said while they were on the train. 'I've got an address for Susan Gosling and Dolly Meek too, both aunts. They are his mother's sisters. Dolly runs a boarding house.'

'I've never been to Dover before,' Jilly said. 'Is it a nice place?'

'I've always found it a bit oppressive,' Charles said. 'You

go to Folkestone, its close neighbour, and that's all light and bright, but Dover has a greyness about it. Maybe it's the castle or just the docks, with the ferries going in and out, or the high cliffs, but the crime rate is higher, and it is a bit sleazy.'

'You've really sold it to me,' Jilly grinned. 'So a fitting town for Edward Reilly to be born in!'

'We'll go and see his aunt Dolly first,' Charles said. 'It's close to the docks, so I think we'll find it's going to be more of a dosshouse than a boarding house.'

'Has Katy's mother started showing any emotion yet?' Jilly asked. 'My mum phones me nearly every day to ask if there's any news, but she went round to see Mrs Speed and she more or less told her to sling her hook.'

Charles shook his head in bewilderment. 'It's not my place to comment on relatives' attitudes. But I am finding it increasingly impossible to understand her.'

'Katy couldn't understand her, either. I think she would've preferred to live in squalor with my family than in her own squeaky-clean and ordered house.'

Charles liked the way Jilly spoke bluntly about her home and family. It was clear she loved them and that they were a very happy family, but he rarely came across such unabashed honesty and he found it refreshing. 'My family don't go in for squeaky clean either,' he said. 'The dogs rule the house, the furniture is old and the kitchen is usually a shambles. I'm actually very suspicious of anyone who keeps a too tidy house.' He went on to tell her what Pat had said about Reilly's house. 'I rest my case,' he laughed. 'Such incredible order shows a twisted mind.'

*

Charles was right about White Cliffs Boarding House. It was by the docks, on the busy road, and it was the kind of guest house that only the most desperate would book into.

It was red brick but painted white; the paint had turned green with mould, and it was peeling off, making the house look diseased. The windows and net curtains didn't look as if they'd been washed for years.

The door was opened by Dolly Meek, who could have been a model for saucy seaside postcards: a huge bust, legs like tree trunks, her grey hair in curlers and a cigarette hanging from her lips. She wore a floral crossover overall that was none to clean.

'Yeah, our Mavis was dumb enough to tangle with Angelo Reilly,' she said on the doorstep, her voice loud enough to act as a foghorn. 'She never married 'im, 'e never stayed around long enough for that, but she changed 'er name to his when she got up the spout with Ed. I told her then, "Get down and see Ma Grady what sorts girls out." But she wouldn't. She said she loved 'im and wanted 'is baby.'

Charles could hardly believe she would boom out such information on the street. He suggested she invite them in, as it was so cold and noisy outside.

'I ain't cleared away breakfast yet,' Dolly said, hiking her formidable breasts up a little higher and throwing her fag end out into the street. 'So you'll just have to take me as you find me.'

The stink of stale fried food and cigarettes was over-powering, but at least the living room she led them into was warm, with a big fire. A large table took up the centre of the room, covered in a red-and-white chequered oilcloth. There were about seven used place settings, cigarettes stubbed out amongst the remains of a cooked breakfast. The whole room was strewn with clutter, everything from old newspapers to boxes of tinned food and a great many bottles, both full and empty.

Dolly swept some clothes off a couch for them to sit down.

'It's really Edward, your nephew, I need to ask you about,' Charles said after a few minutes of Dolly rattling on about how her sister spoiled her chances by getting involved with a worthless ship's stoker who was half Irish and half Italian.

'Our Ed was a good kid, really,' she said, smoothing down her overall and taking a seat on one of the dining chairs. 'Never 'ad a chance, like, not when our Mavis took to the bottle and kept having more sprogs. Ed was the one what did most of the looking after 'em. But 'e got the idea in 'is 'ead that 'e was meant for better things. Always dangerous, that one.'

Charles and Jilly listened to Dolly in amazement. She just spewed out personal stuff about her sister without any embarrassment. 'She'd open 'er legs for any bloke who'd buy 'er a few drinks. I caught her one day in this very room giving one of my boarders a blow job. She'd done it for two shillings. Christ Almighty! I'd need more than two shillings to touch my boarders' cocks, let alone stick one in me gob.'

Charles tried again and again to get her to talk about Edward, and finally she got there. 'Going in the army was a good thing for 'im. I don't think 'e did much fighting, mind you. He used to boast about being trapped in a burning tank and stuff like that. But that was all make-believe. But 'e 'ad money when he was demobbed, so I reckon 'e must 'ave got some kind of fiddle going on in the army. He'd got as 'ard as bleedin' nails an' all. He wouldn't give his mum any money, or any of us. Knocked Mavis about too, broke a couple of her teeth. Then 'e disappeared for some years. He come back once in a flash car and a hundred-pound suit. That time 'e gave us all money, 'e wanted to show off cos he'd got this building firm. But he lost it all, didn't 'e? We read about it in the papers. Came down one time with this girl he'd married. She was probably a nice little thing, but too soft for a bloke like 'im. I told 'er she'd got to stand up to 'im, but she just smiled, like she didn't believe me.'

'Dolly, he nearly killed her, and she finally ran away from him.' Charles felt he had to make the woman see how serious this inquiry was, and he didn't want a trip down memory lane unless there was some point to it. 'Since then he's burned down a house and killed two women in the fire, one of whom was the woman who'd helped his wife escape.'

At this Dolly's mouth fell open, and the cigarette she'd only just lit and stuck between her lips dropped on to the floor. 'Oh my God!' she exclaimed. 'Are the police looking for him?'

'Yes, of course. I expect they'll be searching around here very soon. But my real concern is a young woman called Katy Speed. He's abducted her, and I am afraid he'll kill her, too. So please tell us if you know anywhere in Dover he could have taken her to.'

'I ain't seen him for years. But a mate of mine told me she saw 'im 'ere just before Christmas.'

'Where did she see him?'

'In the 'igh street.'

'Tell me, Dolly, is his mother still alive?'

'No, she died back in 1956. It were the booze what done it. Only other person in our family left here now is our Susan, she's my sister. She ain't like me. She got religion, joined the Sally Army.'

'What about his friends, boys he knew when he was at school? Do you know any of them?'

'There's four or five blokes 'e used to hang around with. They drink in the King's Head. John Sloane is the one to ask for. But be careful what you say to 'im, 'e's got a nasty temper.'

'I want you to promise me something, Dolly.' Charles moved closer to her, looking right into her eyes. 'If Ed should come here in the next couple of weeks, or someone tells you they've seen him, will you ring me or the police immediately? And please promise me you won't warn him I've been asking questions.'

'I promise. I wouldn't piss on 'im if 'e was on fire,' she said, and her washed-out blue eyes flashed, proving she meant it. 'Ain't likely he'll come to me, but if 'e does I'll kick 'im in the goolies and slam the door on 'im.'

'One good thing about seeing a really rough person, in their own grubby habitat,' Jilly said as they walked back into the town to find Ed's Aunt Susan, 'is that it makes you realize you and your family are quite civilized.'

Charles laughed. He found Jilly very refreshing with her complete candour. There was a great deal to like about her. Although not conventionally pretty, she had a good face.

Her height, the graceful way she moved, and her flirty eyes framed with impossibly long lashes, all reminded him of a giraffe. She was wearing a tartan miniskirt and long boots, and she had sensational legs. She'd told him on the way down to Dover that her Auntie Joan disapproved of miniskirts, but she was gradually shortening all her skirts a little at a time so the sudden shock of seeing so much leg exposed wouldn't kill her aunt. Charles was very amused by the things she came out with.

'Dolly was rough, Mavis was a tramp,' Charles said as they neared Aunt Susan's. 'It makes you wonder what their mother was like. Yet I got the idea that Dolly actually had a good heart.'

'Well, let's face it, she had to have something going for her,' Jilly laughed. 'When she came out with that story about Mavis doing that for two bob, I wanted the floor to open and swallow me. But to be fair to Dolly, she probably creates a warm home from home for the men who stay in her boarding house.'

Susan's home was a tiny terraced house in a narrow backstreet. It was a dirty little street with the front doors opening straight on to the pavement, but Jilly remarked that number 9 was the only one with a scrubbed doorstep and dazzling white nets at the sparkling windows.

'But then she's in God's Army,' Jilly added, arching her eyebrows. 'Cleanliness is next to godliness, after all.'

The door was opened by a very small, thin woman with snow-white hair, dressed in black. She looked enquiringly at them.

'Mrs Susan Gosling?' Charles asked. For a second he thought they'd got the wrong house, as it was difficult to imagine this woman coming out of the same womb as Dolly. When she nodded, he handed her his card. 'I'm a lawyer making some inquiries about your sister Mavis's son, Edward, and this is my assistant, Miss Carter. May we come in?'

'Is he dead?' Susan asked as she led them down a narrow passage to a living room cum kitchen at the back. It was a bleak room devoid of any real comforts except for a fire. A plain wooden crucifix hung above the mantelpiece. She beckoned to the chairs around the oilcloth-covered table.

'No, he's not, but he is in serious trouble and wanted by the police. But our real concern is for a young woman, Katy Speed, who he abducted ten days ago now. We are afraid he will kill her.'

Susan Gosling was the kind of elderly woman you would never be able to pick out in a crowd, not unless she was wearing an unusual hat or coat. She had no distinguishing features; just a soft, little old lady sort of face, with a shrunken mouth. Her expression didn't even change at what Charles had said. She displayed no shock or horror, or even any indignation at him saying such a terrible thing about her nephew.

'Ever since he was twenty or so, I've half expected something like this,' she said. 'I knew he had turned wicked, I pray for him all the time. But he never stood a chance, not with my sister Mavis. She was a terrible mother, all her children suffered, but him most of all.'

She offered them a cup of tea and opened the cupboard to get the cups. Charles noted there were just four cups and saucers; he suspected she had very few personal possessions.

'Tell us about his suffering,' Jilly asked. She looked at Charles, as if to remind him he'd called her his assistant. 'Did his mother beat him, or was it your sister's men friends?'

'She took everything out on him, because he looked like Angelo, his father. If that man had loved her as she loved him, she might have turned out a good person. So poor little Eddie took the brunt of all her anger and hurt. She hit him, she belittled him. She even burned him with cigarettes. I threatened to call the cruelty man lots of times, but she used to just laugh at me. She kept having more kids, too. And Eddie, at seven or eight, mostly took care of them as best he could.

'She taught him to be cruel, though I never saw it in him till he was older – all the time he was caring for the little ones he was kind and patient. But then he took up bare-knuckle fighting, and he became a champion. People started to look up to him where once he'd been like the dirt under their feet.'

'He enlisted for the war, didn't he?' Jilly asked.

Susan nodded as she warmed the teapot. 'He wanted to the moment war broke out, but he was just seventeen then. He couldn't wait to go. Who could blame him?'

'How come you are so different from your sister?' Jilly asked. 'I know you are in the Salvation Army, but were you always the good one?'

The older woman smiled at that. 'We all start out the same in God's eyes,' she said. 'It's what happens to us as we grow – the paths we take – that change us. I was married young to Sydney, a farm labourer, and we were very happy in our little cottage over towards Folkestone. First

239

we lost our daughter at the age of two to diphtheria, and three years later Sydney was killed in an accident with the threshing machine on the farm.'

'I am so sorry.' Charles and Jilly spoke in unison.

Susan put the pot of tea on the table and got a little jug of milk from the pantry. 'It was a long time ago now. But thankfully I was helped by a member of the Salvation Army who saw how lost and afraid I was. You see, I had to leave the farm cottage and come back to Dover. I had nothing. Well, I had my two sisters, but I never wanted to be like either of them. Oddly enough, it was young Eddie who was a comfort to me. I regret now I didn't take him from Mavis and bring him up myself. Maybe I could have saved him from taking that wrong turning later.'

They all had a cup of tea, and Susan offered them each a rock cake. She said she'd made them early that morning because she couldn't sleep. 'I must have sensed I was going to get visitors,' she said with a sad smile.

Charles explained to her about Ed's crimes. He said now he had Katy, and they were hoping to find someone in Dover who might have an idea of where he could've taken her.

'Has he come to visit you recently?' Charles asked.

'No, he hasn't. But he wouldn't, because the last time he came here he threatened me. That was around the time his wife left him. I thought he was going to kill me, he was so angry. He really believed I knew where she'd gone, but I didn't. I only met her once, when he brought her here after they were married. I used to write to her, send cards and a little present for the children's birthdays. But I didn't see her. I'm not even on the telephone, so I can't ring her.'

'So what did you do?' Jilly asked.

'I screamed for my neighbour's husband to come. He threw Ed out, but not before I told Eddie that he alone was to blame for Deirdre leaving and he wasn't welcome here any more. He has been back to Dover, people have told me. The last time was around three months ago. But he didn't come here.'

Jilly asked her what she did in the Salvation Army, and she said she helped at the homeless men's hostel, down by the docks, about three or four times a week.

'Dover is a sad town, I realize that now. People arrive on the ferry, hoping for a new life in England, and often they don't leave Dover. We get foreign sailors who've jumped ship, often because of a woman, we seem to have more alcoholics here than other towns, and now drugs are creeping in too, mostly used by the youngsters. If I had been aware of it when I was younger, maybe I would've moved away. But I didn't, so here I am still, trying to help others to find their way.'

'I think the police will be coming to question you very soon. But if your nephew comes to you before that, you'd better phone the police yourself,' Charles said.

'He won't come here, because he knows that is exactly what I'd do. I might be small but I've learned to stand up for myself.'

'Are you sure there isn't a place he might take Katy? Somewhere he played as a child? Somewhere he could've bought when he was in the money?'

She shook her head. 'I'm sorry, I don't know of any such place. But if I think of anywhere, I'll tell the police.'

She asked Jilly then how well she knew Katy.

'She's my best friend, as close as a sister,' Jilly said simply, a tear trickling down her cheek. 'I must get her home safely.'

Susan got up, went over to Jilly and put her arms around her, drawing the girl to her chest. 'I'll pray for you to be reunited,' she said. 'And I am so sorry my nephew has brought you such heartache.'

'She was a good woman,' Jilly said as she and Charles walked back down the street. 'But I couldn't help feeling sorry for Ed. The abused became the abuser.'

'It's off to the King's Head now,' Charles said, ignoring her sympathy for Ed. He felt a twinge of it himself, and didn't want to admit it. 'Let's hope they do some decent food in there.'

16

Charles ordered half a pint of bitter for himself and a lemonade for Jilly from the beefy-looking barman in the King's Head. Although it was only half past twelve the bar was already very full. In the main they looked like men who were out of work, or perhaps dockers waiting for a cargo to unload.

'Do you happen to know if an Edward Reilly ever drinks in here?' he asked as he paid for the drinks.

'Can't imagine why anyone would ask about that sack of shit.' A tough-looking, bald-headed man standing beside him spoke out.

Charles was a little taken aback by the venom in the man's voice. But at least it made it easier to find out about Reilly.

'I'm Charles Stevenson, a barrister. I need to find Reilly fast, as it appears he has abducted a young woman. I was actually looking for a John Sloane, who I believe grew up with Reilly. Do you know him, too?'

The barman gave a little cough to alert Charles. 'This is John Sloane.'

Sloane's belligerent expression changed to a wide grin. He held out his hand to Charles. 'A woman from around here?'

Charles shook the man's hand. He was a little embarrassed, but at the same time relieved that the man seemed friendly. Sloane looked capable of knocking his head off. It appeared he was in the building trade; he was wearing dirt-covered working clothes, hefty boots, and had a pencil behind his ear.

'No, it was in London, but I was recommended to come and chat to you because of your friendship with him as boys. I hoped you might have had a favourite place where you played, made camps – you know the kind of thing – especially if it's somewhere he could be using now to hold this young lady.'

Sloane looked thoughtful. 'We mainly hung around the town or on the beach. We went to St Margaret's Bay quite a bit, though. He liked it there. I couldn't be bothered with the bloke after the war, he'd got too big for his boots, boasting all the time. He told us all so many bloody great lies about his time in service. The truth is he managed to get a desk job, when the rest of us were right in the thick of it.'

Another taller, thinner man with red hair, who had been standing to the other side of Sloane, now spoke up. 'He were in here just before Christmas.'

Sloane looked round in surprise at the other man. 'You never let that slip, Bri?'

'I didn't tell you cos I know Reilly gets your goat. I only spoke to him to be polite. He said he'd bought a property down here a few years ago and he was doing it up. He asked if I wanted some work.'

'Where was this property?' Charles asked, his heart beginning to race a bit.

'He didn't say, and I didn't ask cos he's always been a bullshitter.'

'You could find out for certain if you go into the estate agent's a few doors down,' Sloane suggested. 'Maxwell, the owner, always knows who has bought what in Dover.'

'That is very helpful of you. May I buy you both a drink?'

They both said they'd like a pint. Charles paid for their drinks, but Sloane was anxious to know more. 'He was always weird, had a nasty temper, along with big ideas, and he lied easier than he breathed. Who is this young lady he's got hold of? If you find his place here in Dover, come back for us and we'll go there mob-handed. I've got a few things I'd like to settle with him.'

Charles looked at Jilly, suddenly a little nervous that Sloane wanted to be involved.

Jilly decided to take control. 'Charles, we can't go looking for him now. We've got to catch our train, if you are to make your appointment this afternoon.'

'She's right, I must go now,' Charles said to Sloane. 'I'll leave it to the police. But thank you for your help.'

Out in the street he turned to Jilly. 'Your quick thinking was timely, I could feel myself being railroaded. I'm not sure I should have said I was a barrister, either. Even if they don't like Reilly, they probably dislike the police and lawyers even more.'

'I think they genuinely wanted to help,' Jilly reassured him, aware he wasn't used to dealing with rough men like Sloane and was a little nervous. 'But I think it would be smarter not to give away too much at the estate agent's. People gossip, and let's face it, a local bloke wanted for abduction is pretty juicy. If they found out it was murder too, the whole town would be talking about it.'

*

Charles realized quite quickly that Maxwell, the estate agent, was not the brightest of men. He was around forty, wearing a loud tie and a cheap suit. There was so much Brylcreem on his dark hair that his wife had to be changing pillowcases on a daily basis. He was the sort of man Charles most despised: loud and vulgar, cracking endless, tasteless jokes because he had no real conversation.

Saying he was defending a client in London who claimed to have been working on a property down here at the time the crime was committed, Charles asked Maxwell for a list of people who had bought property from him in the last five years. He said he thought the owner was called Reilly, but that could be wrong.

Maxwell made a great show of opening and closing filing cabinet drawers. He kept saying the name Reilly, over and over again.

'Surely you keep a list of all properties sold? Your accountant would want it.'

'Oh, yes, I do. It's not that, it's the name Reilly. I kind of know it, but can't remember why.'

Charles waited, saying nothing until Maxwell brought out a file. He opened it and ran his finger down a list of properties.

'Ah, that's it! Yes, he bought a semi-derelict property in St Margaret's Bay. It was four years ago. He acted like he was some big shot from London, talked about doing a big development on the site. That's why the name stuck in my head.'

'Could I have a photocopy of that list?' Charles asked. 'I need to let my client see the list and confirm it was the property he worked on.'

'Funny! I remember now that Reilly boasted he could do all trades and he'd be doing it all himself, as he didn't trust workmen.'

'I expect that was just showing off, but just let me have a copy of the list.'

He was surprised Maxwell was prepared to hand over such information without proper authority. Whether this was because he was too dumb to think along those lines, or just impressed that a lawyer had come into his office, Charles didn't know. The man just put the three or four sheets of paper into his photocopier and pressed the button.

'Good chap,' Charles said in his most haughty voice as he took the sheets. 'Much appreciated.'

'You sounded like a right toff then,' Jilly giggled as they walked back down the street. 'Good chap! Do people you know really speak like that?'

'Lots of them,' he said. 'And I have found it's a great way of backing out gracefully from a sticky situation.'

'I'll have to remember that, then,' she said, still amused. 'Only there isn't a female equivalent to "chap" is there?'

'No, not now you come to mention it,' Charles said, feeling buoyed up by Jilly's good mood. 'Come on, we'll get a taxi to St Margaret's Bay.'

'Don't you think we should call the police and hand it over to them?' Jilly said.

'Oh, Jilly, we've come this far, we have to go the extra mile. Besides, there's not a lot of point in calling them if it is just a wreck, we'd only look a bit stupid.'

'For a man who works in the law you don't have much regard for the police,' she remarked.

'I do, actually. By tonight, when the message has been passed on from the Met, there'll be officers crawling all over Dover, but I need to find Katy now.'

'Does your instinct tell you she's still alive?' Jilly asked, her lips quivering.

'I don't know,' Charles said honestly. 'I really want to believe that she is. But you've known her for years, what do you feel?'

'I know she will have fought him, if not with weapons, with her tongue – and she can be pretty scary – but that could have made him even meaner and angrier. All I know is I can't imagine my life without Katy in it. I have always thought when we were old ladies we'd still be going shopping and having afternoon tea together.'

Charles hailed a taxi coming down the road. 'St Margaret's Bay,' he said. He didn't trust himself to look round at Jilly; he sensed she was crying.

Maxwell had said the address in St Margaret's Bay was quite difficult to find, and the taxi driver showed no enthusiasm for helping them find it. He turned them out of his cab on a steep hill that ran down into St Margaret's Bay itself and begrudgingly pointed over to the right. 'I think it's up that lane. Too many potholes to drive up,' he said curtly.

The taxi driver was right about the potholes, and they were all full of water. Both sides of the lane were bordered by bushes, mostly leafless now in early March, but even so it was hard to see what lay behind them. They came to a farm gate on their right. Looking over it, they saw the track winding round, leading down to a somewhat ramshackle farmhouse and barns at least six hundred or more yards further on. It had a sea view, and probably looked idyllic in summer, but today the sky and sea were grey, the wind was whipping tree branches about, and it was very cold.

Another thirty or so yards and they came to a further farm gate on their left. That huge field appeared to be lying fallow, and it sloped up towards some woods.

Charles was just about to suggest they abandon their search, as his shoes and trousers were covered in mud, when they saw a chimney pot just above the hedge.

They had to walk about two hundred yards further to see that the single-storey stone-built cottage it belonged to was set down in a dip. Thick woodland almost obscured the place. The sign 'Dean Cottage' was so faded, and partly concealed by ivy, that it was difficult to read.

'The perfect spot to hide someone away,' Charles said thoughtfully.

There was no car parked up on the gravel-and-mud area in front of the cottage. But there was a six-inch-deep rut made by a car. It was partially filled with rainwater, but it looked as if it had been made recently, as the pattern of the tyre was very crisp.

'Of course there's been frost most nights, so that would preserve the pattern,' Charles said, thinking out loud. 'Come on, let's have a look round.'

'It's not as tumbledown as that estate agent implied,' Jilly said. 'I mean it's got a roof and windows for a start.'

'The roof has been mended, look!' Charles pointed at it.

Jilly saw he was pointing to quite a large patch of new tiles. They were a brighter red than the others. 'The stone wall has been rendered, too,' she said. 'Well, actually, it looks as if he's done the whole front and possibly replaced some missing stones. My dad does work like that sometimes.'

It was very difficult to get round to the back of the cottage. Piles of bricks, old rubble and a cement mixer blocked the way, and the bushes and trees to either side made it impossible to skirt round these objects.

'I get the feeling he doesn't want anyone looking back there,' Charles said.

Net curtains stopped them looking in through the windows. But they banged and shouted. All they could see of the interior was through the letter box. But it was just a bare hall, all the doors leading off were closed.

'If my friend Pat was with us, he'd break in,' Charles said. 'But I daren't do that. That taxi driver could identify us, and Maxwell too. Besides, it will be dark soon and we'll need to walk down into St Margaret's Bay to call for a taxi.'

'Fair enough. But let's stop at the police station in Dover and talk to someone before we get the train back?' Jilly suggested. 'The police here might not know about this place, so when the London police get on to them with the rest of the story they'll be able to go straight there to check it out.'

She turned her back to the cottage. In summer the view down across fields to the sea would be beautiful. She presumed, as Maxwell had said Reilly was going to develop the land, he meant the woods behind and on both sides of the cottage.

Voicing this to Charles, she pointed out that he might have somewhere else, out in the woods. 'I kind of feel Katy's here,' she added. 'But it's too much for us to search thoroughly. Let's go back to Dover and get help.'

Charles put his arm around her as they walked back up the lane. It was very cold and windy, and he could feel her fear for her friend. 'I'm sorry, Jilly, that I wasn't brave enough to kick that door in. Or sensible enough to insist that taxi driver waited for us.'

Her smile was a bleak one. 'Let's at least walk faster, that way we'll keep warm.'

Katy felt that she was dying. She hurt so much that she even hoped death would come quickly to save her any more pain. The faces of her mother, father and Rob kept flitting into her mind, and with each image the memory of some happy event. There was her father breaking off from his work to come and watch her running in the hundred-yard sprint on Sports Day. It was blazing hot and he'd said he doubted he'd be able to make it. But he arrived just as she was lining up for the race. She saw him give her his little thumbs-up signal, which he had said meant he would be running with her in his head, and she took off like a rocket. She won by a huge margin, and she'd heard his cheers for the whole race.

Her mother didn't very often bestow any extra joy on an event, but Katy remembered her crying when she sang a solo in a carol service one Christmas. Katy must have only been eight then, and on the way home her mother had said she had a voice like an angel.

As for Rob, the happy memories with him were so plen-tiful that she flitted from one to the other. Screaming with laughter as they did roly-polys down a grassy bank; swop-ping clothes when they were about five and eight, and going into town dressed like that. She'd tucked her hair into her brother's school cap and could've passed for a boy, but Rob looked ridiculous in a dress, he couldn't fool anyone.

Rob going with her for her first date. She was to meet Peter Hayes outside the cinema and she was too scared to go alone. The plan was that Rob would go home once she'd met Peter, but in a moment of blind panic she asked Peter if Rob could see the film with them. Later that night, Rob said she must never do that again, he'd never felt so awkward, but they both howled with laughter that Peter had agreed and even paid for Rob. Sadly, he never asked her out again.

Rob was the one she played board games with, batted so he could practise his bowling, played tennis in the park, dared each other to swim in the sea at Easter when it was icy. They giggled about things late at night, shared so much, and it was a wrench when he went off to university.

She wouldn't ever meet the girl he would marry, or hold his children in her arms. She'd never get the chance to find out why her mother was so chilly, and she certainly wouldn't see the day when she became warm and fun loving. As for her father, life would never be the same for him without her. She knew in her heart that, although he loved both her and Rob, she was the one who was dearest to him. In fact, once she was gone, the family would break up. Rob would concentrate on his career; her father would immerse himself in his work and probably leave her mother, because there was nothing to keep him there. It didn't bear thinking about what that would do to her mother.

Then there was Jilly. She and her family meant so much to Katy. She had always believed that she and Jilly would be at each other's weddings, be godmothers to their children, share each other's lives until they were both old ladies.

She wondered too if Charles would be sad she'd gone. Had he thought, as she did, that maybe there was something special there? Or was that just her overactive imagination?

Yet however much pain she was in, however impossible escape seemed, a voice at the back of her head was telling her she mustn't give up, urging her to look around her and see if there was anything in the room that could help her to gain her freedom.

While Katy was dwelling on the happier memories of her family, and what Charles and Jilly meant to her, the pair were actually only a few miles from her at the police station in Dover.

Charles wasn't pleased at the reception he was getting. Having first enquired as to whether the Met had sent word to Dover that Edward Reilly was to be apprehended, he got only a blank stare from Desk Sergeant Forbes. Charles explained about Katy's abduction. But even then, despite Charles telling him a young woman's life was in danger, he got the distinct impression that Forbes resented being told what to do by a barrister. Deeply frustrated, Charles began to raise his voice.

'Don't,' Jilly whispered to him. 'It will just make things worse.'

Charles knew she was right – his father had always said when you lose your temper you lose the battle – but he found it hard to believe that the Met hadn't immediately informed the Dover police to do a check on Reilly here.

Pat would've made the situation absolutely clear, explaining that he'd sent Charles down here to make some inquiries, and insisting that if he should come to Dover police, asking for assistance, it must be given promptly.

'Look, I'm not claiming Katy Speed is definitely in that house in St Margaret's Bay. She might already be dead and buried somewhere else. But if she is still alive now, and she dies because you didn't take this seriously, how are you going to feel? She's just twenty-three, a mere girl. If it was your daughter in there, wouldn't you be battering the door down now?' he implored Forbes.

'But we haven't had any instructions from the Met,' Forbes said for the umpteenth time. 'You have no proof she's in that cottage; we can't go breaking into a house on a whim.'

Charles looked hard at the desk sergeant and noted his dull eyes, high colour and how fat he was. He clearly didn't chase villains any longer, and he'd become complacent because most of his work was now related to the docks, immigrants and smuggling.

'This man set fire to a house in Bexhill and killed a mother and daughter. He tried to kill another woman by driving her off the road, and an associate of mine, an ex-policeman, thinks he may have abducted another woman and her children near Eastbourne also. Now he has Katy. So tell me, do you still think it's a whim?'

'Why don't you telephone someone senior in the Met?' Jilly suggested. 'Or just phone Hammersmith police station, who know all about it.'

'Stay here. I'll go and speak to the governor,' Forbes said.

It was getting dark outside now, although it was only

about half past five. Charles had often had clients complain that the police hadn't taken them seriously when reporting a crime, or that they'd said they'd deal with it, then did nothing. Mostly he'd believed it was pure fantasy on his clients' part. But now he was beginning to see it could be true.

He wished he had taken John Sloane up on his offer to go to the cottage mob-handed. In fact, if the police didn't pull their finger out in the next half-hour, he'd go back to the King's Head and get a posse together.

While waiting, Charles telephoned Pat. His friend was shocked that the Hammersmith police hadn't informed Dover; he said it was normal procedure to follow up in another town, if they had information that the suspect came from there or had relatives or associates still in the town.

'Hang on in there, Charles,' he said. 'I'll ring through and put a rocket up their arses.'

'I doubt she is in the cottage. We couldn't see anything suspicious, aside from recent car tracks. But there might be something in the house pointing to where she's being held.'

'They've already searched the Hendon house and got into the garage. I was told they had some interesting evidence, but that's all they would say. I know now why I left the force.'

When Charles got back to Jilly, he could see she was wilting. 'Come on, we'll grab a quick bite to eat while we wait for them to get their act together,' he said. 'I'll just tell the desk sergeant we'll be back.'

*

255

There was a fish and chip shop with inside tables just across the road.

'Hmm, this is good,' Jilly said as she tucked into cod and chips. 'It doesn't taste so good in London. I didn't think I'd be able to eat, my stomach was churning so much, but maybe that was hunger and not anxiety.'

'Things always look better after something to eat,' Charles said. 'I hope I'll be able to go back into the police station and not snarl at anyone.'

'You are funny,' she said. 'I kind of thought you were Mr Calm always. It's good to see that even a barrister can flare up in anger.'

'It's not the barrister flaring up, it's the man who cares for Katy,' he said softly. 'I've got to make them act tonight.'

17

Katy hauled herself across the room to the kettle. Every step hurt, and the plan she had in mind depended on Reilly coming back. She had been willing him to come for the last couple of hours, despite knowing full well just willing someone to do something was unlikely to have any effect.

But she had to be prepared, in case he did come, and the kettle was her only weapon. She filled it up, then plugged it in. Next she had to move the bed away from the door to leave more space when he came in.

Her broken arm and all the other injuries screamed at her to stop, but her determination was stronger than the pain. Luckily, it was a cheap bed and didn't weigh much; she soon had it placed to the side of the room. Now she could sit on it, the kettle right beside her, and the electric fire a yard away from the door ready for him to trip over. Hopefully, as she flung the boiling water over him, he would fall right on to the fire. He'd have the keys in his hand and she could grab them.

All she had to do now was wait and pray.

Waiting for someone when you knew they would come eventually was one thing. Waiting for someone who might never come was quite another. Even worse was to be in pain and be forced to sit upright, poised for action. She knew that after hearing the click of the first lock, it took about ten seconds for him to descend the stairs and open the inner door. She didn't dare fall asleep in case she didn't hear that first click. She also had to keep turning the kettle on to make sure it was boiling hot.

She picked up one of the books he'd left and started to read it again, but she couldn't see clearly enough with her swollen eyes, so she had to abandon that. She took out the five-pound note she had in her purse, and stuffed it down her bra. That was her emergency money. If she did manage to get out, she intended to find a phone and ring the police. She just hoped the address was displayed in the phone box, or how could she tell the police where she was?

Katy knew she would need to move like lightning when she heard his footsteps, and that was going to be hard when she was so badly hurt. She had to be standing, poised with the kettle, and ready to pounce on his keys the moment he stumbled. She needed to be out of that door in double-quick time, and lock it behind her. If she failed, she knew he'd boil that kettle and pour it over her.

Even once he was locked in, she couldn't be a hundred per cent sure she was safe. He might have a second set of keys. But she could lock the outer door and leave the keys in the lock, which would delay him. He was much stronger than her, and wearing shoes, so he could kick the locks in. She had nothing but socks on her feet, so if she couldn't immediately see somewhere safe to run to, she'd have to hide.

It wasn't as if she knew where she was, not even which town she was in. She could be on a main road, in a wood, anywhere. She wouldn't even know which way to run.

Thinking through all these variables made her tremble

with fright. There was so much that could go wrong. At school everyone had thought she was brave, because she always took dares. But she didn't feel brave at all now. She'd been a good runner too, but she was too badly hurt to run today.

'Please God, make me strong, help me if he comes for me,' she prayed.

She'd prayed a lot since she'd been in here. She thought, if she did get away, she'd go straight to church and give thanks. How Jilly would laugh at that. She was always talking about the 'holier than thou' people in Bexhill who went to church every Sunday but were horrified when a couple of West Indian families came to live in the town. But Katy had been brought up to say her prayers at bedtime, and although she'd never actually admitted it to Jilly, she'd never stopped.

She had just put all three pairs of socks on her feet and boiled the kettle again when she heard the click of the lock she'd been hoping to hear. Jumping to her feet, she grabbed the kettle up off the floor and listened intently.

He was fumbling with the second lock, and it crossed her mind he might have been drinking.

The door opened to the left, so it would conceal her momentarily. He'd be confused because the bed, which had been right in front of the door, was no longer there. She hoped that would be enough to catch him off guard.

The door opened. She could smell cigarettes and alcohol on him. Katy could hear her own heart thumping.

'Been shifting the furniture?' he said and moved forward. 'Where are you? Not on the lav?'

'No, just here,' she said and swung the kettle forwards

and upwards so the flow of boiling water caught the side of his head even before he turned to her.

He screamed with pain. Stumbling forward, he did exactly as she'd hoped and fell on to the electric fire.

The keys in his right hand fell to the floor. She stepped over him quickly, snatched them up and was out of the door, locking it behind her.

Just the effort she had put into those few movements had exhausted her. She had to lean on the wall and take deep breaths before she could even attempt to go up the stairs.

'Enjoy it in there,' she yelled back through the door. 'I hope the burns are agony. That should give you an idea what it'll be like to burn in hell.'

She climbed the flight of stairs with difficulty, and then paused to listen before going out through the second door and locking that one, too. He was crying like a girl.

That took away at least a little of her pain.

The second door was very thick; it not only locked with the key but had two big bolts, so she slid them across. He wouldn't get through that.

The door opened into a short passage; at the end of it was a kitchen. She wasn't going to linger and take a closer look. There was a part-glazed door to the left, through which she could see that it was dark outside. But it was locked, and there was no key. To the right was another door leading to a hall. He'd left the light on there, so clearly he'd come in that way. As she got to the front door she almost laughed when she saw the main fuse box. So with great pleasure she shut the main switch down to plunge him into darkness and cold.

Once outside, with the door shut behind her, it took a few moments to get used to the dark. It was really dark too, with no street lighting – not even a glow in the distance from other houses or a town – and terribly cold and windy. She soon realized by the earthy smell that she was in the depths of the countryside, and the lane outside Reilly's garden wasn't even tarmacked.

The stones hurt her feet, and she walked through a puddle without seeing it. So now her socks were wet and her feet were turning to blocks of ice.

His car was there; the bonnet was still warm when she touched it. But although she had the car key along with the cottage keys, she didn't know how to drive, so that wasn't an option for escape.

'The town can't be far away,' she said aloud. The angle at which he'd parked the car suggested he'd come from the right, so she went that way. Every bone in her body was protesting at walking now. Her broken arm was hanging at her side and pulsated agonizingly.

'But you are free,' she reminded herself. 'Even if you don't know where you are.'

Down at the police station in Dover, Charles was being asked the same questions again, for the third time now. Jilly was distraught that no one was rushing up to that house in St Margaret's Bay.

Suddenly she'd had enough of policemen who just stared at her, the smell of stale cigarette smoke, and a background noise of people shouting in other rooms nearby.

She rushed out of the door, down the steps of the police station and up the street to the King's Head. She found

John Sloane, who was still at the bar, and only then did it cross her mind that he'd be no use to her if he'd been drinking.

'Did you mean what you said about going to Reilly's place?' she asked him. 'We went there this afternoon, and Charles is at the police station now trying to get them to act, and get up there. But they aren't doing anything. Would you or one of your friends take me and break in? I know it's a lot to ask, but I've got this feeling Katy is there.'

Sloane swayed on his feet, looking at her with half-closed eyes. 'I'm too drunk to go anywhere, darlin'.'

'I can see that, but can someone else take me? Please, John, I'm afraid Reilly might kill her.'

'What is this, John?' another man asked. He had shoulders as wide as a barn door. 'Where does the lady want to go?'

'St Margaret's Bay, mate,' Sloane said. 'You got your car, Lance? Will you drive us?'

Jilly looked pleadingly at the big man. 'It's my friend, Katy. She was abducted, and I think she's in Ed Reilly's place. It's on an unmade-up lane at the top of the hill, above the town. Please, Lance, I'm so scared for her.'

Lance looked confused. He hadn't been in the pub earlier, so he didn't know the background. Drunk as Sloane was, he appeared to realize this.

'Look, mate, it *is* serious. I'll explain as we drive.'

Faced with Sloane's drunken insistence, Lance agreed, grinning rather foolishly at Jilly.

'So where's the posh boy?' Sloane asked once they were in the car and driving out of Dover. He was in the passenger seat, with Jilly in the back. As he turned to her, he breathed out fumes of whisky but appeared to have sobered up a little.

'In the police station. I just couldn't stand any more indecisiveness from the police,' she said. 'They were going on about the problems of getting a search warrant. I can't possibly go back to London tonight without knowing if Katy is in that cottage, dead or alive.'

She explained a bit more about Reilly. Sloane whistled when she got to the bit about him burning a house down with two women in it. 'Shit! Why didn't you tell me that this afternoon? The man needs stringing up.'

'I know. There's a lot more to it, too. Katy's father was arrested for setting the fire, and so she started doing her own detective work, to prove his innocence.'

'If she's in that place, we'll get her out,' Sloane said firmly. 'And don'cha worry about me being pissed, darlin'. I work best with a bit of jungle juice inside me.'

The cold and the pain made Katy feel very strange. Her feet were so cold and wet that every step felt like walking on daggers. She could barely see out of her swollen eyes. Her arm hurt so much, and she couldn't see the stones in the lane well enough in the dark to avoid the bigger ones. Time and time again, she stumbled.

'You will reach the road soon,' she said aloud. 'Someone will come by and give you a lift.'

But the words were hardly out of her mouth when she fell again, and this time she couldn't stop herself. She felt a sharp pain in her ankle and her forehead hit something hard.

For a second or two she saw stars before her eyes.

Then just blackness.

'This is near it!' Jilly said, leaning forward in her seat to point out a milestone caught in the headlights at the side of the road. 'I remember seeing that just before the taxi driver stopped, so the lane is just along here on the left.'

Lance slowed right down. 'I never liked Ed Reilly. He was always weird, even when we were kids.'

'With his mother being a drunken whore, knocking out little bastards like shelling peas, I suppose he was bound to go wrong,' Sloane said. 'Look there!' He pointed to the lane.

'The taxi driver wouldn't come along here, so we had to walk,' Jilly said as Lance turned into the lane and the car lurched over a pothole. 'God, it's bumpy!'

'I'll bill you for repairs to my suspension,' Lance said. 'Christ Almighty, what's that?'

He did an emergency stop, his headlights playing on the ground ahead. It looked like a sack lying in the lane.

Jilly leaned forward in her seat again. 'Golden hair – I think it's Katy!' She was out of the car like a bullet, running forward, splashing through a puddle.

The men followed her quickly, leaving the car engine running.

'It is Katy, but she's unconscious,' Jilly called back, kneeling beside her friend and smoothing her hair back from her face, which was badly beaten. 'God, she's been in the wars. He's smashed her to a pulp. If it wasn't for her hair, I wouldn't know her. Can we get her into the car?'

'Christ Almighty! She's a mess!' Lance exclaimed as he

reached Katy and struck a match to look at her. 'Should we be moving her?'

'She'll freeze to death if we don't get her away from here quickly,' Sloane said. 'Poor kid! Wait till I get my hands on that bastard.'

In the light from the car headlights he felt as if he was looking at a lump of liver, not a face. He'd seen blokes almost torn apart in fights many a time, but never a woman in such an appalling state as this. 'Take her feet, Lance, I'll take her head, into the back seat and straight to hospital.'

It was only once Katy was receiving emergency treatment at Dover Hospital that Jilly thought to ring the police station and get a message to Charles about what had happened.

Katy's condition was critical; she was drifting in and out of consciousness. She was suffering from a broken arm, ankle and two ribs, plus a chest infection and innumerable lesions caused by the beating she'd received at the hands of Ed Reilly.

Charles arrived so quickly after her phone call that Jilly saw then just how much he cared for her friend. His face was white, his eyes frantic with anxiety.

'They won't let us see her, not yet,' she said, restraining him from going into the ward. The doctor had told her it might be weeks before Katy recovered, and he was afraid the mental scars would take years to heal. 'She is really poorly and needs an operation to fix her broken ankle and arm.'

'I was furious with you when you ran out of the police station,' he said. 'I had the mad idea you'd got the train back to London! I should've known better.' He looked across at Sloane and the big man beside him, both waiting anxiously with Jilly. 'You called the cavalry?'

At Charles's remark the two men grinned sheepishly.

'I can't thank you two enough,' Charles said.

'I'm a sucker for a damsel in distress,' Sloane said. 'You should've let us come with you in the first place. We could've beaten the shit out of Reilly.'

'How did Katy get away?' Charles asked, confused by this turn of events.

'We don't know,' Jilly said. 'We found her lying in the lane. The only thing she said when she came round briefly in the car was, "Is that really you, Jilly?" But she passed out again after that.'

'So we don't know where Reilly is, then?' Charles said. 'After you called the police station, Jilly, the sergeant said they were going straight over there. But he'll probably be gone by now.'

Ed Reilly wasn't going anywhere. He'd managed to grope his way to the bed after all the lights went out. His scalded face and neck hurt like hell and he'd burned his hand on the electric fire when he fell over it. But what really hurt was that he'd been bested by a girl.

He knew he could probably kick the lower door open, but not the second one. That was solid oak – and she would've shot the bolts across, too.

So all he could do was wait for the police to come.

Police Constable Withers slowed right down once they were in Hart Lane. Neither he nor Perkins knew Reilly's place, or even the lane, and they'd been told the cottage was concealed by trees; then there were the potholes, some deep enough to break an axle.

Withers had wanted to come here earlier when the barrister chap was urging them to check if Reilly was holding the girl there. But the sergeant wasn't one for spur-of-the-moment actions, or bending rules. In Withers' opinion he was a gutless wonder. Surely, when someone's life was in danger, rules had to be bent and risks taken.

'There's his car!' Perkins exclaimed, pointing out the parked Jaguar caught in the panda car's headlights. 'Think we'll need backup?'

'Our coshes are backup,' Withers said grimly. 'I'll be happy if he tries to fight us. By all accounts he deserves a good kicking.'

'No lights anywhere,' Perkins remarked as they got out of the car.

'That's a good excuse to kick the door in,' Withers said gleefully, and with one thump from his size eleven boots, the door swung open.

Withers tried the light switch but nothing happened. Perkins shone his torch about in the dark hall and spotted the fuse board. 'The electricity's been switched off. Could she have done it before she left?'

Once he'd switched the power back on they looked in the first room to their right. There was nothing in it but a shabby blue sofa, stuffing coming out of its arms. Several old newspapers were scattered about, the most recent over a week old, and an almost overflowing ashtray had been left on the windowsill. There was a fireplace too, with ashes and cinders still in place. The faded chintz curtains were closed.

The room opposite, across the hall, held only a double bed with a sleeping bag and pillow lying on it.

They pressed on then, heading into the kitchen at the back of the cottage. That was in a pre-war time warp, with an oilcloth-covered table, an ancient coal stove, an old butler's sink and a kitchen cabinet with a drop-down enamel-covered door. Reilly had been using a camping gas ring. There were a saucepan and frying pan next to it, and a few tins of food – baked beans, corned beef and soups – in the cabinet. But it didn't look as if he'd prepared any food recently.

'Maxwell, the estate agent, said he bought it a few years ago to do it up and live in it,' Withers said thoughtfully. 'If that was so, I would've expected to see bags of concrete, lengths of timber and plumbing stuff. But there's nothing. Why hasn't he started the work? And where is he now?'

A faint sound made them turn to see another door in the small corridor. It was a substantial one, quite different from all the other doors. It had two heavy bolts shot across it, and yet keys were hanging from the lock.

'I think he's in there,' Withers exclaimed. 'It must lead to a cellar. Look at those bolts; no one puts those on an interior door unless they plan to lock someone in. By God, that girl must've turned the tables on him!'

'It would be good to leave him for a few days,' Perkins laughed. 'A taste of his own medicine. But I suppose we can't do that.'

They heard a sound again, and Withers drew back the bolts and unlocked the door. The stairs behind it were steep, and there was another door at the bottom.

'Police! Stand back from the door and put your hands up,' Withers commanded in a loud voice. He looked at Perkins and grinned. 'Let him think we're armed,' he whispered.

Perkins unlocked the door, and as the door opened Withers raised his truncheon, expecting Reilly to try and get past them and escape.

But instead, he was sitting on the bed holding a piece of cloth to his face.

He didn't even move or show any emotion when Withers told him he was arresting him for abduction, arson and the murder of two women. He then read him his rights.

'I didn't do any of that,' Reilly said weakly. 'You've got the wrong man.'

'Sure, sunshine, and the moon is made of blue cheese,' said Perkins. 'You captured the wrong girl, that's for sure. She really turned the tables on you.'

Withers put the handcuffs on him none too gently, and only then did they see the burn, right down the side of his face, and his scorched hand.

'Hurts, does it?' Withers asked.

Reilly nodded.

'Well, so it should. You deserve pain.'

Perkins went up the stairs first. Withers pushed Reilly to go up after him and then followed on behind.

'We'd better get the boys up here to collect evidence, sharpish,' Perkins said. 'With the front door damaged anyone could get in.'

18

The first two days in hospital Katy was aware of very little. She vaguely remembered coming back from theatre, after they'd set and plastered her broken arm and ankle, and a nurse telling her she was in a private room. But the pain-killers they gave her were so strong that in between checks on her blood pressure and temperature, she kept drifting back to sleep.

But on the third day she had felt alert enough to ask for a mirror to see her face, and even said she was feeling hungry. The ward sister said that was evidence of recovery. While sympathizing with Katy at the sight of her battered face, she pointed out that the swelling had already gone down and the bruising would soon fade.

Katy felt she shouldn't whinge about her face – after all, she had survived. Besides, looking at all the flowers and cards in the room, she felt truly loved. The extravagant pink roses were from Charles, with a lovely card saying he'd be visiting her just as soon as she was well enough. All the staff at Frey, Hurst and Herbert had sent flowers, and there were more from Joan and Ken, with a note saying they were so relieved she was safe now.

The funny card from Jilly was her favourite. It depicted a woman in bed in full make-up, wearing a fluffy bed jacket and eating chocolates, and said: 'Some people will go to any lengths to get some attention.' Each time she looked at it she smiled.

Then, to Katy's complete surprise, her mother arrived. She was wearing her brown musquash coat and matching hat, which she only ever wore on special occasions. She was also wearing Tweed perfume; it reminded Katy of church on Sundays when she was much younger.

'What are you doing here?' Katy exclaimed.

'It appears I'm visiting you,' Hilda said, putting a bouquet of spring flowers down on the bed and sliding a small suitcase under it. 'The case has clean nighties, toiletries, and clothes for you to come home in. This is a right pickle you've got yourself into.'

If Katy hadn't been so moved to see her mother, she might have been hurt by the accusatory tone she used, especially as she was feeling very weak. But knowing Bexhill was over fifty miles away, it did prove that Hilda cared far more about her than she'd ever let on.

'I'm so pleased to see you,' Katy said, and held out her one good arm for a hug.

Surprisingly, Hilda moved closer and really hugged her. 'It's been so worrying. Rob said he thought the man would kill you.'

'Well, he didn't, and I managed to get the better of him. But at the moment it doesn't feel like much of a triumph, I still hurt too much.'

'Your pretty face looks so sore,' Hilda said, reaching out to gently touch Katy's cheek. 'What a terrible business! And you look so thin.'

'That will soon be rectified, once my mouth gets better.

I feel hungry now.' Katy wanted to grin, but any slight movement of her face still hurt. 'But do sit down, Mum, and tell me how you've been.'

Hilda pulled up a chair and sat down, her handbag clutched on her knees, as if afraid someone would snatch it. Katy waited; she could almost see her mother's thought processes. Should she apologize? Maybe act like she hadn't actually been horrible? Perhaps even hope that her daughter might have lost her memory?

'Well?' Katy said pointedly.

'I'm sorry for the things I said, and for not being more supportive before you went to London. But I was afraid for you, and it looks as if I was right to be.'

Katy wanted to laugh. It was so like her mother to justify her behaviour.

'You were nasty, Mum,' she said wearily. 'But you are here now, so let's draw a line under it. How is Dad? I sincerely hope you didn't shut him out when they released him?'

'No, I didn't,' she said, and at this she looked ashamed. 'He came home and we've had a good talk about it all. He brought me here today. He said he'd let me come and see you first and he'll come up with Rob later.'

Katy was very glad to hear that her parents were trying to make it work, and she was thrilled her brother would be with her in a little while.

'That is really good news,' she said. 'But when I get home we've got to talk properly. There's a lot I don't understand about you, Mum, and I think you really need to explain yourself and tell me about your past. Will you do that?'

'I'll try,' she said and looked down at her lap, as if

wishing her ordeal would end. 'Does that mean you won't be going back to London to work?'

'No, it doesn't, Mum. Even if they don't keep my job open, I'll still want to live in London.'

'Charles, the barrister, is he your boyfriend?'

'I had one date with him, Mum, so I don't know where that leaves us.'

'But he's been chasing around looking for you. He was the one who rang us to say you'd been found. It sounded like he was in love with you.'

Katy did manage a giggle at that. 'I never expected you to become a romantic!'

'I always wanted you to have a kind, loving husband and a nice home.'

'Just like you had?'

'Yes, I do have all that. Perhaps I didn't always appear to appreciate it. Michael Bonham, your father's solicitor, came to see me. He talked about what some women go through with their husbands. I realize now that Gloria Reynolds was a very kind woman.'

'Are you my real mum or an imposter?' Katy asked jokingly. She could hardly believe her mother would actually admit she'd been in the wrong. 'And how is Rob?' Katy thought she had better not push for any further apologies.

'He's okay now you've been found, but he was frantic. Well, we all were. I'll go in a minute and let him and your dad come up.' She paused, clutching her handbag even tighter, and her lips quivered. 'You'll never know how scared we all were. We had begun to think you must be dead. All I could think was that I'd never told you how precious you were to me.'

'Oh, Mum!' Katy's eyes filled up. She had never, not even in her wildest dreams, imagined her mother saying she was precious to her. 'I thought about you a lot, too. It helped me get through those cold, lonely hours in the cellar. But that's all over now, and I can't wait to have one of your lovely dinners.'

Hilda got up and leaned forward to kiss her daughter's cheek and to hug her again. 'I've been very silly, haven't I?' she said in a small voice. 'Michael Bonham told me his wife had a similar problem and she got medication to help her. I'm going to the doctor tomorrow to see what he can do.'

'That's good, Mum. We'll all do what we can to help you.'

'At the moment you are the one who needs all our help,' Hilda said. 'You were subjected to a long and vicious ordeal. You must have thought you were going to die. So you won't forget any of this quickly, if ever.'

'Well, that's a bit doomy, Mum,' Katy joked. 'To think I imagined I'd be out on the town in a couple of days.'

Surprisingly, Hilda smiled. 'You always did have the knack of looking on the bright side. But let me get your dad and brother, they can't wait to see you.'

Rob bounded into the small room, bringing a smell of fried food with him. Her mother and father hung back a little.

'You've had a big breakfast, I can smell it,' she said as he hugged her. 'I could just eat that myself.'

'As soon as we can take you home, that's what you'll have,' Albert said, elbowing his son out of the way so he could hug her, too.

'You look a bit thin,' Katy said. She reached up and

touched her father's cheek; it felt fragile and papery, like a dried leaf.

'The prison food was awful. And of course I was worried about you and your mum. But a few good dinners with you back in the house and I'll be fine.'

As the three of them clustered around her bed, for once all in unison, all there for her, she felt a surge of love for them. She hadn't got the energy to tell them more about her ordeal yet, or even ask them questions. Maybe she'd never want to talk about it much, but suddenly her home seemed like the only place in the world she wanted to be.

'I had a word with your doctor and he won't discharge you for at least a week,' Albert said, as if reading her mind. 'Your chest infection is still there, plus he needs to know you can cope. With both a broken ankle and a fractured arm, it means you really can't manage two crutches. I said we can bring a bed downstairs for you and I can push you around in a wheelchair. But even after me giving it my all to get you home, the doctor still said no – for now, anyway.'

'I so much want to go home,' Katy sighed. 'And it's too far for you to come and visit me here.'

'After I've taken your mum and Rob home, I could come back and stay in Dover somewhere,' Albert said.

'Oh, Dad, you won't like that, you'll be bored stupid.'

'She's hoping Charles will come to visit,' Rob teased. 'From what I heard, the night you were found he hung around here all night.'

'Did he?' Katy asked.

'Not just him – Jilly was here, too. They only left because the doctor said he wouldn't allow you visitors,' Albert said with a wide smile. 'I got that from the receptionist downstairs. I can't wait to meet the man who went to such lengths to find my daughter.'

'Jilly was just as brave and wonderful,' Hilda said. 'She dragged men out of the pub to take her up to that house. She found you, unconscious and out in the cold, in a muddy lane. If she'd waited for the police to act, you might have been dead by then. I'm just so sorry I used to have such a poor opinion of her.'

Katy could only look from one dear face to another, her heart melting with love for them. She knew they wanted the full detailed story, but she felt too weak to attempt to relive it all. She hadn't even got enough energy to ask what had happened to Reilly.

'It's been so lovely to see you all, I just wish I could be a bit livelier for you,' she said. 'But I'm really weary, so I think you should go home now. I'll be back with you before you know it.'

They looked disappointed, but they didn't argue. Rob said he'd be going back to university in the morning, and Albert said it was high time he got back to Speed Engineering. 'I don't want them finding they don't need me any more,' he said with a smile.

Hilda came closer to Katy and hugged her. 'I can't wait to get you home and cook all your favourite meals,' she said.

Katy gave one last wave as they disappeared from view, out in the corridor, and sank back on her pillows. Her mother's final words rang in her head and she wondered whether it would be twice as difficult to leave home next time.

*

'Charles, how lovely to see you,' Katy said, when he surprised her by coming through the door with a huge bouquet.

It was now a week since she'd got away from Reilly, and four days since her parents and Rob came. She'd begun to think Charles had lost interest or was too busy to come so far to see her. Thankfully, she'd got the nurse to wash her hair for her yesterday and she'd put on the new, pale blue frilly nylon nightie her mother had bought her.

'I wanted to come days ago, but the ward sister told me your chest infection wasn't clearing up, and you were worn out by visits from the police.'

She knew then that he must have been ringing the ward daily. Sister was something of a dragon. She'd insisted that Katy rest more, keeping her broken ankle elevated, and that the police officers didn't tire her too much with their questioning.

'The chest infection is almost gone now, thank goodness,' Katy said. 'It was horrible; it hurt when I coughed, and I felt really poorly. I'm so glad they let me stay in this private room. At least when the police come I don't have a whole ward gawping at me.'

'It was important to keep journalists out, too,' Charles said. 'There were a few of them downstairs just now. They don't give up easily.'

Charles sat on the edge of her bed and leaned forward to gently kiss her lips. They were still bruised and a bit puffy, as was her whole face. But despite that, the kiss sent a delicious frisson of wanting more throughout her body.

'Hmm,' he murmured. 'I've been dreaming of kissing you for so long.'

'And you don't mind me looking a fright?' she said.

He put one hand gently on her cheek. 'You don't look a fright to me. You look like the bravest girl I've ever met, each bruise is a badge of courage.'

'Or stupidity,' she suggested. 'If only I'd told someone where I was going, or if I'd left Edna's notebook back at the house with Joan and Ken. But anyway, enough of me! Why are you here midweek? Surely you've got clients to defend.'

'I rearranged things,' he said, smoothing her hair back from her face. 'I wanted to see you too much to wait any longer. So now tell me what's been happening. Have the police been driving you mad?'

'Making my statement was the worst thing; they went over and over it. What he said, what I said, how he hit me and why, every last thing. I think I confused them even more by saying he was nice sometimes.'

She went on to tell Charles about the night she was sick and Ed stayed with her, bringing the eiderdown and the electric fire. 'I don't think he knew how to kill me,' she explained. 'I suspect he hadn't got it in him to do it close up, like stabbing or strangling. Will he hang?'

Charles shrugged. 'I doubt it. The anti-capital punishment brigade are gaining support, and in general I'd say rightly so. But when I look at what Edward Reilly has done, it's hard to offer up a reason for reprieving him.'

'So he'll get a life sentence, then?'

'Yes, but that won't happen overnight. There is still so much the police have to look into. They think he may have committed other crimes. The doctor's wife from Hampstead is missing, with her children; it seems he was seeing her when she was living near Eastbourne. They are also opening up old, unsolved cases that are similar. What I am intrigued by is how he managed to track down Gloria, Edna and the doctor's wife, yet didn't find his own wife, Deirdre. Could the almoner back at the Whittington Hospital have spilled the beans? Or was it the older lady in King's Cross who told him? We won't get anything from her now, as it turns out she died last year.'

'Perhaps he'll confess all,' Katy said.

'I somehow doubt that,' Charles said. 'I'd love the opportunity to interview him and get to the bottom of what made him how he is. What I learned about him from his aunts, and Deirdre too, was fascinating. And then you said he could be kind, and you don't think he knew how to kill you. All such compelling stuff to me!'

'Well, I don't want to think about him any more,' Katy said firmly.

Charles smiled and stroked her cheek. 'No, I don't suppose you do. It was tactless of me to talk about him. Besides, I'd much rather talk about us.'

'Us?'

He smiled at her puzzled expression. 'There I go again, speaking out loud without thinking it through. It's just that ever since you went missing I haven't been able to think of anything but you. I kind of hoped you might have been feeling the same. But I suppose staying alive was the only thing on your mind?'

'Actually, you did flit in and out of my mind quite a lot,' she admitted, blushing furiously. 'You took my mind off the possibility of dying of hunger.'

Charles grinned. 'Now there's a first! No one has ever claimed that of me before.'

Katy giggled. 'There can't be any "us" for a while. I'll be back in Bexhill, waiting for my ankle and arm to heal. That's going to take about six weeks or so.'

'I can come down there at weekends.'

Katy's heart leapt with joy. 'I'd like that, but I doubt you'll enjoy being around my mum. She's hard work.'

'I can stay in a guest house and call for you, even push you around in a wheelchair. Please don't put up obstacles!'

'I'll try not to. I suppose I'm afraid you'll get bored waiting for me to get back to normal.'

He leaned closer to her on the bed and put his arms around her. 'I want to help you recover. Not just your ankle and arm, but the whole of you. No one gets abducted like that, locked in a room in fear of their life, and just returns immediately to how they were before. That's why you need to be with your parents, have the security of your home, and know that you can talk it over with me whenever you feel the need. It might take six weeks, or six months, but I want to help you through it.'

Katy leaned into his shoulder; it felt so good to be close to him. In just the same way as she had managed to forget her misery in the cellar for short periods by thinking about him, she could now quell the feelings of panic by breathing in his smell of soap and cedar aftershave. She hadn't told anyone, not the nurses or doctors, about these moments of panic. She felt if she did admit to experiencing them, the moments would just grow longer and stronger.

A policewoman who came to talk to her soon after she came round, after being in theatre, asked if Reilly had raped her.

'He wasn't like that,' was how Katy had answered. She

sensed the woman didn't believe her, and thought Katy was denying it because she was embarrassed. But Reilly really hadn't made any sexual overtures. The time he slept on the bed with her, when she'd been ill and vulnerable, he didn't even attempt to cuddle her. Yet in some strange way that made his violence towards her worse.

But then he hadn't abducted her because he wanted a woman, only because he had to prevent her exposing him. Then he was stuck with her, and didn't know how to get rid of her.

She kept thinking about the day she escaped. What would he have done to her if she hadn't attacked him? Might he have come up with some way of killing her? Or would he have just left her there, once again – unable to kill her, yet unable to let her go, either.

He was a puzzle, and she would probably never get the answers to all her questions about him.

Did that mean she would never be free of him?

19

'How wonderful to be going home at last.' Katy sighed happily as her father drove along Shakespeare Cliff towards Folkestone.

It was a beautiful, cloudless day, the sea below the cliffs on her left reflecting the blue of the sky as if telling them spring was almost here. Here and there they saw almond blossom, banks of crocuses, daffodils and camellias in full flower. But the sunshine was deceptive, and it was still very cold.

Wearing her own clothes again felt good, too. She'd always liked the black-and-white striped polo-necked sweater her mother had picked out, and the black slacks hid her plaster cast. But it felt very odd to be wearing only one shoe. Just a woolly sock over the other foot.

'It will be great to get you home,' Albert said, smiling at her. 'Your mother has been in a delirium of baking for days. She's made enough cakes to hold a street party. But maybe we'd better throw one, as everyone has been calling to ask how you are.'

'They just want to know the gruesome details,' Katy said. 'Funny that they didn't come calling to offer support when you were arrested.'

'Now, now, don't be like that,' Albert reproved her. 'It's been good for your mum, she actually chats to other women now. Besides, there are lots of people in our road who are genuinely fond of you.'

Katy wasn't convinced, but she let it drop; her father was one of those people who saw the best in everyone.

'How are things between you and Mum now?' she asked him. 'And I want honesty, please.'

'Much better,' he said. 'She can't change overnight, but she is trying. I wish I could unlock whatever it is inside her that makes her so –' he stopped, perhaps unable to say the word.

'Difficult? Savage? Unreasonable?' Katy suggested. 'Pick any one you like! But I intend to get to the bottom of it. I shall be like a dog with a bone. They sent a psychiatrist to see me the other day. I got a few good pointers from him.'

'What did he ask you, then?'

Katy shrugged. 'How I felt about Reilly, was I having nightmares about him? All the usual stuff. So I asked the psychiatrist what might have happened to Reilly that would have turned him from taking good care of his younger siblings into becoming a wife beater and eventually a murderer. The shrink said he felt it was hatred of his mother, and then he saw the women in his life turning into her. But I can't see that that makes sense. Charles said Deirdre was a gentle, quiet woman, she wasn't a drunken floozy. Anyway, nothing that shrink said explained why Reilly wanted to kill Gloria and Edna.'

'Presumably just because they'd taken Deirdre away from him? Even though it was his behaviour that drove her away in the end. So what good pointers did you get that might apply to your mum?'

'She never talks about her childhood, does she?'

'She can't talk about anything in her past. I've tried to

get her to, but she changes the subject. And if I keep on, she gets angry.'

'Well, I'm going to try and make her talk to me about it.'

'Good luck with that.' Albert made a little snigger. 'I'll keep out of the way, in the shed, while it's going on.'

He was silent for a little while and then sighed. 'There is something, Katy. Something big. But it isn't my place to tell you; she'd never forgive me. But I think you're right, it is time to pull the skeletons out of the cupboard. Tomorrow I'll be at work all day, so it might be a good opportunity. But please don't be angry with me if it all goes pear-shaped.'

Katy felt a rush of pure delight as she got home. The front garden was bright with daffodils, and the big camellia growing against the house wall was covered in bright red flowers.

The door opened before her father had even turned off the ignition, and her mother darted out, her broad smile a joy to see. She opened the passenger door. 'It's so good to get you home,' she said, with all the warmth she normally lacked.

'I'll just get the wheelchair out of the boot,' Albert said.

Katy wasn't surprised to see her father had made a little ramp to get the wheelchair over the threshold; he had always been good at thinking of everything. She managed to do a one-legged hop from car to chair, and he wheeled her in.

'Your father said he thought you'd rather sleep upstairs,' Hilda said, once Katy had been wheeled into the kitchen.

'Yes, I would. I can go up and down on my bottom.

284

But I only need to do it once a day, as we've got the down-stairs lav.'

'Will you be able to get in there?' Hilda looked doubtful.

'Of course I will. I can hop with the one crutch. Stop worrying about me. I'll soon get used to it.'

'Well, I must say, I wasn't keen on bringing your bed down here,' Hilda said, proving she hadn't changed that much, she was always one for order. 'Now, tea and cake, and then you can tell me any news. Has the chest infection gone now? Does your ankle – or arm – hurt?'

'Chest all better, and just twinges now and then in my arm and ankle. I just hate the plaster; it's so hard to sleep with it at night.'

'It must be,' said Hilda, looking hard at her daughter. 'You are still very pale and thin, but your face looks a lot better, and the remaining bruising should fade soon.'

Katy thought she looked a fright. Other people might try to convince her she looked fine, but she had every colour of the rainbow around her eyes, from purple through to yellow. But she had promised herself she wasn't going to moan about it. After all, she was lucky to be alive.

But that night she didn't feel lucky. First hauling herself up the stairs on her bottom, then hopping into the bathroom, only to find she'd left her toothbrush in the bedroom. Another hop back there, then the return to the bathroom to clean her teeth. After that, back to the bedroom, by which time she felt exhausted.

Once in bed, the leg plaster caught on the sheets and scraped against her other leg. Then her plastered arm made it impossible to lie on her right side. She was forced to lie on her back, and the prospect of spending at least another five weeks like this was hideous.

Once she'd turned out the light, the memories surfaced. The smell of that cellar, the cold, the hunger and the fear. She felt every blow Ed inflicted on her, and couldn't help but remember the mad look in his eyes. Yet there was the gentler side of him, too. He'd been so kind when she was ill – in fact, she'd thought they had turned a corner and he would let her go.

But it wasn't just the ordeal in the cellar that concerned her. She longed to be able to have a bath, to wear something pretty. To be able to walk outside alone.

To be normal again.

It was the following afternoon before Katy tackled her mother. Hilda wasn't one for sitting down during the day. She kept herself busy cleaning, polishing, washing, ironing, cooking and washing up. Katy had learned from an early age that nothing deterred Hilda from her routine. Even if she had a cold or sickness, she battled on regardless.

But after they'd had lunch of home-made French onion soup, and the washing-up was done, Katy asked Hilda to come and sit with her by the fire.

'I've got some ironing to do, and I must pop down to the Home and Colonial for some cheese,' she said, twisting her hands nervously, as she always did when someone asked her to do something unexpected.

'The ironing can wait, and by tomorrow you'll need more from the shops than just cheese,' Katy said. 'Now sit down, Mum, it's important.'

Hilda perched on the edge of the sofa, her hands clasped in her lap.

'Sit back and relax, Mum. You look like you are here for a job interview.'

'What is so important?' Hilda snapped. 'Is something wrong with you?'

'Not me, Mum, it's you. Back in hospital you promised me we'd talk, and today we are going to do just that. I want you to start by telling me where you grew up and about your parents.'

She saw her mother's face tighten. She didn't want to talk about anything other than the recipe for her fruit cake or the fact that the spare room could do with new curtains.

'There's nothing much to tell,' Hilda said with a deep sigh. 'My parents had a smallholding near Salisbury. They grew vegetables and kept chickens. We sold the goods in a little shed by the gate.'

'Brothers, sisters?'

'I had an older brother, Richard, but he died when I was twelve. Something wrong with his liver. My folks never got over it.'

This was a major bit of news, and Katy wondered how anyone could keep such a thing to themselves for years.

'Did your parents make you feel guilty that you were healthy?'

Hilda looked thoughtful rather than cross at the question.

'Yes, I suppose they did. They needed Richard, you see, for the heavy work, digging and stuff. I felt they thought I had no use, even though I did the weeding, fed the chickens and looked after the bedding plants we grew from seed and sold in the summer. As soon as I got home from school, I had to work.'

'How did that make you feel?'

Hilda frowned and looked hard at Katy. 'Feel? When I was a girl no one cared how you felt. You didn't expect them to.'

'Maybe so, but how did you feel?'

'Put upon, I suppose. I used to daydream about having a life where I could go for walks, lie around reading books, wear pretty clothes and have lots of friends. I didn't really make friends, because I never had any time to be with them.'

'And did your parents keep on and on about Richard dying, to the point where you wished it had been you who died?'

Hilda looked astonished at that question. Her mouth opened and closed, but no words came out.

'I know that sounds harsh, but was that how it was?' Katy asked.

'Yes, it was,' her mother said, somewhat reluctantly. 'I felt I didn't count for anything. Sometimes I wished I could get sick so they'd make a fuss of me.'

'So when did you leave school, and what did you do then?'

'I left school in 1929. I was fourteen. I worked three days a week as a laundry maid for the Colridges, they had the big house in the village, and the rest of the time I worked for my parents. But my mother died suddenly in 1931; they said it was a heart attack. She used to get herself very worked up about the Depression. Things were getting tight for everyone, men losing their jobs and such, but it wasn't going to make our lives change much. My father was always telling her that we'd never starve, as we grew our own food and sold enough to buy anything else we needed. But she was a worryguts. Always had been.'

'I'm sorry. So you were left with just your father? How was that? You were too young to be without a mother.'

A tear trickled down Hilda's cheek. 'It was awful. He used to go down the pub every night, and sleep half the day. I had to try and keep everything going on my own. He didn't do anything. We had no money for chicken feed, so he sold all the hens and drank that money away. With no eggs to sell, and gradually fewer and fewer vegetables to eat or to sell, we were done for. He was so nasty to me; he demanded the money I earned doing laundry and he just drank it away. Often he hit me, too. Finally, when he hadn't paid the rent on the property, we were evicted. Mrs Colridge felt sorry for me and took me in as a maid of all work. She had got rid of most of the other staff because times were hard for her and her husband, too. So it was just me doing everything in her house.'

Katy felt she'd been handed the answer to much of her mother's odd attitudes. The penny-pinching, the disapproval of drink, and her inability to relax. She put her hand over her mother's and squeezed it. 'No wonder you don't ever talk about those times,' she said. 'It must have been so grim.'

'It was better with the Colridges than being with my father,' she said. 'At least I was well fed, living in a decent place, and no one shouted at me or hit me. In fact, Mrs Colridge was quite kind. She relied on me, she was a very weak woman.'

'And your father?' What happened to him?'

'He drank himself to death.' Hilda spat that out, revealing she was still bitter towards him. 'He tried to get money from me a few times, but I didn't earn much and I wasn't going to give it to him for drink. He was found dead in the woods, just before war broke out. Living like a tramp, filthy dirty, a real disgrace.'

Katy understood now why her mother had such high standards of cleanliness, of order and self-restraint. But she wanted to know the 'big' thing her father had mentioned, and so she needed to move Hilda along.

'That must have been so awful for you, Mum,' she said. 'So humiliating and sad, too. Did you move away then to do war work?'

If Hilda felt she'd been cut short on the subject of her father, she didn't show it.

'Yes, I enrolled for war work and I got sent to a factory in Southampton.'

'So you were twenty-four then. What did you think of factory work? It must have been strange after living in a quiet village?'

'I liked it. I was earning good money, I had other girls for company, and we were all away from home so we had a lot in common. The work was repetitive, noisy and dirty. We were making small parts for tanks, planes – all sorts, really. But we'd go to dances on a Saturday night, and I liked sharing a house with other girls. I was the one who always cleared up.'

Katy smiled at that. She could imagine her mother taking on the role of housekeeper. 'What about romance? Any boyfriends?'

'There were a couple of lads, but I was too shy to be comfortable with them. I wasn't pretty, either. I felt awkward.'

'We all feel like that at first,' Katy said. 'I was terrified at my first few dances. I used to tell Jilly I wasn't going to any more parties. So what changed for you? You met Dad and everything was fine then?'

'What's behind all this? Why are you interrogating me?'

Katy was alarmed at her mother's aggressive tone. She had thought it was all going so well.

'Interrogating you?' she said. 'I was just interested in hearing about your past, how you met Dad. How you were as a girl. We need to talk about these things, Mum. They all affected you, made you the person you are now. The horrible experience I had with Reilly would probably affect me badly if I didn't talk about it.'

'Why do you assume I had a horrible experience?'

'Because you're hiding something, Mum. People don't hide good things.'

'You think you are so clever,' Hilda snapped, getting to her feet and looking down at Katy with a look almost of hatred. 'You always did think you knew it all. Well, you don't, and some things that happen to people are best left in the past.'

'Mum, I only want to understand you,' Katy said quietly. 'I prayed a great deal when I was locked in that cellar. I thought about you, Dad and Rob a lot, too. Because I thought I wasn't going to live, it made me see that if God spared me, then I must get through to you. That I must find out what makes you so unhappy sometimes, and maybe then I could make it better for you.'

'No one could make it better, and if I was to tell you about it, you'd hate me.'

'Did you kill someone? Did you rob an old lady, or hurt a child?'

'No, of course not,' Hilda said angrily. She sat down again but remained on the edge of the seat.

'Well, those would be the only things I could hate you for,' Katy said. 'I wouldn't care if you'd robbed a bank, drowned a cat, or danced naked on Hastings Pier. Everyone has done something that they think people will hate them for. And they are usually wrong.'

She put out her hand to take her mother's, but Hilda pushed her hand away. 'Leave me alone, Katy. You don't want to know this; it's terrible.'

Katy saw that her mother was crying. She wasn't making any sound, but huge great tears were rolling silently down her cheeks. 'I do want to know. I don't care how bad it is. I promise I will still love you just the same,' she said, and put her arms around her mother and drew her to her chest. 'Now come on, whisper it, if you can't bear to say it out loud.'

Hilda said nothing for some time. Her shoulders were heaving and Katy could feel the wetness of her tears on her jumper, but there was no sound.

'I was raped!'

It came out as a whisper but, as quiet as it was, Katy heard it clearly.

'Tell me about it,' she said.

'I can't.'

'Yes, you can. Just explain where you were, who you were with. I expect I'll understand the rest without you going into any detail.'

There was a long silence. Katy waited patiently, as she sensed her mother needed to tell this story.

'Four of us went to a dance in Aldershot,' she said eventually. 'Nancy, one of the girls, had a boyfriend stationed there and she arranged with someone for us to have a lift there. I had made a new dress, it was pink with white flowers on it, and the girls said I looked pretty. I felt good, too. It was a warm night, and I thought something good was going to happen.' She paused.

Katy didn't attempt to prompt her because she sensed her mother was reliving that night.

'It was good, too. They had decorated the hall with paper garlands and balloons, and the band was first class. I danced with lots of men that night and I drank a fair bit, as we'd taken some gin with us. I thought I'd finally stopped feeling awkward and I was really happy. But it got very hot in the hall, and I went outside for some air.'

She broke away from Katy and sat up, looking into the distance as if she was back at that hall.

'The hall was on a country lane and, of course, it was all dark because of the blackout. But the moon was bright that night and I walked away from the hall. I could hear ducks quacking, even over the music inside. There was a pond, and the moon shone right down on the water and the white ducks swimming around, making it as clear as day.

'Then suddenly this man was there. He wasn't in uniform, he was wearing an open-necked shirt and dark trousers. He said how bright the moon was and asked me where I was from. He had a very posh voice, and he was nice-looking, with fair hair that shone in the moonlight. I flirted a bit with him. He suggested we went for a little walk. I don't know why I agreed, I didn't even know his name, but I suppose I thought it would be something good to tell the other girls, like a little adventure.

'But it wasn't an adventure at all. He took my hand and he drew me away from that lane into the bushes. He started kissing me, and I got scared then and said I had to go back. Then he punched me right in the face. He hit me so hard I fell back on the ground.

'He had one of those scarf cravat things round his neck and tucked into his shirt. He whipped it off and tied it round my head, gagging me. Then he did it to me. It hurt so much, and I tried to fight him off, but he was too strong and he hit me again and again.

'When he was finished, he got up and kicked me really hard in the stomach, then disappeared into the bushes.'

Katy could hardly believe what she'd heard. It would be shocking to hear this had happened to anyone, but knowing it had happened to her mother — a very private, particular and restrained woman — made it even more devastating.

'Oh, Mum, that is terrible!' Katy was crying now, too. She pulled her mother back into her arms. 'What did you do?'

'I managed to get the scarf off and I called out. I tried to get up but I couldn't seem to get my balance, my stomach was hurting so much. Then suddenly this soldier was there; he came running into the bushes and helped me up. I didn't need to tell him what had happened. My knickers were on the ground where the man had torn them off. He helped me put them back on.'

'So did you get the police?'

'No, I knew how they'd be. They'd think it was my fault, because I'd gone into the bushes with the man.'

'But didn't the soldier who helped you want to get the police?'

'Yes, but I wouldn't let him. I told him it would just be worse for me. I might even lose my job if it got out.'

'Lose your job! A man rapes you and suddenly you are the bad person?'

'That's how it was, back then,' Hilda shrugged. 'I don't suppose it's much better even now. Anyway, the soldier went back into the hall and told my friends he was taking me home, and he did – in an army jeep. He was so kind.'

'So did you ever find out who it was that raped you?'

'No, I didn't tell anyone else what had happened. I was in bed by the time the others got home.'

'But how could you live with such a dark, horrible secret?'

'I had someone who knew about it. The soldier who helped me. I talked to him about it and he came back to see me again and again.'

'What was his name?'

'Corporal Albert Speed.'

Katy thought for a moment that her mother was mixed up.

But Hilda repeated the name and looked pointedly at Katy.

'Dad?' Katy exclaimed. 'That's how you met him?'

20

'Dad!' Katy whispered his name, deeply shocked that something as awful as this had brought her parents together.

'Yes, Albert. But for him I would almost certainly have killed myself. Believe me, Katy, I was the most innocent of girls. I had no real understanding of anything to do with that!'

Katy knew her mother meant *sex*. She had rarely spoken openly on the subject, just vague innuendoes, usually uttered through pursed lips, as if even the thought disturbed her. Katy had got all her knowledge of human reproduction and male–female relationships from books and her friends. Jilly's mother had filled in any gaps in a cheerful but blunt manner.

Now Katy understood why her mother couldn't speak about it. Yet surely having had two children since then should've helped her?

'So did Dad take you to the police?'

'He wanted to, but I wouldn't let him.' Hilda cocked her head up in a defiant manner. 'I couldn't talk to a man about such things. And anyway, I was afraid they'd say it was my fault. I'd been drinking, and I'd let him lead me away from the dance.'

Katy could understand that. A friend of hers from school had gone to the police after being raped, and the police had said she shouldn't have accepted a lift home from the man. They had shown no concern, either.

'When was this, Mum?' Katy asked.

'The end of June, 1940. The reason we went to the dance in Aldershot was because my friend's boyfriend was one of the many soldiers, along with Albert, who had been in the retreat from France and were rescued from the beach at Dunkirk. They were both lucky to get home unscathed.'

Katy hadn't even known her father had been at Dunkirk. But then he only ever made jokes about his time in the army.

'So what did you do? Did you just carry on as if it hadn't happened?'

Hilda looked at her daughter with bleak eyes. 'I tried to. But there are some things you just can't forget. It was Albert who kept me going. He wrote to me, and three times he caught a train to come and see me.'

'Was England being bombed then?' Katy asked.

'Not then, we'd had what we called the Phoney War, when nothing really happened. But after Dunkirk the Germans swept through Europe. Holland, Belgium and France all fell. Then, at the beginning of July, we had the first daytime bombing in England. The London Blitz began on August 23rd, but our worst time in Southampton was from the end of November.'

'Did Dad remain stationed in Aldershot?'

'No, his mob were sent out to North Africa. At the time, I didn't know where he'd gone – they couldn't tell you stuff like that – but he wrote to me. I went back to work, and it was very scary when the bombs fell on Southampton. It was a major target, not only because of the ships and the harbour, but because the factories were making everything from guns to tanks. We all lived in a constant state of anxiety. I suppose that was why I didn't cotton on that I was expecting.'

'Oh, Mum,' Katy exclaimed. 'The rapist made you pregnant?'

'Well, I certainly hadn't done it with anyone else,' Hilda retorted with indignation.

Suddenly, like a lightning bolt striking her, Katy knew the truth. She had been born in March 1941.

She was the child of the rapist.

It felt like falling down an unseen hole. Fragments of childhood memories flashed past her, as if she was being given one last glimpse of things she'd held dear before they were snatched away forever.

'So Albert married you out of pity?' she said in horror. 'And you've let me believe all these years that he was my father? How could you do that?'

In the heat of the moment Katy forgot her broken ankle and, wanting to get as far away from her mother as possible, she got up off the sofa. But as soon as she took a step, she fell back on to the cushions. She began to cry then. She couldn't escape, and her whole world had come tumbling down.

'I'm sorry, Katy. I was too blunt; I should never have told you what happened to me. But in telling you part of the story, I had to tell the whole of it. You said you wanted the truth about me. Now you've got it.'

'All these years! All that pent-up nastiness I had to deal with, you watching me like a hawk, criticizing every move I made. So you saw all that's man's evil in me, I suppose?'

Hilda was crying now, tears streaming down her face. 'No, I never saw any badness in you. I didn't even think of him being your father – not once you were born, and I held you in my arms. Albert has always been your father in every way that counts. He wrote to me all the time, wanted to know what you were like, and when he came home in July of 1941 he asked me to marry him.'

'So what did he get out of the marriage?' Katy was so angry with her mother, she wanted to hurt her. 'A cold, bitter woman with a rapist's child. For as long as I can remember, you were always picking on him, nothing was ever good enough for you. Why on earth did he want you?'

'He said he fell in love with me as he drove me home that night after the dance. But I didn't believe him. How could any man want spoiled goods?'

'So you just used him? Is that what you are saying?'

'It wasn't like that, Katy. I fell for him, too. He was so kind, so gentle, but strong too. If I'd never been raped and I'd met him first and fallen in love with him, that would have been wonderful. A dream come true. But the rape spoiled everything. But please don't think I used Albert. I did lean on him, because I had no one else, but I loved him then and I still do.'

Angry and hurt as Katy was, she could hear the truth in what Hilda was saying. But she wasn't prepared to let her off lightly.

'All those times I asked why I had red hair and green eyes when you, Dad and Rob were all brown-eyed with dark hair, you could've told me the truth.'

'You tell me how you tell a child her daddy isn't her daddy? Or make a distinction between a brother and sister? Don't you think it felt like a sword in my side? You are Albert's daughter in every meaningful way. He changed your nappies, he helped you take your first steps, taught you to swim and ride a bike, helped you with your homework. Don't tell me you don't know that he loves you; he has shown it every day of your life. I often feel jealous that he loves you more than me.'

'I wish I could get out of this house and away from you,' Katy snarled and turned herself round on the sofa so she couldn't see Hilda. She could hear her mother crying but she wasn't going to turn back and apologize.

After a while, Hilda got up and went into the kitchen. Katy pulled the wheelchair nearer to her and hoisted herself into it with the aid of her crutch. Then she wheeled herself to the stairs, got out and shuffled on her bottom up the stairs.

She slammed her bedroom door behind her, locked it, then crawled on to her bed to cry.

It seemed to Katy that her whole life was one big lie. If her real father had been killed in the war, and then her mother had met Albert and married him, she could've borne more easily the pretence that Albert was her father.

But to be conceived by rape! How could she ever get over that? And who was this nameless man who had raped a young woman and abandoned her in a wood? What traits had she inherited from him? How could she ever feel comfortable with Rob and her father now she was only a half-sister and stepchild.

This devastating news hurt so much. She had believed, once she'd got away from Reilly, that all her troubles were over. She wished now that he had killed her. Nothing could be as bad as knowing your real father was a rapist and your mother was a liar.

At half past five her mother came knocking on the bed-room door and begged Katy to come down for supper.

'Your father will be in soon, and he's going to be so upset that you are locked in here,' she said. 'Please, Katy. I am sorry about what I told you, but you said you wanted the truth.'

Katy ignored her mother and put the pillow over her head. She felt too miserable to think of eating anything, and she didn't want to see Albert, either.

Albert came home around six. Katy heard muffled voices, Hilda's voice growing more shrill as she told her husband what had happened. Then there was silence.

Katy wondered if they could've gone out. The house wasn't normally ever that quiet.

Then, just after seven, she heard Albert coming up the stairs. His step was plodding and weary, which told her how troubled he was.

'Open up, Katy,' he said firmly at the door. 'I've got tea and sandwiches here for you and we must talk.'

'Go away, I don't want to talk to you or eat sandwiches!' she shouted back.

'If you don't open the door and behave like an adult, I'll kick it down. There are two sides to every story and you are going to listen to mine, even if I have to restrain you to keep you listening.'

He only ever used that fierce tone when he was very angry. Katy knew she must open the door or he would carry out his threat. Reluctantly, she hopped to the door and turned the key, before slumping down on her bed again.

Albert shut the door behind him and pulled up her dressing-table stool to sit down on.

'All our married life Hilda knew she must one day tell you the truth,' he began, his face tense and his eyes troubled. 'Keeping it locked inside her has made her miserable, but she found it impossible to tell you. I would've told you myself, but it isn't my story to tell. But seeing as you've reacted so badly, I am going to tell you my side of it.'

'What did you both expect? That I would say goody, goody, how great to have a rapist for a father?'

'Don't be ridiculous, Katy,' he reproved her. 'But how about trying to look at what happened from a different viewpoint – your mother's?'

Katy crossed her arms and looked defiantly at the ceiling.

'Hilda had a hard, miserable childhood. She endured things you, with your privileged childhood, can't even imagine. Finally, she is set free by her parents' death and she goes to work in a factory in Southampton, and for the first time in her life has fun with other young women in the same boat as her. The war is a threat, but in late June of 1940 it isn't on the doorstep, and she and her friends travel to Aldershot to a dance. Nearly all the soldiers there that night, including me, have been rescued from the beaches at Dunkirk, and are in high spirits because of it. I remember spotting Hilda as she came into the hall. She looked a bit scared, but very pretty in a pink dress, her chestnut hair tied back with a pink ribbon. I sensed she wasn't used to dances, that she was shy, and was probably wishing she'd never come. But just as I was about to go and ask her to dance, I was called away. Two men from my regiment were fighting outside, and as a corporal I had to sort it out before the MPs turned up.'

Katy sniffed. Albert was always so bloody reasonable, telling a story so well he could change anyone's mind. She was determined he wasn't going to weaken her resolve.

'As it turned out, I was gone for nearly two hours; one of the men had sustained quite a bad injury and I had to get him back to base. By the time I got back it was dusk, but I looked for Hilda. She was with a man I knew quite well, Roy, a good bloke, and she was drunk. It transpired her girlfriends had brought gin with them and had been lacing the orange squash. But I told myself I'd missed my chance, and Roy would take care of her. I started dancing with another girl, and it was some time before I noticed Roy was alone and Hilda had gone. So I went outside to look for her.'

'So why did you think you needed to be responsible for a total stranger?'

'Oh, Katy, you of all people know why some of us look out for the weaker ones. You did it all the time at school. Anyway, I couldn't see her. There were a handful of couples necking, but no Hilda. Of course, I didn't know her name then. So I asked a bloke I knew if he'd seen a girl in a pink dress, and he said she'd gone down the lane with a civilian. I hadn't seen any civilian men in the hall, so I just had a feeling I'd better go and look for her.'

'But you were too late, the deed had been done?'

'Yes, tragically. She was several hundred yards away from the hall, in the woods, lying on the ground crying. The rest you know.'

'It's the rest I don't understand. I get why she was scared

to go to the police – let's face it, they don't have much compassion for women – and I get why you took her home. But Mum is not Miss Personality, so why get permanently involved?'

Albert gave her a long, hard, disapproving look.

'Why did Charles search for you? You'd only had one date with him,' he retorted. 'What was so special about you?'

Katy felt ashamed then, and couldn't reply.

'The truth is, I fell for Hilda that night. Okay, maybe it was mainly sympathy, but not all. And something else took over. I met up with her three times before I was shipped out to North Africa; at each meeting I became more and more certain she was the one. Obviously, I had to be very careful with her – she had been through something terrible – but she was warm and funny, and she wanted to put what had happened behind her. I told her I loved her in a letter just before I left England.

'When she found out she was expecting, she sent me a Dear John saying that, as fond as she was of me, and despite feeling indebted to me for my kindness, she didn't want to ruin my life. I was shocked, but there was no way I was going to abandon her, and I wrote and told her so.

'She was so brave all through her pregnancy; her letters to me were warm, she didn't whinge about her situation, and she worked right up until two days before you were born, too. She had the bombing in Southampton to contend with, and then having to move into a grubby little room when you were born, the only place she could get. She had no money, her friends from work had disappeared like smoke, but the moment she held you in her arms she loved you. I've still got the letters she wrote to me at that time. She stressed that although she'd like me in her life, she didn't want to tie me down, and I owed her nothing. But when I got some home leave and saw her again, I knew I wanted to marry her. It was just love, I wanted both of you, forever.'

'But she was such a cow. Have you forgotten, Dad, that you said you were going to leave her?'

'No, I haven't forgotten. But nearly losing you changed things and made me realize what is important and what isn't. It was keeping the secret about you that soured her, even made her a little mad. Can you imagine having something like that gnawing away at you?'

'Sort of,' Katy agreed reluctantly.

'I should have been the strong one and told you the truth years ago. But Katy, when is the right time to tell such things? A child who knows nothing about sex wouldn't understand, and the older a child gets the more difficult it becomes. Look at how you've reacted today. You nearly died at the hands of a madman, yet you are horrified by this and cannot trust the two people who love you the most.'

'What did you expect? That I'd say okay, Dad, so you aren't my dad, mine's some filthy pervert who ruined my mum's life. Was I supposed to cuddle Mum and say it doesn't matter that she lied to me for twenty years?'

Albert sighed deeply with frustration. 'I think you should consider what you would do if Reilly had raped you and now you were pregnant. I know he didn't, and you aren't pregnant, but what if?

'Your mother and I would, of course, take care of you.

We could probably get you an abortion in a private clinic, or maybe suggest adoption. But it is far more likely we would persuade you to stay here so we could bring up the baby together. But Hilda didn't get any of those options. Maybe, at the back of her mind, she thought I only married her because I felt sorry for her. But that isn't true. I loved her then and I love her now.'

The bedroom door opened, and there was Hilda. It was clear from her expression that she'd heard what her husband had said.

'You haven't drunk your tea or eaten your sandwiches, Katy. If you think a hunger strike will make me feel worse than I already do, you are wrong. I couldn't feel any worse. But don't blame your father; everything he did was for love. I just hope that one day we'll be in church to see you marry a man with such fine qualities.'

She turned on her heels then and went back downstairs. Katy felt she'd just had her face slapped.

'Well, Katy?' Albert moved to sit beside her on the bed. 'Are you through with hating me?'

Katy hung her head. 'I couldn't hate you. As Mum pointed out, you were the hero. And I will admit there would never have been a time to tell me this when it wouldn't have been painful. I want you to be my father.'

'I am, my darling,' he said, drawing her into his arms. 'In all the important ways. Let me tell you something. At the end of the war, countless men came home from the fighting to find a child at home who wasn't theirs. The vast majority accepted that child. They knew that war makes people do extraordinary things; maybe some of the men had turned to another woman while they were away, and they knew how lonely and scared their wives must have been. But, above all, the child of that union is innocent of everything. It deserves to be accepted and loved. From the first moment I held you in my arms, I loved you. Nothing you've ever done or said has changed that. I just wish that I'd made Hilda tell you this years ago – not just for you, but for her. A huge wrong was done to her that night in Aldershot, and she's carried the blame inside her for twenty-four years. Be the bigger person now, Katy, and free her of that guilt?'

Katy stayed sobbing in his arms for some time. Her anger and hurt were gone now; they couldn't survive when she was being held by such a wonderful man.

Eventually, she sat up, blew her nose and dried her eyes. Then she ate the sandwiches.

Albert lifted one eyebrow questioningly.

'I can't tackle Mum on an empty stomach,' she said.

Katy trundled the wheelchair into the sitting room, where her mother was waiting. With the curtains drawn and a fire lit, it felt warm and cosy, as it always had.

She hoisted herself out of the chair and on to the sofa, beside her mother. 'I'm sorry, Mum, you didn't deserve me to be so nasty to you. I should've put myself in your shoes.'

Hilda smiled weakly and held out her small, thin hand to take her daughter's. 'When you went missing, I feared the same had happened to you, but that he would kill you afterwards. I became paralysed with fear. I couldn't telephone anyone, or visit your father, I couldn't even eat. I knew I must appear to be uncaring, but it was the exact opposite. But thankfully that monster didn't rape you or manage to kill you. Suddenly I could breathe again, and I resolved that I must tell you about my past.'

'I understand, Mum.' Kate let her mother embrace her. 'You have issues with showing affection, not just because of what happened that night in 1940, but because of your childhood. But I also understand now that all the baking, making lovely meals and keeping the house spotless is your way of showing your love for all of us. You can let up on that a bit now, just sit and chat, laugh with me and Dad. When Charles comes to visit, try to smile more.'

Hilda smoothed Katy's hair back from her face and smiled. This time it lit up her eyes.

'I think I finally understand just how lucky I've been,' she admitted. 'Shall we let it all go now?'

Katy nodded. She felt that if she said one more word, she might start to cry again.

21

'Is it alright for Charles to come this weekend for my birthday?' Katy asked her mother on Friday afternoon. 'I said I'd ring him back if it wasn't.'

'Of course it is, dear,' Hilda beamed. 'It will be lovely for him, the weather is improving by the day. Spring is finally here.'

A week had passed since the startling family revelations and during that time Katy had become much calmer, more mobile, and her facial bruises were finally disappearing. Only yesterday Hilda had wheeled her down to the hairdresser's so she could have a badly needed trim, wash and blow dry. They had passed her old firm of solicitors and dropped in briefly to say hello. It had been good to see her old workmates, and she got offers of a night out from some of the younger ones. Katy had laughed and said she wasn't going anywhere until she was out of plaster and could dance again.

She saw that Gloria's shop had been sold. A sign on the window said it was under new ownership and closed for refurbishment, but the girls in the solicitors' office had said they'd met the new owner. She was one of Gloria's old suppliers, and had a similar personality.

But the main development during the past week was that Ed Reilly had finally admitted his crimes to the police. Along with setting the fire that killed Gloria and her daughter, and attempting to kill Edna, he also admitted that he had had a relationship with Margaret Foster, which began when she was still in Hampstead, then was briefly revived when she moved to the village near Eastbourne. However, he insisted he hadn't hurt her, or abducted her and her children, and he had no idea where she was now.

This information had come from Michael Bonham. Katy was anticipating the police would be visiting her again before long to tie up any loose ends. But for now she was excited because Charles was coming for the weekend.

'I'll go and make up the bed in the spare room and put a hot-water bottle in it so it's aired,' Hilda said that evening. 'It will be so nice to meet him properly at last.'

'Just don't be too pushy,' Katy warned her. 'I know I really like him, but we have only had one date so far. So it isn't a big romance.'

Hilda smiled, as if she knew otherwise.

She had been like a different person since revealing her secret: jolly, chatty, smiley, and with none of the old displays of nervous hand-wringing, or cleaning incessantly. There had been a couple of wet days earlier in the week, and she and Katy had sat in the living room going over a box of old family photographs and putting them in albums.

Looking at pictures of the family when she and Rob were little brought back many happy memories, and it was quite startling to see that before Hilda began getting very thin, she had been pert and pretty, just as Albert had said.

'You were about twelve when I started becoming nervy and losing weight,' Hilda admitted. 'I remember putting on a summer dress one day and being shocked that it was far too big. I got into the habit of always keeping a cardigan on, as my arms were scrawny, and I never put on a swimsuit ever again. You know Albert was always on at me to go to the doctor's, but the more he did, the crosser I got. I suppose I was scared the doctor would question me.'

'Well, by this summer we are going to fatten you up and you will put on a swimsuit.' Katy picked up one black-and-white snapshot of her mother paddling with both children. Hilda was slender, but with a lovely shape. It must have been taken in the summer of 1946, because Albert had been demobbed and had taken the picture. 'You can be like that again!'

Hilda laughed. 'Oh, look at that awful costume. It was all ruched up with elastic and when you went in the water it filled up. I had to press myself all the way down as I came out the sea.'

'I had one like that, too,' Katy remembered and rifled through the old pictures till she found it. 'It was bright red, and I thought it was wonderful, so much better than the knitted one I had before.'

The photographs from 1953 onwards showed Hilda's escalating problem. In one taken at the Coronation Day street party it looked as if Hilda was almost in tears.

'There was a woman living along the road then called Alice Manders,' Hilda explained. 'She kept remarking that day how different you and Rob were. She even hinted that perhaps I'd been "naughty" during the war. She spoiled the whole day for me, and I just seemed to get worse and worse from then on.'

'I found you crying in the kitchen that evening,' Katy recalled. 'You claimed you'd got something in your eye. I knew that wasn't true and I thought you were disappointed in me because I'd shown you up by being greedy and eating far too many cakes.'

'How could you even have thought that? The sugar rationing was stopped for the Coronation, and all of us mothers were thrilled to see our kids tucking into the kind of party food we'd almost forgotten existed. I made about two hundred butterfly cakes for that party, not to mention ten big trifles.'

It was so nice to finally be forging a real relationship with her mother, to find the softer, more thoughtful side of her, and – even more surprising – her sense of fun. Taking Katy out in the wheelchair, Hilda had run while pushing her, and at times had laughingly threatened to let go of the handles.

Mealtimes were no longer fraught with tension as her mother banged pots around. Once, Katy had rarely watched television in the evenings with her parents, because Hilda was like the censor, disapproving of anything even slightly risqué. Now she laughed at comedies, almost as if her formerly non-existent sense of humour had finally come back to her. She didn't even baulk at slightly blue jokes.

But as good as it was to have a much nicer mother, Katy still felt saddened to think Albert wasn't her biological father. She wondered whether she should tell Rob next time he came home. Would he feel differently about her? She was sure not, as he was always so level-headed, but it did worry her.

It was, of course, lovely to be at home now while she still had limited mobility. But she really wanted to get back to London, to have Jilly's company, and of course to see more of Charles.

She spoke to Jilly most nights on the phone. She was now going out with a chap called Guy who worked at the zoo, and burning to get a flat of her own, mainly because she admitted she wanted to go to bed with Guy. His land-lord didn't approve of lady guests, so they couldn't go there. Jilly was due a few days off and intended to come home to Bexhill towards the end of next week. She made jokes about getting Katy drunk even if she was in a wheelchair.

But seeing Charles again was scary. Really exciting on one level, but being stuck in a wheelchair made her look a bit pathetic and not at all sexy, so maybe once he saw her like that he'd go off her. So much had happened since their date, she couldn't even be sure how she felt about him, either. It was all a bit of a fantasy, like he wasn't real.

She'd told Jilly her fears, but her friend had just laughed. 'Go on with you, he's bloody gorgeous. And all he wants is you.'

Perhaps that was so; she just had to hope for the best.

Charles arrived on Saturday morning, wearing the biggest smile and carrying a huge bouquet of spring flowers.

Albert let him in and Katy wheeled herself to the door-way of the sitting room to greet him.

'Jilly was right,' she thought. 'He is bloody gorgeous, and thank heaven I got my hair done and the bruises have faded.' It didn't hurt that she was wearing a new pink twin-set her mother had bought her. She was forced to wear trousers to cover up the plaster, but at least her top half looked fresh and attractive.

'Hello, Charles,' she said and introduced him to her

parents. He had spoken to both of them on the phone, but hadn't met them in the flesh.

'I'm so very pleased to meet you at last,' he said as he kissed her mother's cheek and shook her father's hand. 'You certainly went through hell in all this.'

'The horror disappeared as soon as we knew Katy was alive,' Albert said. 'But as I understand it, that was mostly down to you and Jilly, not the police.'

'Don't let's dwell on that,' Katy said. 'I think we've said all there is to say on the subject. Come on in, Charles, and sit down, you must be tired after the long drive.'

'Yes, indeed, Charles. I'll put the flowers in water for Katy. Would you like a cup of tea?'

'That would be lovely, Mrs Speed,' he said. 'But the flowers are for you. Katy's present is still in the car and will stay there till tomorrow.' He gave the bouquet to Hilda, who blushed like a schoolgirl.

As they sat in the sitting room, drinking tea and sampling some of her mother's home-made shortbread, Katy wished her parents would disappear so she could just kiss Charles. She loved the way he looked at her mother, eyes bright with interest, the way his lips curled up at the corners as if secretly smiling. He was so undeniably well mannered. No doubt he was already wondering how he was going to get through a whole weekend of small talk. Yet he appeared completely engaged.

'It's such a lovely day, maybe we should get out in the fresh air?' Katy ventured nervously. 'I mean if you don't mind pushing my wheelchair.'

'Mind? I'd love to!' He leapt to his feet. 'Is it far to the sea?'

'Not at all. But just make sure you are back for lunch at one,' Hilda said.

'I hope it's not a big lunch, Mrs Speed, as I thought I'd take Katy out to dinner tonight – that is, if you don't mind,' he said. 'I made a reservation at the Grey Goose, in Battle. It's very highly recommended.'

'Very expensive, too,' Hilda said, with just a tinge of her old waspish tone. 'But I'm told the food is lovely.'

Charles helped Katy on with her coat and into the wheelchair and smiled graciously as Albert opened the front door. Then he pushed her chair out, and said they'd be back for one.

He paused at the gate, looking across to Gloria's burnt-out house. The scorched timbers and the walls had all been pulled down now, but not taken away, and it remained a real eyesore.

'The worst of it is, the attached house where Mr and Mrs Harding used to live is to be demolished, too,' Katy said. 'It was too badly damaged internally for them to return to it. They have been moved to a bungalow at Cooden Beach. So sad, as they were almost like grandparents to Rob and me. As soon as I can walk again, I must go down to see them.'

'Any news of what is happening to the site?' Charles asked.

'Rumour has it the developer wants to build a huge detached house there. Some of the neighbours are protesting about it. But I think it's better to have a big, smart house than flats or something.'

'Someone always protests at change,' Charles smiled. 'I don't know why people just can't embrace it. In London there are so many projects getting started to clear away war damage and slum areas. I find it exciting. But many people see it as a threat.'

'We'd better go,' Katy said. 'Or Mum will come out with a blanket to put over my knees. She does that – like I'm eighty!'

It was warm in the sunshine and as soon as they got down to the seafront, Charles found a shelter out of the wind and wheeled the chair into it. 'That's better,' he said as he sat down. 'Now I can look at you.' He leaned forward to kiss her lingeringly, and all the bubbly fizzing feeling Katy had experienced with her first kiss from him came back.

'I thought of nothing but that on the drive down here,' he said. 'I can't wait for the plaster to come off your ankle and arm and to whisk you away somewhere.'

Katy felt a pang of fright at that. Did he mean he wanted to sleep with her? She wasn't ready for that yet, and neither did she want to think that was all he wanted.

'I've got news of Reilly,' she said, moving on to safer ground. She told him what Michael Bonham had told her. 'I'm a bit confused about the doctor's wife, though. How did she come into the picture? And where is she now?'

'I spoke to the officer who interrogated Reilly,' Charles said. 'It seems Reilly had known Margaret Foster since he did a small building job in her house in Hampstead. This was a few years back, and he had a brief affair with her. She told him at the time that her husband beat her but she didn't know how to get away from him. Reilly said he really liked her, but what she told him made him scared: she had two children, her husband was a very ruthless, powerful man, and of course Reilly was married to Deirdre. So he told Margaret that although he'd like to help her, he couldn't, and he ended the affair.'

'Very gallant!'

Charles smiled in agreement. 'Anyway, he said in his statement it was another eighteen months before he saw Margaret again, still in London, and she confided she was about to leave her husband because she had been put in touch with two women who helped beaten wives start a new life. She told him their names and that they were in Bexhill. Reilly pretended he still had a thing for her and wanted to keep in touch, because he suspected these same two women might have helped Deirdre leave him.'

Katy pulled a face. 'How horrible, to use one damaged woman to find another one,' she said indignantly. 'And Margaret could've been signing her death warrant!'

'Exactly, but the police officer doesn't believe Reilly did anything to Margaret at all. In his opinion, and I'm inclined to agree, Reilly only visited her to pump her for information about Gloria and Edna. When Margaret read in the local paper about Gloria dying in a fire, she was scared and that's why she did a runner.'

'Funny she hasn't let her parents know where she is, though.'

'I'm sure she will now that the story about Reilly is all over the national news. There was a sighting of a woman who sounded much like Margaret, also with two children, on the cross-Channel ferry about the time she disappeared from Eastbourne.'

'Let's hope that's the case, her parents must be frantic,' Katy said.

'He certainly was an excellent planner,' Charles said. 'He claimed he'd broken into Gloria's house months before he set the fire, looking for information about where Deirdre was. But he didn't find anything. He spent a lot of time watching and following both women, and it was anger that made him set the fire. Of course he said he didn't think Gloria was at home, so he will plead not guilty to murder.'

'I shouldn't think a jury would believe that,' Katy said. 'But thank goodness he got caught before he tracked down anyone else in Edna's book. Do you think he wanted to do that?'

'I don't know.' Charles looked thoughtful. 'He's never going to admit to it, even if that was his plan. If I was defending him, and thank God I'm not, I would suggest that he acted when the balance of his mind was disturbed. I have to say, it's going to be tough on you when you are called to give evidence.'

'I'm not too worried about that. I mean I haven't got any dark secrets to be revealed under cross-examination.'

Charles smirked. 'That's a shame. I was looking forward to interrogating you this afternoon!'

Katy laughed. 'More seriously, I would agree he was unbalanced; he was almost like Jekyll and Hyde. When he was calm he was really nice, charming even. I could see how a woman could be taken in by him.'

They moved on then down the seafront and had some coffee, before turning back for home.

'Are you still having nightmares,' Charles asked as they turned into Collington Avenue.

'Only occasionally now,' she said. 'It feels good to be

back in my old room, at least until I'm all mended. Then I'll come back to London; there's only so much mothering I can take.'

Charles laughed. 'I could sense how intense she could be.'

'There is a great deal to tell you about my family,' she said, turning her head to look up at him. 'But not all at once, or you might run a mile.'

'I'm not running anywhere, except here,' he said, breaking into a fast sprint and pushing her till she squealed.

'This steak is so good!' Katy said, later that evening, when they were at the Grey Goose. They had a corner table close to an open fire and, with the good food, the wine and Charles sitting opposite her looking so handsome, Katy felt she'd died and gone to heaven. They hadn't attempted to take the wheelchair; she'd hopped with one crutch and Charles supporting her on her other side.

'So tell me the family secret,' he said. 'I sensed something momentous had happened last week when I rang. Also, your mum didn't seem to quite fit with what both you and Jilly had said about her.'

'No wonder you went in for law,' Katy said. 'You've got a nose for intrigue. Now if I tell you, don't let it slip to my parents, I think that would really upset them.'

'My lips are sealed,' he said, making a zipping gesture.

She told the story as briefly and succinctly as she could. Charles looked shocked.

'That must've been awful for you, and even worse for your poor mum,' he said, putting his hand over hers on the table. 'I'm so sorry.'

'It was terrible when she first told me. But Dad made me see how it was for her, and what keeping such a thing inside her had done to her.'

'You are remarkable,' he said with a smile. 'So much compassion, so much common sense too. Of course your father is a real hero, and I suspect much of your strength comes from him. I believe we inherit things not just from shared genes, but by living with someone.'

'Yes, I think that's true. I've always had a strong bond with Dad. I always knew how he would react to things. What was important to him.'

'I think one of the most amazing things about him was that he wrote to your mother, telling her to register your birth in his name. He hadn't even seen you then; he might have been killed in North Africa, but he was thinking ahead and wanted to protect you both, whatever happened to him. Such a noble man.'

'He told me he fell for Mum the night he found her in the woods. Do you believe love can happen just like that?' she asked.

'Yes, I do.' He smiled and reached out to run his finger down the side of her face. 'I knew you were the one for me on that first date with you.'

'You couldn't have,' she said reproachfully.

'But I did. I couldn't get you out of my head the next day. I wanted to see you on that Sunday so badly, that's why I rang Jilly's relatives. After hearing you'd gone out on Saturday night and vanished, I knew I wouldn't rest until I found you. I was so scared he was going to kill you, but I hung on to the belief you were still alive. So did Jilly, she's a great girl.'

'She thinks you are pretty special, too,' Katy admitted. 'I don't know what I'd do without her, such a steadfast, good friend. I can't wait till she comes down next week, I've missed her.'

'And what about me, will you miss me?'

'I'm sure you know perfectly well I will.'

'You looked a bit worried when I said about whisking you away somewhere to be alone. Why was that?'

Katy blushed. 'Because I haven't ever done anything, you know, with a man.'

'You mean you are still a virgin and you're a bit scared of what it entails? Or that you are against premarital sex?'

'You are very blunt. The first one.'

'I will never push you into doing anything you don't really want to do,' he said. 'But I do believe there comes a time when two people can't help themselves any more.'

Katy looked into his soft brown eyes and sensed she was almost at that point; only the plaster on her leg would act as a deterrent.

On the way home, Charles pulled over to the side of the road. 'I just want to kiss you,' he said. 'I know we won't be able to when we get back to your house.'

He was just the best kisser she'd ever known. Her whole body ached for more, and when he slid his hand inside her blouse, and cupped his hand around her breast and gently rubbed her nipple between his fingers, she wished they were in a hotel room with nothing at all to stop them.

'We must go home,' he said after a little while.

The car windows were all steamed up, and Katy's ankle was throbbing because she couldn't stretch out her leg properly.

'If we don't go now, you'll be getting the third degree in the morning. I shall be lying in that spare room tonight wishing I dared creep into your bed.'

'You won't, though? Mum has got ears like a bat.'

'No, I won't, but I shall fantasize about what I'd do to you if I was in there.'

She wanted to get him to tell her what that would entail, but she wasn't bold enough for that just yet.

Charles left to go back to London on Sunday evening at eight. It had been the best birthday Katy ever remembered.

Charles had bought her a beautiful silver bangle, and from her parents she had received a cream trench coat-style mackintosh, which she'd admired in a magazine while she was in hospital. Rob had sent her a tiny china teddy bear with a crutch.

'A souvenir,' she said when Charles looked puzzled. 'When we were little we both liked little china bears, and we used to buy each other appropriate ones. He always had ones with footballs or cricket bats. I'm surprised he took time off from his studies to find a bear with a crutch.'

They had roast beef with all the trimmings for lunch, then Charles and Albert took her for a walk in the wheelchair. When they got back, Hilda had laid the birthday tea: salmon salad, toasted teacakes, a birthday cake with candles, and trifle too.

'I haven't had a tea like this in years,' Charles said gleefully. 'My granny used to do what I called the Big Tea. I used to dream of it when I was at boarding school. My mum's were poor affairs, just bread and jam and seed cake.'

Albert lit the candles on the cake. 'I can't believe you

are really twenty-four,' he said. 'It seems like only yester-day you were five and you had to kneel up on a chair to blow out your candles.'

'Don't forget to wish,' Hilda barked out as Katy got ready to blow the candles out.

Katy wasn't going to forget to wish. She wanted to marry Charles, to live in a country cottage and have four children.

She did wonder if that was a bit greedy.

Epilogue

Tunbridge Wells, 1972

Katy came in from taking the dry washing off the clothes line, put the basket on the kitchen floor and with a huge sigh eased herself down on to a kitchen chair.

It was July, yet another very hot day, and her baby was due in a week's time. Her pale pink cheesecloth dress with its gypsy-style embroidery down the front was sticking to her with the heat. She fanned her face with an old envelope in one hand, and with the other she stroked her bump.

'Won't be so long now, little one,' she said. 'Daddy will be home soon and we'll all go and sit in the shade in the garden and drink that home-made lemonade I've put in the fridge.'

'Talking to yourself is a sign of madness.'

Katy looked up to see it was June Pettigrew at the open door. She was smiling and holding on to her own bump. Her baby was due in a month, and she'd been staying with Katy and Charles, along with her two children, Matthew and Angela, since her husband beat her to a pulp some three months earlier.

'The council have a house for me,' June said jubilantly. 'I have to hand it to you, Katy, you were right about pester power. I think they were so sick of seeing me at the council offices, they caved in.'

'That is wonderful!' Katy exclaimed. 'What's it like? Have you seen it yet?'

'I went straight there. It's lovely – three bedrooms, a garden – and it's been looked after, a painter was just touching up bits while I was there. I couldn't believe it was so nice, I thought they'd give me a hovel.'

Katy explained to June that she would be able to get a grant from Social Services to cover essential items like beds, cooker and fridge. But she also had a contact with a second-hand shop owner who helped women in difficult circumstances with furniture.

June suddenly leapt forward and hugged Katy. 'What would I have done without you and Charles?' she said, her eyes filling with emotional tears. 'You took us in when we most needed sanctuary; you fed and clothed us, advised me of my rights, made the kids smile again. You gave us a new life. How can I ever repay you?'

'You finally finding happiness is all the reward we want,' Katy said. 'You know the background of why we've helped woman in your position? Although we're about to have a baby of our own, we hope we will be able to continue to help people. Luckily, thanks to people like Erin Pizzey in her Chiswick refuge for battered women, and all the publicity she managed to get about it, people are becoming much more aware of the kind of cruelty you had to live with. But now you've got a home of your own, it's a brand-new start.'

'And I must make a start on packing. I'm getting the keys tomorrow,' June said. 'The kids are having a sleepover at Marlene's.'

Marlene was another woman who had spent a few

months with Charles and Katy, until she got a council place. She still helped Katy with cleaning and laundry at the Old Rectory, and befriended and advised the latest residents.

Once June had gone upstairs, Katy sat down again and thought back to how her life had changed since her twenty-fourth birthday. At that time her biggest preoccupation had been waiting for the plaster to come off her leg and arm, and hoping the nightmares about Reilly would soon vanish.

Charles and Jilly were responsible for her rehabilitation. They were on the phone, sending her letters and coming to Bexhill to visit her – her friends and comforters when she most needed it. Jilly made her laugh, painted her nails, told her tales of what her friends at the zoo were up to. Yet it was the wonderful feelings Charles evoked inside her that really pushed the darkness aside. The excitement of seeing him, just the touch of his hand, his lips on hers, made her forget to be afraid. Instead of lying in bed remembering how it had been in the cellar, she found she could only think of how wonderful it would be to spend a whole night with him.

As it happened, Charles wouldn't hear of it until she was out of plaster, and back working in London. He made jokes about her irate mother catching them and throwing him out. But in her heart Katy knew he needed her to be absolutely sure it was him she wanted.

Jilly found them a cheap but rather grotty two-bedroom flat in Camden Town, which they painted and smartened up, but Katy didn't go back to Frey, Hurst and Herbert at the Inns of Court. Both she and Charles thought their relationship might prove problematic. Instead she found a legal secretary's position with Whitehouse, Gibson and Alton, a firm of solicitors in Chancery Lane.

The biggest hurdle in 1965 was Edward Reilly's trial. Murder trials always attracted a great deal of interest, and the press were voracious. Fortunately, they never discovered where she and Jilly were living, or where Katy worked. But poor Hilda and Albert had a pack of journalists at their door when the trial began.

Reilly's claim that he'd committed the crimes while the balance of his mind was disturbed didn't hold up. The eminent psychiatrist who gave evidence made it quite clear Reilly knew exactly what he was doing. Although he offered mitigating circumstances, in that Reilly's youth had been blighted by cruelty from both his mother and her male friends, the man was sane.

Katy was only in the witness box for an hour, but it seemed far longer to her. She hated the way Reilly never took his eyes off her, and she found it irritating that the defence barrister hammered home the kind acts Reilly had done, like providing a kettle and a fire. He even pointed out she'd used the kettle as a weapon to burn his face, directing the jury to look at the still scarlet wound.

She wanted to shout out that no one in the court had any idea what it was like to be imprisoned, to be beaten and starved. Wouldn't anyone use the only implement at hand to make their escape?

But however painful it was to her, Charles pointed out that she had the sympathy of everyone in that court, and the prosecution barrister said that she had been both clever and brave to outwit Reilly.

There had never been any real expectation that Reilly would hang. The anti-capital punishment lobby was too powerful and vocal by then. Katy had always thought hanging was barbaric anyway, so when she heard he'd got a life sentence she felt vindicated. Finally she was able to move forward and be just another young woman enjoying her life in London.

London was an exciting place to be that summer of 1965. Skirts grew shorter by the week, men were growing their hair longer, and new clothes boutiques selling outrageous clothes popped up like mushrooms everywhere. There were discotheques and rock concerts to go to. For the first time in her life she was really living, not marking time as she had in Bexhill, with Saturday night at the De La Warr Pavilion the highlight of the week. She didn't spend all her spare time with Charles, because he often had to handle cases in other cities and stayed away overnight. He said he wanted her to go out and have fun, so she did, with girls from work, Jilly and many of her new friends from the zoo.

It was on the August bank holiday, nearly six months since she'd got away from Reilly, that Charles told her he loved her. He and Katy had gone to Southend on the train for the day, together with Jilly and her boyfriend, Guy. It was a very hot day, and Katy was wearing white shorts and a skimpy white top.

They queued up to get on the Wild Mouse ride, a terrifying roller coaster with narrow cars so you sat behind one another rather than side by side. 'I love you,' he said, just as they were clambering aboard, Katy in the seat in front of him.

It was hardly an appropriate time to make such a statement and although she had been itching to tell him she loved him for ages, she didn't reply.

'I want to marry you, too,' he yelled out just as the ride began.

The little cars hurtled along at breakneck speed, turning so sharply on corners that Kate screamed, thinking the car was coming off the tracks. But Charles was leaning forward towards her, she could feel his warm breath on her neck, and as the cars made their final terrifying descent, he whispered in her ear.

'I mean it, will you marry me?'

That summer Katy had already discovered that Charles had more sides than a threepenny bit. There was the calm measured barrister, a product of public school and wealthy parents; that Charles wore Savile Row suits and bought his shirts from Hawes & Curtis in Jermyn Street, spoke with a plummy accent and had impeccable manners.

But away from the courts Charles liked to wear Levi's jeans, desert boots and T-shirts. He listened to loud rock music, and liked what he called 'vulgar entertainment', meaning fairground rides and going to the dogs. He was one of the first lawyers to give up on the 'short back and sides' haircut, too. He could be argumentative, stubborn, and always believed he was right. But he was also tender, passionate and kind. Proposing to her on the Wild Mouse ride was typical of his sense of fun. Not for him the formal proposal on bended knee. Maybe he intended to give Katy a wild ride, too!

Katy didn't agree to marry him straight off. Not because

she had any doubts that he was the right one, but because he was taking her away to a country hotel near Tunbridge Wells the following weekend. She had already lost her virginity to him, at his flat, just a couple of weeks after she returned to London, but this weekend in Tunbridge Wells was to be a romantic, first whole night together, and she had managed to persuade her doctor to put her on the new birth control pill. They were only supposed to give the pill to married women, but she twisted the doctor's arm by saying they were engaged. And he agreed the pill was prudent.

That weekend was just perfect on so many levels. Their first chance to be entirely alone, thrilling lovemaking, the weather was glorious and so was the hotel. Katy agreed to marry him the first evening there, over dinner. While wandering around pretty Tunbridge Wells on Saturday morning, looking for an engagement ring, they both felt this was the place where they would like to spend their entire married life. It was easy to get to London on the train, and easy to visit her family in Bexhill and his in Hampshire.

Charles bought her an engagement ring, a beautiful sparkly single diamond. They decided they would get married the following spring. And they would buy a house in Tunbridge Wells.

They found the house the second time they went to the town. It was called the Old Rectory, a large ramshackle mellow red-brick house with a veranda around the front, and a large overgrown garden. It had a slightly Gothic flavour, with arched windows and a couple of funny little turrets over the bedrooms on either side of the house. Because it was in poor condition inside, they bought it for just £2,000. An absolute snip.

The wedding had to be delayed, and the easiest and most cost-effective way to get work done on the house was to let some of the tradespeople stay until they'd finished their work. People advised them against this. But in fact it worked like a dream, as they attracted talented, sensitive tradespeople who were not purely motivated by money. The house became like a commune, people coming and going, a fun place full of laughter and music. Charles fixed the price for each job, and Katy ran the house.

Their neighbours referred to them as 'hippies', or 'flower children', and remarked that they all slept on mattresses on the floor and believed in free love, but neither Charles nor Katy cared. 'Peace and love' was in the air, and they wanted to embrace it.

It was early in 1968, when the building work was finished, that both Charles and Katy woke up to realize they had to make changes. People were becoming dependent on them, dropping in at any time for advice, meals or a place to sleep. They couldn't go on being responsible for other people.

'It's been great fun, but we need to have a purpose in our lives,' Charles said firmly. 'We always said we were going to help women escape from violent marriages. I believe that is what we must do. But first we must get married; we'll buy proper furniture, and become respectable.'

Katy laughed so much at the 'respectable' bit. At work and in court Charles was always that, and no doubt some of their snootier neighbours had been puzzled by the smartly suited man who left the madhouse each day carrying a briefcase.

Luckily, at that time, they only had one lodger, Tom;

everyone else had drifted off on the hippie trails to Morocco, India or Afghanistan.

Charles explained the situation to him, and Tom took it very well. 'It's been a blast,' he said cheerfully. He had hair down to his shoulders and, in the summer, he wore nothing but a pair of shorts, not even shoes. He had done bricklaying, plastering and some plumbing for them and he'd been with them for nearly a year. 'But all good things have to come to an end, and you two need time alone again.'

Tom was right, they did need time alone. They had both been working five days a week in the City, and their weekends were always full of household chores, cooking, organizing building materials, and just listening to other people's problems.

They both took time off in March, and spent the whole two weeks looking closely at their house, making lists of things that still needed to be done, itemizing furniture and curtains to buy, and then they spent the rest of the time in bed making love.

Katy remembered one day sitting outside in the spring sunshine under the cherry tree in full blossom, just looking at their house. They had loved it when they'd bought it, but all this time there had been so many people about, they had been sidetracked and forgotten what the attraction was. They could see it now so clearly: the lovely old red brick, the quirky windows and turrets.

'It's waiting for a family,' Katy said. 'Imagine a pram out on the veranda with a fat brown baby kicking its legs. And a little boy climbing the trees while his bigger sister is on the swing.'

'So three children, is it?' Charles smiled. 'Why stop at three?'

'Let's decide that at a later date,' she said. 'Now about the wedding?'

'I thought we'd have it in June,' Charles said. 'That gives us time to get everything shipshape here. The garden is beautiful in summer, so we could have the reception out here in a hired marquee and get married in the local church. We'll get caterers in.'

It was good to hear Charles making plans again. He had been drifting for some time.

Jilly came down to see them during that fortnight, and she was very pleased to hear they'd finally seen the light. 'You filled the house with fun people, we had some memorable parties here, and the very best of times, but now it's time for just the two of you.'

Guy had moved in with her in Camden Town, and they too kept talking about getting married, but they never got beyond the talking.

'How many people are you going to invite to the wedding?' she asked.

'We'll avoid asking the hippies,' Charles said with a smirk. 'They might not leave afterwards.' He looked at Katy questioningly. 'Let's announce that it's family only, plus our closest friends and a few work colleagues. How does that sound?'

'Just great,' she said. 'We can have your two little nieces as bridesmaids because they are cute. And Jilly as matron of honour.'

That was just how it was. They got the house tidied up, bought proper furniture, and the wedding day went splendidly. Katy wore a very simple, cream satin long dress, and the little bridesmaids and Jilly wore pink. Pat was Charles's best man, and Albert gave Katy away. Even Edna came up from Broadstairs.

Yet rattling around in a big house on their own wasn't really their style. So, soon after the wedding, Katy spoke to the almoner at the local hospital and to a couple of social workers, telling them she was willing to help any women anxious to escape from violent marriages.

It began with a trickle – one woman and her baby, who only stayed for five nights before returning to her husband – but then it was two, three, and upwards. Sometimes they had as many as eight women, with up to sixteen or so children between them.

For Christmas of 1968 they had only two mothers, Pat and Gwen, with five children between them. Charles said that to see those children's joy at opening their stockings and pulling crackers, safe and relaxed, away from their violent fathers, more than made up for the mess and noise they created.

It gave Katy even greater satisfaction to see Pat and Gwen, two women who had only bonded through shared adversity, become real friends and soon afterwards set up home together with their children. She had a strange feeling that Gloria was looking down and applauding.

Katy gave up her job in the early part of 1969, as the number of women coming to them grew. Often these women had been badly hurt, and however much they hoped for a secure home, even one room, they needed help and nursing until they were able to cope again. Sometimes there were as many as ten children on

334

mattresses in one room, and their mothers were packed like sardines in other rooms, too. Katy would go to jumble sales or beg women's groups like the WI or Mothers' Union to donate both children's and women's clothing to her, as so often the women fled their homes with nothing more than what they stood up in.

She became accomplished at persuading greengrocers and bakers to let her have any goods left at the end of the day. By talking to some of the more affluent women in Tunbridge Wells she persuaded them to have coffee morning to raise cash for the cause, too.

Charles, meanwhile, gave free legal advice to the women who needed it, sometimes reclaiming the family home for them or seeing that their husbands were charged with grievous bodily harm.

People often remarked that they didn't understand how Katy and Charles could let their home be taken over by others – meaning, without saying, by women from very rough backgrounds.

Occasionally Katy would look at Charles and wish he'd say it was time to stop, they'd done their bit. But he wouldn't because, like her, he felt they must carry on. They were the only safety net for these women. There were a few hostels opening up by then, but Katy heard they were often frightening places, where women would turn on other women. The children had been through enough; maybe it was crowded at the Old Rectory, but it was a real home, and the children soon learned to treat it with respect.

Katy found it had its rewards too: supporting women like June who, in turn, helped others just as she had once been helped; seeing frightened mothers finally get a safe place of their own to live; knowing they'd shown children that violence in the home is always wrong, and that they weren't somehow responsible for the bad things.

Then just before Christmas of 1971 Katy realized she was pregnant. She'd dreamed of it, she'd hoped for it, and had even begun to think her role in life was to be a kind of universal aunt forever.

'Can things get any better?' she said to Charles the same night she'd told him, as they were going to bed.

'Yes, and they will when we've filled this house with kids,' Charles laughed.

Now, as Katy sat in the kitchen caressing her bump and thinking about the past, she wondered if Hilda had felt the way she did today, when she was nearly due.

Oddly enough, for all Hilda's cantankerous attitude, she had been remarkably enthusiastic about Charles and Katy's plan to open the house to beaten women. She often came and stayed for a week or so; she would give the older children lessons on cake making, clean everything in sight, and polish the windows till they shone. But the most unexpected thing was seeing her with small babies. She really loved them, and she would rock one in her arms for hours, given the chance. Which was why Katy wanted to know how Hilda had felt when she was due.

She felt compelled to ring and ask her.

They had never spoken about Katy's birth before; Rob's had been mentioned, but not hers.

'Hello, dear,' Hilda said. 'It's not like you to call me in the middle of the afternoon. Are you having pains?'

'No, Mum, I was just sitting here in the kitchen stroking

my tummy and talking to the baby, and I wondered if you did that with me.'

'Of course I did,' she said, without even a pause for thought. 'I used to tell you what the weather was like, what I was having for tea. Everything.'

'So you didn't resent me, then?'

'Of course not. To be honest, in the last weeks of the pregnancy I went into a kind of bubble. I was happy, nothing outside affected me. I had my letters from Albert – he'd tell me all the things we'd do together when he got back. I used to daydream about us walking you in a pram down to the park. Things may have started badly, dear, but once I felt you move inside me, I knew I was going to love you.'

That was all Katy had wanted to hear. Charles had been right. It didn't matter who her biological father was.

After she put the phone down she continued to sit. The kitchen felt cool in the hot weather; the red quarry tiles were a joy to walk on when it was hot, even if they were a devil to polish with Cardinal.

All at once she felt a great sense of calm wash over her, a feeling that all was right now in her world. She did still watch her neighbours from the upstairs windows, and wonder about their lives. Charles sometimes called her Keyhole Kate, the nosy character in *The Dandy* comic. Actually, she wasn't really nosy, she only wanted reassurance that the families in her street had happy lives.

She and Charles would go on welcoming battered women and their children at the Old Rectory. Maybe they'd only have one or two staying at a time, rather than the hordes they'd had in the past.

She would invite her mother and father here often – she wanted them to grow close to the new baby.

She didn't even think about Ed Reilly any more. That whole sorry saga was one she'd put to bed when he was sent to prison.

But then she'd been lucky, just as her mother had been. They'd both found good men who didn't want to bully them, who treated them as equals.

She stroked her stomach again. 'If you are a girl, make sure you pick a man like your father,' she said. 'And if you are a boy, I'm going to train you to be perfect husband material.'

Acknowledgements

Thank you to Louise Moore and Yasmin Morrissey of Penguin Books for all your help, support and, above all, your boundless enthusiasm. I couldn't have done it without you both.

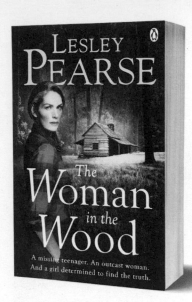

The Woman in the Wood

Fifteen-year-old twins Maisy and Duncan Mitcham have always had each other. Until one fateful day in the wood . . .

Dead to Me

Ruby and Verity become firm friends, despite coming from different worlds. However, fortunes are not set in stone and soon the girls find their situations reversed.

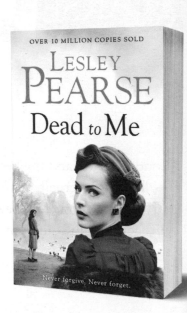

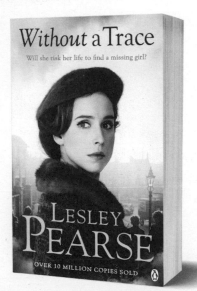

Without a Trace

On Coronation Day, 1953, Molly discovers that her friend is dead and her six-year-old daughter Petal has vanished. Molly is prepared to give up everything in finding Petal. But is she also risking her life?

Forgive Me

Eva's mother never told her the truth about her childhood. Now it is too late and she must retrace her mother's footsteps to look for answers. Will she ever discover the story of her birth?

Belle

Belle book 1

London, 1910, and the beautiful and innocent Belle Reilly is cruelly snatched from her home and sold to a brothel in New Orleans where she begins her life as a courtesan. Can Belle ever find her way home?

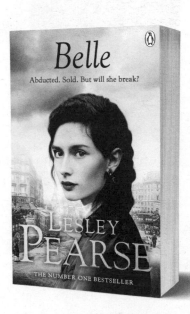

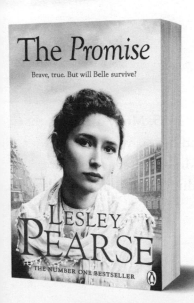

The Promise

Belle book 2

When Belle's husband heads for the trenches of northern France, she volunteers as a Red Cross ambulance driver. There she is brought face to face with a man from her past who she'd never quite forgotten.

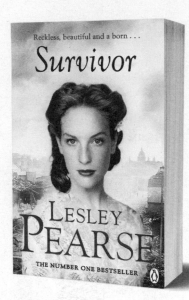

Survivor

Belle book 3

Eighteen-year-old Mari is defiant, selfish and has given up everything in favour of glamorous parties in the West End. But, without warning, the Blitz blows her new life apart. Can Mari learn from her mistakes before it's too late?

Stolen

A beautiful young woman is discovered half-drowned on a Sussex beach. Where has she come from? Why can't she remember who she is — or what happened?

Gypsy

Liverpool, 1893, and after tragedy strikes the Bolton family, Beth and her brother Sam embark on a dangerous journey to find their fortune in America.

Faith

Scotland, 1995, and Laura Brannigan is in prison for a murder she claims she didn't commit.

Hope

Somerset, 1836, and baby Hope is cast out from a world of privilege as proof of her mother's adultery.

A Lesser Evil

Bristol, the 1960s, and young Fifi Brown defies her parents to marry a man they think is beneath her.

Secrets

Adele Talbot escapes a children's home to find her grandmother — but soon her unhappy mother is on her trail . . .

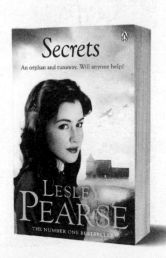

Remember Me

Mary Broad is transported to Australia as a convict and encounters both cruelty and passion. Can she make a life for herself so far from home?

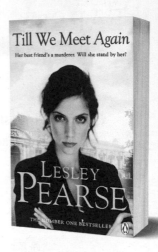

Till We Meet Again

Susan and Beth were childhood friends. Now Susan is accused of murder, and Beth finds she must defend her.

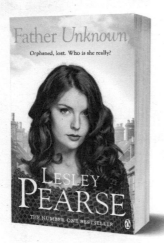

Father Unknown

Daisy Buchan is left a scrapbook with details about her real mother. But should she go and find her?

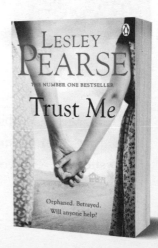

Trust Me

Dulcie Taylor and her sister are sent to an orphanage and then to Australia. Is their love strong enough to keep them together?

Never Look Back

An act of charity sends flower girl Matilda on a trip to the New World and a new life . . .

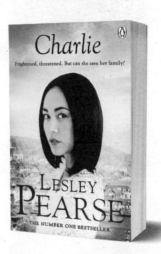

Charlie

Charlie helplessly watches her mother being senselessly attacked. What secrets have her parents kept from her?

Rosie

Rosie is a girl without a mother, with a past full of trouble. But could the man who ruined her family also save Rosie?

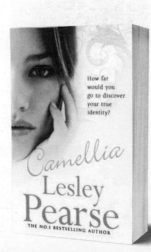

Camellia

Orphaned Camellia discovers that the past she has always been so sure of has been built on lies. Can she bear to uncover the truth about herself?

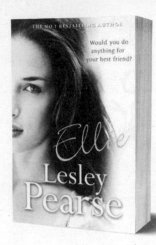

Ellie

Eastender Ellie and spoilt Bonny set off to make a living on the stage. Can their friendship survive sacrifice and ambition?

Charity

Charity Stratton's bleak life is changed for ever when her parents die in a fire. Alone and pregnant, she runs away to London . . .

Tara

Anne changes her name to Tara to forget her shocking past — but can she really become someone else?

Georgia

Raped by her foster-father, fifteen-year-old Georgia runs away from home to the seedy back streets of Soho . . .

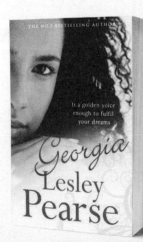